WHAT LOVE BECOMES

For Ron

Love of My Life

WHAT LOVE BECOMES
A novel
By Jan Marin Tramontano

Published by Adelaide Books, New York / Lisbon
adelaidebooks.org

Editor-in-Chief
Stevan V. Nikolic

426p.

For any information, please address Adelaide Books
at info@adelaidebooks.org
or write to:
Adelaide Books
244 Fifth Ave. Suite D27
New York, NY, 10001

ISBN 10: 1-949180-47-6
ISBN 13: 978-1-949180-47-3

Printed in the United States of America

What Love Becomes

A novel
by

JAN MARIN TRAMONTANO

Adelaide Books
New York/Lisbon
2019

"I tell you this during another night

of living next to you

without having said what was on our minds …

Love doesn't look too closely"

The Ecstasy

– Philip Lopate

Headline: Florida Teens Critically Injured in Parasailing Accident

As children, we run, extend our arms, pretend to be Superman. Soaring birds mesmerize us. Our eyes trail a jet until it disappears into the clouds.

I could never see myself jumping out of a plane but there is something appealing about parasailing. Why? With the right conditions, you can rise hundreds of feet above the water, be as close to a bird as you'd ever want to be, but you're tethered—attached by a long line to a boat.

That would certainly give me a modicum of confidence.

Except.

It can be risky. Parasailing is an under-regulated business. There have been accidents before this one. A man died after the towboat propeller failed and his parachute lost buoyancy, hurling him into the water. A mother of two was killed when she was dragged over beach umbrellas and into a volleyball pole when her line snapped. And now, two teenagers were critically injured when winds from a storm swept up, breaking their line. They zoomed through the air until they smashed into a high rise and landed in a parking lot.

These girls placed their faith in a company that should have known better than to send them up into strong winds.

Bear with me now.

The idea of flight while being tethered made me think of something else that's been on my mind.

Parasailing might be a perfect metaphor for what we want from marriage. We want to be held but we want the hold to be loose. We want our partner to admire our speed and grace in flight but not to tug on the towline. We need to make sure the line doesn't tangle or knot. We try to balance who gets the flying time and when.

It's complicated. With marriage — also an unregulated business— we have a fifty percent chance to reach the *death do us part* finish line, and that doesn't count those who want to fly away but don't.

We are creatures grounded in blind faith. To parasail, we sign a release form exonerating a company we know nothing about to take us up in the air. To get married, we sign a legally binding contract for life, not knowing how sickness, health, richer, or bad decisions will play out, because we think love is enough.

Ah, the lure of magical thinking.

When we find ourselves flailing, maybe we think we can change our fate by doing one new, unexpected something. But just maybe the day will come when we cut our own towline knowing that the free fall may land us in just the right place.

Part One

The Accident
2012

Chapter one

Willow never thought she could be the kind of woman to leave a wounded warrior, yet, she's on her way home to do just that. *My tour is finally over and I'm not reenlisting.*

Her husband, Denny, is not a Vietnam vet who'd be living in a cardboard box without her nor is he a soldier who lost his legs or suffered a brain injury as a result of an IED explosion in the second Iraq war. The consequences from his war —the first Persian Gulf War— are different. It was a war fought without adequate defense against an invisible enemy—nerve gas, deadly chemicals, and pollutants.

Denny is chronically victimized by his environment now. Triggers are unavoidable. The scent from a woman's perfume, a fresh coat of paint on a neighbor's house, even spring pollen, can set off days in the dark with migraine or debilitating allergy attacks.

The bouts come and go. Jobs come and go. Yet, Willow stayed.

From the day he flew to the Middle East and beyond, Willow and Denny lived on shifting sand. Iraq, Saudi Arabia, Philippines, were once countries whose shape Willow would trace on a map. What happened to him there changed the trajectory of both their lives. Whether it was oil fires, searing heat, smoke, desert sand lodged in every pore, or the pills he was forced to take didn't matter. Pick one or all.

The lingering chronic leg pain and limp he suffered? That's another story all together.

He blindsided her when he joined the Marines just when they were about to get married. When she remembers that day now, she's enraged she didn't run. But then, it never crossed her mind she had a choice.

"I'm sorry, Willow, but I couldn't tell you until it was a done deal. It's something I have to do and I didn't want you to talk me out of it."

Willow's tears streaked her contorted face. "No. Denny, this is not something you had to do. We had plans. What about our life? I thought that's what you signed up for. What about that, Denny?"

"I'm sorry, babe. I really am. Think of it as me going off to college for four years. It isn't as if there's a war going on. It's a good thing. When I come back, we'll do everything you want."

But there was a war. What's more, it never occurred to her that if he could do this, there might be other equally arbitrary decisions he might make.

After recovering from the first blows— enlisting without telling her and coming back as he did— the second more deadly strike was his unilateral decision that they would not have children.

Now stopped at a traffic light, Willow grips the wheel. Her grief resurfaces again, red and raw, as she remembers the second worse day of her life with Denny.

"Are you kidding me, Willow? The pills they gave me cause birth defects. It would be a crime to bring a child into the world knowing that."

"What?" she gasped. "No. We always talked about having a brood. It's all I've ever wanted."

"That was before, Willow. Get your head out of the clouds for once. You're a librarian. Read about what's happening to the babies born to PGW vets. You could do that to a kid? Maybe when I'm better, we can adopt." He stomped out of the room. Conversation over.

Willow was sure she'd stop breathing. When she told her sister that she felt something inside of her tear, she meant it. Autumn was infuriated. "I told you to leave the loser when he joined up and now this? You are not staying with him. You are moving in here with me. That's all there is to it."

But she stayed.

Winding her way through the city streets, Willow puts her hand on her racing heart, willing it to slow down. *Stop thinking about the past, concentrate on how to begin, what words to use.* She silently practiced her speech to him all afternoon but now can't remember a word.

For a moment, she pushes the bad memories aside and sees the Denny watching her as she walked into high school, her first day in a *real* school. She knew no one. Groups of students hung out together, relaxed with one another. Apart from all of the noise was Denny. He was leaning against a wall wearing a football jersey, ragged jeans and when he saw her, a wide grin. She could never explain it but from the moment she first saw this redheaded, freckle-faced guy, she was his for life. They didn't date right away, just gravitated toward each other when passing to the next class, then after school. She'd watch him at football practice, captivated by his skill and speed.

They'd sit on the grass behind school cross-legged, facing each other. She'd tell him stories of her wandering childhood living in communes. He'd laugh, twirl her light golden brown curls around his finger, stroke her cheek. He'd call her at night. They'd do homework together. Before a single kiss, they became each other's world.

Blinded by her idea of them, she never saw the restlessness pulsing beneath his skin.

As one year bled into the next, she knew she would never have the husband and family she dreamed of. Those losses devolved into blame. Implacable, he was defeated and wanted only to turn his back on that time and accept his limitations.

She never knows how he'll be when she comes home from school. Moody. Agitated. Apologetic. Energetic. Sometimes even loving. Yes, sporadic sightings of her Denny remained. The occasional flicker in his eyes let her know the Denny she fell in love with was still in there somewhere.

In the wide swatches of time she had to think about her marriage, she decided that when the terms become skewed, when worse exceeds better, and cherishing is long gone, it should become null and void. It slowly dawned on her that it came down to this — when the balance of happiness to unhappiness tips all the way over, it's time to rip up the pledge and heave it into the black hole that grew deeper each year.

At least that's what she told herself now.

She felt her unhappiness keenly as it insidiously spread, a pool of dark sludge coating her life with sticky residue. Then, one day something small and unanticipated happened. She had an epiphany:

she wanted and deserved more. A single pinprick of happiness was enough to startle her back to life.

Sometimes change starts small but it begins to take up more and more space until it's too large to ignore, as if you don't know how cold you are until you feel the sun, or when the simple joy of careless conversation or sharing a meal with light banter makes you happier than it should.

Willow's feelings for Blake, were slowly aroused. At first, it was just chatter about work. He was her boss, the school principal. She liked being around him and sought him out whenever she could. He made her see that she could fill herself up with something bright to balance the pull-down of Denny.

Chatting became coffee. Then a drink. Dinner. And when they could no longer stand not touching one another, they became lovers. She expected to feel guilty but she didn't.

A fling. Something to look forward to. When it's over, at least I'd know I chose life while holding on to my sinking ship.

But it didn't happen that way. There was no going back.

Willow and Blake decided this would be the day they would each tell their spouses they were leaving. She would go home and tell Denny; he would tell Jillian. Willow supposed it was a fitting day for what they were about to do. Sunny while they were together. Now, it was raining in big, sloppy drops.

"We'll tell them and then meet at the Beverwyck Inn." Blake said. "Or maybe I should be there, waiting outside your house, just in case."

"No. It'll be okay."

He pulled her close, stroking her hair. "Just get in and out. Fast."

"Yes," she nodded. "I know. What about Jillian? Do you know what you're going to say?"

"No. But I don't want to let her turn it into a harangue. I want a hit and run, I think."

"No, you don't, Blake."

Willow eyes the interstate signs and considers taking the long route home. She looks at the clock. Five–fifteen. The traffic on I-90 should be picking up. She could sit in bumper-to-bumper traffic pretending she's a commuter anxious to get home to prepare dinner

or play a game of catch with her kids. The other drivers would probably curse the crawl while she'd hope traffic would come to a dead
stop.

*No. That's silly. It's too far out of the way. The sooner I get this over
with, the sooner I get to Blake.*

She turns on the radio, pushing the button to change the dial
from NPR to rock. *You're a heartbreaker, dream maker, love taker. Pat,
oh did you got that right. Denny in spades.*

Maybe she should stop for a cup of coffee to concentrate. She
has to choose the right words rather than have a torrent of incoher-
ence spill out. What she says does matter. She needs him to understand this is best for both of them. She must be gentle but firm. He
has to understand she won't change her mind.

Willow has no doubt she is doing the right thing. Yet, she can
see his face crumble as soon as he understands what she's saying.
Despite everything, sadness wells up inside her.

Stopped at a light, tears blur her vision and stream down her
face. She thinks of him alone in their dark house. *Where is the damn
Kleenex?* She looks over her shoulder and sees the box on the floor, on
the passenger side. It's wedged under her umbrella out of reach. She
turns around, letting go of the wheel for a second to flip the box toward her. Stretching, Willow's foot slips out of her shoe and the heel
gets caught on the gas pedal. Twisted, she pulls herself back to face
front when the car lurches forward, accelerating into the intersection.

She hears tires screech, a crashing sound, and the blast of a
horn. Willow feels impact. Then nothing.

Chapter two

Blake Golden locks his file cabinet. He neatens his desk and looks around his office. *When I come in tomorrow, everything will be different. Willow will sleep in my arms tonight and tomorrow night and after that.*

He leaves work with a clear mind. His job isn't an easy one but he knows he's good at it, a stark contrast to his home life. Jillian thinks him incapable of doing anything right. She treats him as an irascible child, charting chores on a dry erase board in the kitchen.

Before leaving the house this morning, she laid out the evening. "Chelsea is going to the library with Sara after her 5:30 rehearsal. They're eating at The Point. Plan on dinner for us at seven. The grocery list is on the table."

"It's all on the board, Jillian," Blake sighs, "I got it."

He always chafes at the specifics of her instructions, but when left to his own devices, his meals are never up to her standards. He makes great chili, is good with any kind of meat, but never really mastered the fine art of al dente vegetables and low-to-no-fat cooking. She'd carp, "For heaven's sake, Blake, you know I need to eat well and you could use a little trimming around your gut. And let's not go into Chelsea's atrocious eating habits."

Tonight, his assignment is chicken with brown rice and a salad— arugula with mixed baby greens. Simple enough. They had it so often, he could hardly mess it up. The only variation was the seasoning on the chicken. Maybe tonight he'd slather it in jalapeño or wasabi. Make sure it burned all the way down. That would be a good *I'm out of here* meal. Or he might overcook tasteless chicken until it was dried out, puck-like. Just like they were.

What is he thinking? He's not going to fix dinner. He's going to go home, pack a bag, stash it in the car, and tell her as soon as she walks through the door. Keep it short. Avoid accusation and blame. Just tell her he's leaving and get to Willow.

He flinches and rakes his fingers through his thick dark hair. It's been hard to ignore how cowed Jillian's been since she came back from her soul-searching trip to New York. He hoped she'd come back telling him she wanted out but that didn't happen. No surprises there. Leaving in her mind would be admitting failure. Something she could never abide.

It's mind-boggling how the very qualities that first attract you become repelling.

Blake flashes back to the first time he saw Jillian. The image of her walking across campus fighting the wind, her long silky black hair flying behind her, is still sharp. Her lithe body held the ground. She marched as if she knew exactly where she was going in life.

She was intense. Her large, dark almond-shaped eyes sparkled, and she had a deep, throaty laugh. Jillian intended to become a professional dancer but was ordered by her father to major in something practical. By the end of her freshman year, she didn't care what her father wanted. "Daddy will have to understand, Blake. Ballet companies want young dancers. I can't afford to wait just to placate him."

She left college and went to ballet school in Manhattan. Blake took the long drive every weekend to visit her. He never tired of watching her work at the ballet barre, admiring her drive and tenacity.

Jillian was exquisite and he fell hard. And so did she. "I've never known anyone like you, Blake. Not many would be willing to put up with all the time dance takes."

"It's who you are, Jillian. I get that. It's not a problem for me."

When she reserved studio time, he always went with her to watch. Sometimes she'd ask him to hold her or raise her into the air so she could practice her balance and arm work. For him, it was an opening, however slight, into her sacred space. In the chaste, bare studio, he was overwhelmed with unceasing want. All he could think about was how he felt inside of her.

Her father, however, saw nothing but problems. "Teaching is woman's work, Golden. I want my daughter to marry a provider. Bad enough she thinks she's going to be a ballerina," he barked. "You don't have my blessing and I'm not going to support you. I worked hard for every dollar I've earned. You should do the same, boy. With someone else's daughter."

At first, their friends were surprised they were a couple. "What's a girl like her want with a guy like you?" his roommate, Mike, asked. "You don't see it, but I'm telling you, she looks down on us. You're smart and you might be good in the sack for now, but you are us, man. I can't see you with a season subscription to the symphony sipping white wine. Yankees? Yes. Nirvana or Pearl Jam? Yes. Yo-Yo what's his name? No way."

Mike held his hands, palms up, moving them off balance, "Easygoing, normal guy versus tight-assed, snobby ballerina. It's a no-go, buddy." Mike might have been right but it took years for Blake to remember that conversation.

His friend, Mindy, merely asked, "Why would you settle for second place?"

He never saw it that way and more importantly, never doubted Jillian was the one. He was eager to make her dream his. It gave him purpose and direction when he was still flailing after his sister's death. Blake understood she had to see things through and that meant living in New York. After graduation, he had an offer to teach history at his hometown high school in Albany. He'd get his masters at night. Save some money. Then, he'd go to New York, too.

"Are you sure, Blake?"

"It's no sacrifice. It'll be exciting. Hell, it's New York. It's not so bad being long distance for a couple of years when we know we'll have the greatest life."

It never occurred to him to think about what their life would look like in ten or fifteen years, if she made it. More importantly, he never considered what it might mean for them if she didn't.

Blake was very happy during their early years together. His beautiful wife and daughter took his breath away. They bought a comfortable house. He was a teacher who loved his job. It was more than enough for him.

Not so for Jillian and over time, their marriage curdled.

She pushed him to interview for the principal's job. It had more prestige in her mind. At first, he resisted. He wasn't eager to leave the classroom and he felt it was important for someone to be home with Chelsea at night. But now he was glad.

Despite the fact it was her idea, it, too, became a problem. "Do you have to go to every performance of *Our Town?* I need time to work with a student tomorrow night. We have a recital coming up and she's not ready. Surely, the show will go on without you."

"No, Jillian. That's not the way it works. You've known about the play run for months. Besides, Chelsea is expecting you to go to dinner with Sara and her mother. Have you forgotten? You've already cancelled twice. It's on the damn kitchen board."

Blake never imagined he'd be the one to leave, let alone because he'd fallen in love with someone else. He accepted his life as it was just as Willow had until one afternoon after school dismissal, Willow appeared and the earth's axis changed. Tall and thin, appearing weightless to him, she glided into his office wearing a blue gauzy dress, her burnished hair carelessly piled on top of her head.

She extended her hand and smiled. "I'm Willow D'Angelo, your new librarian. You signed off on a trade with Angie Smithson. Angie told me you set high goals and I'll be expected to perform miracles," she laughed.

And so, you did.

Is she home yet? Blake wonders, wary of Denny's reaction. Off kilter for years, Blake only knew the old Denny from pick-up games when they were young. He was ultra-competitive which made him fearless in many ways. The games were low-key but Denny would take chances, as if his life depended on a winning play. Odd. Now, Denny could have had a sign painted on him—Beaten.

Blake sees him occasionally around town but Denny never looks up, never invites conversation. He moves with purpose, despite his limp—a fast shadow. It's hard to be angry with a man who suffers, but someone who radiates sunlight the way Willow does, should not be with a man like that.

He picks up the phone. "Jillian, make sure you come straight home right after class. Don't dawdle. We need to talk."

"You haven't wanted to talk since I got back from New York. Now, it's a demand?"

"Just come home right after your last class." *No candles, Jillian. Just a spray of ice water.*

Blake locks his office and stops to pick up Chinese take-out on his way home. He'll tell her and walk away from Jillian's sharp tongued recrimination once and for all.

Chapter three

Standing in line at Starbucks, Lily Lerner shakes her head, still stunned she's on a leave of absence from her life, her real life. Once a successful international journalist, she is now on her way to cover a local board meeting. The contentious agenda item—rezoning a residence on a commercial strip to allow for a new local business. Unbelievable.

After fifteen years based in London at WNN, she began to unravel. One bleak location merged into another. And then the unthinkable happened. She froze right in the middle of Montague Street.

"C'mon, Lily." Ian, her videographer, pulled her arm. "You know the drill. We've done it a million times. What's wrong with you?"

She didn't seem to hear him. Immobile, Lily stared at a woman lying on the sidewalk. Her leg was shattered. Bloody bone and bits of metal protruded where smooth skin had been moments earlier. The woman begged, "Find my daughter. Please. Joanna. Her name is Joanna." Her plea penetrated the babel of noise. "Please. Someone. Find her."

A bomb exploded during lunch near the crowded Blue Door Bistro in Russell Square. Lily had seen it all before—the dead on the street, the maiming, the animal like cacophony emanating from the wounded, the blare of sirens, the rushing to help, bodies once whole, split apart. But before today, she repressed the horror of it all and adrenalin kicked in. She covered war zones and reported on terrorist bombings on what had been peaceful city streets. In fact, she covered a bombing weeks into her internship at WNN. Lily had never seen anything so shocking. She whispered to herself over and over, *you can do this*, and she did. Her producer told her she was astonished at her composure first time out.

Lily was deliberate in her method. She'd rush to get in as close as she could without being obstructive, scan the scene to search for the most compelling story, get the best possible all around accounting from victims and witnesses. Even when she felt clammy with fear, dizziness, or pure revulsion, she did her job.

But not this time. She choked on the smoldering smoke and crouched down to hold the woman's hand. "They'll find your daughter," she murmured, blinking away a wavy vision of a dead, Ethiopian child from her mind. "Help will come. They'll find your daughter."

Lily knew the medics would search for the most critical first and this woman would lie on the sidewalk with head lacerations, and scrapes and burns, her leg blown open for who knows how long. She wouldn't leave her.

Ian roughly pulled Lily to her feet and shook her, "Lily, pull yourself together. We have work to do."

But she couldn't.

Her boss told her to take six months. "It happens."

"Not to me," Lily said.

"You've been going nonstop. Take a breather. Then, I'll find a temporary, less stressful assignment for you."

So here she is— exhausted, defeated, and unsure of what's next. She took a leave of absence. Suddenly, London no longer felt like home. She wanted to go to the place where she grew up, where she visited in between assignments, where her boyfriend, Stephen, now lived. She hoped family and the oak and maple treelined streets would settle her and send her back to her real life. She was a woman who should live in a city like London. Not a podunk city in upstate New York.

But in truth, Lily felt homeless.

Stephen was done with long distance. They'd been together, in a manner of speaking, for ten years. Fearless at work, Lily skirted relationships in her personal life. She knew she loved Stephen, but until now the ocean separating them felt just right.

When Lily first came back, she told him she needed some space for a few weeks to get herself together. She'd first stay with her mother to catch up and rest and then crash with her friend, Amber. Three months later, she stayed on and off with Stephen but still hadn't left Amber's altogether. Time was running out. It seemed to her the decisive person she used to be seemed to have been left on that London street.

Lily took a short-term job at the local TV station to stay busy and not go crazy. But she is going crazy. *A zoning meeting, for God's sake. Gag me.*

Jolted out of her spiraling thoughts, Lily jumps. She hears a crash just as the barista is spooning foam to top off her coffee. Instinctively, she reaches over and snatches the drink, spilling some on her sleeve. "Sorry. Gotta run."

She bolts out of Starbucks, latte in hand, licking the foam off her fingers. The sirens grow louder as they approach. On autopilot, she pulls her phone out of her bag. "Hi, Rich. It's Lily. There's been a crash at Wolf and Shaker. Luke's in the area? Good. I want to get some shots of the scene. I'll be ready say 6:10 as a breaking story but that will cut it too close for the meeting. How about sending the intern, Erica? She'll do a great job."

Slipping the phone into her pocket, she realizes she's responding like the old Lily. She didn't panic when she heard the crash. She isn't sweating. She doesn't feel light headed. She's in control.

She walks toward a policeman standing near the intersection holding back the gawkers. "What happened here?" she asks.

He pointed to the intersection. "A woman driving that sedan was broadsided by the van. Hey, you in the blue shirt, get your ass back and put your phone down or..." He turns back to her. "Poor woman, distracted for a second and her life, as she knows it is over. If she survives at all. Hey, wait a minute, you're that TV reporter. How'd you get wind of this so fast?"

"I was in the area on my way to a meeting." She sips her latte. Offhandedly, she asks, "Did you see what happened? Know who she is?"

"No and no," he snarled. "Didn't you say you were on your way somewhere?"

"I called in an intern. She was happy for the opportunity," Lily flips back her long, brunette curly hair. "How long do you think it will take to get her out?"

He shrugs. "Not long, I hope." He turns away from her to stop a group of teenagers from getting any closer.

Two ambulances and a fire truck turn the corner and screech to a stop. Behind them, another police car arrives to manage the traffic and the crowd at the scene. An EMT jumps out of an ambulance and rushes to the car, pushing through the crowd of rubberneckers who pour out of Starbucks and Moe's. A woman runs out of the nail salon blowing on her nails.

Four paramedics trail behind with two stretchers. The driver of the van is conscious. Lily watches him speak to the medics as they strap him onto a stretcher and whisk him away in the first ambulance.

Meanwhile, the firemen jump down off the truck and quickly assess the situation. They disconnect the battery, put the car on blocks, and use the *Jaws of Life* to get her out.

A muscled, long-haired, twenty-something guy with a video camera on his shoulder walks toward her.

"Hey, Luke. Glad you were so close. Let's see. Get some shots of them getting her out of the car."

"Got it while you were pumping the cop."

She points to the parked cars stuck in the lot. "How about we go over there? Use the crash scene as background."

They approach a couple leaning on a blue Civic. "I'm Lily Lerner, Channel 2 News. This is Luke Burke. Did you see the accident?"

The woman, leaning on her husband, is shaken. "We were in the parking lot walking to our car when we saw it. I noticed it because of all the bumper stickers. She seemed to be turned around reaching for something in the backseat. I said to my husband, what's she doing in there, all twisted around? And then, the car suddenly flies through the light and gets hit by the van. Poor woman."

"What do you mean she was reaching for something?"

"Well, I couldn't really tell but she was definitely turned around."

Her husband interrupted. "It looked like she needed something on the back seat but she was stopped at the light. That's all."

"Your names, please?"

"We're Cindy and Al Black. We gonna be on TV?"

"Maybe. Can't promise." Lily smiles. "Thank you so much."

Lily and Luke walked over to a man sitting in a pickup with the door open. "And you, sir? Your name and what did you see?"

"Jerry Littleton. I was behind her, stopped at the light. And then boom, the next thing I know she's through the light and gets t-boned in the intersection. I couldn't believe my eyes. I wonder if something was wrong with the car. You know like the Toyota thing. Damn shame."

25

"Thank you, sir. Drive safe."

Lily walks closer to the crash site to see if she could hear what the police or medics are saying. "Luke, do your thing. I'll see you later. We'll see what else we can get for the ten o'clock. Something doesn't seem right."

"Sure thing, boss," Luke smirks and walks toward the other side of the crash scene to get some different footage.

Why did she shoot through the light like that when she'd already stopped? Lily moves in as close as she can to the medics and overhears the woman is alive. "Call it in. We better take her to Lourdes."

She sprints to her car. Luckily, she'd parked in the lot away from the scene and can get right out. By the grace of God, she drives down the same street minutes before an accident, escapes it, and then manages to park in the right place. Lily thinks that a lot lately. For years, she tiptoed close to disaster and remained unscathed. But now she wonders. How much bad news can you witness without having it taint you in some way? Is that why she's here thinking about settling down with Stephen and covering zoning board meetings?

It's been five months since she cracked up— two in London and now three here, but she's still not making any progress. Last week, there'd been a school shooting. The first local story close to the kind she was used to. The shooter was only thirteen and decided he didn't want to kill anybody— just wound them so they'd be scared to death the rest of their lives. It was his well thought out revenge for being bullied.

The shooting took place in the cafeteria of the middle school Lily had attended. Dazed, she saw herself sitting at the far table near the wall, where she and her friends ate lunch for the three years she attended school there. She blinked away the faces of her friends who for a moment took the place of the newly wounded.

For the first time— and she'd seen a lot of terrible things—Lily vomited in a wastebasket. Disgusted with herself, she thought, good thing Christiane Amanpour didn't see that. She never seemed to lose her composure. Through her time abroad, Lily adopted Christiane as both her silent witness and not so silent critic. Her unattainable bar: *What would Christiane do?*

Ashamed, she was scared she'd never be the reporter she once was. She needed to do something real around this story and pitched a follow up—a segment on the adults in this boy's life to try to figure out how nobody saw any red flags. Her producer said no.

"C'mon Rich. These stories keep popping up all over the country and all anybody does is say, gee, I guess he was kind of strange and quiet. Yeah, he was a loner. We report the school holds grief counseling and the parents are sad and then relieved their own kids are okay. That's crap. We need to go deeper. An in-depth story could do more."

"No, Lily. That is not what you were hired to do. Listen to me carefully. I don't want to have to say it again. I give you assignments and you do what I tell you to do. Period. You knew this was the gig when you signed on. Be grateful for the leeway I do give you." He hesitated. "You only signed on for six months. Deal with it."

But now, she's grateful for the adrenalin rush she feels for the first time since London. She heard the crash and didn't freeze. The wail of sirens didn't send her heartbeat into frenzy. Even if she's chasing an ambulance, it's something. She's going to get there first and dig for the real story. Her gut tells her there was more to this accident. All the rest of her grit may have deserted her, but there was still that.

At the hospital, she finds an inconspicuous place to stand where ambulances come in. There is too much commotion for anyone to bother with her. First, a heart attack is rolled in, then a kid knocked out during football practice. A few minutes later, a flurry of medical staff surround the accident victim's gurney. A resident snaps orders. "Alert the OR. We've got to stop the internal bleeding. Looks like blunt abdominal trauma. She's in acute respiratory distress. We'll take care of what we can and get her to surgery stat."

A nurse approaches the medics who brought her in. "Do you have ID?"

"Here's her purse." The strap was torn, the leather stained brown.

The nurse takes it in her gloved hand. "Poor woman."

Lily hovers in the background trying to get close enough to hear what they're saying. Although she can't risk moving in too close, their body language and expressions are clear. The driver is in bad shape but alive.

She waits for family to arrive. It gives her time to figure out how to approach without being offensive. Lily is certain there's a story here beyond the accident.

Chapter four

Denny glances at the clock. It's after five. Willow should be home soon. But lately, he's never really sure when she'll finally get here. When he presses her, she's evasive. She's taking on more responsibility at school, has errands to run, is meeting a friend for coffee. 'I'll be home when I get home' is all she says.

Who can blame her for not rushing home?

During his marathon migraines, Willow sleeps on the couch. She always leaves the living room immaculate but today everything is in disarray. A sheet and afghan are twisted on the couch. A half-filled coffee cup, an empty wine glass, a stack of novels— bookmarks in all of them— are on the coffee table. Still dragging from the dregs of the headache, he's determined to straighten up.

The headache battered the right side of his temple and face. Sound and light attacked him. He heard a lawn mower whirring inside his head. Black edges narrowed his vision, framed like strips of old photo negatives. He could do nothing but brace himself against the pain, lay in the dark, drift in and out of sleep.

Denny's recurring nightmare always finds its way into the throbbing crevices of his brain. Alone in the desert, on watch, sand whips and stings. The dream has no end, just a middle that holds him. In reality, he was sent out with a small unit to set up a base camp but in the dream he's alone, lost in a hostile place with snakes, tarantulas, infinite sand flies and infernal sand for company.

Willow knows the headache drill. Leave him the hell alone. But she doesn't. Denny knew she was angry because he waited to take the Relpax. "Stop nagging me, Willow. I know when to take the fucking pills." She hardly talked to him lately but never held back when it came to his headaches.

If she could imagine the burning sensation in his head from the pill while it worked, maybe she'd stop telling him what to do. She read. She heard. The doctor said. Denny didn't want Willow's annoying advice disturbing the cocoon of darkness and silence he needed to get through the headache.

"Goddammit, Willow. Let me be."

Now that the headache was gone, he cursed himself all afternoon. Lashing out at Willow was unfair. Always making up. Never doing anything right the first time around. Self-flagellation has also become one of his new unattractive qualities. *Stop this. Get your shit together, man. Pretend to be worth keeping around.*

It seems all his pain, residual and new, has become who he is. He may not be able to verbalize what happens when Demon—his name for it— enters his body and takes control. It's Demon who slams him without warning and makes him foul.

Denny knows he's living on the brink of something he doesn't want to happen. He can feel Willow's gloom settle in alongside Demon. He has to buck up and make all her disappointments fade.

She badgered him to go for therapy. "It's enough, Denny. Get help."

"Just how is a shrink supposed to help? It's not like I'm crazy. Or is that what you think?"

Exasperated, she sighed, "How many times do we have to have the same conversation? Psychiatrists are trained to help you deal with things like chronic illness and recurring nightmares. I don't know what else to say."

Knowing his apologies would never be enough, he relented. "Fine. I'll go."

Willow found him a therapist who counseled vets. Assessing the shrink at the first session, Denny pronounced him unqualified for such a specialty. It was obvious that this guy didn't have a clue about what it was like over there or what it was like to be sick. What a shmuck, sitting, nodding, like he got it. Maybe the shrink should take Demon on as a patient. Anything else was none of his business.

He wouldn't go back. Willow was disappointed, but hey, he gave it a shot, didn't he? Now, Denny went to group therapy at the Vet Center. What more did she want from him?

Work is the one thing that never lets him down. He loves everything about it —the smell of the wood, the design, the cutting, the required accuracy. It makes him a good craftsman. No matter what, he hasn't lost that.

That is not to say there is ever clear sailing. Finish work is his biggest problem. He does everything he can think of to ward off an allergy attack— opens all the windows, runs big fans to circulate the air, wears a military issue mask. His head pounds, his lungs burn, but he gets through it. He concentrates on bringing up the luster. Make it shine. Even when his leg throbs, he just pops a few more pain pills and keeps working. He should get some credit for that, right?

He'd come a long way. Local contractors are less leery of hiring him. He's getting more work through the Vet Center. Custom home office furniture is becoming his niche. He just got an order for a custom desk and bookcases. She has to give him credit for that.

Tonight, Willow will come home from work, smell dinner cooking, hear the sander buzzing. Norman Rockwell couldn't do better. Determined not to mess up another night, he'd make her favorite pasta. He'd show her tenderness.

Maybe he could make tonight the start of something better.

Chapter five

"Hi, Georgia, it's me. Blake just called." Jillian gulps, "He demanded I come home right after class. He wants to talk. He was, well…It's going to be bad. I know it is. Call me when you get this, okay?"

She hangs up the phone and shudders, unnerved.

Jillian came back from her solo trip to New York several months ago determined to get things back on track but all her lame attempts to morph into the kind of wife she thought Blake wanted didn't seem to matter. What he wasn't saying or doing, alarmed her. She wouldn't allow herself to think beyond getting through a day. And now this. Jillian imagines it's the tone he uses when calling parents about their child's misbehavior.

She sits at her desk and absently turns the pages of a costume catalog. For a moment, the years disappear. She is still the young dancer and he is totally devoted—understanding what ballet meant to her, respectful of the time she devoted to it, never resentful. It was Blake who came up with the long-distance marriage plan. The important thing then was he never wanted her to choose.

He was different from other boys. Aside from his great looks — curly dark hair, blue eyes, athletic build—he listened, was funny, smart and most of all, believed in her. Blake even studied anatomy to understand whatever strain or injury she suffered while dancing. Who does that?

Jillian shakes her head. What did she expect? That they would always be two young kids in love? The very nature of their personalities put them at odds. Her supportive, loving husband took laid back to a whole new level. Her rigid need for order pulled at the threads of their life, threatening to unravel all of it.

She hates that she simmers and stews and sinks into her own quicksand, that everything needs to be done her way, on her timetable. *I can't be someone I'm not, can I?* Jillian thought she'd come up with a brilliant solution. To put a stop to her constant nagging, she hung a dry erase board in the kitchen to list Blake and Chelsea's daily tasks. Slowly, she understood what she had done. Hanging over their kitchen table, it loomed down at them as a declaration of war, challenging them to do something drastic to stop their destructive, nitpicking clashes entirely. But nothing changed. They just lived each day locked into a state of restless unhappiness.

Her mother always warned her that her need to be right would be her undoing. *Well, Mom. Right again.*

Jillian never dreamed of anything but becoming a world class soloist. The way some girls dream of fairy tale wedding dresses, Jillian imagined elaborate ballet costumes. When that dream collapsed, she skidded through her life. She never thought she would become one of those women who would "have it all," even though it appears she does. Instead, she feels constantly under siege, made worse by a husband who lives in a different time zone.

It didn't have to be that way. The rollercoaster off-switch might be stuck but they can figure out a way to stop it. Why couldn't they undo the minutia that was burying them and remember how they began? Of course, they could.

Jillian had two loves in her life. Ballet failed her. Blake would not.

Tonight, will be the night they begin fixing things, she thinks. Yes. She'll make it happen. She'll convince him. Blake is all she knows.

Jillian promises herself that all she'll do is listen and channel the Blake she wanted to be with forever, the man who used to make her laugh at herself, who told her that she could be a professional ballet dancer, run a dance school, or anything else she put her mind to. The man who told her he would love her forever.

She aches to see that Blake tonight. She wants to be that Jillian. They will remember their best selves. She'll make sure of it.

Chapter six

The sauce simmers on the stove and the kitchen table is set. Denny clipped some crimson and gold mums from the garden to put on the table. Willow is late but that gives him time to regroup from the effort. He actually made dinner. *One small step for mankind.*

He sits in his worn lounge chair to wait for her, remembering to turn on the pole lamp beside him. Willow is always on his case if he's watching TV in the dark when she comes home.

Sitting with an unopened Patterson mystery in his lap and the TV set on, Denny tries to remember if she said she had something to do after work. The news ticker reports an accident tying up traffic. Maybe she's held up in that. She'll be glad to come home to a hot dinner.

He must have dozed off and is startled awake by the doorbell. *What are the damn kids selling this time? Why can't everyone leave me alone?*

The heavy rapping on the door lifts him to his feet. He sees a cruiser in the driveway.

"It's the police, sir. May we come in?"

Denny opens the door. Two police officers stand on the top step. "Mr. D'Angelo? Willow D'Angelo's husband?"

He nods and opens the screen door for them to come in.

The policewoman sniffs, "Is something burning?"

Denny runs into the kitchen. He thought he'd turned down the flame but hadn't. The boiling sauce scorched the bottom of the pot. "Shit," he mutters.

The police follow him into the kitchen. "I'm Officer Donovan and this is Officer Moore."

To support his buckling legs, he leans against the counter. "What happened to Willow?" Denny asks so quietly he's barely audible, his face drained of color.

33

"She was in a car accident and is in surgery at Lourdes Hospital. That's all we know. We'll take you there."

He shudders. "Not the accident on the news?"

"Yes, sir. I'm afraid so."

Wordless, Denny follows them out the door. With the siren blaring, the ten-minute ride to the hospital takes five but still feels interminable. Hunched over, he holds his head in his hands. *Willow, you can't leave me. God, please don't take her from me*, he silently prays. But it's reflex. When has God ever been good to him?

Chapter seven

Lily stands near the entrance of the emergency room waiting for the family to arrive. The waiting room is crowded with listless children snuggled on their mothers' laps; a woman howls that her husband is being ignored; a teenager holds an ice pack to his head.

While waiting, she calls Albany Memorial, the hospital closest to the accident scene. She assumes the other driver was taken there because his injuries were not life threatening. Lily wheedles some information. They won't give her a name but she manages to find out he didn't sustain any serious injuries and would soon be released.

Two police officers arrive with a doleful looking man. The woman officer holds his arm to steady him. He's tall and lanky with reddish hair pulled into a ponytail. He wears a faded plaid flannel work shirt and his belt is pulled tight to keep up his faded jeans. To Lily, he looks worn down despite his ramrod straight posture. A nurse greets him, lightly touches his arm. Lily stands back knowing she has to stay inconspicuous or they'll kick her out.

The nurse wrinkles her forehead as she speaks to them. Lily can only partially hear what she's saying —accident, injuries, surgery, trauma. The officers look grim. The man's face is stone.

The policewoman says, "Good luck, sir. I hope your wife comes through this okay." The policeman shakes his hand.

Lily follows the nurse and the man upstairs to the surgical waiting room. "This is going to be a long night, sir, and it will be quiet. Your wife's our only emergency surgery for now. If you need anything at all, Vicky is the charge nurse. She's right down the hall."

"Okay," he nods.

Lily trails behind them, then sits across the room to give him space. He has to be her husband or lover, although she doubts the latter from the looks of him. She tries not to stare at the rumpled man. He shifts in the chair trying to find a comfortable position. Leaning back, he stretches out his long legs and then doesn't move a muscle. He sits frozen in place. Every once in a while, he rubs his knee and repositions his leg.

Lily takes off her blue silk suit jacket and folds it on the chair next to her, noticing the coffee stain on the sleeve. *I'll just hold the mic in my right hand for the ten o'clock*, she thinks. *Amber is going to kill me if I can't get the stain out.* She takes a hair tie from her purse and cajoles her long curls into a loose bun and rolls her neck to work out the kinks.

Her instinct is to comfort the man but all his signals scream stay back. Studying him, she thinks he's good looking in an unconventional way. His auburn hair frames a lightly freckled, weathered face with green eyes set in deep pockets. He looks like he hasn't slept well in years.

Not what I was expecting, Lily thinks. On the drive to the hospital, she began writing the lead in her head, assuming this would be a story of sudden tragedy in a suburban family. But from the looks of him, he's not part of a suburban family and is already in ruins.

Lily clears her throat. "Excuse me, sir."

He appears not to hear her.

"Sir, is there someone I can call for you?"

He looks at her, surprised someone else is in the room with him, shakes his head and looks down at the floor.

"Just let me know if you need anything."

He doesn't react.

Lily itches to get some kind of new information but knows she needs to suppress the urge. *Make yourself useful.*

She walks to the nurses' station down the hall. A woman with sandy colored permed hair looks up from her paperwork. "What can I do for you? Hey, wait a minute. I know you. You're that Lily reporter, aren't you? You did that school shooting story. Oh my God, what a scary story… my kids went there…"

Lily cut her off. "Vicky. You're Vicky, aren't you?" She checks her name badge. "Listen, I wonder if you could find out if that man in the waiting room has someone you can call? He shouldn't have to wait alone."

"You shouldn't be here, Lily. I can call you Lily, can't I? No media. That's the rule."

"All I want you to do is check in with the man waiting for his wife to get out of surgery. I'm sure that wouldn't be too much trouble. Find out if you can call someone for him."

She huffs, "I don't see how that's any of your business."

Lily snaps, "Just see if you can help the guy. That's all I'm asking."

"Don't take that tone with me." She stands and walks around the nurses' station to face Lily. "Lily, I'm sorry. But you have to leave. I really don't want to call security. Our families need privacy and you have no business being here."

Chapter eight

Denny, can you hear the baby? I can hear his muffled cries. I'm under water. It's murky and I can't surface. I'm trying to kick but my legs won't move.

Make sure he's swaddled. It will make him feel safe. We had a beautiful baby even though you refused. Did we name him Matthew? It means gift of God. Did you know that? It's a name to protect him. No matter what you may see, Denny, he's perfect to me.

That's what I was telling you when you said those awful words. Once they hit the air, you wouldn't take them back. You broke my heart. I could feel it crackling into shards. My heart fell out of place and just dangled. I'd put my hand to the place that once held it and could feel the change. Even the rhythm of the beats was different.

I am a mother. Even though you said no. No baby for us. TOO RISKY. That's funny, Denny. Mr. I-Need-Risk-to-Feel-Alive. Zoom Zoom Zero to Sixty.

But it was all a bad dream. Matthew is reaching for me but I can't take him. The water is too deep and my legs are tired.

But you can, Denny. Don't you dare say you won't.

Chapter nine

Blake stands in the kitchen looking out the back window. There is so much work to do in this yard every season. *How is this going to work? Move out and then come back to do the usual chores? There are so many things I haven't considered.*

His stomach flips when he hears Jillian pull into the driveway. He heads toward the front door but stops. Turning around, he walks through the kitchen and out the back door onto the deck. It now seems the only place to tell her.

Blake wipes off the chairs, still wet from the rain, and sits down. Though partially hidden by a cloud, the sun, low in the sky, warms him. He searches for the right words to begin the conversation but nothing comes. *How long are you going to sit in the car, Jillian? Let's get this over with.*

Finally, he hears the car door slam.

She walks into the kitchen, puts down her ballet tote. Through the garden window, she sees him sitting bent over, looking down, with his elbows resting on his knees. He's in classic Blake worry stance. She knows trouble is waiting for her. When she woke up, she expected a routine Tuesday. As she made her mental list of tasks—a trip to the costume store, a pointe class, their menu for dinner— it never entered her mind that her life could be inextricably altered by evening.

And the irony of Blake calling the shots is not lost on her.

I'll try to keep my mouth shut for once. No. I'll grovel. No, I'll... at that moment, she's at a total loss.

She pours herself a glass of Shiraz, opens the screen door, and lets it bang shut behind her.

Blake turns toward her and gestures for her to sit across from him.

"I prefer to stand. What's going on?"

Blake doesn't look at her. "When we first moved here, Chelsea was how old? Four? She ran in circles, arms wide open, and when she spotted the swing set and slide, she squealed, 'I have my own playground.' Remember that, Jillian?"

"Of course, I remember… her little legs pumping hard." Jillian looks past Blake to the area where the swings used to be. " 'Mommy, push me higher!' And she'd sing at the top of her lungs, never in tune." He didn't return Jillian's wan smile. "Of course, I remember," she sputters.

"Ancient history." Quietly, he says, "I have something to tell you."

She slugs the wine. "Do you want a glass? Let's just have some wine first."

He shakes his head. "No… I don't want to drag this out." He looks straight at her. "I'm done. I'm leaving you, Jillian …right now. Tonight. I want a divorce."

Jillian swallows hard. She tries but can't contain the anger bubbling beneath the surface. "That's it? You just stand there and tell me you want a divorce? You said you wanted to talk. That's not talking, Blake." Her voice rises, "No. Absolutely not. We're not getting divorced."

He stands. "No more commands, Jillian. Just think about what the last years have been like."

"Don't go there, Blake. Don't turn this all on me." She struggles to find her breath. "Things have been a little off lately. We can fix that…" She rambles, "I went to New York to sort things out. I never had a chance to tell you what happened there. What I did, what I learned…"

He walks toward the gate.

"Wait, stop, you can't leave yet."

Her insides quake, the wine backwashing into her throat. She straightens her spine and glares at him. "You're so calm. Definite. Wait a minute. There's only one reason that…oh my god… you've met someone, haven't you? You're leaving me because you've found someone else. You're having an affair. That's it, isn't it?" Her voice is shrill even to her own ears. She looks hard at him and sees nothing in his face to tell her it's not true. She lunges toward him and slaps him hard.

He rubs his cheek, undeterred. "We're over. Have been for years even if we didn't do anything about it. In a few days, when you get over the idea that it's me leaving you, you'll probably be relieved."

"Don't patronize me. Who is she? You have to tell me." She stands and begins walking back and forth on the deck. circling the chairs. "I can't believe it. How could you? How? When?" She grips the back of a chair to steady herself.

He walks towards the driveway.

"Wait. You can't just leave like this. We have to figure this out. Okay. You had an affair. It happens. Just say it's over and we'll..."

He turns to face her. "We should have separated years ago but we didn't. I wasn't looking for anything. It just happened. We'll talk tomorrow and tell Chelsea together."

She grabs his arm to keep him from going. "I want to know who she is. You owe me at least that. Who is she?" She hears herself speaking but doesn't recognize the strange voice.

He pulls away from her. "No. I'm not going there, Jillian. This conversation is about us."

"Conversation? Look at me, Blake." She shrieks, "You can't just make an announcement that ruins our lives and then run."

"I'm not going to dignify that remark. I've never run. I've always been... well, never mind. Think what you want. Chelsea will be off to college soon. She's no dummy. We haven't fooled her. You know that, don't you?"

Jillian's mind spins with images of Blake with someone else, someone not her. "What does she know? This can't happen now. Not just before she leaves, too. No. Please, Blake."

"Chelsea will be okay. She's an amazing kid. Happy, involved, has lots of friends, is a good student." He glares at her. "For a teen-ager, she feels pretty good about herself, in spite of..."

Stung, Jillian's eyes well up. "Can't wait to get to her," she moans. "Don't do this to me. To us."

"Call Georgia. Tell her to come over. I picked up Buddha's delight for you and Mongolian beef for her. Your favorites."

Chapter ten

Lily attacks the elevator button, pushing it over and over. *Fool. What would the world do without us? They wouldn't know a damn thing about what's going on, that's what. That's the rub. The total rub.*

Power walking to the cafeteria, she buys a cup of coffee, sits at a corner table and pulls out her cell phone. "Amber, are you on tonight?"

"Where else would I be?" she asks. "Why are you wearing my most expensive suit? You better not spill anything on it."

Lily puts her arm behind her back and stands, scanning the cafeteria. "I don't see you."

"At the cash register. Will I be glad to see you?"

Amber is tall but gives an even taller appearance. Her smooth, mahogany skin, high cheekbones, and wide oval brown eyes are framed by straightened shoulder length hair.

Lily can see her bright smile from across the room. "Of course, you will. I'm pure delight."

Amber and Lily are close as sisters as are their mothers, Lisa and Marika. Amber, six years older, always looked out for her. When Lily came back from London adrift and depressed, one word about not being ready to move in with Stephen right away and Amber immediately offered her spare bedroom.

"It feels great to sit." Amber stretches out her long legs and massages her stiff neck. "What's up? Why are you here?"

"I was on my way to cover a meeting. Stopped at Starbucks and while I was waiting, I heard a crash." She takes a breath. "Amber, I heard the crash and the sirens and didn't turn into a puddle. I think I'm on my way back."

"I hope so, Lily. That's a good sign." She yawns. "I heard someone came in with major trauma. I don't think I'll ever get used to seeing how people's lives are mangled in a nanosecond," Amber shakes her head. "Makes me happy I'm in obstetrics."

"Absolutely."

She peers hard at her. "So why are you still here? Even I know the drill. You go back to the station, file your report, and then see what else is happening in our exciting town for the next broadcast."

Lily shrugs, "When I was on my way here, I had this whole scenario in my head. Mother is on her way to daycare or some kind of sports practice—depending on her age. She's a soccer mom with a husband, two kids, blah blah. But now, I know I was dead wrong about that. The man I think is her husband looks like he's been through the ringer already and from what I can see is as comatose as you can be without being unconscious."

"That's my Lily. I don't know what you're doing as a reporter. You should write novels instead. I tell you when my practice is big and fat, I'm setting you up. With your work ethic and imagination, we'll make a fortune."

Lily ignores her. "I know I should leave but I can't. I'm going to keep an eye on him until someone comes. I can't explain it but something isn't right with him or with the accident. There's a story here…"

Amber squeezes some mayo into her chicken wrap and blows on her tea. "No, there isn't. I know you're desperate to feel the work again but ambulance chasing? Uh, no. It was just a sad, unfortunate accident like they all are."

"Amber," Lily interrupts. "When I heard the crash, I reacted. I didn't stand around like my feet were lodged in wet cement. There's a reason I was there. There is something odd about the accident and that guy…"

"A reason? Sure there is," she rolls her eyes. "Okay, never mind. Hey, why is there a honking brown stain on my favorite blue silk jacket?"

Lily rubs it. "I'll take it to the cleaners first thing in the morning. Sorry."

"Damn it, Lily. Wear your own clothes. You got enough of them crowding my closets," she retorts, sipping her green tea. "And the answer is no, I'm not going to find anything out for you."

"I didn't ask…"

"You were getting there. Why else would you be calling me? Here, you want a bite?"

"No thanks."

"Okay. New subject. What's up with Stephen? You're there a lot. He's got to be thinking you're ready. Are you finally all in?"

She reaches over to Amber's plate and takes a chip. "I thought I made up my mind this morning. When I woke up, I looked around the room. Uncluttered, but comfortable. He has a fluffy, blue comforter his grandmother quilted for him. In one corner of the room, his guitars are on stands, arranged just so. The way the sun streams in mornings, makes you feel, well... grateful. He just added a bookcase that he left half empty for me. It's beautiful. He had it made by some carpenter he heard about at the Vet Center."

"The Vet Center?"

Lily smiles, "Stephen volunteers twice a week. He writes letters, tries to get them through bureaucratic mazes and runs a writing class. He says it's the least he can do. It wasn't his butt on the line in Iraq or Afghanistan."

"Yes, I can hear him saying that." Amber nods, taking the last big bite.

"He overheard a conversation about a Marine who fought in the first Gulf War, with a flailing carpentry business. Stephen glommed right on to that and hired him. Thus, the new bookcase. Turns out he's a really fine craftsman. He wants to have him make a bureau. Something with long, deep drawers since the closet space is so pathetic."

"Hmmm. So, let me see if I've got this. You woke up, the sun is warming your face. You're in a featherbed surrounded by custom furniture designed for you and you say, 'Self, I could get used to this but I better not. I might become too happy. Or worse yet, dependent.'"

They both laugh.

Lily hesitates.

"Spill it, Lily. When nothing comes out of your mouth, something I don't want to hear is about to burst out."

"Smart ass. ... I got a call yesterday."

"I got a woman in labor. Tell me fast."

"Long shot job."

"Lordy, spit it out."

"I'm a finalist for a job at NPR. National Public Radio. Based in D.C."

"I know what NPR is. That's radio. You're a TV reporter."

"It's serious in-depth news, Amber."

"Sounds like same old without hair and makeup. You realize it will completely screw things up with Stephen. Total self-sabotage." Amber narrows her eyes, "Never thought you'd be such a chicken shit— either personally or professionally."

"Is that what I am? Gee, and I thought I was exploring options because I had a nervous breakdown."

"Don't go drama queen on me. Talk it through."

"A job like that is who I am. I'd be back doing international news. But… if I do this, Stephen and I are done. He's made that clear. I know I love him. He's been so great through my… transition. But you know how I grew up. Maybe I'm not cut out for the day to day."

"I was there, girlfriend. Never did a girl grow up with more love and security."

Lily shrugs, "Maybe. But my parents couldn't make it work."

Amber said, "Excuse not a reason. You and Stephen are not remotely like your mom and dad."

"Anyway, I know something isn't right about this accident. I can feel it. I definitely think it might have been a sign that I was there and witnessed it."

"There you go again changing the subject," Amber sighed. "Really, Lily. A sign? A reason? Remember how we used to laugh at all those stories your mother would spin about your great grandmother and her superstitions? Now, you're beginning to sound like her. It's pathetic. There is nothing here for you. It was an unfortunate accident and you don't know anything about the people involved. Making it into more than that is not your way back into anything."

Amber finished her tea. "I've got to run so I'm giving you the short version of the speech I've given you for years. You're just plain scared of living your own life. Time to do that instead of observing everybody else's. Stephen is a good man who is waiting for you to run out of excuses. If you don't want to move to the next step, you'd better tell him. You owe him that. Quit dragging this out."

"I know that. My doubts never ever occur to me when we're together."

"Did you hear what you just said?"

Lily muses, "I guess because I'm in job limbo now it makes me feel unsure about all my choices."

"He'd support you if you wanted to go back to school or start something new."

"Absolutely not. It has to be an equal partnership."

"I'm just saying…you never know what you might find. I heard something interesting today. A patient is applying for a fellowship at the Dart Institute for Journalism and Trauma. I think it's at Columbia. Ever heard of it?"

"No."

"They focus on ethical reporting on violence, conflict and tragedy. Check it out. You're killer on writing and research. Or find something where you could be based here and travel on assignment. Broaden your focus, little sister. Haven't you heard? We live in a digital world." Amber put her plate and cup on the tray. "Anyway, I have to go." She stood. "Wrap this story up. Do a straight report for the ten o'clock. Then, go to Stephen's. Time to start living your own life instead of watching everybody else's."

"I hear you, Bossy." Lily agrees. "But still, I have to listen to my intuition. I know there is a story here for me."

"You call it intuition. I call it imagination. Diversion. Or maybe even desperation. Anyway, gotta run. I'll call you later."

Chapter eleven

Where is that bright light coming from? It's surrounding me. Denny? Are you there? I can't see you— it's blinding— but I know you're there. I can feel you. I can always sense you staring at me even if I don't let on.

I'm still being carried through water. Can't kick or paddle. Arms and legs don't move. Whoosh! The current is moving, carrying me along.

Don't let me drown. My dress. The blue one we bought in Cape May is all wet and gritty from the sand. The one I always wear for luck. It's sticking to me and I want to rip it off. But I can't. So much for luck.

Denny. I see your gleaming motorcycle. You'll rub off the paint if you keep at it. Silly boy. Shiny, shiny, so shiny... then just a heap of crumbled metal. Maybe that light I see is the same one you described. What did you say? It calmed you. Yes. I get that now.

Voices echo. They are near and far. Crowding around me. Men and women, pushing and pulling. What do they want from me? I want to help them but I don't know how.

The current is carrying me faster. We're coming to a beautiful waterfall. I wonder what's beyond it.

Chapter twelve

Willow should have called by now. She promised to let me know when she was on her way to the inn. An uneasy feeling takes Blake right to her house. He feels conspicuous sitting in his car across the street, but the husbands and wives coming home from work, focused on pulling bicycles, baseball bats, and soccer balls off driveways, don't seem to notice him.

Denny's truck is in the driveway but her car is not. He calls her cell phone repeatedly but it goes straight to voice mail. He leaves yet another message. "Come on, Willow. Pick up, will you? Please, sweetheart. I'm beginning to worry."

As the sun begins to fade, he circles the block and rolls past her house again. There's one dim light coming from the living room in the otherwise dark house.

Willow said she wasn't afraid to tell Denny. Her only concern was that she tell him in the right way. Blake didn't have the heart to tell her the how and the what didn't matter. He'd only hear that she was leaving and who knows how a guy like him will react?

Blake gets out and walks up the long driveway past Denny's truck. Peeking into the garage and into the back of the house, there is no sign of either of them. He walks up the back porch stairs and looks into the kitchen. It's in order. There are pots on the stove. Blake sees the table is set complete with a bouquet of flowers.

But no one is home.

He walks back to the car and calls another five times. *There has to be a good reason she can't pick up. Maybe I should just go to the inn as we planned. I can't stay parked in front of her house.*

He's sweating despite the coolness of the late day. Blasting the air conditioning helps. He turns on the radio and hears a traffic report suggesting alternate routes. There's been an accident and traffic is backed up.

At the Beverwyck Inn, Blake stands in the doorway and scans the lounge, willing her to be casually sitting at a table waiting for him. But, of course, she isn't there. *I'll just wait a bit*, he thinks. *Maybe she's in the ladies' room.* He stands too long at the door.

The bartender calls out, "Hey, man. Come on in. We don't bite."

Blake smiles. "I'm waiting for someone."

"Why don't you have a drink while you wait? You look like you could use one."

"Good idea," Blake says, unconvinced. He positions himself at the bar so he can still see the lobby.

"What'll it be?"

"Scotch and soda." Blake takes off his tie and slips it into his jacket pocket. He rolls up the sleeves of his blue shirt, the one Willow comments on every time he wears it. It reminds her of the ocean, she always says. Brings out the blue in his eyes.

The bartender smiles at him, pulls at his trim beard. "You look familiar. I pride myself on never forgetting a face."

Blake runs his hand through his thick hair. "I don't think so. Never been here before." His leg shakes; in one hand he clutches his phone, the other his drink.

"Give me a minute. Wait. I got it." He grins. "Knew I'd get it. You're the principal at my kids' school. I try to go to as many of my son's games as I can. My daughter goes there, too."

"What's the name?"

"Frank. Judy and James Frank."

"Great kids."

"They are. Judy's on the honor roll every quarter. And my boy. We're hoping for a football scholarship."

"You have good reason to be proud." Blake swigs his drink.

"This is none of my business but you don't look so good. You okay?"

"Sure. I'm fine." Blake tries to smile. "Just don't tell your kids I was in a bar on a school night."

The bartender laughs, "Good to see a principal without a stick up his ass. Oops, sorry. Bad language. Anyway, let me know when you're ready for another." He pauses. "And don't worry, buddy. I never saw you. If anyone asks, you were never here."

Blake nods, nursing the rest of his drink. Still, no Willow. Finally, his phone rings. "Willow? Are you okay? Where are you?"

"So that's her name. Willow. Willow what?"

"I'm sorry, Jillian. I thought…"

"I can imagine what you thought. What am I supposed to tell Chelsea? I think we should do it together. Be back here at nine," she orders. "That's her curfew tonight."

"No Jillian. We'll tell her tomorrow. Calmly."

"Can't leave your girlfriend to talk to your daughter about leaving us?"

"Don't get ugly, Jillian. I'll see you tomorrow." He clicks off.

The bar is filling up. Marking time there is even worse than sitting at home waiting to tell Jillian. He pushes images of everything that can be wrong out of his mind. He can already feel the drink and knows he shouldn't have another. He pays his bill and goes to the desk to check in. Sinking into the bed, he realizes how weary he is, and closes his eyes. *Wouldn't Jillian love to know I'm stood up? She could add it to the list of things her husband couldn't do right.*

The only other time he'd been to an inn was when he and Jillian were first married. They spent their honeymoon at a bed and breakfast on Lake Cayuga, one of central New York's Finger Lakes.

The owner asked them to call her Ms. Aurora. Her long honey-colored hair was held by a wreath of flowers. She walked gracefully and was light footed, despite her fleshy body. She looked ageless.

"Everyone should rename themselves when they understand who they are. Perhaps, you'll think about that during your stay. I'm Aurora, for the Aurora Borealis, the sky's natural light display. It's created by the collision of charged particles in the atmosphere as was I. My own aura is luminous and I emit life changing healing rays. Open yourselves to my positive energy field, my darlings."

She was a collector of music boxes, Chinese urns, erotic pencil drawings, and delectable food and spices. The smell of baking scones and patchouli lingered in the air.

Ms. Aurora insisted they inspect every available room. They were all different, decorated in single color themes with corresponding baskets of lotions and oils. The bathrooms were mirrored and had big claw foot tubs. Before Blake and Jillian made their choice, Ms. Aurora asked them to lie down on each bed to see how it felt and whether or not they liked that particular view of the lake.

When Ms. Aurora finally left them in a lavender room, Jillian tittered, "Freak show."

"But don't you love how she cares about the smallest detail?"

Jillian pushed him onto the bed. Pulling her dress over her head. "I suppose. How did we do? You like this view?"

"Exquisite. Just spectacular."

They never left their room. Ms. Aurora left trays of croissants with butter and jelly, strong, hot Kona coffee, cheese and crackers, fruit, pate, artisanal salads—all on fine china. In the late afternoon, she'd leave sparkling wine in crystal goblets, and elaborate flower arrangements. She'd knock and then leave the tray by the door.

Before they left, she asked, "Would you like me to do your numerology?"

Jillian forced a smile. "We really need to get on the road."

"Oh my darling, I don't want to trouble you but I see tension surrounding you, Jillian."

"Not at all."

"I'm a gifted intuitive. I sense things, even the smallest vibrations. When things become hard for the two of you —and they will— remember the time you spent in my home. Marriage is hard, my dears, but love is not. People become unhappy because they forget that. Come to me."

"We really have to go." Jillian took Blake's hand.

"Jillian, don't be afraid," she chided. "Since you are rushed, I will do a brief smudging ceremony. It's been performed for centuries to remove negative energy as well as for centering and healing. It will only take a moment."

Ms. Aurora gently pulled them to her. She placed her hands on their heads and mumbled something they didn't understand. She then took smoking sage and marked the space around them.

When she finished, she handed them a bag of candles and oils. "Smudging is a sacred Native American custom. It will keep you in balance. Don't forget the time you spent here. When times are hard, come back to me."

She hugged them both, pulling them to her as a mother might.

"Thank you, Ms. Aurora," Blake said. "We couldn't have chosen a better place to spend our honeymoon."

Walking to the car, Jillian asked, "Blake, you don't believe in that clap trap, do you?"

"I don't know. But I like what she said about remembering our time here. Let's not ever forget it, promise?"

Jillian laughed. "I should have known all her weirdness would appeal to you." She kissed his nose. "Come on. Let's go. Let's not waste another minute before I have to leave for New York." She twirled to the car.

Blake wonders if Ms. Aurora is still in business. Willow would love everything about the place. On the long drive home, they would imagine renaming themselves and what that could mean for them. He felt his eyes closing.

Before he gave in to sleep, he checked his phone one more time to see if he could have possibly missed her call.

Chapter thirteen

Denny paces stiffly, looping back and forth around the waiting room's perimeter. There's been an attempt to make it comfortable. The chairs are in groupings. There is a counter tucked into the corner with a Keurig, an array of coffee pods, and a basket of granola bars. Under the counter is a small refrigerator. Off to the left, a consultation room. Old *People* and *Sports Illustrated* magazines are neatly piled around an arrangement of silk flowers on a coffee table in the center of the room.

But the room's purpose can't be disguised. Institutional comfort. Antiseptic hospital smells permeate the space along with anxiety, relief, and sorrow.

Denny's fear liquefies and rushes through his veins. Life without Willow? No. He can't go there. Won't.

Willow, I cannot be without you. Hang on. Forgive me. Give me a chance to make things up to you. I've always loved you. Despite… His eyes water and he blinks hard to clear them.

Buck up, man, he thinks.

"C'mon, Denny." Willow pulled him down the walk toward a white, green-shuttered house with an open porch.

"Slow down. Renting a house seems…well…like too much responsibility. What's wrong with a small apartment?"

"No. This is a perfect beginning for us. It even has a two-car garage for your workshop."

He pursed his lips. "I think you're jumping ahead of things."

She kissed him. "I see us here, Denny. This is where our life begins." She skipped up the front stairs onto the porch and sat down on a wicker chair. "When we have babies, they can play outside and I can keep an eye on them while I sit right here."

"Babies? Whoa. We're still kids ourselves, Willow."

"That's our future. Why not think about it now when it's such a beautiful story?" she assured him.

A car pulled into the driveway. "Hello, Willow. You must be Denny. I'm Lorraine Madigan." She got out and shook their hands. "This is the deal. It's a rental with option to buy. The owners aren't ready to sell yet. They want to be sure that if they don't like Florida, they'll still have their home. But seriously, have you ever known anyone who would trade 80 degree Februarys for our Nor'easters?"

Willow smiled. "See Denny. It's just as I explained. Rent while we're in college. Buy later. Let's go in."

Her description to Denny was spot on. It was a light airy place, well cared for by the owners.

"Our dream house." Willow squeezed his hand.

Denny asked Lorraine. "No crime to speak of here?"

"Nothing to worry about. City but safe."

He forced a smile. "If that's the case and I don't have to worry about you, we'll take it."

Willow looked at him quizzically. "It's not like I'll be living here by myself."

"Just being thorough," he muttered.

Willow opened her wallet. "Okay. I brought the deposit. Do you have the lease?"

After they signed, Denny and Willow drove to the Corning Preserve and strolled hand in hand on the path. "It's dirt cheap. We can manage it even…"

Willow interrupted. "It's fate. We were meant to have it."

"I don't think fate bothers itself with house rentals. I always thought your mother's crystal readings damaged your brain. Now, I'm sure of it," he teased. "You may be the most beautiful woman on the planet but not the fastest. Race you to the bridge."

Breathless, they ran. Just behind him, Willow grabbed his hand. They fell together on the grass. Canoes and kayaks dotted the river.

She let some time pass. "Den, something's going on. What's up? Tell me right now," she demanded.

He looked across the river, away from her. "There is something I have to tell you and I don't know how." He stammered, "You know I'm a lousy student. Community college isn't for me."

"Did you fail stats? It's no big deal. You can just take something else. You'll find the right thing."

Unable to look at her, he said, "I already have."

Her voice quivered. "What are you trying to say? Tell me right this minute." She turned to face him and yanked on his chin to make him look at her.

"You know I want to spend my life with you," he faltered. "I did something yesterday you're not going to like." He was breathing hard. "I'm not meant for college. I hate it. And if I don't make it as a carpenter, I need a career."

She squeaked out, "What kind of career?"

He sucked in a big breath. "I joined the Marines."

All the color drained from her face. She screamed at him, "What? You're a jerk and a liar."

She stood, turned around and walked away from him. Then, she broke into a run. Her long legs carrying her away from him and what he'd just told her. She was fast, but he was faster. He caught up to her, pulled on the sleeve of her lacey shirt to stop her. "Willow, please stop. Listen to me. I didn't tell you first because I knew you'd be mad but it's something I have to do."

Her eyes flamed. "You want to be some tough guy, maybe get blown up or something. You go right ahead." She pushed him. "Get the hell away from me."

She sprinted away. He called after her. "I'll get leave. It's only for a few years. Then, I'll be ready."

He threw their life off track with one stupid, misguided decision.

Chapter fourteen

Georgia pulls Jillian into her arms. "I came as soon as I could."

"You know the last thing he said before he ran out the door? Call Georgia. I got your favorite Chinese. Jackass."

"Poor Blake. He doesn't even know how to be spiteful. It's not in his nature."

"Spare me your Blake Golden cheerleader routine tonight. Okay?"

Georgia ignores her and puts her bag on the table. "I'm sleeping over. And I brought wine and tortilla chips which you will eat tonight."

"I would get stinking drunk if it weren't a week night."

"If tonight isn't a drinking night, what is? I'll get us some glasses. Sit down, honey. We have time to talk before Chelsea gets home." Georgia walks toward the kitchen.

Jillian cries out, "He left me for someone else."

Georgia spins around. "What?"

"You heard me."

She shook her head. "That's not possible. I don't believe it."

"Her name is Willow."

"He told you about her? Willow as in tree? What kind of name is that?"

"I don't know. He wasn't going to tell me about her at all," she grumbles. "He was going to let me believe it was just about us."

"So how did you find out?"

Weepy, Jillian said, "I just knew. And when I accused him, he didn't deny it."

"So, who is she?"

"He wouldn't say anything about her when he was here. Tried to keep it about us. But I called him. I shouldn't have but I did.

Demanded he come home so we could talk to Chelsea tonight." She shook her head slowly. "He thought it was her, said her name so gently, like it was a goddamn prayer. It made me sick."

"What did he say when it was you? Was he flustered?"

"No. He sounded worn out. Said we'd talk tomorrow and hung up."

"You should probably figure out what to tell Chelsea together. Calmly."

"How is that supposed to happen?"

"This may not be as bad as you think, Jilly."

"Trust me. Things couldn't be any worse." Jillian leans back into the white leather couch and pulls her knees up to her chin. "I came home right after my last class. When I pulled into the driveway, I saw he beat me home. His car was parked in the street. That should have been the tip off. He didn't want me to block him in. I knew what I was walking into but tried kidding myself, thinking he'd never have the guts to tell me he wanted out," she sniffles. "I thought I could stall him. Keep him from telling me what I didn't want to hear."

She swirls the wine in the glass Georgia handed her. "I sat in the car, took down my hair and brushed it out—didn't want to look severe. Then, I went into the kitchen to get a glass of wine. When I looked out the window and saw him, I knew. I hoped the weaker part of him, the part of him that never wants to hurt anybody, would prevail. I steeled myself for bad news but thought I could make nice."

She shreds a balled-up tissue. "He didn't say much. We haven't been happy, I think he can't do anything right, I'm a bad mother, Chelsea will be going off to college, blah blah…" Jillian draws in a deep breath, "Then, he flat out announces he wants a divorce." Jillian sighs. "Whenever I thought about leaving him, I couldn't imagine it. I would cast out those thoughts because I couldn't envision being without him and alone."

"Jilly, I'm so sorry."

She cries, "Georgia, he looked tired under the weight of it all. I knew there was nothing I could say. I could see it was too late."

"Maybe it's too soon for me to say this, Jillian, but this is no real bombshell. That it was Blake is the only real surprise."

Jillian snaps, "You're right, Georgia. I don't want to hear it."

"Jilly, honey, I'm only saying that you haven't been happy in ages. It burns that he's found someone else. Never saw that in Blake's DNA but," Georgia steels herself. "Have you forgotten about Philip?"

Bitterness rolls off her tongue. "That was nothing. I never would have let it get that far. Everybody thinks Blake's such a saint. Well, he's not, is he?"

Georgia ignores her. "This is what I'm wondering…"

"What?"

"Isn't any part of you relieved? I mean how many Thursday nights out did we talk about how frustrated and mismatched you were?"

Softly, she admits, "That's all it was. Talk. Truth? I'm scared to death. I don't remember a damn thing before us. We've been together half my life." She drains her glass.

Chelsea bursts through the front door. Her face is streaked with tears. Georgia rushes to hug her. "What's wrong, love bug?"

She puts her head on Georgia's shoulder and looks over at her mother whose tear-stained face matches her own.

Chelsea looks at the two of them. "What's wrong, Mom? Why are you here, Georgia? Did something happen? Where's Daddy? Is Grandma okay?"

"Everyone's fine. Daddy. Grandma. All fine." Jillian puts down her glass and walks to her daughter. "What's wrong?"

"We were at the library. Sam rushed in. He looked like he was going to cry. He told us he was getting something to eat at *Moe's* when he heard a loud crash. He ran out to see what happened and it was terrible. A car and a van crashed into each other. Look." She opens her phone and clicks on a video. Jillian sees the smashed car, a limp, bloody body lifted onto a stretcher, the medics running to the ambulance.

"I'm sorry you had to see this. Why would anyone record that? It's a terrible accident but you can't take these things to heart. Bad things happen. They…"

"You don't understand. That's not just anybody. That car belonged to our librarian, one of the coolest people in school. What if she's dead?" Chelsea wails.

"We'll turn the news on later. Maybe there will be an update and it's not as bad as it looks."

Chelsea bristles. "It's bad, Mom. Didn't you see?"

Jillian sighs, "I only meant maybe her injuries aren't as bad as we think. Do I know who she is? From open school night or something?"

"No. I never had her for a regular subject. It's Mrs. D'Angelo. Everybody loves her and we all know her car." Chelsea weeps. "She pasted bumper stickers all over it: *Commit Random Acts of Reading. So Many Books, So Little Time. Never Judge a Book by Its Movie.* Stuff like that. Everybody knows that's her car. They all make fun of it, but they don't mean it. She even feeds the kids who come to school hungry."

"She sounds wonderful."

"She is. She doesn't have to but she runs book clubs for us after school. I love her!" Chelsea howls. "She's always helping us. She's so beautiful. What if she's dead or in a coma or paralyzed? Why did it have to happen to her?"

Jillian tells her, "Life can sometimes be cruel. It always seems worse when bad things happen to good people."

Georgia interrupts. "Come. Dad brought home Chinese. We'll all try to eat something and we'll wait for the news."

"Where is Dad? He'll be so upset."

"Of course, he will. We know how much he cares about everyone at school." Jillian catches Georgia's eye and mouths, "Not tonight."

Georgia warms the Chinese food in the microwave. Chelsea picks at the food. Jillian hardly tastes a bite, keeping a firm grip on the stem of her wine glass. Only Georgia eats what Blake brought. "The Buddha from Mongolia has outdone himself. Come on, guys. As my mother would say, 'You'll feel better after you've eaten something.'"

Chelsea picks up her chopsticks. "What's going on? All that wine and Mom, you never cry but your eyes are swollen."

"I'm fine. Georgia and I just couldn't wait until Thursday to have girl talk."

"Yeah, right. What's going on, and where's Daddy?"

"Don't get all high-handed with me. He just has stuff to do tonight."

"Oh right, sure. I'm the high handed one," Chelsea mumbles.

"Come on you two. Not now. Mom and I were just going to watch a movie. You know the ballet movie your mother has seen forty-two times?"

"Of course, you are. It's hard being Shirley MacLaine when you want to be Anne Bancroft, isn't it, Mom?"

"Watch your tone. Why would you say such a thing?"

"Because it's true. Maybe it just makes me sad that you didn't have the life you wanted because of me."

Jillian frowns, "That's a crazy idea. You have nothing to do with what happened to my career. Besides, you trump everything. Don't you know that?"

"Yeah, right, Mom."

Georgia jumps in. "If you must know, the real reason we watch it is for the great cat fight. I've always had this fantasy I could pull your mother's beautiful long hair while she'd have to settle for a few short wisps."

"I'd kick your butt, Georgia, if you touched a single strand of my hair."

"Stop. You're both so lame." She looks at them and shakes her head. "I'm going to my room. Let me know when the news is on, okay?" She balances her plate and glass in one hand, and clutches her phone in the other. Jillian jumps when the plate clangs into the sink.

Georgia sighs, "If bad things come in threes, what else can happen tonight?"

Chapter fifteen

I have to be somewhere. Someone is waiting for me. I think I can see him at the end of a long bright road. Mama, I don't want to be late. He may get impatient and leave.

The light is too bright to see. And there is noise. People are talking but I don't know what they are saying. The tones are urgent. I don't want to let them down.

There is a man standing in the shadows away from the confusion. Do I know him?

I'm drifting.

Now, I'm with Autumn in the big summer garden. You know the one. We're still in California. We're supposed to be picking vegetables for dinner. Autumn picks zucchini and she yells at me for picking the big golden flowers. She says, no, Willow. Don't pick those. More zucchini will grow from them. But I like them, I tell her. She says, too bad. Zach won't like it. Well then, I don't like Zach. She says, but what if he's your father?

All the ifs. If this, then that.

But now, she's fading. Can't see where she went. She disappeared among the sunflowers that I can never reach. They almost touch the sky.

Mama, I hear that waiting song in my head. The one from the French movie we watched. Remember the song we used to sing? If it takes forever, I will wait for you. Why didn't the girl from the umbrella shop wait for the boy who went to Algeria? But I waited, didn't I? Waited and waited. Even when my boy came back to me.

I'm still waiting. and I don't want to wait forever. Not for a thousand summers or a hundred moons.

Now, someone is waiting for me but I don't know who he is and what he wants. I think it's good. Mama. Am I right?

I'm sorry about the zucchini and tomato flowers I picked. Zach never knew, did he? Is that why we had to leave?

Ssh don't tell Autumn. She loved it there.

Chapter sixteen

After Amber leaves the cafeteria, Lily pulls out her cell phone and calls her videographer. "Luke, I'm still at Lourdes. Come back. We're doing an update at ten."

"Hey, Flower. Love you madly but not coming until you clear it with Rich."

"About to. He'll say yes. Called you first so you have plenty of time to get here."

"Sure you did. I'm thinking you got nothing more than we got at the scene and you're stalling while you figure out how to bullshit him. Call me back when he says yes. This may be a temp gig for you but not me. I'm thinking he'd rather have footage from the zoning meeting. You know, where something's happening."

Lily calls Rich. "I'm at Lourdes. Tell Luke to come. I'm going to do an update on the rush hour crash."

"Whatcha got?"

"Enough."

"Specifics, Lily."

"The florist's driver is doing okay. Not a broken stem in any of his arrangements. The woman's still in surgery."

"That's about two seconds. What else?"

"I'm getting background on her from her husband. It's a sad story. I think we need to jump in first." She hedges. "I think he's a vet."

"You think he's a vet? That's what you got? I'm giving the intern tonight's lead. You should have been there. A huge fight over a controversial project. A story that will dominate over the next few weeks, Lily. Not like a car accident. You sure you know what you're doing? Going from the big pond to the little one is bad enough. But you're making it worse. Doing nothing but puddle jumping."

"It's all good, Rich. Really it is. Erica will be a great reporter someday. Trust me on this one. And give your okay to Luke. Okay?"

"Okay. Don't pull this again. I give you an assignment. That's what you do."

She texts Luke: *It's a go. Meet you at the front entrance ten minutes before airtime.* She adds her lily of the valley emoji.

Next, she texts Stephen: *I'll be late tonight. On story.*

Lily buys the last two pre-packaged sandwiches, a bag of chips, two cans of soda, and two large coffees. She assumes he probably drinks it black but picks up every possible combination just in case—*sweet n low,* sugar, creamers, and a container of skim milk.

She ducks past the nurse, Vicky, who is looking at a magazine. Speed walking down the hallway, she sees a doctor heading toward the waiting room. She catches up with him and they collide in the doorway.

"I'm so sorry."

He smiles, "I don't have that much to report."

Lily doesn't want to dissuade him from thinking she's part of the family. "After you, doctor."

He walks over to Denny who's standing at attention. "Mr. D'Angelo?"

Denny croaks, "Yes. How is my wife? She's not..."

"No. No. No. I'm Dr. Whiteman, a surgical resident. Just wanted to let you know your wife is still in surgery and is holding up pretty well. Her surgeon, Dr. Horan, will come to talk to you when she's out of surgery and in recovery."

"How much longer?" Denny asks.

He shrugs, "Everything takes time. I know it's been a long night. Hang in there."

He leaves and Lily follows him. "How bad is she?"

"You a relative?"

"No. Mr. D'Angelo is by himself and... I don't know. I just couldn't seem to leave him."

He peers down at her.

"Okay then. I'm a news reporter," she admits. "I came here to get some additional information about the accident when I saw Mr. D'Angelo waiting all alone. I'll be doing a report at ten since the accident made rush hour a mess but it will be straight forward and I'll respect keeping her anonymity if that's what Mr. D'Angelo wants."

"I should throw you out but the man looks like he could use those sandwiches," he says over his shoulder as he hurries down the hall.

Lily walks back into the waiting room. "I picked up some sandwiches. Not much variety at this hour."

Scowling, he says. "I heard. You're a reporter?"

"Guilty. But in my defense, I'm here because, frankly, I didn't want you to be by yourself through the long wait. True, I'll have to report something to justify sitting here while I'm supposed to be covering something else, but you can tell me whatever. I'll totally respect your privacy."

He grabs a sandwich and a can of soda. Sitting back down, he rips open the package and eats half a sandwich in two bites.

"Can I call someone for you? This is too big to be alone."

"No." He finishes the soda, and then opens the coffee lid. "Maybe. I guess. I don't really want her around but Willow's sister should know. Her name is Autumn Wells. She lives in town."

"I have permission to call her?"

"I just told you to," he barks and then polishes off the rest of the sandwich.

Lily hands him the other sandwich. "I'm not really hungry. Take this one, too. Can I tell her to come?"

"Only if you stay. I don't want to deal with her."

"Okay. After I call her, I'm going downstairs to file my report. What can I say?'

He doesn't answer.

"Mr. D'Angelo?"

"My wife's name is Willow. She's 38. She's a school librarian. Everyone loves her."

"Where?"

"Where what?"

"Where does she work?"

"At the high school. Willow's worked all over the district but loves high school best. She says she finally found her home." He looks away. "She loves those kids. Teenagers are hard. But not for Willow."

"Do you know where she was going?"

"Home," he whispered. "She was coming home."

"Okay. Thanks. I'll be back in about a half hour. Think about what the doctor said. She's hanging in."

Lily walks into the hospital courtyard, gets the sister's number and calls.

"Hello. Is this Autumn Wells?"

"Yes. Who is this?"

"My name is Lily Lerner. I'm calling to tell you your sister, Willow D'Angelo, is at Lourdes Hospital. I'm sorry. She was in an accident and is in surgery."

Autumn panics. "Oh my God! Is she okay? How bad is she?"

"She's still in surgery but we've just been told she's holding up well considering…"

Autumn interrupts, "It wasn't the accident that bolloxed up the commute, was it?"

"Yes. I'm afraid so."

"Why am I being called so late? Who are you? What did you say your name was? Why didn't that husband of hers call me right away? How bad is it? What am I saying? Of course, it's bad. How could it not have been? My poor, baby sister," she rambles.

"Mr. D'Angelo asked me to call."

"Nice of him," she sputters. "I'm on my way. Lourdes, you said, right?"

"Yes. The surgical waiting room is on the second floor."

Lily then finds the ladies' room to fix her hair, put on some makeup and smooth out her rumpled suit. She walks to the front of the hospital to wait for Luke, making notes.

First up is Erica's report from the zoning board meeting.

Lily gets her cue.

"This is Lily Lerner reporting from Lourdes Hospital. During today's early evening commute, a floral delivery van from *Pansies & Poppies* broadsided a sedan at the intersection of Wolf and Shaker Roads."

The footage of the car accident shows emergency personnel prying the car apart to get the driver out.

"The driver of the van, 26-year-old Nick Evans, was treated and released but the driver of the sedan was seriously injured. The woman has been identified as 38-year old Willow D'Angelo, a beloved Albany high school librarian. She is still in surgery. According

65

to witnesses at the scene, there is some confusion about the accident itself."

A repeat of witness reaction is shown and Lily concludes her segment.

"Why did Mrs. D'Angelo's car, presumably stopped, go through the red light? The cause of the accident is under investigation. We'll have an update tomorrow morning on *Wake Up News* at six with Holly Holmes."

"Thank you, Lily!" the news anchor chirps. "Now, we'll turn to a report about the abuse of twenty-seven cats in Glenville."

Lily calls Stephen.

"Tell me you are on your way over. You look exhausted and I bet you haven't eaten. Can I tempt you with the exquisite tortellini I made us for dinner?"

She sighs, "That sounds heavenly but I'm going to be a little while longer."

"C'mon, Lily. There is no reason for you to stay."

"I just want to stay until someone comes to sit with the husband. He's a mess and all alone."

"So, now you're taking on babysitting, too?"

"I'll explain everything when I see you. Now, go to sleep. I know you have a heavy load tomorrow. Do you want me to wake you when I get home?"

"When you get home? Is that what you said?"

"I guess I did. A slip of the tongue," she backpedals.

"No such thing. In that case, I won't give you a hard time."

"I'll try not to be too late."

"See you later, then. Love you."

She closes her phone. *What would Freud say about that slip?*

Chapter seventeen

Blake wakes with a start. It takes a minute for him to remember where he is and why. *Drinking scotch on an empty stomach was not the best idea I ever had.*

With a jolt, all the events of the day collide, one smashing into the next. Part one of today's plan was accomplished. He told Jillian he was leaving her. But part two has gone to hell. Where is Willow? He grabs his phone hoping for a message. Nothing. Should he call the police? What could he say? He's having an affair, tells his wife, and his girlfriend goes missing?

Something terrible must have happened.

Blake turns on the TV. It's about time for the ten o'clock news. Maybe Denny reacted badly and had a meltdown. That would hardly be newsworthy, but you never know.

He barely listens to the lead story. But then he sees the wreck. There's no question it's Willow's car. When the reporter says her name, he can barely catch his breath. He sweats and shakes at the same time.

Chapter eighteen

Georgia knocks on the door. "Chelsea, it's almost ten."

She comes out wearing her Mickey Mouse pajama bottoms and t-shirt, *Dance Your Heart Out,* from one of her mother's recitals. Her dark hair is pulled into a high ponytail. She squeezes in between her mother and Georgia. When Lily comes on, Chelsea whispers under her breath. "Please let her be okay. Please let her be okay."

As Lily reports the accident details, Chelsea wails, "Noooooo."

Jillian feels lightheaded. She absentmindedly strokes her daughter's head but hears nothing past the name —Willow D'Angelo. Willow. This woman that Chelsea's crazy about is the same woman Blake loves. Vomit creeps into her mouth. She runs to the bathroom and heaves all she has lost in a single day.

Chapter nineteen

Denny paces. His cadence and posture is unmistakable, save the drag of his right leg. Walking back and forth across the small room, he doesn't notice his bum leg, his burning gut, the background headache inching its way toward his right temple. He wants to scream but knows he won't or punch a wall but knows he can't.

A Marine doesn't admit fear even when his orders put him out in the goddamn desert to set up base outside Kuwait City, or when he waits for orders to evacuate embassy personnel during a political uprising. He can control his fear by refusing to give in to it. A Marine doesn't give in to fear even when his wife might die.

There is only one thing this Marine is powerless to control. His need for the adrenalin rush. In that, he's an addict. It overpowered his love for Willow and made him half a man. He's failed her in every way that counts.

After four years serving in the Marines, Willow expected him to be the same guy he'd always been.

"Relax," Willow said. "You're home now."

"Coming back…it's not that simple, Willow."

She wasn't listening. "I spent four years alone. Now, you're back and you disappear for hours at a time so I'm alone again. Waiting. Always waiting for you to come back."

"I'm never gone that long."

Willow kept on him. "All that time, I had to wonder whether or not you were dead or alive. You promised me when you came back, we'd be together and happy again."

He put on his jacket and opened the door.

"Wait. Where are you going? I'm talking to you."

He muzzled that voice in his ears, the warning voice, the un-Willow-like voice and walked out on her. Careening out of the driveway on his motorcycle, he watched the speedometer needle push past sixty, seventy, eighty. Just him and the road. Nothing but the wind pounding his ears, the cold, clean rain. Just how fast could he push it?

The slick road didn't slow him down. Neither did the nearly solid sheets of rain making it virtually impossible to see. He couldn't seem to go fast enough. It was getting harder to get the rush. The training was unrelenting. He was always on guard. Waiting for action that never came. It was an air war. He never saw combat. The uprising that fizzled as they stood on high alert. The slow build up, tension rising, without climax. It was all inside him.

He floored the gas pedal, needing release.

The next thing he knew he was lying in a hospital bed looking up at a fluorescent light.

He could feel Willow sitting beside him, but he couldn't look at her.

Without opening his eyes, he asked, "What happened?"

"The police said you were going ninety," she thundered. "They said you should be dead. If you wanted to kill yourself, you blew it."

Quietly, he asked about his injuries.

"A concussion. Your leg is a mess. Breaks. Pins in your ankle. You'll never walk right. They say it's a miracle your injuries weren't worse. You're a bigger idiot than I ever realized, Denny D'Angelo." She left the room.

His leg would always hurt. At first, he thought he deserved this daily reminder of his colossal stupidity. But enough is enough. How cursed can they be? If she survives this, will her life be like his? A life with Demon?

Autumn rushes into the waiting room, her bobbed blonde hair uncombed, her cashmere sweater buttoned wrong. "Tell me everything you know," she demands.

Denny doesn't look at her. "A while ago, a resident came in and told us she was still in surgery. I don't know what time that was."

"Of course, you don't. What did he say?"

He ignores her. For him, time has stopped.

"God, Denny. Why didn't you call me? At least I'd find out what's going on rather than sitting here like a dummy."

She rushes to the nurses' station. "What can you tell me about my sister, Willow D'Angelo? She can't still be in surgery all these hours, can she?"

The nurse, Vicky, quickly pushes her Sudoku magazine into a drawer. "Um, sorry, I don't know when the surgery actually began. Some injuries take time to repair. The surgeon will come and explain everything to you."

Her voice trembles. "Can somebody survive… a crash like that? Can they?"

"They can and they do. She has the best trauma team working on her," Vicky soothes her.

"I'll be in the waiting room. You'll let me know if you hear anything at all?"

"Of course."

When Lily comes back upstairs, Denny and Autumn are sitting on opposite sides of the room. *I guess there's a reason he didn't call her. Wonder what that's all about?*

"Hello, Ms. Wells. I'm Lily. I called you."

"I know you. Thought the name rang a bell. You covered a verdict on one of my cases last month." She narrows her eyes. "What are you doing here?"

"I came just to establish your sister survived the crash and then when I saw Mr. D'Angelo alone, I couldn't seem to leave, but now that you're here…"

Autumn rubs her temples. "I haven't talked to him in a long time and don't plan to start now. Consider yourself still on duty."

"Oh, I see."

"You see? What could you possibly see? My sister is the sweetest, most loving person ever to walk this planet. And then she marries that loser. It should be him lying on that table now." She starts to cry. Lily sits beside her and takes her hand.

In the near silent, low-lit waiting room, rapid footsteps in the hallway coming toward them echo. Denny and Autumn rush to the door. The doctor, still in his scrubs, comes in to the waiting room and motions for them all to sit down.

71

Chapter twenty

Autumn, you know the house I used to draw as a child, the one with the green shutters, and the porch and the symmetrical windows with the lace curtains. I found it. Even the silly looking skinny tree is here. Only the round sun with lined spokes in the corner is missing. You always said suns don't have spokes, anyway. You said they had rays that don't look like that.

Yes! The house I imagined was a real house and I moved in. It's my one and only house. The only one I ever lived in that was mine. It was nothing like any of the places we lived in. Only trouble is it's filling up with water. It's up to my neck. I used to be a good swimmer but I think I've forgotten how. I hear voices. Can you tell whoever it is to hurry? Maybe tell them to bring a raft?

They are close. I hear them. But if they don't come soon, I'll drown.

My throat is blocked. But you can hear me even when we're not together. We're magic sisters. Better than twins. I love you, Autumn. Find Mama. Bring me our Mama Grace. Please. And then come to me. If you're both with me, I won't be scared.

Chapter twenty-one

Blake is unsteady. The floor beneath his feet seems to be moving although he knows it can't be so. His shirt is drenched. The flowered wallpaper is closing in on him; the charm of the chintz and potpourri cloys in the airless room.

The day that would change his life has done just that— in the cruelest of ways.

Willow often talked about karma and fate. Just as some children were raised to believe in the resurrection and the Holy Ghost, her mother believed in dharma and reincarnation. Willow thought most of it farfetched. Nor did she think happy or tragic accidents had anything to do with fate.

"To avoid accidents, you just have to pay attention, Blake." she said with certainty.

Surely, she was the most attentive person he'd ever known. But not today. Only one thing could have made her drift into the intersection. That drive home had to have been overloaded with worry, crowding her mind. She was distracted trying to figure out what to say to that pathetic husband of hers. How could he not have seen it was too much for her to handle?

What am I doing here? She needs me.

He is about to change his sticky shirt but thinks no. She'll wake up and smile as she does every time he wears it. That thought carries him.

Blake runs down the stairs, through the lobby, and onto the street. He doesn't think. There's a rushing in his ears and he's breathless from the weight in his chest. Before he realizes how far he's walked, he follows the signs to the emergency room and walks through the doors.

Chapter twenty-two

Chelsea stands outside the bathroom door. "Mom, are you okay?"

"Yes, just try to get some sleep. Tomorrow's still a school day." Jillian's curled in a fetal position, her hot cheek against the cool tile floor.

"I'll wait until you come out."

"No. Please go to bed, Chelsea. Really. I'm fine now."

"Sure you are, Mom. I heard you. You threw up. I'll get you some water."

Georgia is making peppermint tea. "This should help settle your mother's stomach."

"What's wrong with her? And where's Dad? He's always home by now."

"I think Mom threw up because she drank wine on an empty stomach."

"Doubt it. She's got plenty of practice," Chelsea retorts.

A pale Jillian walks into the kitchen. "Let's sit down and have some tea."

Georgia sets two mugs on the table. "I'll be in the living room."

Jillian tries to cleanse the pungent taste of the words as they form in her mouth. Swallowing hard, she speaks slowly. "This isn't easy so I'll just say it, okay?"

Chelsea nods.

"Dad told me today that he wants a divorce. He didn't get into a big tirade or go into any details. His suitcase was already packed." Jillian hiccupped. "There's not much to say at this point. We were going to tell you together tomorrow."

"What? No way. I can't believe he didn't tell me," she snivels. "He doesn't jump into things. He must have been planning this. Unless..." She stares down at the steaming tea. "There's more, isn't there? There has to be or you wouldn't be throwing up."

"Isn't us splitting up enough?"

Chelsea stares into her tea. "It's not really a shock, Mom. But if it happened, I never thought Daddy would be the one to leave." She looks up. "What really happened, Mom? You did something that put him over the edge, didn't you? What did you do?"

Jillian stands. "What do you mean what did I do? Are you kidding me?" she roars. "Your father walks out, and you have the audacity to blame me? I never did stand a chance against the two of you."

"Don't put this on me, Mom. Be real. You act like you hate him most of the time." She adds, "And me."

Georgia rushes into the kitchen. "Please don't argue. That's the last thing either one of you needs after all that's happened. Everyone is distraught. Why don't we all just call it a night?"

"Good idea." Chelsea runs to her bedroom, slamming her door.

"I'll lose them both, Georgia. I know I will. The woman gets into a horrible accident either before or after she's told her husband about Blake. Whether she lives or dies, he'll blame himself. I know him." Jillian's voice wavers. "And my daughter adores her and hates me." Panicked, she sobs. "What am I supposed to do now?"

Jillian couldn't face going into their bedroom. *There will be time for that,* she broods. She wraps a blanket around her and goes outside to sit on the deck. There's a chill in the air—it's cool but not too cold. A sliver of moon lights the sky. She stares up at a ribbon of stars.

Blake knows the constellations. He'd bring Chelsea out with him at night from the time she was about five. They'd unroll their sleeping bags and get in, snuggle close, as he'd point out a group of stars. Sometimes, they'd just look up at the sky and watch the show. Chelsea would point with glee, 'I see the moon, does the moon see me?' Her version of a poem they'd recite every night. She loved that Chelsea was growing up with that kind of father, one so unlike her own.

But, what kind of mother was she? A negative nag. The one with the lists and schedules—bedtime, bath time, mealtime, home-work. Later on, appropriate clothes, curfews, makeup ... They always teamed up against her.

Sonofabitch. When did he have time to have an affair? There didn't seem to be much of a change in his schedule. Wait a minute… they could skip out whenever they wanted. She was the librarian with no friggin' classes. The blood rushed to her face. Plus, all those meetings, and concerts and games he insisted he had to attend. He'd said if she was so hot on him taking the principal job, that was part of it. Whenever they'd fight about it he said… she drew in a deep breath… he said it was the kind of principal he wanted to be. Well, wait until this gets out. Wait until everyone knows that he was two-timing his wife with the librarian. Ha! What kind of principal will he be then?

But when they hear that it's Willow, he'll still get all the sympathy. Wonderful Willow and Blameless Blake. No morality play. A damn Greek tragedy. Did Willow's husband, the other fool in this mess, suspect something was up? Or was he as dumb as she was?

I have to go to the hospital. See who she ditched for my husband. Find out if she's dead… Blake surely can't be there. But wherever he is, he must be devastated. Goddamn him.

Georgia comes outside and drags a chair next to Jillian's. She holds her hand. "Talk to me."

"I'm going to the hospital to see who her husband is."

"You are not. You don't even know if there is a husband." She shook her head. "In any case, it's just a terrible idea."

Jillian griped, "Blake isn't even thinking about us now. Twenty years together and poof! Plunked himself in a new life. God, I hate him."

"If you keep that thought, it'll make the whole mess easier to deal with, won't it?" Georgia smiles.

"Get me Chelsea's yearbook, will you? It's on the bookshelf in the living room. I want to see what she looks like."

"No. Let's reset your thinking, okay?"

Jillian looks at her. "To what? Do you know how many years we've been married?"

"Of course, I do. I was your maid of honor, remember? Tell me something. When did you start having doubts? First time." She looked at her sideways.

Jillian didn't answer right away. "As my mother was zipping up my wedding dress, she said, 'Jillian, it isn't too late to back out.

You can just walk out of here right now and think about the life you really want.' She just put it out there. In a way, it surprised me because she was crazy about Blake. So that wasn't it." Jillian rubbed her forehead. "I think she felt I romanticized life with Blake just like ballet." She paused. "She was oblique then—rare for my outspoken mother. Even with the dance dream still firmly intact and his accepting, no, embracing that, I pushed any doubts away— yes, I did have doubts— but focused on how much he loved unlovable me."

Jillian looks up at the moon. "What would my life look like if I listened to wise old Mom?" she shakes her head. "But Blake took my breath away. I felt lucky. He was amazing back then." Jillian's tears stream down her face and neck. "I want him back. I want things to be the way they used to be. I gave up everything for him."

"Stop that, Jilly. You did not and you know it. You must be exhausted, though. Time to end this miserable day. See if you can get some sleep."

Jillian couldn't go back in the house. Snippets of their lives flash through her mind like an endless movie reel and all of Blake's failings magically disappear.

Chapter twenty-three

"D'Angelo family? I'm Dr. Horan." The forty-something, shaggy-haired surgeon plops down in one of the chairs. He takes off his rimless glasses and rubs his eyes. "Feels good to sit."

Denny sits in the chair next to him and Autumn perches forward on the coffee table. Lily sits a couple of chairs away from Denny, hoping to fade into the background. Fighting her instinct to take notes, she sits on her hands.

Halting, Autumn asks, "Is she...?"

"Her injuries were extensive but I think we got everything. She did hit her head, though, so it is likely she suffered a concussion with that kind of impact. Could be more but we're hoping not. We'll get a consult with a neurologist in a day or so."

He shifts in the chair. "She came in with a collapsed lung, probably punctured by broken ribs. There was fluid collecting in her belly so we did an exploratory laparotomy to find the source of the bleeding. We removed her spleen and repaired many small tears to her intestines. Given the direct impact, she avoided some life-threatening scenarios. There is no apparent damage to her liver or heart. The intestinal repair was slow going, accounting for some of the time in surgery, but we're hopeful we got all the tears. We're not out of the woods yet. There may be some problems we didn't find or complications along the way. But so far, we've determined most of the injuries were confined to her abdomen. She also has some broken bones and ribs, lacerations. In an instance like this, it's always a wait-and-see game. Things come up. More surgery isn't out of the question."

"Like what?" Autumn asks.

"Every case is different. And there is always the possibility of more bleeding. That being said, let's say we're cautiously optimistic that won't be the case."

"Can I see her?" Denny asks.

"For a minute."

"I'm going, too." Autumn rises.

"Of course." The doctor yawns. "Be prepared. Seeing her could be a shock. Her face is extremely bruised and we needed to remove some shards of broken glass from her cheek and forehead that are now stitched and bandaged. We're keeping her in an induced coma. It's important to her recovery. When we think she's ready, we'll cut back on the meds to start waking her slowly."

"The ventilator is noisy and a bit disconcerting at first. She'll stay closely monitored when she gets to the ICU. The nurses are only assigned two patients. The ICU doc on this week is a pulmonary guy. So that's good given her lung issues. Other specialists will be brought in as needed." He stands. "So, look in on her and then I suggest you go home to get some rest. She will be out of it and won't know if you're here. You have to keep up your strength because in these kinds of circumstances time seems to stand still." He rolls his neck to stretch out the kinks. "Questions?"

Fearful, Autumn asks, "You removed her spleen. Is there anything else she'll have to live without?"

"Don't worry. She won't miss her spleen. Other organs, particularly the liver, take over its function. It's one of the amazing things about the body. I was slow and steady stitching up the intestinal tears so hopefully, we're good there. But you never know what might come up. As I've told you, she was pretty banged up. It's possible we might have missed something or new problems could arise. But let's not worry about that now. One thing at a time." He heads for the door and looks back. "Just go down the hall. The nurse will bring you in."

Lily hangs back as Autumn and Denny follow the doctor out. Blake is outside the waiting room listening. Denny bumps right into him but doesn't notice.

Chapter twenty-four

Lily gathers up her things. In the hall, a man pasted against the wall has a fine sheen of sweat on his face and neck. He's raking his clammy fingers through his unruly hair and is in need of a shave. His breath is ragged when he chokes out, "Please tell me what the doctor said. I couldn't hear him well enough to understand what he was saying."

"Excuse me, sir. I didn't quite catch what you said."

"What did the doctor say?" he demands.

"I'm sorry. Said about what?"

"Don't play games," he barks. "I have to know about Willow. How bad is she? Tell me," he insists.

"You'll have to speak to the family. Maybe you can catch them…"

"Please. You must have heard something. Even if you're here for somebody else." He has a firm hold on her arm. "Tell me."

Lily pulls away from him and twists her hands. *The surgeon's report was meant only for the family. I shouldn't even have been listening.* She looks at him closely. Does she know him? He looks familiar. "Wait a minute…I know you. You're Blake. Blake Golden. What are you doing here?"

He stares at her.

"I'm Lily. Lisa's daughter. Lisa Stern? Your next-door neighbor? Never mind. It's not important. I'm sorry. I really can't tell you anything. Autumn and Denny went in to see her. They'll be back here any minute."

He looks at her trying to place her. Lisa Stern? He's too tired. The name sounds familiar but he can't visualize her.

He steps closer. "Just give me the broad strokes. It will be on the news tomorrow anyway, I guess. Hey, wait a minute. You're the TV reporter who was just on. What the hell? Never mind. I need to know now," he pleads.

Lily's unnerved by the man's despair. She holds her breath, releases it slowly. "She came out of surgery okay. They fixed most of what was wrong. There was blunt force trauma caused by the impact. Can't really say more." Looking at him, she adds, "He said she's strong and did well."

Blake tries blinking the tears away but can't stop them. She steers him toward the door. "Sir, I don't think you should be here. The family will be right back. Listen, there's a *Dunkin' Donuts* across the street. Let's go there. Staying here in the hospital is not a good idea. Let's go."

Wordlessly, he follows her. The night sky is clear. Stars shimmer and the moon is bright. Blake looks up and stares into the open night sky.

Lily watches him, imagining he's saying a silent prayer.

Once inside, she steers him over to a table and goes to the counter to get coffee.

Blake stares out the window.

She sits down, flips off her tight heels, and rubs her feet. "Here." When he doesn't take the coffee, she slides a cup across the table. "My mother bought the house next to yours when I went to college. She needed a one floor house for my Aunt Isabela who recently... Well, anyway. She's very fond of your daughter, Chelsea. And your wildflowers."

Distracted, he says, "Of course. Lisa."

"You understand what I told you about Mrs. D'Angelo is between us. I came to the hospital to report on the accident. But I overstayed. I shouldn't have been there and shouldn't have heard."

"Why did you stay?"

"I needed to get the story on her condition but Mr. D'Angelo was distraught and alone. I didn't want to leave him alone in case... well... I sat with him for a while before he let me call Mrs. D'Angelo's sister."

He spat, "Has that effect on women." He looks away. "But not Autumn. She has his number."

"Yup. He told me I could only notify her if he wasn't left alone with her. When she got there, wow, no love lost there." She shrugged, "Not knowing him, I'd declare him a mess."

"You don't know anything about it," he snarls.

She's quiet for a minute. "So where do you fit into all this? You must know her very well to be ..."

He changes the subject. "So, here you are in the middle of the worst day of people's lives. You must see this all the time."

She vacillates. "This is the thing. From a news angle, something feels wrong about the accident. She stops at a red light and then for no apparent reason accelerates through the intersection."

Lily sees sweat trickle down his face.

"Is that what happened?" He gulps hard. "I should have known this was too much for her. I could have driven her, waited down the street, kept her safe..."

"Safe from what?" Lily probes.

He doesn't answer.

"Never mind." She drinks her coffee. Grateful for a distraction, she watches the guy behind the counter flirt with two young girls wearing dresses that barely cover their butts, who think everything he says is hilarious. She turns back to Blake. "Do you have any idea why she might have sped through the light? What might have caused the accident?" She sees anguish in his eyes but keeps going. "Sounds like you know Denny and Autumn...how..."

"Stop, Lily. Please. Just stop." He looks away from her.

She knows she's not going to get anything more out of him. Exhausted, she wants nothing more than to feel Stephen's arms around her. After a night of hanging around with people she doesn't know, she has more questions than answers. An accident that doesn't make sense and some kind of poignant love triangle unfolding. Her eyes close and she forces them open. "Here's my cell." She slides her card across the table. "Call me if you need someone to talk."

"Yeah, Lily, right," Blake sighs.

Chapter twenty-five

Lily calls Amber from the parking lot.

"You still here?" Amber asks.

"I'm just about to go home." She relays the surgeon's summary of what happened.

"I can't believe you stayed and eavesdropped. You've got some nerve, Lily, but I guess that's what's kept you in the game for so long. Back to the injured woman, I'd say that's pretty good news given the nature of the impact."

"Yeah. That's what the doc told the family. Now, do you want the intrigue?"

"No. I don't. Go home and go to bed. Intrigue. Lord, Lily! Do you ever listen to yourself? Talk to you tomorrow, I've got to go. Woman in labor delivering twins."

"You're no fun. Good luck to you, or should I say her."

She then texts Stephen to let him know she'll be there in about twenty minutes. Regardless of whether or not she's ready to commit, she knows she wants— no make that needs him tonight.

Chapter twenty-six

Jillian can't stay home another minute. She tiptoes out of the house so Georgia doesn't hear her and drives down the street. Picking up speed, her anger flares hotter. *He's probably shacked up with his girlfriend while I'm in New York trying to fix things... working my ass off while he's having his afternoon delight. The punchline in all the wife jokes.*

She slowly rolls by the hospital but knows she can't go in. Instead, she notices a *Dunkin' Donuts* across the street. She decides to have some tea. Pull herself together before she goes home.

Jillian sees Blake right away, sitting in a booth in the front window, staring at his coffee. She is transfixed, staring at this familiar looking stranger. She knows it's him but he doesn't look anything like her Blake. He doesn't even look like the same man who walked out on her earlier today. The man she sees looks frail, a hunched old man. His face is folded in sorrow. She feels sucker punched. There will be no reversals. Ending their marriage isn't even a blip on his radar. All his grief is for her. This Willow.

Jillian opens the car door, bends over, and vomits.

About to back out of her parking space, Lily watches a woman get out of her car. At first, she thinks the woman is drunk but when she straightens up and steadies herself, she recognizes Jillian. The ballet bearing and assurance is wobbly, but the lithe woman's elegance is still evident. Lily watches Jillian hesitate, stopping to look at Blake through the window. She then takes a slow, deep breath, opens the door, and walks right over to him.

Chapter twenty-seven

Pulling up to Stephen's moss green bungalow, Lily tries to leave everything she's witnessed at the door. The low lights he left on for her in the living room cast a warm glow. She tiptoes into the bedroom and watches him for a minute, marveling at how well he sleeps — deeply, never restless.

With a glass of Malbec in hand, she looks through her playlists. This is a Jacqueline Du Pre playing Elgar's *Nimrod* night. Those mournful cello tones seem just right for what she's seen over the course of the evening. Sinking into the deep sectional couch, she arranges the multi-colored throw pillows under her head. Lily closes her eyes but her mind spins. She knows she has to find out what caused the accident. This wasn't just some accidental crash. It might even have been a suicide attempt. She just knew something was up.

Lost in thought, she doesn't notice Stephen standing in the doorway watching her. He scratches the back of his head, flattening his tousled blondish gray hair. "When did you get home, babe?"

She opens her eyes. "Oops, sorry. I hope the music didn't wake you. When I looked in, you were sleeping soundly. I always envy how still you are in your sleep."

He shrugs. "I sleep with a clear mind. And yet, here I am. You must be exhausted by all that went on tonight. Ready to come to bed?"

She regards him and smiles. Tall and lean, he's wearing his Springsteen *Born in the USA* T-shirt and the palm tree boxers she'd bought him when on assignment. "Not yet. I thought I'd have some wine to calm down my swirling mind."

"That'll be the day," he laughs, sitting down. "Want to talk about it? Tonight was peculiar even for you." He looks at her squarely. "You're acting desperate. But you're not, you know."

Lily shrugs. "Do you want some?" She offers him her glass.
"No, I'm good."

She twists her long curls into a bun and pushes a pencil through to hold it and leans back into the cushions.

"Stretch out your legs. I'll massage your feet," Stephen offers.

She closes her eyes, feels the tension release. "It's not all about how the accident happened. More about why it happened and what's going to happen next." She is quiet, takes a deep breath. "Ah, yes, right there. Put some pressure on my arches."

He massages deep into her left arch with three fingers. "How's that?"

"Heaven."

He shifts to work on her other foot. "Wait a second. I didn't make the connection when I heard your report. D'Angelo. Is the husband's name Denny?"

"Yes." She sits up. "Do you know him?"

"Relax. Lie back down. I'm not finished."

She scrunches back down into the pillows. "Well?"

"He's the guy that made our furniture."

"The vet having a hard time of it," she muses. "It fits. Hmmm. A little deeper into my arch? Those damn shoes kill me. Oh yeah. Right there," she sighs.

He massages her feet and then starts to work up her legs.

A few minutes later, she says, "Another man shows up at the hospital. None other than my mom's neighbor, Blake. He's probably Willow D'Angelo's lover. And then…" Her eyes widen. "When I think this drama can't get any more complicated, Blake's wife, Jillian, pulls into the Dunkin Donuts across from the hospital. She's a mess, throws up in the parking lot."

Stephen sighs, "You just can't make this stuff up." He massages her calf. "Tell me what really pulled you in. Besides of course, the most important thing— no panic attack when you heard the crash and sirens."

"Well… it brings up a lot of things. Like my stupid job. The fact that there was an accident isn't the real story. What really happened in that intersection is that two marriages collided. For me to spend my days reporting on the physical wreckage without the why is well, pointless."

86

He moves his hands up her legs to massage her thighs.

"Lordy, Stephen, you have the best hands," Lily moans. Her body quivers as he moves his hands up and down one thigh, then the other.

"Maybe you should be a barista until you find the right thing," he jokes. "Many stories lurking among Starbucks dwellers.

"Yeah. Can you picture that?" she laughs. "I spilled coffee on Amber's favorite silk jacket. Tried hiding it while we met in the hospital cafeteria." Lily grins, "Busted right away, of course. Nothing gets past her. After berating me, she told me about something that might be a good fit."

Stephen laughs. "Amber is never short of ideas either, is she? So what is it?"

"A patient told her about Columbia's Dart Center for Journalism and Trauma. They have a program on the science and psychology of trauma and its implications for news coverage."

He chuckles, "How do you know this already?"

"Was curious and googled it, of course! Listen to this. To improve coverage of violence, they have a program for senior and mid-level journalists. Amber wasn't suggesting I do this particular thing. She just wants me to think about other possibilities."

"Her favorite word, I've noticed."

"That and *definitely*. She's been sure of herself since she was a kid. I wish I had her level of certainty about things."

"You always did. It'll come back."

"The one thing I thought I was sure of in my life is a big fat question. Rich was not happy I chose this over the council meeting."

"I'll bet. But back up a sec. What's different about this? All the stories you report on are dark. Men beating up their wives, animal abuse, car accidents, shootings. You report it and then move to the next story."

"I think seeing another example of marriage misery rattled me. I couldn't bear it if that happen to us." She ruminates, "Just when I was getting to yes about moving in."

"What do you mean, getting to yes?" He pushes her legs off his lap and sits up straight.

"You know I don't come from a *Happy Days* family like you do."

"For god sake, Lily. We've been over this a hundred times." Exasperated, he sighs. "Here it is again. Not everybody is like your parents. We are not those people you saw today. It's about time you realized we're just plain lucky us. You can't keep doing this."

She sighs, "I know."

They're both quiet. "I've decided I'm going to teach a course on the triumph of love in my survey lit class next semester. Or maybe I'll do one on long, happy marriages."

Lily snickers, "If you can find any books. Wait a minute. No. Don't. I can see the girls lining up hopeful and in love with their dreamy prof. Especially if you put *Fifty Shades of Gray* on the syllabus."

"I said literature. I think you should take it, too, my jaded girl. Give you better perspective."

"I'll consider it, sir." She closes her eyes. "Listen." She hadn't realized Leonard Cohen's *Dance Me to The End of Love* was on the playlist. "*Dance me through the panic/Till I'm gathered safely in.*

Stephen murmured, "I'm trying, Lils. That's exactly what I'm doing."

"So, you're willing to take a chance on us, no matter what? Even though I'm unsettled about my work. What if something came up?"

"Like what?"

"Like...oh I can't think right now." She wanted to tell him about the NPR job but the words were stuck in her throat. "You're pretty set but me? I should be also... before..."

"That's commitment, Lily. Not all marriages have the same model. When are you gonna get that? It's as simple as this. I understand how important your work is. You wanting to change jobs or go back to school aren't deal breakers. Sometimes you'll need more from me, other times, it'll be the other way around." He sighs, "No more equivocating, Lils. No more excuses. Time to stop being afraid of the one thing in life that matters."

"We are lucky." She flips over to sit on his lap and starts to kiss him, his mouth, his forehead, his eyes. "Let's always be like this," she whispers. "Promise me."

Chapter twenty-eight

Blake doesn't notice that Jillian has come in and ordered tea. With her back to him, she feels a pillar of wretchedness in all its un-yielding angles. Turning to face him, she sees his jaw working double time, dread distorting his mouth, his breathing labored. His eyes are hooded and the dark wavy hair he always meticulously combs is a tangle. Just as his physical misery is visible to her, she assumes his mind must be shut down.

She tries to draw warmth from her cup of tea. Watching him, she realizes she's never seen him so clearly. Two thoughts attach themselves to one another as they circle her mind. She hasn't really seen him for more years than she can remember. And he doesn't love her anymore.

Jillian sits down across from him. He looks up and then past her.

She doesn't trust herself to say anything. She could never say the right thing in the best of circumstances, let alone now.

After a protracted silence, he says, "What are you doing here, Jillian? Go home."

"I couldn't sleep. I'll leave in a minute. Chelsea came home from the library in hysterics. Somebody took a video of the car. Evidently, they all know it." Jillian adds, "I was going to wait for you to tell her about us but she knew something was wrong and wanted to know where you were. I had to tell her." She sighs deeply. "Not about you and her. Just that you wanted a divorce. I guess you should know she was more upset about her precious Mrs. D'Angelo than her parents splitting up."

Dully, he says, "The kids will be grief stricken. I hadn't thought about that."

"How bad is she? Is she still alive? The way that car was…"

Blake interrupts, "Please, Jillian. Just let me be. Go away."

She reaches across the table but he jerks away from her.

"I was too late, wasn't I?" she hisses. "When I came back from New York, I thought everything might be different. But you were already with her."

Blake doesn't answer.

"Does Chelsea know about the two of you?"

Blake frowns. "Of course not. Jillian, you have to control yourself. Be careful of what you say. You have to be there for her in ways that you've..."

"Fine one to talk about control," she sneers. "Of course, I'll be there for her. Do you think I'll abandon her, too? You realize, don't you, that the accident changes everything. You won't be with her now. Even if she pulls through, she'll go home to her husband."

Blake's eyes cloud with anguish. "I don't know what will happen now that Willow's been hurt. But regardless, we're done."

She glowers at him, "Okay, Blake. I get it. Always the hero."

Deflated, he says "You've never understood a thing about me."

"Just what are you going to do now? They won't even let you in. ICU is for family, Blake. She isn't your family. We are."

"You've had the last word. Are you happy now, Jillian? Have some mercy and leave."

She stands up, swallows her collecting tears. She won't allow herself to cry in front of him. Her sorrow, masquerading as vitriol, leaves a bitter aftertaste in her dry mouth.

Wordless, she walks to her car. Gripping the steering wheel, she looks through the window at Blake. Clearly embedded in a world she knows nothing about, his eyes are riveted on the hospital.

She wonders if regret has a half-life. Or if she will always suffer its consequences.

PART TWO

The Long and Winding Road

*"We always deceive ourselves twice about
the people we love—first to their advantage,
then to their disadvantage."*

– Albert Camus

Chapter one
1998

When Denny was agitated, his limp was more pronounced. Waiting for Willow to get ready, he paced their living room, circling the oak coffee table, the yellow and blue print couch, around the navy blue club chair. He was trying to figure out how to talk her out of visiting Joe and Tess. Denny would flinch watching Willow's fingers twitch, aching to hold their poor, deformed baby.

Spending time with them dredged up the same tired argument. Willow refused to accept the obvious fact that it was wrong for them to have a baby.

"Not this again, Denny." Willow shook her head. "I don't want to hear about it anymore. No way are you going to make me believe that everything we always wanted was left in that desert."

"As usual, you're in your fantasy world. You live everyday with the way the pills poisoned me but you ignore it when it suits you." Exasperated, he added, "How can you think my sperm weren't affected, too?"

"Everything will be fine. All pregnancies have risks. You just have to hope for the best."

"Yeah, right."

He wasn't about to get himself backed into Joe's life with a baby that looked like he should be in a circus side show. They took those same pills, didn't they? Goldenhar had been a rare birth defect until PGW vets started having babies.

It was bad enough that those damn PB bills caused all his problems— the migraines, allergy attacks and crushing fatigue. He'd never even had a headache before his service. Why would he be spared a deformed baby?

Willow hurried into the living room. Fresh out of the shower, her golden, honey colored hair was damp and her pale skin glowed. "No more pacing, Mister. Tess and Joe are expecting us. We're going and it'll be great."

He smiled half-heartedly "You're right. Let's go."

Denny didn't think much of himself for the way he felt but he couldn't bear to look at that baby's screwed up face. All he could think about was the cruel teasing and bullying the boy would suffer at school to say nothing of the operations he'd undergo to help him look normal. Which would never happen.

One night, after too many beers, Joe said, "Fuckin' Marines. One of the guys in line refused to open his mouth. The CO sneered at him. 'This ain't a fucking democracy. Open your goddamn mouth.' Those tiny white pills, no bigger than an aspirin, and look what they did to my baby. I'm a pussy. Can't bear looking at my own son." He slammed his beer bottle on the bar. "Kicker is, we were never exposed to any nerve gas, were we? I'm in hell now for no goddamn reason."

When Jason was born, their doctor explained to Joe and Tess that in Goldenhar syndrome, parts of the face may not completely develop or the chin and jaw line may not meet as they should. Sometimes, there's extra skin covering the ear opening. He said their baby had mild, treatable problems by comparison but still, the child would face obstacles. He had an underdeveloped ear, mouth droop, mildly uneven facial structure, and a cleft palate. Different specialists would fix the problems, one at a time, as he grew.

"If something happened to me," Joe confessed to Denny, "I wouldn't be saddled with all this guilt. You're paying the price yourself. That's rough, man. But to have my kid be born like this is killing me. I try but I don't know how to love this kid. All I see is misery. He won't die from it but his life will be doctors and operations, speech therapy, maybe hearing aids and who knows what else as he gets older. He'll be like a rebuilt car. You know, trying not to look damaged, when he is." He choked up. "I go into his room at night when he's sleeping just to look at his face, see past it. I fuckin' can't."

Denny understood what his friend was saying. He couldn't make himself look at the baby either.

Tess stood on the walk with Jason on her hip. "It's so great to see you both. Isn't it Jason?" She picked up the baby's hand and they waved.

Looking over Jason's head, Denny asked, "You look great, Tess. Where's the big guy?"

"He's out back waiting for you."

Denny hightailed it to the backyard.

Willow pursed her lips but Tess shrugged. "It's okay, Willow. Used to it. Do you want to put Jason down for a nap? I'll make coffee. While the guys catch up, so can we."

She took the baby to his room. "Hey, Jason. Here's one more bear for your zoo." Jason grasped Pooh and looked up at her. She kissed his forehead and took off the hat with a flap that covered his malformed ear. She touched it. "Poor little guy. You work so hard to get what we take for granted."

Willow sang *Mockingbird* to him and by the time she was through, he was fast asleep. "Your little lopsided mouth makes you look like you're always smiling, baby love. Sweet dreams," she whispered, covering him and arranging the toys in his crib.

"What smells so good?" Willow asked, looking around the kitchen.

Tess took a pie out of the oven. "Glad you reminded me."

"Really, Tess. A homemade pie?"

"I was in the mood and I know how much Denny loves my blueberry pie." She sat down across from Willow. "I have to tell you something."

Willow furrowed her brow. "I'm listening."

"There's no easy way to say this. Joe and I are separating."

"What? No way."

"I'm disgusted with his attitude toward Jason. But that's not the whole story."

Willow groaned, "Not an affair? Impossible." She picked up a knife and walked toward the back door. "I'm going to kill him."

"I love you," Tess laughed. "Now, sit down."

She reached for Tess's hands.

"Sometimes, when the rope is pulled too tight, you just have to let it go." She pulled away and sipped her coffee. "You know, in some ways, it's a relief. Since he can't deal with the baby, the doctor visits, the procedures, it'll be easier without him." She fluffed her streaked blonde pixie cut. "For the past month, he's been coming home late. Dummy me thought it was because he waited until Jason was down. We'd have dinner together. Try to remember who we were."

"Didn't it piss you off that you're alone with the baby all day and he can't even help at night?"

"I didn't go there. I was just glad to have some time with him when he was my Joe, not the stranger with the frozen face trying to hide his revulsion. I thought if I talked about our day, he would start believing Jason was a little person, not just a freak show."

"So how did you find out?"

"I took Jason to the plaza near Joe's office because he loves watching the needles move on the Calder sculpture. It started to drizzle so I picked up coffee and the scones Joe loves from the Concourse bakery." She skipped a breath. "When I got to his office, his secretary jumped out of her chair and said, 'why don't you wait in the conference room and I'll tell him you're here.' Normally, she greets me like an old friend, but she was obviously flustered. Without knowing, I knew what she didn't want me to see. I blew past her before she could stop me and opened his office door. There he was with his beautiful, long-haired blonde assistant having lunch. They weren't kissing or anything but I could see they were intimate."

"What?"

"I didn't give him a chance to say anything. I whipped the stroller around and left. He followed me and I screamed at him to go away, I couldn't stand the sight of him. I left him standing in front of his building in the rain with his hands in his pockets. We talked that night. I told him he wasn't the man I thought I married and he could go somewhere to figure himself out but he had to support us. I can't possibly go back to work."

"I don't believe this."

"You know I went to a support group a couple of times. Alone, of course. Desertion is common. Our culture values beauty above everything. I don't ever want Jason to feel Joe's disgust… or whatever it is. To me, it's Joe who's the ugly one."

"Whatever happened to love conquers all?" Willow moaned.

"I'd put that in the trash bin with the rest of the rubbish we were fed."

"This is temporary. He just needs time to come around. Face his fears and guilt."

"Doubt it. She's got huge breasts, is about a size 2, and wears stilettos."

"That's not a good match for a teddy bear who wouldn't know a Jimmy Choo if he fell over one." Willow sighed. "You know Denny won't even talk to me anymore about having a baby and it's all I want, all I think about. My biological clock is ticking away. Tick. Tick. Tick."

"It's not ticking. It's prime time. But think hard. Isn't taking care of Denny enough?"

"I think he's getting stronger. He's taking a migraine med that seems to work better."

"You always see the upside of things. Sometimes you don't face facts, my friend."

Willow bristled. "I know the difference between facts and suppositions. There is only one fact I'm sure of. Time is marching on and the older you get, the harder it is to have a baby." She finished her coffee. "What do you think would happen if I got pregnant without telling him?"

"That's insanity. Look at the wreckage around you and learn from it, Willow."

On the way home, Denny said, "You can't be surprised by this. Joe's been fucked up ever since that baby was born. He's ripped up inside. Anybody can see that. Even you, Willow. This is proof we shouldn't have a baby."

She didn't answer him. *Yeah, buddy. That's what you think.*

Chapter two
1994

Breathless, Jillian rushed into the ballet mistress's office right after class. It was cramped space, not much larger than a closet. "You wanted to see me?" she beamed, certain she got the part.

"Come in. Close door." Olga faced her. They were close enough for Jillian to smell her onion breath. "There is no reason to beat the bush. When I tell you come…you think you got part. I am sorry but no." She shook her head, a slight smirk brushed her lips. "I call you in to tell you truth."

The almost imperceptible curled lip, the one Jillian worked to avoid in class, was set. Jillian braced herself for a severe critique of her audition.

"Jil-y-an. You work hard. Harder than others. Think you will become soloist someday. But I tell you no. Technical skill good. This I admire. And discipline very good. But you miss something." She stared at her, slowed her speech so each word would have impact. "You do not become music. No artistry. That is soul of prima ballerina. This gift cannot be learned."

Madame Olga tilted Jillian's chin up to look at her directly. "You have will. Ethic. Maybe make corps of good company. But soloist. Never. All dancers important. Not just stars." Jillian caught the edge of satisfaction, the terrible pleasure this woman took in humiliating her students now focused on her alone. She willed herself not to cry.

"I tell you now because you must face. You thank me someday. You dance in showcase but not Swanilda. Never Swanilda."

She didn't hear anything more. The words *no artistry* burned through her. Her eyes filled. *You do not become music.* If she could not imagine what that must feel like, how could she achieve it? All the practice would never make her the dancer she wanted to be. It was true. She saw it every day. Not many, but the ones she tried to emulate, had natural lightness and fluidity. They were ethereal. They were grace.

Madame Olga's disdain was palpable, her jackhammer-like tone crushing. Taunted in class, Jillian pushed past her embarrassment to accomplish what Madame demanded. She willed away creeping doubts and kept working.

Obviously, she never made the transformation.

Now, here it was. Condemned to the chorus line. Gasping for air, she flew out the door, leaving the ballet mistress in mid-sentence. She had to get out. Jillian ran down the dimly lit staircase— past the lumpy plastered walls, away from the smell of sweat and dreams and disappointment, the faint sound of a piano, the rhythmic patter of feet hitting the floor, the snap of a teacher's fingers— out the front door.

On the crowded street, she ran for several blocks, weaving around anyone blocking her way. Panting, she slowed down and walked until all the familiar streets fell away. She pushed past couples with linked arms, tourists with cameras dangling from their necks, boys and girls with backpacks. The whoosh of traffic, cabbies leaning on their horns, the babble of unfamiliar languages became white noise.

She walked until she couldn't. Finally, she plopped down at an empty table at an outdoor cafe. Realizing she still wore her ballet slippers, she tore them off, hurled them into the street and watched a tow truck run over them. She reached into her bag and pulled out street shoes and a sweatshirt to put over her leotard.

Where was the server? Didn't anyone see she was waiting? But really, how could that matter when a boulder had fallen smack into the middle of her life without the courtesy of crushing her?

She looked around. This is what normal people do. They stop for a drink on the way home from work. They come home and watch the news. They have children. Their feet don't hurt. Their toes don't bleed. Their tendons aren't stretched. They eat what they want. They—

Life suddenly looked easy.

When the orange-haired, gangly server finally appeared, she ordered a cheeseburger and fries instead of sparkling water and a salad. She couldn't remember the last time she'd eaten anything that heavy. When he placed the juicy burger on the grilled roll and salted fries in front of her, she laughed out loud. The plate had more calories than she'd eat in several days. She'd subsisted for years eating five small meals a day— fish, skinless chicken, tofu, vegetables, carefully balanced carbs. Always eating the right food to sustain energy. Food as fuel. Never pleasure.

She ate halfway through her burger and knew she'd be sick. Dashing to the curb, she vomited in the street. She wiped her mouth with the back of her hand, found some bills at the bottom of her backpack and wedged them under the plate with her half-eaten food.

Dizzy, Jillian steadied herself and walked home in a trance. Thankfully, her two roommates had class. She brushed her teeth and drank some water to get rid of the vile taste in her mouth. Then she undressed, and slid under the cool sheets.

She woke up at about nine, put on a robe and looked out the window. The neon sign across the street was flashing. Her upstairs neighbor was practicing the cello. Restaurants on her street were filling up. She never noticed the life whirling around her.

Jillian had a fleeting thought— maybe she should try another school. But the thought of starting over sickened her all over again. No. No. No. She didn't have it in her. Olga said she would be in the showcase. Maybe someone would see she was more than—no. That would never happen.

Blake would be home by now. Should she wait to call him? There was nothing to think about. It was over. She'd never solo. Never dance the best parts. Never experience the imagined acclaim riveted into her brain, pushing her to practice, day in and out, when she was too tired to live.

What she finally allowed herself was that she knew it all along. Madame Olga, the merciless slave driver, was right.

Jillian called Blake.

"Hey, Jilly. Don't you have class tonight?"

"I did a morning class instead," she lied. "How are things?"

He laughed. "All is well in the life of Blake except his wife isn't here. If you were, I'd…"

"Can you take your mind out of the bedroom for one minute?"

He smiled, "Don't you want to know exactly what I have in mind?"

"Believe me, I know. Listen, I have to tell you something."

Blake's light tone shifted. "You sound serious. What's up?"

She swallowed hard. "I want to live like a normal, married couple." Jillian looked down trying to imagine a baby bump growing in her small, taut body.

"Something happened. Tell me."

"Nothing happened." She looked out the window, hypnotized by the blinking neon sign. "I miss you. Just seeing you on weekends is getting old. I want to come home."

"Whoa. Back up a minute. Just last week you were on fire about the showcase and that role. Swan something or other. You talked about making the Company. This is crazy."

Her palms were so wet, the phone almost slid out of her hand. Taking another class with Madame Olga, even facing her classmates ever again was out of the question. *Maybe I could pretend to think about it. I could sightsee. I've been in in New York for years and I've never set foot in a museum. But my roommates? They'd want to know what was going on.* "Then you don't really want me to come home?"

"Don't be an ass. But this doesn't make any sense. You've always said New York is the only place for you."

"It takes too much. Besides, how much longer are you going to put up with an absentee wife?"

He sat up in his chair. "Whoa. Stop right there. Let's get this straight. This isn't me saying come home."

After a protracted silence, Jillian said, "I'm done."

"That was an awfully long hesitation, Jilly. It's too sudden. What aren't you telling me? You've been excited about that showcase for weeks."

She sighed, pushing all thought of that aside. "Sometimes you just know," she gulped, "when it's time to give up the silly dream."

"That silly dream has been everything to you, Jilly. You're in a competitive world. You can't let it get you down if you don't get every part."

She snapped, "It's not that, Blake. I'm tired and I want to come home. That's all." She sighed, "I thought you'd be ecstatic."

"I just want you to be sure." His voice softened. "We'll talk it through when I get there tomorrow. I'll still come as I always do." He started to hum their song, Madonna's *Crazy for You.*

Jillian forced a laugh and joined in, "*You're so close but a world away…* "

"Listen to me, babe. If it's just the tired talking, I get it."

"I don't think a good night's sleep will change anything." Jillian hung up.

It's done. I'll never tell a living soul what happened. And now, I can be a ballet teacher like all the other wannabes who never made it.

Blake hung up, stunned.

Jillian called a few weeks ago, animated. "I can't believe it. I'm trying out for Swanilda in *Coppélia* for the student showcase. This is critical for the move to the Company. I know this part, Blake. It was written for me."

"What's it about?" he asked.

"Love."

Blake imagined the dreamy look on her face after they made love.

Jillian gushed, "Swanilda and Franz are getting married but she thinks he's paying too much attention to a girl named Coppélia who sits on the toymaker's balcony. He's mesmerized by her beauty and Swanilda is hurt."

"So what happens?"

"*Coppélia* isn't real. She's a doll. The toymaker needs someone to die to bring her alive."

"Do they live happily ever after?"

"Yes, Blake," she sighed. "They live happily ever after."

At the time, he wondered what made her suddenly irritable. But maybe things were beginning to pile up and he hadn't seen it.

Getting a beer out of the refrigerator, he thought about his last visit. She'd been in the bathroom for a long time.

"You okay?"

"Don't come in. I'm working on my foot and it's gross."

He opened the door anyway and gasped. Bloody band aids and gauze pads were on the floor. Blake could never get used to Jillian's battered feet but today they were worse than ever. "When did your toenail fall off? And those blisters are screaming red. They look infected. We have to see a doctor."

"It's nothing, Blake. You just push through."

"You should rest for a few days. Losing a nail must really hurt. Give those blisters a chance to calm down."

"What? Take a day off? I'd lose my edge. No way."

Last weekend she's bleeding in the bathroom not caring how much her feet hurt and now, she decides she's done. Something had to have happened she's not telling me.

He clicked on the TV. *But if she wants to come home, life is good.*

Lily
1996

Dear Mom,

Sorry I haven't written sooner. I've been working like a mad woman.

Touching down at Heathrow was a pinch me moment. Hopefully, I will live here in London for a long time. I know you're thinking, oh Lily, you're getting ahead of yourself again. But relax, Mom. I know the internship is only a six-month promise, but the optimist in me thinks I'll turn it into a hire —despite what I'm up against. The other interns are a tribe unto themselves. Most of them went to Ivy League schools, spent summer vacations building houses in Brazil, volunteering in schools in Johannesburg, perfecting their French in Paris. You know— the opportunities of the rich. The odds are stacked against me. I can't compete with the experience money can buy so I just have to work harder and learn faster. I'm hoping that will count for something down the road.

The intern program arranges housing. I was placed in a three bedroom flat furnished in British bland. My room barely fits a bed but it's near work and in Soho. Who can complain about that? I don't spend much time there. My flat mates are easy to get along with. Patty is a photo journalist intern and Juliana works in advertising. They got here a month ahead of me so they think they're native! When I arrived, they insisted we go out right away, giggling that I had to get the touristy sites out of the way because now I was a Londoner. As if they are… Patty is from Wisconsin and Juliana is Dutch. Anyway, it was a good welcome and we all get along. We don't have much in common so I don't see any real friendships developing but it works for now. I'm hardly home anyway and when I am, I crash.

I love the walk to work. Hearing all the conversation around me. I'm trying to pick up on common expressions but there are so many new ones I hear each day, it's almost like learning a foreign language. I hardly knew at first what people were talking about but I'm acclimating. I've worked out the pound/dollar exchange and if I'm careful, will have enough.

At our orientation, they made it clear this was no glamour job. The interns are here to support —through research, sourcing, fact checking, getting lunch, anything that's asked. We were told a thousand different ways we were the lowest of the low but that's okay with me.

My supervisor's is Hildie Ward and I like shadowing her. I couldn't ask for a better mentor despite how hard she is on me. She's very tall and thin with the most beautiful, angular face, framed by straight pitch black short hair. Model beautiful and the most intelligent person I've ever met. What presence. She commands attention with just a look so she doesn't have to use her deep, roaring voice which rumbles through the newsroom all day long. She is tough and nothing gets by her. My new goal: I want to become her.

I work very long days. I want to be the one who's always here just in case something out of intern realm comes up. I finally had my chance. I thought she was going to send me out on a breakfast run when she barked, 'want to see if you have the stomach for this, Lerner? Come on.' She took me to the Docklands IRA bombing. Unexpected.

Other news. The network is trying to build up an online presence and their website is pretty thin. There was an intern meeting to brainstorm ideas. I suggested doing a blog post about the human-interest side of a news story. Hildie said, 'Hmmm, okay, show me something.' She liked it and put it up. I know computers are not your thing so I enclosed it. Don't let it alarm you. What I saw hit me hard but I promise I'm okay. It was really an extraordinary experience and the kind of work I've always planned to do. I liked writing it. Maybe it will help me keep things in perspective. So, I added one more task to my long list.

The rest of my time has been doing typical intern work. It's fine. Every day is different. I can start a day getting background on a low-level diplomat from an unpronounceable African country and end it by getting the scoop on the politics of a new outdoor market in a growing ethnic neighborhood. I love everything about the network from the energy of the newsroom to the people I work with. It's all good. What a start for my big adventure.

I'm going to follow your lead, Mom. Stay on track with work. Take every opportunity. Not let anything—especially a guy—sideline me. I learned my lesson getting involved with Josh when I was at the Globe. There is always time for that later, isn't there?!?

Try not to worry. Kisses to everyone.
Love, Lily

Wrong Place, Wrong Time or How Your Life Can Change in An Instant

Weeks after I began my internship at WNN, I witnessed the aftermath of a bombing, ending the latest IRA (Provisional Irish Republican Army) ceasefire. This moratorium, lasting seventeen months, gave people enough time to let their guard down and go about their lives in peace.

It is rightfully referred to here as *The Troubles*.

Understatement.

A large bomb made of fertilizer and sugar was detonated from a truck at the South Quay Station on the Docklands Light Railroad in the Canary Wharf area of London. The IRA called in a warning 90 minutes ahead so the area could be evacuated but it wasn't enough time— two men died and another 39 were hospitalized from blast injuries and falling glass. The bomb caused about 100 million pounds (about 242 million dollars) in damage. If causing economic hardship was the IRA's intent, they were successful.

An IRA spokesperson pronounced the deaths and injuries to be caused by a security failure. In response, the Metropolitan Police Commissioner retorted, "it would be unfair to describe this as a failure of security. It was a failure of humanity."

Yes, sir.

As a new intern at the network, my supervisor took me to the site with her to observe how to record the damage and observe witness and victim interviews. The explosion left a huge crater almost eleven yards wide and three yards deep. The rail station itself had extensive damage and three other buildings were destroyed. While it was fortunate the warning saved the lives of most in the area, the destruction was breathtaking.

It's not that I haven't covered terrible things. I've been called to the scene of an apartment building explosion caused by a gas leak, cars mangled in a crash. But this was the first time I witnessed major damage, death, and injury born out of politics—or maybe plain hate.

The senseless scene at Docklands today perpetuates the Troubles. The blistering hatred festers on both sides and new, previously neutral people, are unwittingly recruited. Being in the wrong place at the wrong time makes you collateral damage in a fight you may have been sitting out. From that unfortunate bit of fate, how you live your life maybe inextricably changed. A man bleeding from his head and face from flying glass moaned, "This isn't my fight. They didn't kill me but they might've. Bastards."

And that's aside from healing wounds and attitude toward safety.

Acts of terror like this are cowardly. Maybe someday I'll learn to ask the right questions to try to get at what people think they'll accomplish by killing and maiming to make a point.

In the meantime, the ceasefire is over. Retaliation is inevitable. The only question is when and where.

Chapter three
2000

Sitting at a window table in the *Daily Grind,* Willow and Autumn shared a blueberry scone and are drinking their second cup of coffee. Resolute, Willow said, "I have to have a baby. No matter what he thinks or says."

"You better think hard about this. It's straight out of our darling mother's playbook. We don't even know who our fathers are." Autumn reminded her, "You are not our mother. You chose a different path." She smiled, "You actually got married."

"Maybe I'm more like her than you think." Willow stacked the creamers one on top of the other, knocked them over, and stacked them again. "Grace never let anyone get in the way of what she wanted."

Understatement," Autumn snorted. "Okay. Tell me how you got to this."

"You sure?"

"Yup. Lay it out for me."

"First off, I'm sorry Denny suffers but I'm sick to death of sorry."

"Specifics?"

"I'm sorry he came back from the military sick with allergies and migraines. Not really sorry about his leg but we won't go there." She knocked over the creamers and began piling them again. "I'm sorry he took pills he thinks cause birth defects, too. But he's known from the very beginning all I've ever wanted was children." Her voice rose. "I'm not going to let him deprive me of the only thing I want because of the trauma HE let into our lives. And, can you believe this? It's the argument he uses NOT to have a baby."

"I didn't realize your anger was still so raw." Autumn arched her eyebrows. "You need to leave him. Cut your losses before it's too late."

"No, Autumn. I don't want to decimate my family. I want to add to it."

"If you actually think he'll come around, you're deluding yourself. Do I have to lay out the facts for you?"

Exasperated, Willow asks, "Is it necessary for you to go all lawyer on me?"

"Can't help it," Autumn shrugged. "One, he's convinced himself that if you have a child, it will have a birth defect because of the pills. His evidence: Joe and Tess's baby. Two, he knows he isn't physically up to the responsibility. Evidence: His sick days and loss of income. Three, don't get mad at me. He's too selfish to share you." Gathering steam, she went on, "Just thought of something else. This probably should be at the top of the list. This is Denny's way. Do what you want. Tell your partner later. It's who he is, not who you are. Don't stoop."

"Maybe it's not right, but a baby may be the one thing in my life that would turn things around." She looked away. "The one good thing out of all the bad."

Autumn clasped Willow's hand. "No, sweetie. He'll never come around to it. Why can't you see that?"

"What I can't see is my life either without a baby or without Denny. I didn't run away when he did what he needed to do. He'll do the same for me."

Autumn shook her head. "And make you miserable."

Pulling away, Willow looked beyond her sister, biting her lip so she wouldn't cry.

"All right." Autumn broke the silence. "So how do you do it? Will you be honest? Tell him that the baby may have a birth defect but you don't care? Or do you just plain deceive him. Tell him you're on the pill or something?"

Willow shrugged.

"That's what I thought. I don't always agree with Mama but when she says 'regret is a powerful destroyer,' I can't argue. And you will regret this."

"What do you think she'd say if she were here now?"

Autumn softens her voice and sing-songs, "It's a big world, my lovely Willow. Go out there and find the right man to give you happiness. If you think that's outside your possibility realm, then you do what you need to for your own well-being. Seduce him and make yourself a beautiful baby."

Willow laughs. "Exactly right."

"I hated the way she moved us around when we were kids. But looking back on it now, I have to admire that she never gave up trying to find her bliss."

"Having a hippie mother certainly broadens your thinking. I totally rejected that world but maybe she had a point."

"You must be truly desperate to say that. So, don't do a thing until you've really considered the disastrous implications. Sorry, but I've got to run." Autumn motioned to the waitress for the check. "Just don't let him shut you down. You need to say everything to him that you just told me."

Willow hugged her. "What would I do without you?"

"Damned if I know." She held her sister tight.

The curtains were drawn across the living room windows to block out the late afternoon sun. *Apparently, Denny's headache hasn't lifted yet.* Willow rolled passed the house and drove to her neighborhood park. She watched a group of teens playing Frisbee, then younger boys and girls organizing a game of kickball. One boy in particular caught her eye. He had Denny's coloring—auburn hair, freckled face, but with her blue eyes. He reminded her of the Denny she first fell for. She suddenly thought of something else, something she wouldn't say to him — that she was beginning to resent him for refusing her the only thing she ever wanted. What she would say instead was he was going to give her a baby regardless of his mistaken ideas.

When she got home, the aroma of tomatoes and chicken simmering overwhelmed her. Denny was in the kitchen humming as he slathered garlic butter on a loaf of rustic bread.

"You must be feeling better," she exclaimed. "Whatever you're making smells divine."

He smiled, hugging her. "Much."

"I didn't realize how hungry I was until I walked in the door."

The table was set and they sat down to eat. "From now on, I'm taking advantage of every day I feel well. That's a promise."

"Spectacular idea. I hope so, Den. I really do."

"While I was at it, I made a pot of chili for us to have later this week."

She put down her fork. "What happened? You even look different. Did you find some magic pills while I was gone?"

"I wish. All I know is that instead of the drag I usually have after the headache, I had energy. Demon was totally gone. I even finished the cradle for the Wilsons. They'll be relieved to know they'll have it before their baby's born. I thought we could bring it over after dinner and get some ice cream."

Her eyes sparkled. "Let's not push our luck. You've done more today than you have in weeks."

"No worries. I can handle ice cream."

"Rocky Road on a waffle cone, then." Willow smacked her lips and started to clear the table.

"Let the dishes go. I'll do them in the morning."

She could hardly take her eyes off the woman's belly when they delivered the cradle. *How beautiful she looks. Soon, I will have life growing inside of me, too.*

When they got home, she stood in the bathroom with her diaphragm in one hand, and the tube of jelly in the other. She knew she should use it. Tricking him seemed wrong. But with Denny feeling this well, it might be the best time to make a healthy baby. She was about to put it back in the case but hesitated. *Duplicity wasn't the way. At least, not yet.*

When she got under the covers, he asked, "You were in there a long time. Are we all set?" Code for having her diaphragm in. In time, she could pretend it meant something else— that she wanted to make love, that she was ready, something...

He kissed her neck and slowly worked down her body. He knew exactly where her tender spots were, her pleasure points, how to transport her to pure release. He whispered how he loved the taste of her skin, the pale pink peaks of her nipples. When he entered her at last, Willow felt as if the world that had been lost to her might once again be within her grasp.

114

Chapter four
1995

When Jillian left the rigidness of ballet, she was desperate to fill her days, empty her mind, and sleep without Madame Olga's cruel, disembodied face floating toward her. From the time Blake left in the morning until he occupied her evenings, she struggled to make her flight from New York her decision. But, when those devastating words crept to the surface, she'd bubble up with self-hatred. Evenings with him helped push away the grief that overcame her without warning. She knew she'd have to do something to nail this past life shut.

Georgia nagged. "Blake is coddling you. Telling you to take your time, enjoy yourself, is not going to work. Brooding, or worse, pretending to be the happy housewife, is a disaster. Go to a ballet studio and get a job. Take some classes. Do something familiar."

"Are you kidding me? I'd rather die."

"Cut the melodrama, Jilly. Time to stop moping and get on with it."

Blake insisted one of their three bedrooms become her studio. He painted it pale lemon and salvaged a mirrored wall and ballet barre from a defunct studio. But the door remained closed. Sometimes she would find herself standing in front of it but couldn't go in.

The other bedroom was for the baby. Getting pregnant was intentional yet it surprised her, as everything did in this new, unfamiliar life. She loved being pregnant and unlike any woman she'd ever heard of, dreaded the actual day when the baby would leave her body. Was it fear about the responsibility or something worse? She couldn't go there, either.

When Chelsea was born, she was numb. She'd stare at the wrinkled little face framed with thick dark hair and wait to feel something. When the nurse helped the baby attach to her breast for the first feeding, she knew she was in real trouble. She wanted to fling the baby across the room.

Okay, Jillian. This is what's gonna happen. You will fall in love with this baby. There are no ifs. The books say sometimes it takes time to bond. It'll happen when I learn how to take care of her without my stomach clutching or my instinct to run surging when Chelsea cries. Maybe nursing is making everything worse. Insist on bottle feeding no matter what Blake says.

Her mother stayed for three weeks. Jillian carefully watched how she took care of Chelsea noting how she swaddled the baby to calm her, the way she held Chelsea's head while bathing her, how she soothed her when she cried. Nothing came naturally to Jillian but she was a good student. She mimicked her mother in the same way she would learn a new dance wondering, as with dance, if what she lacked was teachable.

Her mother, Ruth, reassured her. "You'll be fine. You'll know what she needs and wants. Trust me. When you were born, Nana came in and took over. Just like the general she always was. And then… she left and I was alone and scared to death. But I learned and so will you."

"Chelsea likes you better. I think you should move in."

Her mother hooted. "Never thought I'd ever hear that from you. We all just do the best we can. Can't ask for more than that." Ruth's smile faded. Her face which mirrored Jillian's in every way, became serious.

"What, Mom?"

"I was always afraid ballet would break your heart. I don't know what happened but it's time for you to talk. You'll explode if you don't. Or worse." She gently pulled Jillian's chin toward her. "Look at me. You need to tell the truth. Not some fairytale you concocted. Something insurmountable had to have happened to make you turn your back on the only thing you ever wanted. I don't know why you thought getting pregnant so fast was a good idea but now that you have Chelsea, you'll have to deal with all of it at once."

Jillian forced a smile. "Oh, Mom. Stop. Nothing happened. I'd just had it and I missed Blake."

"Right. You never were much of a liar." Her mother looked around. "Now, you have all this new responsibility. Jillian…"

"This is getting old. There's nothing to tell so just drop it, will you? Oh, listen. Hear the garage door open? Blake's home."

"Saved. But I'm not leaving until you tell me."

Jillian looked toward the door. "Nothing to tell. I guess you will be moving in."

Just as Blake walked through the door, Chelsea woke up wailing. He kissed Jillian and pecked Ruth's cheek. "My baby girl is calling." He rushed into the baby's room and the crying stopped instantly. He came out, rocking the swaddled infant, singing: *Woke up, it was a Chelsea morning . . .*

Ruth was amazed. "You're so good with her. Frank couldn't even bring himself to hold Jillian at two weeks old, let alone change a diaper and quiet her."

"His loss," Blake said, never taking his eyes off the baby.

Jillian threw herself into motherhood with the same discipline she put into dancing. She kept records of Chelsea's feedings, nap times, outings, facial expressions. She filled the air with chatter hoping to advance her language skills, reported her day in detail to Blake when he came home from school. She stroked Chelsea's soft thighs, nuzzled her neck, kissed her cheeks. But felt nothing.

Many days she spent hours walking Chelsea in the stroller, blinking away the tears that still flowed when she missed dancing so much her body ached. She pushed away the steady flow of tears when Chelsea cried for her and she didn't want to hold her or change another diaper or feed her again. And more tears on those days she could see how happy Blake was —a happiness that eluded her.

It was only to take off the baby weight that she was able to first peek into the room with the ballet barre and mirror. It took days after that to actually go in and work. It was painful at first but as she moved, she thought about nothing but the stretch of her legs, the position of her arms, and the beautiful music that always transported her.

"Hi, Blake. It's Jessica. How are you?"

"Great. How are things going?"

"Killing myself as usual," she laughed. "Don't ask me why! Is Jillian there?"

"Nope. She just took a run to the supermarket."

"I miss her. She doesn't want to talk to me. I get nothing. Yup. Nope. Fine. Great. Even if she doesn't want to talk ballet, we can still be friends," she complained. "We were roommates for so long."

Blake confided, "I don't know. The long distance was hard and it's great having her home, but it's all hard to figure —one minute she's flying on star power and the next, just quits. Do you know what happened?"

Jessica told Blake that Madame Olga was sadistic and probably abused or insulted Jillian, maybe told her she didn't have the chops to make it. The word at the Academy was that Olga crushed her, chasing her away.

Jillian walked into the living room. "I'm home."

"It's Jessica," he answered, handing her the phone.

"Hey, Jess. You've caught me at a bad time. I'll call you back, okay?" She hung up, closed her eyes, and sat on the couch for a few minutes before going into the kitchen.

Blake was putting ice cream in the freezer. "That was quick. You two used to be good friends. Had so much to talk about."

"We don't have anything in common any more. The last thing I want to hear about is what's going on in that world. Okay? It's history."

"Maybe you should join a mother's group or something. Since Georgia is working, you need company during the day. At least until Chelsea becomes a good conversationalist," he quipped.

"Right, Blake. A whole afternoon talking about the color of baby poop."

"That's harsh. It was just a suggestion. There are other…"

"Since you have this covered, I'm going to lie down."

"Okay. By the way, Chelsea had a great afternoon. I think I saw a real smile."

"Glad," she mumbled, walking away from him.

Stacking cans on the pantry shelf, he shook his head. *What could that woman have said to her? Jillian would never fold that easily and yet, she has that look of fear on her face. Like my sister, Emma, when she thought we weren't looking. The one she tried to hide from us toward the end, that haunted, knowing look. She knew her life was over even if none of us could face it.*

Lily
2000

To: lilylerner@aol.com
From: asinclair@brighamandwomens.org
Subject: Are you really ready for Africa?

I'm thrilled and scared for you at the same time. I was hoping Hildie would keep you on domestic stories for a couple more years. But if I know you, you've been carping at her to make good on her promises to send you places where you think the 'real stories' are. And now, you're off.

Well, girlfriend, since I've never been one to mince words, I have to tell you I'm worried. Don't let what you see break your heart. The cultures, the wars, the evil people are capable of—seeing that first hand will be devastating— if you let it. Do your job well and then leave it there, okay?

Don't let it dampen your lively spirit. Enough. You get my drift.

Also, I'm not one to talk with my grueling schedule, but I never hear about you doing anything fun. What's the point of living in London if you don't see any of it and you don't date any loveable, bumbling but handsome Hugh Grants or smart Jude Laws? It's all I have to suggest. I don't get out much either.

I haven't been home in an age but Mom keeps me posted. She gives your mother's relationship with Evan to the end of the year. He's supposedly successful, handsome and of course, smitten, but she's getting itchy. Subtext: He's too conservative, too dependable, too whatever it is that always makes her move on.

Let's not be her, okay? We don't have time for men now but when we do? Promise me.

Love you. Be safe. Be smart.

Amber

Chapter five
2002

Willow obsessed. She convinced herself she needed a baby as much as she needed air or water. She tried every approach she could think of to make Denny understand that but nothing would move him. He didn't get angry; he just went cold or changed the subject.

"Nothing's changed since the last time you brought it up, Willow," he said, coolly. "We have us. That's more than enough."

The ticking inside her, warning her that her eggs were dying away one by one each month, was getting louder. She couldn't waste any more time.

Once she made up her mind, her deception was total. She made sure he didn't suspect anything so he wouldn't want to make love. Her diaphragm stayed in its case. She periodically squeezed contraceptive jelly into the toilet so the tube would look used, in case he became suspicious.

She focused on how right she was. Denny's health was better. His headaches and fatigue seemed to be in retreat. She searched for statistics on birth defects. The risks were higher for women vets. He'd have to come around. This was their shot at the life she wanted for them.

"I think we should paint."

"Really?" Denny asked. "You never wanted to spend anything on the house. We've never even made the extra bedroom usable. I always thought you'd want to set it up as your library."

She looked at an old water stain by the dining room. "It's time. We could also use a good coffee table and Denny-quality book-shelves. Maybe even a rocking chair like you made for the Fishers."

"I have just the wood for a coffee table left from a job. Maple. Why haven't you asked before?"

"Time just feels right, now." Willow looked around. "Mike, the music teacher, has a brother-in-law with a painting company. He says business is slow so he could probably come next week."

"Sounds great. I wonder how I'll do with the primer and stuff, allergy wise."

"Why don't you go stay with Joe for a few days? He could probably use some company."

"You wouldn't mind?"

"Not at all."

"What are you thinking for the living room? Not purple, I hope," he smiled.

"I'm thinking some kind of green for the living room. Maybe a pale blue for ours and a soft yellow for the other bedroom." Willow wanted to tell him she was pregnant but kept losing her nerve. She was only in her eighth week. She still had time.

"Great. Apple or sea green would be nice in here. Nothing too minty."

"Agreed. I'll get some paint chips at Home Depot on my way home from school tomorrow." She put her arms around his neck. "I think you're through the worst. From here on, everything will be different. Our life will be just as we'd always planned."

"Maybe it would be all right for me to stay. Latex paint is water based and dries quickly."

"Let's not take a chance."

"Okay. I'll call Joe and see if he has room for me in that shoebox he rented. If not, I can go to Aunt Jen's house. Haven't seen her much since Uncle Carl died."

"Sure. That might be better anyway."

"You don't want to sleep on the old twin bed in my cousin's room?"

She smiled, "I think all six feet of you will fill it up nicely."

She scheduled the painter to come later that week. Then, she called Tess. "Can you can meet me Thursday night for dinner?"

"With or without Jason?"

"It doesn't matter. I just want to talk to you. Why don't we go to *Maggie's*? It's pretty quiet during the week especially on the early side."

"How does 5:30 work?"

"Perfect."

The school day dragged. She didn't feel right. She was crampy and had a dull headache, as if she were getting her period. By the time she got home, she had sharp pains. Willow called Tess. "Please come over. Right now."

Alarmed, Tess asked, "What's wrong?"

"Everything."

"I'm on my way."

She made it to Willow's in minutes. Tess rang the bell but there was no answer. She tried the door handle. It was unlocked. Carrying Jason through the living room to the back of the house, she thought she could hear her; the sound was unnerving. Panicked, she called out, "Willow, I'm here. Where are you?"

Tess found Willow lying on the bathroom floor crying and saw instantly what was wrong. She had bled through several pads that were in the trash. In the toilet was a clot of bloody tissue.

She put Jason down in the hall just outside the bathroom and tossed him his trains. "Play here with Thomas and Percy, honey."

Tess got down on the floor and cradled Willow in her arms. "I'm so sorry, honey. Just let it out. I'm here."

"It serves me right," Willow convulsed. "Denny has no idea. I'm being punished. "

"No. You're not being punished. It happens more than you think. Most women who've had miscarriages go on to have babies. Many babies."

She wept, "I was fixing up the house. Denny isn't sick all the time. I thought maybe we were through the worst. We'd have a fresh start. Now…it's all gone." Tears ran down her face, her throat, her shirt.

"Ssh, it's okay," Tess rocked her. "Everything's going to be just fine. You'll see. I'm sorry. Sorry, sweetie."

The two women sat on the floor while Jason sat quietly watching wide-eyed, his lopsided mouth looking sad.

At least for the moment, Willow was cried out. "I'm okay," she said. "Let's have some tea."

While Willow changed her clothes, Tess scooped the clot from the toilet into a sandwich bag. She then brought it and Jason into the kitchen. Laying down his activity mat, she sat him on the floor with some toys. "There, sweetness. You play for a bit while I talk to Aunt Willow."

Jason dumped the blocks out of the bag.

A drawn Willow came into the kitchen in sweats, her hair pulled back away from her face. Her eyes were swollen.

"I thought maybe a slug of this might be good. I found some bourbon in the cabinet." Tess poured the amber liquid into a juice glass.

Willow sipped and scrunched up her face. "I forgot how this stuff burns." Her puffy, blotchy face turned red.

Tess fixed her a sandwich.

She pushed it toward Tess. "I can't eat. You take it."

Tess reached for half the sandwich. "You have to tell Denny."

She shook her head, "No way."

"And you have to go to the doctor. You may need a D&C. It looks like you might have expelled the whole thing but you have to make sure. It's in the fridge."

Willow tried to smile. "I guess once a nurse always a nurse."

"I'll go with you. Just tell me when. Now may not be the time to say it but what you are doing is no good. You can't say, 'Surprise, I'm pregnant,' like you're giving him a gift or something. You don't tell him and you'll end up like me, for God's sakes."

"And what's wrong with that?"

"Everything and you know it. I'm alone. I have full responsibility for the baby. Joe walks around like Quasimodo, weighed down with all his disappointment in himself and the detour our life has taken."

Willow asked, "You still love him, don't you?"

"I'll always love him. Right now, though I can't wrap my head around the way he thinks and feels. I know he can't help himself but he's really hurt us." Tess broke off a piece of sandwich. "Thing is, I'm not going to count on it but I think he'll buck up someday and be the man I always loved."

"After everything, you'd take him back?"

"I miss him. I haven't had a good night sleep since he left. Think about that Willow. You finally are seeing glimpses of the old Denny. You have no idea what this could do to your life. Don't romanticize it."

Willow shook her head. All she knew was that she had a big, gaping hole where the baby she loved used to be.

Lily
2000

To: asinclair@brighamandwomens.org
From: lilylerner@aol.com
Subject: Out of Africa

Amber,

Just back from Ethiopia. Grateful for a working toilet and other overlooked luxuries of home. In my own bed but can't sleep. Unfathomable pictures swirl in my mind. Coming from a country overdosing in abundance, the paradox is dizzying. What we saw was the convergence of drought, poverty, and total disregard for human suffering.

When I first started, Hildie counseled me. She said if I want to stay in this for the long haul, I'd have to build walls. 'I can't tell you how,' she said. 'Everybody does that differently. Avoid sentimentality. Just tell people what you'd want to know if you couldn't see things for yourself. Try to be objective. Ignore your subjective lens.' Ha. Impossible.

Wherever we go is bad. It's just a different kind of awful.

For a quick minute, I could see you at the refugee camp clinic in Danan tending to the children here with Doctors Without Borders or something. Your bright smile diffusing some of their misery. But what could you do at a clinic with virtually no medicine or supplies?

No. Stay where you can actually treat people.

Sorry for this but talking to you always helps me. I'm still stunned by avoidable misery. So... I have to focus on the fact that if we didn't go in, no one would know.

Anyway, I'm back home and glad. Hopefully, I can stay put for a bit. And stay grateful for a hot shower and working toilet.

Fingers crossed that you get the rotation you want next in your immaculately clean, state of the art American hospital.

I'll be back for a visit in March for Mom's birthday. She'd kill me if I missed her big 5-0. Hopefully, you'll have time for me. I'll send you the details when I have them.

Love you, Amber. Your annoying (and sometimes comforting voice) is always with me.

Lily

Famine Sweeps Ethiopia…Again

Fifteen years since the last famine, Ethiopians are starving again. The fact that people are starving in Africa is nothing new to us. Generations of American children have grown up with that fact cavalierly communicated at dinner time. *Eat your vegetables,* mothers across the country would say. *Children are starving in Africa.*

Grave suffering is packed into that one small sentence.

Drought is a part of life in many African countries. It is expected. It is part of their calendar, how they refer to a season. And it is deadly. During the last famine in Ethiopia, one million-people died. The mothers I met in Ethiopia repeatedly face what mothers should never experience—watching their children die.

And shame on me. What was I thinking? I was impatient that the trip took too long and I'd miss something. What? I wouldn't see a child take his last breath? And then, when I'd catch myself. I'd try to imagine what it would be like to walk for days in the hot dust, without food and little water, with all my measly provisions strapped to a donkey, carrying whatever child was the weakest. That put me in my place.

I followed a middle-class family devastated by famine. Their losses were gradual—first their livelihood, then their home, their village, then one by one their five children. We arrived at the camp an hour after their four-year-old, Aman, died. Wrapped in his mother's colorful orange and gold headscarf, this child's now peaceful face is all sharp angles of bone. His father stands over him swatting flies.

His mother cannot speak. His father says, "We pray to Allah but we need help. Tell the other nations they must send us food and medicine or we will all die."

Now that I have seen the faces of the children starving in Africa, I don't think I'll ever look at a plate of food in the same way. I've written this in the hope that you won't either. NGOS and government agencies must figure out a way to get appropriate food and medical care to the dying. Immediately.

In an age of accomplishing remarkable things—space travel, genome mapping, instant worldwide communication, there must be a way to figure out how to get food and clean water to starving people.

I'm as certain of that as of the next drought cycle.

Chapter six
1999

Ordinarily, Jillian hoped Blake would be asleep when she came home from dinner with Georgia and Claire. But not tonight. She had news that couldn't wait.

He was sprawled on his recliner. *Law and Order* credits were rolling. "Hey, babe. Good time?"

"Always."

"Chelsea was a stitch at bedtime. First, she needed to find Babar, then she didn't do a good job brushing her teeth and wanted to do it again, then she wanted to brush her toys' teeth. Finally, I said enough and she was sleeping within seconds."

Jillian scowled. "Blake, you let her get away with too much. It throws her off."

"Can't help it. Routine will become her life soon enough."

Jillian sat down and took off her heels. "We have to be a team. Not good cop, bad cop."

"It's not like that, Jilly. You worry too much. Anything new with the girls? Claire must have something to report."

"She's going away with the new Mr. Hunk this weekend to an inn near Tanglewood. They're going to see James Taylor. Unbelievable, isn't it? Given what her life was like just a year ago. But listen to this. She heard about a teaching opening at a ballet school."

"You should definitely follow up. Maybe working in a dance studio you approve of will help move you into the happy column." He yawned. "Time for bed. Coming?"

"In a bit. Just want to get a few things ready for the morning."

He kissed her. "Feel free to wake me anytime," he grinned.

Jillian was in no hurry to go to bed. She brought a glass of wine into her studio and sat cross-legged against the wall. In her mind's eye, she envisioned a line of little girls standing at the barre, eager for her to take them into the magic.

Jillian woke up before her alarm, her heart thumping. Too anxious to make the call after she dropped Chelsea at nursery school, she went into her studio and stretched at the barre. Still procrastinating, she put on her toe shoes and pirouetted across the room and back. Even now, she heard instruction — *head up, shoulders back, turn your left foot out, first position, go on.*

Wiping the perspiration from her face, she chastised herself. *Enough. Just make the call.* Jillian couldn't believe how excited she was over a potential teaching job. Had she imagined this scenario several years ago, she would have cringed. Now, she tingled with anticipation.

Shrugging off her nerves, she dialed. The call was brief. A heavily accented woman told her to come tomorrow at ten.

Maybe she could become a good version of Madame Olga. It's not what she imagined for herself but anything was better than her current job— teaching at a dance mill in a studio wedged between thumping tappers and hip hop dancers shaking their hips to *Salt 'n Pepa.*

The ballet school sign hung over the heavy wooden door of a three-story brownstone. It was simply called *Ballet Academy*. The waiting room had worn brocade upholstered French provincial dining chairs. Posters of Anna Pavlova and Margot Fonteyn hung above a dark wood storage cabinet with cubbyholes for shoes. On the opposite wall were movie posters: *The Red Shoes, Turning Point,* and Baryshnikov's *White Nights.*

She took off her shoes, slipped them into her bag, and walked to the office. A slight, angular woman motioned Jillian to sit down while she finished writing on the single open folder on her desk. Behind her was a credenza with an electric teapot, two china cups, and several binders. Otherwise, it was stripped bare.

"Okay, now. Good morning. I am Sima Orlov." She shook Jillian's hand. "You teach ballet?"

"I've studied since I was eight. Attended year-long classes and summer sessions before four full years at the New York Academy. I teach part-time now but would prefer to be in a school devoted to ballet. Particularly one that may have some serious students."

She held Jillian's gaze. "Many disappointed ballerinas. Different stories. Same ending. Can you live with yours?"

Jillian didn't answer. What could she say? She allowed a moment to pass. "I've heard that you would like to teach less and hoped I could help you do that."

She looked at Jillian's tote. "Let us see. Go change. First door on right."

Sima was tall, ballet thin and sculpted, with gray and black streaked hair pulled into a bun. She had high cheekbones and large gray eyes outlined in black kohl. She wore a wrap skirt over black leggings and a neatly pressed white blouse.

They walked together into the studio nearest the office. The floors were polished; the mirrors gleamed. "Okay. I will teach you first as advanced student, then beginner. Then, you teach me."

"Fair enough." Jillian began to stretch at the barre.

They spent an hour together. The first half, Sima treated her as she would any student— critiquing, turning a leg, raising an arm, lifting her chin. She then had her move across the floor as she called out commands.

"Now, I am student. Teach."

Jillian's anxiety vanished as soon as she began to move. It was as if her phantom body, the body that floated around her but couldn't settle, was back home. She took Sima through the paces as she would any student knowing she needed to show her skill, style, and strengths.

"Good. *Ca suffit.* Let us have tea."

Sima laid out a plan. Jillian would teach late afternoon and early evening classes three days a week. Before the beginning of the next session, she would come in two hours a day to go over teaching plans, learn Sima's philosophy and expectations and to practice. She would be paid for her time.

Elated, Jillian hurried home and ran straight into her studio, turned on her music and leapt across the room. She hadn't remembered the last time she had this much energy. She picked up Chelsea from nursery school, took her to lunch and raced her around the playground.

"Mama, stop," Chelsea called out, breathless. "Swings now. Push me to the sky."

As she pushed Chelsea, she could see bright-faced little girls waiting for her instruction. At home, she hummed as she cooked Blake's favorite dinner — steak with fried onions, smashed potatoes, and garlicky green beans. For herself, she made a skinless chicken breast and steamed vegetables. Listening for the sound of the car pulling up, she ran out as soon as she heard the door slam and rushed into his arms.

He hugged her tight. "Mmmm. I like this." He kissed her deeply, slowly releasing her. As they walked arm and arm into the house, he said, "I take it Madame saw how impressive you are."

"Sima reminds me of my old teachers, ones who could take you down with a look. She is a real pro unlike that ridiculous Marguerite I work for now." Jillian gushed, "The school is in a brownstone. Looks just like the schools I went to in New York. Only smaller. She is a no-nonsense Russian. I auditioned— well it felt like an audition— and that was that."

Blake plopped down on the couch and Jillian moved to face him.

"Daddy!" Chelsea beelined for Blake's lap.

He nuzzled her neck. "How's Daddy's girl?"

"Good, Daddy." She pulled his arm. "Can we have a tea party with Babar? Puhleeze."

"In a bit. Did you know Mommy got a new job today?"

"Ha-ha, Daddy! Knew before you. Hey, I'm going to get Angelina Ballerina. She dances too. Maybe Mommy can bring her to class."

"Great idea. Now, go on." He patted her bottom as she slid off him.

His eyes followed Chelsea skipping into her bedroom. "She's a masterpiece, Jillian."

Jillian laughed. "Objectivity, sir. Okay. Let me tell you. First, I was Sima's student and then she was mine. When we were finished, she brewed tea, gave me the terms. I start tomorrow morning."

"Terms?"

"Before classes start, I go in mornings to prepare. She wants me to understand her expectations on a student-by-student basis."

"Interesting. Not wanting you to draw your own conclusions. Sounds regimented and Russian. You should do very well there," he teased.

Jillian smacked him lightly on the shoulder. "Very funny."

"Did you give Marguerite notice?"

"Oops. I'll call her in the morning."

"Is the pay the same?"

"I didn't think to ask." *Who cares? It will help me get some part of myself back. I've spent the happiest part of my life in places just like Sima's.* "My classes won't coincide with nursery school."

"Really? No Saturday classes like now?"

"Not this session. I'll have to find a babysitter until you get home from school."

Chelsea ran back into the living room clutching Angelina Ballerina.

"Why don't you two play until dinner is ready? We're celebrating tonight. The Blake Golden Steak Special."

"Me, too? The Chelsea Golden Especial? But I don't like steak, Mommy. What else is special?"

"Maybe you'll have some of Mommy's chicken with vegetables, salad, and smashed potatoes."

"Why are you smashing them, Mommy? Are you mad?"

"No, Chelsea. To make them creamy."

"We'll open that bottle of wine we've been saving," Blake added. "Love you, Jillian Ballerina. I hope this is just the thing."

Chapter seven
2003

Beat, Denny lay on the couch and closed his eyes. A football game droned in the background.

Joe grabbed four beers from the refrigerator and walked into the living room. He handed Denny two. "Here, bro." He plunked down on the worn love seat across from Denny and put his feet up on the coffee table. "Jason's sleeping. Pizza should be here soon. What's the score? Giants doing anything?"

Denny yawned. "Losing. 17—zip in the third." He lay his arm over his eyes.

"They suck this season," he snickered. "Man, I don't know how Tess does this. I'd be ready for the loony bin if it were me. Whose bright idea was telling them to go away for the weekend?"

"They both needed it." Denny sat up, thinking about how miserable Willow's been looking lately. "Willow has it in her head that motherhood would be her bliss." He sighed, "Back in the day, I used to be that for her." Denny downed a beer and belched. "Thing is ... even then, I knew I wasn't cut out to be anyone's daddy."

Joe resettled his thick, muscular body on the sagging love seat. "About time to talk. Give it up."

Denny put down the empty bottle and twisted the cap off the second. "I wanted to buy into her happy dream," he said, vague, looking past Joe into the cluttered dining room. "You didn't know me before boot camp, but I was never any great shakes. My senior year, Willow came along sure the sun rises and sets on me." He shook his head. "I wanted to be the guy she was seeing." He swallowed hard. "I'm talkin' way too much."

"About damn time. You've been there for me through all this shit with Tess and the baby. Your turn." Joe looked directly at Denny, who focused on the ring the beer bottle left on the coffee table.

Denny drifted. "Truth? Willow believes on a whim one day I went down to the recruiters' office and signed up. I let her think that it was one crazed flash that wrecked her fairy tale."

"I wondered about that. My recruiter worked on me for days getting me to sign."

"Yeah," Denny nodded. "It never happened like I told her. But I figured it would be all right. I'd come back and handle the whole *if I were a carpenter and she were a lady* thing. Back then..." he paused, "I thought I could want what she wanted. But the closer it came, the more I wanted to run. Can you believe what a jackass I was? Scared of life with Willow so I change it up and join the Marines," he scoffed.

Chuckling, Joe got up to grab a six-pack from the fridge. He tossed Denny two more. "My dad was all for it. Lived the discipline and purpose of the Corps himself."

"Me. Just believed the hype." Denny leaned his head back on the couch. "The one thing I wanted was to ride in an AAV. Thought that'd be so cool. Met my idea of something that made the whole thing worthwhile. I'd say it and the drill sergeant would sneer, 'life expectancy in battle —seventeen seconds.'"

Joe snorted.

"So, what did I get? Combat Engineer. The guy hauling barbed wire, explosives, and land mines. I said I didn't want to walk. Big mistake. That's all I did. Ha. The worst. Life expectancy dropped from seventeen seconds to ten. Tortured me with that every day. Christ, on top of having to walk everywhere, I carried land mines makin' my load heavier than everybody else's." He polished off another beer. "Willow and her *Leave it to Beaver* life suddenly didn't seem so bad."

Joe burped. "World a tinderbox and we had agreements all over the friggin' place saying we'd help."

"Yup, got that sittin' on standby in the China Sea in case there was another Tiananmen Square and we had to get our diplomats out in a hurry. Great odds—300 Marines to about a billion Chinese."

Joe nodded. "Me. I got that when I landed in Iraq."

Denny's shame washed over him. He cringed, remembering the day he told Willow he joined up. She's full of her happy plans about houses and gardens and kids and all he can think about is getting on that bus. Coming back but getting the hell out for now. He still sees her face when he told her. The face that shows up when he's lost in his desert nightmares and she wanders in and out of the dream. He's panicked when he loses sight of her but other times he doesn't want to find her because of that look on her face.

Joe flashed, "We knew dick back then about Iraq. Now Islamic jihadists are everywhere. Cold hearted mother-fucking killers. More than willing to blow themselves up to target innocent civilians."

Joe and Denny were quiet, lost in their own thoughts.

Denny slugged the rest of his beer. The bell rang and Joe got the pizza. They polished it off quickly, folding slice after greasy slice and stuffing their mouths, as if still uneasy.

Denny rubbed his temples. "Do you remember Tony Bartelli?"

"Nope. What about him?"

He blurted out, "He warned me."

Joe frowned, tossing the greasy box onto the dining room table. "About what?"

"The PB pills, that's what. Walking to the showers with him one day, he said he knew about them and no way was he taking them."

Joe sat up straight. "What? No way."

"Yup. Said his sister's a research doc and the pills, Pyridostigmine Bromide, were developed for myasthenia gravis, not to counteract Sarin or soman or whatever the hell else Saddam Hussein had cooked up."

"Myas what? Never heard of it."

"An autoimmune disease that weakens muscles. Nerve gas messes up the enzymes that make your glands and muscles work so if you're hit, your muscles seize up and you die. Defense department had nothing. They were desperate and figured if the drug could boost muscle function, it was worth a shot. FDA approved it as an investigational drug and we were the guinea pigs."

Denny sighed, "I figured it was better than nothing. Not that we had a choice since they checked our mouths to see if we swallowed them."

Joe slammed his hand on the table. "I should have known they didn't know what they were giving us."

Denny scowled. "The shitheads won't own up. Didn't want to but Willow made me go through all the tests the VA had to throw at me. Signed up for their useless registry. And then the bastards send me home because I didn't meet their damn criteria."

Joe swallowed hard. "Tess just looks at me and without saying a word tells me that I'm nobody's idea of a hero. Not even much of a man. More like a pathetic loser. Wanted to show her this weekend I was up to acting like a father to that messed up kid of mine. But my skin is crawling. I don't know what the fuck I'm going to do."

After a long silence, Denny said, "The worse thing is I came back the same old shit I always was. All the sleep deprivation. The aimless walking. Cleaning the weapon I never used every day. The soaring adrenalin when we were in the desert, looking out at Kuwait City only to be pulled back. All of it and I'm still the fucking loser I always was."

"She's your world, man. Where would you be without her?"

Denny shrugged.

"Well, buddy. You better figure that out. She's your fuckin' life-line. If you let her go, you've got nothing. Look at me and Tess." He got up. "I'm going to go check on Jason."

Easy for Joe to say fix it. He and Willow were broken from the start because of him. One lie heaped on another. But there was no going back. He was who he was. Nothing was going to change that. He had to find some way to sidetrack her from this baby obsession. He looked around the cramped living room piled with toys and shuddered. No way. No matter what it took, there had to be a way to steer her off that course. He wasn't cut out to be anybody's father under normal circumstances. No way was he up for having a baby with Jason's problems. Of course, their baby would be born deformed. Wasn't he suffering headaches and allergies from those pills himself? He'd just have to make her see that. She's always stuck by him. Wouldn't she always?

Chapter eight
1998

Jillian stood in the kitchen. She put her coffee cup in the sink and leaned against the counter. "I'm sorry, Blake, but it's sick. Actually, if I were you, I'd be choking on the 'Emma' cookies you have to eat every year. It would be better for all of you to just move on."

Blake scowled at her. "Think about it. One day, Emma was my healthy, big sister. Then, from what seemed like a flu, we watched her fight for her life when she should have been at dances, dating."

Jillian sighed, looking squarely at her husband. "All I'm saying is that after all this time, there has to be another way to acknowledge the anniversary. This ritual sends the three of you careening down a tunnel."

Blake muttered, "This is the first time I didn't go to the cemetery with them."

"Maybe you could skip the whole deal. Think about all the time your parents spend focused on her instead of you."

"Jillian, that's heartless to say nothing of unfair."

She softened, "Blake, I'm sorry your sister died. I can't imagine what that must be like for all of you. But it's enough. She's been dead for years. From all the Emma stories I've heard, she'd hate all this. And that garden. Why didn't they just bury her in the front yard?"

"Stop right now. Maybe if you could bring yourself to be nicer to my mother, maybe she'd..."

Jillian huffed, "She makes me want to scream. If it made your mother happy to see Chelsea playing with the old toys, it would be one thing. But she doesn't. She doesn't remember all the fortresses or towers you built with those blocks. Instead it's Aunt Emma made this. Aunt Emma made that. Let me show you what your Aunt

Emma made when she was your age, Chelsea. It creeps me out and shortchanges you. What's worse, Chelsea thinks she has a real Aunt Emma who's going to pop in someday."

"Jillian…"

She stiffened. "I'm the one who has your back."

"This isn't about me. It's about my poor mother whose only daughter died."

"Just do what you have to do and come home. I'll try to cook a decent dinner tonight."

"Can hardly wait." Distracted, he kissed her and left.

She watched him walk to the car. *No wonder just being alive is enough for you. Want something, Blake.*

Blake pulled up to the house he grew up in, a blue Dutch colonial with black shutters. A graceful maple shaded one side of the house. He sat in the car for a minute looking toward the sprawling, flawless moon garden his parents planted along the driveway fence line. Neither his mother nor father ever called it Emma's Garden yet there it was. White flowers bloomed in all the growing seasons—spring daffodils, tulips, lily of the valley, moving in summer to roses, phlox, and peonies, to fall white spider mums and clematis— draping the post and rail fence. In all the years since the garden was planted, Blake's parents never allowed a weed to sully the enriched soil nor would they leave a spent blossom.

As time went on, Blake wanted to mow it over and scream at them to stop. But he never said a word.

He grabbed a bakery box from the passenger seat and went into the house, banging the screen door shut behind him. "Mom?"

"In the kitchen."

Dressed in the black sheath she wore to the funeral and every anniversary since, his mother sat at the table. She hadn't aged much since the day Emma died but her hair, still shaped into the same neat bob, had turned from brown to silver. Blake strongly resembled her—they had the same thick hair, penetrating sapphire blue eyes, narrow nose and wide, warm smile. But today, she wasn't smiling and her eyes were swollen and dull. A puddle of cream floated in her coffee and the newspaper neatly folded in quarters to the crossword puzzle was blank.

She stood to give him a lingering hug.

"I was in the neighborhood so I thought I'd drop by."

"Liar." His mother faked a smile.

"Busted." Blake exhaled and poured himself a mug from the pot. "Sorry I didn't go to the cemetery with you. I got hung up at school," he stammered. "But I stopped by *Leona's* to get Emma's lemon cookies. Even they remember. She had a box ready for me no charge."

"They didn't remember. No one does. I called them earlier this week."

"Mom."

"On the good days, Dad would stop at *Leona's* to buy them. Emma was apologetic when she could only manage a bite. It's enough I would say. Taste the sweetness."

"I know, Mom. Where's Dad?"

"He's out back mending the hammock." She shook her head. "You should have come with us. Nothing could be as important."

"I can go to the cemetery any day. It doesn't have to be today."

"But we always go on this day as a family," she said, her mouth drawn.

Blake shrugged and opened the box. He handed his mother a lemon frosted cookie. "To Emma."

"Why doesn't it get easier?"

"I miss her too, Mom."

Blake picked up the pencil and started the puzzle. His mother slid it away from him. "No sir, that's mine for later."

"Didn't anyone ever teach you to share?" he quipped.

She picked up her cup, peered at him. "We never get any time to talk anymore. What's new with Chelsea? How are you? And Jillian?"

"Chelsea's speaking in paragraphs. She loves that alphabet book you gave her. *A is for Albany*. Every time, she recognizes somewhere she's been, she's squeals, 'We went there, didn't we, Daddy?' She is a very happy child."

"And Jillian? Is she... um, happy too?"

"She's great. The job at the ballet school is good for her."

"But is it good for you?" she mumbled.

"What's the problem, Mom? Come on, out with it."

"She doesn't know how lucky she is. Every day with that little girl of hers is a gift. And all she cares about is the career she wishes she had. I want to shake her."

"Mom, I wish you'd try a little harder with her. I know you were hoping you'd find a daughter in whoever I married. Maybe that will happen in time." He looked out the window. "After Emma died, I was flailing. All through high school, it was all about Emma —the next test, a new medication, your nightly sobbing. Then, it was over. She was gone and I was at college with no one but myself to think about."

He wrinkled his forehead. "When it was happening, I couldn't wait to get away. But afterward, I was in a complete fog. That is… until I met Jillian. Like Emma, Jillian was vibrant, focused, strong. She brought me back to living."

Incredulous, she exclaimed, "You married her to feel alive?"

"Of course, it was more than that. I'm just trying to give you some context, Mom. Some understanding of what drew me to her. Maybe we're so impaired by Emma dying that we don't know much about living. I don't know about you but I'm still content with a day when nothing bad happens. When I come home from work, I think I hold my breath until I see Jillian and Chelsea are okay. I'm glad she's not like that."

"I can't talk this now. Today isn't the day for that."

"Maybe it's just the right day for it."

"Blake," his father walked in, interrupting them. "Hi, buddy. What have we here? Ah, the cookies."

"Yeah, Dad, enjoy them because I just made a decision."

"What's that, son?"

"It's the last time I'm bringing them. And it's the last time you're ever going to have one either. Emma would hate this. Keep the morbid garden if you have to but it's time to just start remembering Emma with happiness. Not this."

His father frowned, "If only it were something you could just decide."

"It is, Dad. Think of it this way. If Emma tasted one of these cookies, she'd be honest. She'd say Leona's forgotten something. They don't taste right." He took another bite and screwed up his face. "Nope. 'Still yucky,' as Chelsea would say."

Blake's mother laughed, "You know something is missing. I thought it was me. The thing Emma liked was the sweetened lemon and these are tart. I wonder if she changed the recipe."

"So now, you come empty handed, hoping for your mother's chocolate chips?"

"*Leona's Bakery* has a whole case of goodies to choose from or maybe next time I'll bring Chelsea. She'd love to start baking with you, Mom. Or maybe you could teach her to cook. Jillian could use all the help she can get," he smiled, thinking about her tasteless repertoire.

"She still hasn't figured out there's more to life than dancing."

"Irene, stop."

Blake chuckled remembering the cookie disaster for Chelsea's birthday. She insisted that Jillian make homemade cookies like the other moms. Jillian bought slice and bakes thinking that would be good enough. They came out uneven—some thin ones burned, the thicker ones raw. Chelsea was stricken when she saw them. 'Mommy, what happened?' Her lips began to quiver. When Blake started to laugh so did Chelsea and they all threw them one by one into the trash saying goodbye, ugly cookie.

Jillian saved it by buying beautiful pink frosted cookies and taught the kids a dance. 'Mommy's a great ballerina!' Chelsea later exclaimed, twirling, not too gracefully around the living room.

"I've got to get going. Think about those baking lessons, Mom. It would be fun for you both." He quickly hugged his parents and grabbed the bakery box.

He stood in the front yard surveying the garden. Blake crumbled the cookies in his hand and spread them for the birds. Crushing the box, he looked at the white stillness of the garden. A sudden burst of anger rose up in him and before he realized it, Blake walked through the bed and trampled the peonies. Bending over, he pulled a cluster of zinnias from their roots and picked up the flattened dahlias. He stared at them wondering what to do next. He could bring them to Emma's grave or perhaps, give them to Jillian. But imagining the look on her face, maybe he'd just go for a long drive and toss them wherever he ended up.

Chapter nine
2004

Denny worked through lunch on cabinets he should have finished and delivered three days ago. By two thirty, his stomach growled and he began to feel light headed. He put down his sander, vacuumed his work area, and opened his small refrigerator to slap bologna and cheese between two pieces of bread. His cellphone rang and he followed his *Can't Get No Satisfaction* ringtone to a rag pile.

"D'Angelo Carpentry."

"Where the hell are my cabinets?"

His hand shook. "Tim, I…"

"I can't work on your easy does it schedule, Denny. When I tell you I need something by Monday, I mean it."

"It's almost…"

"I don't work on almosts and neither do my customers. I've cut you as much slack as I can afford. You deliver the cabinets to the job site tomorrow morning seven sharp or we're done. I've got a business to run and a reputation to keep."

Denny's temples throbbed. He paced the length of the garage. *Damn that glitch with the wood delivery. And the two days I couldn't do anything right. But today, I'm cookin'.* He looked at cabinet frames on one side of the garage and the stack of doors in various stages of readiness on the other. *I can get it done if I work all night. It's only two-thirty. Sixteen hours. It's enough time.*

He wolfed down the first sandwich, then made a second, brewed a pot of coffee, and set to work.

When Willow came home, she poked her head in. "Hey, Den. Just wanted to remind you it's dinner and a movie night. We're meeting Jane and Will for dinner at six."

Denny looked up. "Have to give me a rain check."

Willow clenched her teeth. "No, Denny. You promised. If we don't go, it'll be the second time we backed out on them last minute. I have to work with her, you know."

"Extenuating circumstances. Tim called this afternoon to tell me if I didn't get the cabinets over to his job site tomorrow morning, I'm finished. That could ruin me. Once the word got out, that would be it. Tim gave me a shot when other contractors wouldn't touch me. Can't afford to let him down."

"How could he? He knows putting pressure on you is a bad thing."

"It's business and I'm not going to blow it. Bad enough it's come to this. Why don't you go without me? I only said yes because you wanted to go."

She scanned the workshop and said slowly, "No. I don't think so."

"There isn't anything you can do here. I have everything I need. I'll just eat the leftovers from last night or have sandwiches. I'm good, Willow. Really. Go." He forced a smile.

"No. It was more about our socializing than the movie. I thought maybe you'd connect with Will."

"Nothing I can do about it." He flipped down his safety glasses and turned on the sander.

Willow walked into the house and flung herself down on the couch. She sighed, grabbing the phone from the end table.

"Hi, Jane. I'm sorry but we're going to have to cancel tonight. Denny's on a deadline and will probably have to work through the night. Maybe it's for the best. I'm exhausted. What was with the kids today?"

"Damned if I know. I actually had to break up a scuffle third period. And I made the mistake of having too many stay after school today for homework help. I tell you something was in the air."

Willow laughed. "And I thought I had a bad day. I was looking forward to seeing *Everything is Illuminated* just for the title."

Jane chuckled. "We could all use some illumination. Particularly into the minds of our kids. I'm tired too. Maybe we can postpone to the weekend. Hope the work isn't too much for Denny."

"You and me both. He can't disappoint this particular contractor. He gives him too much work. And as much as I'd like to say yes to the weekend, it's doubtful. Denny can't deal with the crowds."

"Willow, I give you a lot of credit. Things aren't easy for you and you give off the impression that all is right with the world."

"I try to keep things in perspective, Jane. It's only a movie."

"Yes, yes. Of course, you're right. Well, anyway. Maybe you could come over for dinner Saturday, then."

"Thanks. I'll let you know."

"See you tomorrow."

Willow hung up and made a face. Jane's pitying tone annoyed her.

After a short nap, Willow lay on the couch thinking at least for tonight she'd fill up the space with her own energy. Listen to music and read, or watch a movie classic in a bright room. Denny's needs always seemed to trump hers.

Autumn often said she hated feeling lonely when she was with someone. That was her flashing red to get out of yet another relationship. *Not as easy for me.* But then she smiled, *I'm going to have a perfect Willow night.*

She ordered pizza and brought it out to Denny.

"What's this? You didn't cook?"

"Nope. Took the night off."

"Thanks, babe. I'm starving." He shoved a piece into his mouth.

"How's it going?"

Chewing, he said, "Great. I'm on a roll. I'll get it done no sweat."

Willow glanced around the room, skeptical. "Nice to see you so positive. And while you're working hard, I'll be lounging on the couch spending the evening with Cary Grant and Humphrey Bogart. I'm watching *North by Northwest* and *Casablanca*."

He laughed, "Movie night after all."

She kissed him lightly on the cheek. "Now, get back to work, Bud. No slacking off. Just get it done."

"Yes, ma'am."

On her way out, she said, "By the way, I've rescheduled our double date for the weekend."

"Great," he muttered and turned back to the drawer he was working on. *Just focus.* He pushed away his worries— losing Tim and the threat of steady work disappearing; disappointing Willow again; having to socialize with the bores she works with; the faint pain behind his right eye that he decided was just stress. *Don't think. Just work.*

He finished with a few hours to spare and loaded the truck but was too jazzed to sleep. He peeked in on Willow who was sound asleep. She had thrown the covers off and lay across the bed. His beautiful Willow. Stretched out her t-shirt rose, exposing her flat midriff. He reached across the bed to push the hair from her face but saw even in sleep, she seemed troubled. A slight frown marred her face.

He couldn't help himself. He took off his clothes and got in bed, nestled in close, and stroked her belly.

She half opened her eyes and pushed him away. "Stop, Denny. I need to sleep." In the split second before she turned her back to him, he saw the same flicker of betrayal frozen on her face— the mix of anger and disbelief he first saw all those years ago.

He rolled on his back to give her space. Despite fighting it, he fell into a deep sleep. Within minutes, he was smack in the middle of the dream that never went away.

He's in Saudi Arabia, transferred to the King Abdul Soccer Stadium, now a military base they call the Scud Bowl. Exhausted, he's not sure if it's early morning or late at night. He crashed for a few hours and then was one of a dozen marines picked to go who knew where. Their mission was to establish a base close to the Kuwait border.

The small unit drives into emptiness for about an hour and then stops abruptly. Although, they're still nowhere, it's their destination. They set up a perimeter for what will be a makeshift base in this nothingness. They have no tents so they dig holes. It's hot as hell—well over 100 degrees. But at night it's so cold they sleep fully dressed in sleeping bags, covered with a blanket and their rain gear. Still they shiver. He thinks they'll never warm up again until morning, when the relentless sun comes up and burns through his skin while he fills sandbags.

That's all they do—fill sandbags and stand on guard duty. Hot food is dropped once a day. Without it, they wouldn't have food or water.

At night, they can see lights in Kuwait City far off in the distance. One night, while he's on watch, he realizes he's alone. The buddy he's on guard with disappeared. Everyone is gone.

He panics. There is no food. There is no water.

Stay calm, Denny. He says over and over. He has to stay calm. His unit will come for him. There will be replacements. No man left behind, he repeats to the wind. The sand in the dream batters him. He hallucinates a rainbow of color when the sun rises. His throat is so dry he can barely swallow. He struggles not to sleep. He doesn't want to miss anyone.

He screams but doesn't know if he made a sound. The lights of the city beyond taunt him. He has to stay alert, on watch for when his unit comes back. He waits and waits. But no one comes.

Denny was jolted awake. His body was drenched and it took him a moment to focus. A night light allowed him to see a dresser, windows with curtains. He was in a bed. There was a woman beside him. There was no sand. His breath slowed.

He got up quietly, gulped two large glasses of water, took a shower, and then sat in the living room to wait for morning.

Chapter ten
2001

"Jillian, a moment of your time after class?"

"Is everything all right?"

"Of course."

Jillian glanced at the clock every five minutes. Pushing away dread of what Sima might say, she concentrated on slowing her breath. When her class finally ended, she dashed to Sima's office.

"Sit down. I made some tea and brought some of my Russian tea cakes."

Jillian sat round-shouldered at the edge of the chair.

"These are my husband's favorites. I have to keep him from kitchen when they come from oven and I roll in sugar. Or he eats before they are ready."

Jillian chuckled, "Somehow I never pictured you baking."

Sima smiled. "Yes. I do many things. That is reason for talk today."

Jillian's cup rattled when she put it down on the saucer.

"Every day teaching I am reminded I am no longer young. And reminded again by my husband who would like to see more of me. He wants me to retire as he has. I always say no but now, I think right time."

Jillian gasped, "No, Sima."

"Relax, Jillian. You have helped the deciding. Maybe you buy? Then, I retire. My school stays on."

For a split second, Jillian thought her heart would leap out of her chest. "Oh, Sima. If only. But I don't see how it's financially possible."

"Just think about it. Talk over with husband. See if you want and maybe we work out."

"Yes. I will. I am honored. How soon do you plan to retire?"

"I will see year through to recital. The mind is strange. You think about something long time going back and forth about what to do. Should I, should I not, and then once mind is made up, with snap of fingers, you want it done right away. Let me just say, Jillian, that I would like it to be yours. But if you cannot or do not want, I will look for buyer. There was interest before. I hope there still is, now that I am ready. Think. Talk to husband. We get together again in week."

All afternoon, Jillian was alternately elated thinking about the studio as her own and devastated that it was unattainable.

When Blake came home, she was huddled on the couch. Alarmed, he asked, "What's wrong? Where's Chelsea?"

Jillian hiccupped. "She's fine. Everyone's fine."

"Then what's wrong?"

She told him.

"What are you crying about? Let's try to make it work. Ask Sima what she would be willing to do to pass on her business to you. You know how picky she is. She wants you to take over. Her husband owned a big real estate firm. The money may not be that important."

"I don't want to sound like a charity case. It's humiliating."

"Frame it so it's in her best interest. You'll figure it out."

Jillian couldn't wait the week. The next day, she asked Sima if they could talk some more about the studio?"

"So quick?" Sima remarked. "Well?"

Jillian's carefully rehearsed speech flew out of her head. She rambled, "We can't afford to buy you out, regardless of the price. But might we try to work something out? My husband thinks there may be ways. I don't know much about financing…"

Sima nodded. "Ah, you do want. That's what I needed to know. Where would I have been when I come to this country if I had no help? I'll call accountant and see what he can work out. Dear girl, look at you." She shook her head. "You must be more positive. Don't think so much about what cannot be. It ruins your posture."

She flung herself into Sima's arms and held on until she felt Sima's rigid body return the hug.

A few weeks later, they reached a deal. Sima would hold the mortgage and Jillian would be her tenant until she either could pay it out or buy the building outright. Jillian's mother surprised her with a substantial down payment.

Jillian now spun a new dream, supplanting the one gone cold.

Chapter eleven
2004

Willow's desolation deepened each month. When she could barely drag herself through a day, she finally got pregnant again. She promised herself she would tell Denny the evening the doctor confirmed it, but didn't. Never told him about the miscarriage either. Her resolve was there but her tongue twisted around the words she needed. She tiptoed through her days, careful not to lose this baby, too. But it didn't matter. She could not sway fate.

While working with a student, Willow felt a sudden, deep twinge. *No. This cannot happen. I won't let it.* She held her breath and the pain passed. Slowly, she exhaled.

"You're doing great, Nate. *A Separate Peace* is one of my favorites. *'You have to do what you think is the right thing, but just make sure it's the right thing in the long run.'* So many quotes to live by in this book, aren't there?" She took another deep breath. "We have time for one more chapter. Go ahead: ... *Like all good,*" she prodded.

Nate read haltingly, "*Devon did not stand i-so i- so lated be...*"

The searing pain cut through her again. Don't move, she warned herself, knowing she was powerless to stop it. Another pain shot through her, low and hard, the unmistakable needle-like twinging of an ovary under attack.

She whispered, "Go back to your classroom."

Nate looked up at her. "Mrs. D'Angelo, you look awful. Should I get someone?"

She shook her head and darted through the empty hall to the faculty bathroom and saw, as she knew she would, a dark red stain.

After the first miscarriage, Willow reserved a small space for hope the baby was still viable. It was only when she was lying on the cold table holding a nurse's hand while the doctor scraped the remaining cells of what had been her baby, did that invisible line where physical and emotional pain meet, rupture and snap her to her senses.

From that loss to now, she imagined the child she would have. She saw her daughter's face, framed with thick auburn hair, a trace of freckles and Denny's green eyes. Love surged in these fantasies. Willow could call up the parade of changing facial expressions that would let her see into her child's soul. She was a living, breathing being, as real to her as anything in her life.

Would it be possible for her to dig in and refuse this loss? An acute stab and wetness between her legs pulled her back. What was left of her baby now slid into the toilet.

When she'd wrung out the last tear, Willow ran out of school to her car and spun out of the parking lot on two wheels.

She couldn't go home. Every time she passed her secret nursery, her heart quickened. Now, it would remain a dark, lifeless space.

Several miles out of town, she realized she was driving to her sister's house. Willow could not bear to hear the truth in what Autumn said and thought about Denny. But she needed her now.

Autumn moved often and would always press a key into Willow's hand. "When you finally decide it's enough, come anytime, night or day. Stay as long as you want. Move in with me."

As she wound her way through the hills, she thought she'd have time alone before her sister got home from work but Autumn was home. When she saw Willow's ghostly pallor, she didn't say a word. She just pulled her into the house and held her. With Autumn's arm around her, they walked through the living room, avoiding books piled on the floor, boxes, and bubble wrap.

"What's…"

"I'll explain later. The kitchen's intact. I just made coffee."

Willow followed her sister to her cheery Provençal blue and white kitchen. Their mother painted a mural of an apple orchard on the wall surrounding the sliding door. It always made Willow smile, but not today.

Cupping the mug of coffee, Autumn said, "You look like death."

Willow braced herself. "I had another miscarriage today," she sniffled.

"What do you mean another? This isn't the first? You're doing this despite the fact that Denny wants to remain an only child?"

"If you're going to be like that I'll have to leave and I don't want to. I need you, Autumn."

"Sorry. No commentary. I promise."

"He doesn't know."

"Doesn't know you miscarried?"

Willow sighed, "Doesn't know I was ever pregnant."

"And you've had more than one pregnancy?" Autumn arched her eyebrows. "Was it his?"

Willow shot her a look.

"Sorry."

"I had to keep it from him."

Autumn winced. "Tell me."

Willow's hand shook. She blotted the spilled coffee slowly, staring at the brown shapes on the napkin. "His health is much better. He's working steadily. But he won't budge on having a baby. I can't live with that."

Autumn nodded. "Yes. I know." She sucked in a breath. "Do you think your miscarriages could have something to do with those pills he took? Maybe there's a physical reason the pregnancies aren't holding?"

"No. Absolutely not. I've read everything I can get my hands on. Besides, a quarter of pregnancies end in miscarriages. This is just my bad luck."

The phone rang.

"Sorry. I have to get it. I'm expecting a call from a client."

Willow nodded.

"Grace!" Autumn nodded. "How did you know? She's right here. You're a marvel, Mama-san. Do your magic."

Autumn handed Willow the phone.

"Mama," she sniffled.

"Something's wrong. I felt it."

"I've just lost my second baby."

"I had no idea. I thought that… well, Denny told me there would be no children."

"Did he?" She inhaled a sharp breath. "I can't bear it, Mama," she wept.

"I know, sweetheart. I had one before I conceived your sister. It was a terrible time for me. I thought the world was coming to an end. Our commune was full of babies. I remember not being able to stand the sight of any of them." She shuddered. "It was a painful time. But then… you and Autumn came to me. You, too, will have your babies but don't deceive Denny. Dishonesty is poison."

"According to him, this is non-negotiable. If he knew what I was doing, he might get a vasectomy. So what do I do?" she halted. "Leave him? Sleep around? Join a commune?"

"Don't be harsh. It wasn't like that for me. Not even at The Farm. And you girls are better for it. Though you rejected that life, it appears to still be part of you. As Thich Nhat Hanh said, *"If we believe that tomorrow will be better, we can bear hardship today."*

"Your guru's platitudes are not helpful, Mama."

"He's not my guru. His words just make sense. They show us how to live better. You'll see. Let Denny share your grief. He also says: *In true dialogue, both sides are willing to change.*"

"Mama. I can't talk now. I'll call you tomorrow." Willow hung up, rolled her eyes. "Quoting the master."

"Sorry about that." Autumn smiled in spite of herself. "You always surprise me. Just when I think Denny's totally crushed you, you do something entirely unexpected. How did you keep it from him? You can't have sex right after a miscarriage, can you?"

"Karma. He got the flu, then bronchitis. Then I got it," she smiled, wan.

Autumn laughed.

She shrugged. "What's with all the boxes?

"I'm moving back to town. I bought a rehabbed Victorian. I work such long hours, I'm hardly home anyway."

"You love this place. Something happened." She felt another twinge. "I'll be right back."

She ran into the bathroom. The globby blackish blood seeped through her panties. She called to Autumn to get her a pair of panties and pads, if she had any.

Back in the kitchen, she put her bloodied panties in a plastic bag and threw it in the garbage. "It's finished. Don't think I need to go to the doctor this time."

"You should, anyway," Autumn counseled. "Take some Advil and go lie down."

Willow fell into exhausted sleep. When she opened her eyes, she was disoriented until she scanned the painted French country furniture, the watercolor landscapes, and the orderly dressing table. She knew she could only be in her sister's photo-shoot perfect bedroom. The stabbing reality of why she was there came rushing back.

Moving from one experiment in communal living to another made Autumn and Willow very close. Yet, they grew up with differing sensibilities. Willow, more like their mother, took to the idea of breezing through their life on the go until she was a teenager. Autumn hated being uprooted. While Willow wanted a husband and children, Autumn only wanted a home of her own without anyone telling her what she couldn't do, want, or have. Let alone share.

Their mother Grace was gentle and always looked for the best in people. She never knew for certain who her daughters' fathers were. She didn't think it mattered. The whole group of men, women and children were family until they weren't. Then they would go somewhere else. 'That is how life should be, my darlings. If you think something isn't right, move on. It's a big beautiful world.'

For their mother, it was. They moved from Tennessee, to New York, to California and Oregon, to Idaho, and then back east, in farming collectives, communes welcoming society's drop outs, mountain communities, social experiments. Willow and Autumn never attended a traditional school until they were in high school. Depending on the situation, they were home schooled in makeshift classrooms or libraries, fields, or porches depending on the subject, the weather and the particular situation they were in. One of the hardest things for them both was no matter where they went, they were always around so many people. Always among a gaggle of children, Autumn and Willow, less than two years apart, moved through it all as one.

They invented a game of trying to figure out who their fathers were. There were a couple of men they fantasized were theirs. One of them, Jonathan, had clear blue eyes, bright smile, and endless supply of chocolate in his pocket. He never passed Willow without tousling her hair. He made her feel special and she adored him. She wanted it to be him and was convinced she had his eyes.

Autumn would always say, "No way. Timing, Willow. Mama didn't know him back then."

"You don't know that," Willow asserted. "He could have been at one of the early places, too."

"Sure, I do. Can't be him because it's Howie. He is your father. No question about it," Autumn goaded.

"Ew. No. Not him. He's gross! You're just jealous that I have Jonathan and hawk nose, hairy-eared Elliot is your daddy. He's short enough."

Autumn would inevitably tickle her to change the subject.

Willow smelled cinnamon. Whenever Autumn needed to think, she chopped and kneaded her way through stress. Had her colleagues known that their competitive colleague with a kill instinct in a courtroom was accomplished in the kitchen as well, they'd be astonished.

Willow walked into the kitchen. "Hmm. My mouth is watering."

Autumn smiled. "Raisin cinnamon swirl. You're favorite."

She picked some crumbs off the plate. "I'm sick of myself for now. It's your turn. What happened? It has to be something major for you to leave here. And where was I in all this?"

Autumn sighed, "A convergence of things made me decide. I began to dread the hour ride home on these dark roads. And... well, it's okay now. I didn't want to tell you while it was happening."

"Didn't want to tell me what? We had an agreement, didn't we? Nothing major happens to either one of us without a consult."

Autumn shot her a look.

Willow put up her hand. "Okay. Just tell me why you're selling paradise."

Autumn slathered butter on her bread and watched it melt. She looked up at Willow. "A client was harassing me. We lost his case and he blamed me. Well, we didn't really lose. The settlement was just less than he expected. He had a lot of debt and was counting on an unrealistic pay out. He threatened lawsuits— me, the practice, whoever else he could blame— promising to ruin us. The firm scared him against filing suit but that only turned him into a stalker. I didn't think he'd really hurt me but he kept showing up. I'd be at the gym and he'd be there. At a restaurant with a friend, he'd be staring through the window. It freaked me out so I got a restraining order. Last month, I heard he moved out of town."

"My God, Autumn. Why didn't you tell me?"

"What could you have done but worried? It unnerved me. Made me question the wisdom of living alone out here, particularly with my late hours. I sold it quickly, above my asking price. That gave me enough to buy a house in the city that has a renovated kitchen with a commercial stove, a large enclosed porch with floor to ceiling windows and a front wraparound porch. It's a beauty. There's plenty of room for you should you ever... well never mind that. I sold this place for way too much and still have enough left over to buy something more modest in the country for weekends. I'm not sure I'll do that. But it's a thought. Don't look at me like that, Willow. It's all good."

"And Carl? What does he think about the changes? Happy you're moving to town?"

"Gone, too. I knew I'd never marry him so I told him to find someone who would."

"I wish I were more like you."

"Maybe you are." Autumn laughed. "But for the most part, we are Gracie's yin and yang. You're sweet. I'm sour. You're soft. I have hard edges. You see light where I see dark. We're made for one another. Will you marry me?"

Willow snorted, "You're not dark. I know the hard-shell act. What really happened with Carl?"

"I kept thinking why can't I commit? He's the total package—smart, dreamy handsome, successful. He loves me. He started pressuring me to get married." Autumn took a bite of bread. "I kept making excuses and then slowly realized I didn't love him enough to give up my independence. Even with this very sweet man, I wasn't good at compromising and I realized, once again, I don't like to share." She nibbled a corner of the bread. "You know, what you're doing right now is more my way than yours. Doing what you want can have dire consequences. It can get very lonely."

Willow said, "Aside from Denny, I've never wanted anything so much."

"I know, love. Call him and tell him you're mine for the night."

"Okay."

The sisters sat up talking late into the night. Autumn convinced her she had to come clean.

Early morning dew glistened and the mourning doves cooed their lament from high up on the wire across the street. Denny sat on the porch steps, head in hands. His work shirt was rumpled and buttoned wrong, his hair unwashed. He thought things couldn't be better. Tim contracted with him regularly. He was in demand for heirloom items like cradles and specialized furniture. The headaches and debilitating allergy attacks struck less frequently. Life was good.

So why was Willow at that bitch Autumn's all night? he fumed.

"Denny, you're a weak, selfish bastard," Autumn spit. "You'll never even make it through boot camp, you pitiful excuse for a man. You ever hurt her like that again, being a marine will be a cakewalk. God, I hope she meets somebody else while you're gone. Asshole."

While Willow forgave him, Autumn did not. He thought it drove a wedge between the sisters but evidently not. When something's up, who does Willow run to?

Denny couldn't sit still and walked around the house. He hadn't noticed how neglected the gardens were. It was Willow's domain. She fussed over them, methodically designing her beds each season. There was never a time, except in winter, that there weren't flowering plants. Nothing made her happier than working with the earth and having a house full of flowers to show for it.

But now, it looked like an unkempt weed patch. The spent flowers, dead on their stems, were disturbing. He got a clipper to deadhead the sorry looking daffodils, now a papery thin brown. Tulip petals had fallen to the ground. He cleaned them up and weeded around them. *Don't think. She'll be here soon.*

Lately, she'd been a bit touchy, Denny ruminated. But on the other hand, she wanted to make love much more than she had in years. He sure didn't want to question that.

He heard a car turn into the street and ran to the curb. It was just the newspaper delivery. Then another. Willow. She pulled into the driveway, looked over at Denny, and sat motionless in the car.

He walked over and opened the door. Willow's eyes were bloodshot and her face was still splotched in red patches. "Hi, kiddo. Come on." He took her hand and pulled her from the car.

She nodded and walked with him to the front porch swing. They sat quietly.

"School called. Caroline wanted to know if she should get a sub for today. She said she hoped you felt better. You scared her yesterday, the way you ran out of school."

Willow still said nothing.

He stroked her cheek. "Are you sick? What's wrong? Why would you go to Autumn's? That's what I'm here for."

She looked at him. "I had a miscarriage yesterday."

"A what? You were pregnant?" He was incredulous. "Are you kidding me?"

"Joke's on me, Den."

"I mean how could you be? Didn't we decide?" He stood up and paced from one end of the porch to the other.

"Oh, we decided all right. Except we decided different things." She blew her nose into the crumpled tissue in her hand.

"What are you talking about?"

Willow flashed, "See what it feels like to be on the receiving end." Her voice cracked. "I thought we were getting married to begin our lives together, which by the way, you seemed to be agreeing with. Only we're not. You decided there wasn't enough excitement in *us* so you joined the Marines. Then, you came back a mess and decided to make it worse by going on a joy ride." She quivered. "So, it's okay when you do whatever the hell you want. And you know what? I don't feel one shred of sorry for trying to get the only thing that matters to me."

"The only thing that matters to you?" he repeated. "Dupe me? Seduce me night after night, not because you want to make love, but because you're determined to bring a fucked up baby into our lives? I don't believe it." He opened the front door and slammed it behind him.

She didn't move, knowing he'd pace, trying to calm down. He'd come out again when he was ready. Willow hoped he'd take his sweet time. She didn't want to talk to him or even look at him.

Minutes later, he came back out. "You're really something. You should get an Oscar. I actually believed you finally forgave me and we were good again. But it was just a ploy. I didn't think you had it in you to be so devious. Autumn or Grace give you lessons? You're all pathetic."

Willow didn't answer him. There was nothing to say. He could throw a fit for all she cared. The only thing that mattered was she'd lost another baby.

Lily
2002

To: lilylerner@aol.com
From: asinclair@brighamandyoung.org
Subject: Hey

Lordy, Lily. I just read your last blog, **The Grief of Mothers Who Are No Longer Mothers.**

You always nail it by finding the most poignant, personal tragedy to show the sweeping truths of war. I could see it all. But more than that I could feel your own personal grief in every word compounded by what you witnessed in Ethiopia.

What did this story do to you? Put motherhood into the loss column? Take you one step deeper into the dark side? Now, you'll probably think twice before you go into a grocery store just as you did train stations after Docklands.

It's enough. You've done stories you can be proud of and you've accomplished what you set out to do. But you've got to take a step back before you crash and burn. I know you, Lily. You take everything to heart. There is other worthwhile work you can do. Think about it.

In the meantime, stop working eighteen hour days. Start dating. Fix up your flat. I bet even your colleagues have lovers, husbands, children, fun. I know ambition. I have it too. But you are waving huge red flags whether or not you see them.

Come home. Get refreshed. You need some distance for a bit.
Love, Amber

April 3, 2002
Blog Post: *As I See It*
Lily Lerner, WNN.com

Bearing the Unbearable Burden of History: The Grief of Mothers Who Are No Longer Mothers

One of the first stories I covered as a new reporter was a bombing. For a young girl who had never seen anything like it close up, the senseless targeting of people on their way to work made me think of my own mother and the fears she must have had with a daughter choosing work that put her at risk. For me, it was the first of my 'it could have been me and for what' scenarios, I've played out in my head over the years.

It has been said that having a child is like wearing your heart outside your body. Far too many mothers have had those 'outside hearts' shattered.

Today I want to tell you about two mothers—one Israeli, who had a daughter named Rachel; the other Palestinian, whose daughter was Ayat. On a Friday afternoon, Ayat strapped on a bomb, walked into a market and killed herself, Rachel and thirty others.

Perhaps Ayat was tired of barricades, checkpoints, refugee camps, daily humiliation. Maybe she suffered from teenage angst with escalating rage. Maybe she was just a vulnerable teen seen as useful by Hamas. We'll never know.

Rachel had none of those worries. She just wanted fish for dinner.

There is an added component to this all too common event. What makes it unusual is that Rachel's mother asked to meet with Ayat's mother.

What could these grieving mothers who now carry the heavy burden of history and politics on their backs and in their hearts, possibly say to one another? Whether or not the two mothers sharing their grief will result in any real healing is doubtful. But the idea is uplifting or at least hopeful.

Too many childless mothers carry the weight of cruel political actions. Whether Sinn Fein, Hamas, Al Qaeda, the child soldiers in Africa, it seems to me to be a cowardly way of conducting a war.

And I wonder how anyone who had a mother could dream up these unholy acts.

161

Chapter twelve
2006

Blake raked out the vestiges of winter. Despite wearing an old blue flannel plaid shirt, he felt a chill in the air. With smooth, steady sweeps, he picked up speed. Lost in thought, he remembered the day his father first showed him the house.

"This doesn't feel like an aimless walk, Dad. I can barely keep up with you."

His father smiled, finally stopping in front of a house with a for sale sign. "I'm only showing you this because it's a jewel. Underpriced because it's over improved for this neighborhood. It has a finished basement that would be perfect for Chelsea's friends and space for Jillian to practice her dancing. And you know how good the schools are. Do you remember all the barbeques here?"

"Sure. Every Memorial Day. Best burgers and badminton games ever. But we're fine where we are, Dad."

He peered into his son's eyes. "There's something..."

Blake cut him off. "We're fine."

He patted his son's shoulder. "Of course. Let's not go back just yet. How about a look in the house? Marilyn and Bill's car is in the driveway."

"No offense, Dad, but a house here?"

"It's not like its next door to us."

Blake ignored him. "Even if it is a good deal, I doubt we could afford it."

"You never know. We should find out the asking price."

"I don't think so, Dad."

"Before you reject it outright, know that it would be no hardship for us to help with the down payment. Think of it this way. It could be an early inheritance we can see you enjoy. We have more than enough because…" He stopped himself.

"No, Dad," Blake said, "I have no problem living within my means."

Blake knew the house well. It had an open layout with eye-catching built-ins. There were three good sized bedrooms in addition to a room Jillian could use for dance. He knew he could never afford a house like that. Yet, maybe if she didn't feel so dissatisfied. She was at him every day about what fixes their house needed. But in this neighborhood? He could imagine her sneer, "Why don't we just move in with your parents?"

While they were reading in bed that evening, he broached the subject.

"There's a house for sale in my parent's neighborhood. It's big and in great shape."

Jillian was curious. "Is it on the same block?"

"No. A couple of blocks away. On Hawthorne. It's gray, with black trim, has a big front porch."

She closed her book. "I know it from walking Chelsea when she was a baby. That house is terrific!"

"I didn't think you'd ever consider a place that close to my parents. Was I wrong?"

"Well, I wouldn't pick it. That's for sure. They always act like they're disappointed you married me."

It would be nice if you tried a little harder. "Problem is you never let them know the real you. You don't let them in."

"And what is the real me, Blake?"

"*Hold fast to dreams /For if dreams die/Life is a broken-winged bird/That cannot fly.*"

She put her head on his chest. "Blake Golden, you get that?"

"You underestimate me."

She kissed him. "Oh, I'll let you in," she tittered.

Later, she asked, "Those lines of poetry, they're not yours, are they?"

"I wish. Langston Hughes beat me to it. I should pull out what I remember from my old poetry prof more often. Never thought of it as foreplay. Babe, that was great." He kissed her throat, between her breasts.

Jillian purred, "Tell me about that professor."

He kissed her neck. "She told us it was important to memorize poems. 'When everything else is taken from you, they will be part of you and be your solace.'"

Jillian wondered, "What did she mean by that?"

"She was from Czechoslovakia. Lost a lot."

"Maybe she's right. What's inside of you, the real you, can never be lost or taken away. Blake, you'll love me forever, won't you?"

"I can't see that ever changing." Blake nuzzled her breasts.

Jillian looked up at the ceiling. "Maybe we should at least take a look at that house."

From the beginning, he wasn't sure it was the right move for them. While priced well below its value, it was more than Blake thought they could comfortably afford. But Jillian was unconcerned. She simply wanted it. When she walked through the rooms, she had the look on her face he'd glimpsed when she was dancing. She gushed, "The house oozes charm and the extra bedroom. You never know. We might need it."

"What does that mean? You've been very clear about not wanting another child."

"Well, Blake. I couldn't imagine it in our little house but the space may change my mind."

He bristled. "Don't play me, Jillian. I know you want the house. Leave it at that."

"We belong in a house like this, Blake."

Blake stiffened. "There is nothing wrong with our house. Sure it needs some work but it's comfortable."

Caustic, she reminded him, "What needs to be done is beyond your skill set. The bathroom and kitchen need to be gutted for starters. That's big money."

"But still less than this. You have no problem taking money from my parents?"

"Not if it means living here. And the more I think about it, the more I like the idea of your mother being close by. She can get Chelsea off the bus if I'm working later or detained."

"Whoa. You'd really have to discuss that with my mother. She's finally free to enjoy her retirement."

"You're right, of course. But she knows the neighbors and could at least suggest babysitters."

They walked to the big window in the dining room. Blake remarked, "The yard is a great size. There is plenty of room for a swing set and monkey bars. Plus, a vegetable garden."

"Then it's a yes? Please, Blake."

He watched a sparrow taking a dust bath in a patchy spot on the lawn. After a long pause, he said, "We'll put in a low bid and see what happens."

"Terrific." She pecked his cheek. "Now, I've got to run or I'll be late."

"Can't have that," Blake muttered. He watched her zoom out of the driveway.

Once they put a plan in motion, Jillian vanished from the whole bloody mess of moving and selling the old house.

The realtor was a childhood friend. "Blake, the sellers are nuts. They could easily get another twenty-thou. You better move on this before they realize."

"Tammy," he chided. "Doesn't the price of the house impact your commission?"

She flirted, "But it's for you, Blake. The first boy I ever kissed."

"I was not. There was a lot of spin the bottle before I came around," he laughed.

"Yes. But I mean the real thing. You were my first long kiss with lips and tongues and banging noses. The best. Ruined me to this day," she exclaimed. "I'm dying to meet the lucky Mrs. Blake."

"Jillian's great. You'll love her."

But their meeting was strained. Jillian was brusque and not the least bit interested in making a new friend. She nitpicked all the house's imperfections, in an attempt to get Tammy to consider an even lower offer. Tammy threw him a look, unmistakable in meaning. Oh, Blake. How did you end up with her?

Remembering that first time Jillian saw the house left him unsettled. There was something off. He knew it then just as he knew it now. Blake could feel himself sinking and decided yard cleanup could wait. In the house, Chelsea was curled up on the couch reading.

"Whatcha reading, Chels?"

She held up the cover.

"*The Outsiders*. Hmmm. I think I might have read that way back."

"It's so cool. It's everything… it's about a boy who thinks the world is divided into two groups—greasers and socs. One has everything, the other group is on the sidelines. Then there's a murder and…"

"Glad you're excited about what you're reading, but it's turning into a really nice day. Let's pack a picnic and take it to the park. By this afternoon, it'll probably be warm enough for paddle boats on the lake."

"Really? Can I call Sara to come with us?"

"You don't want to spend a beautiful Saturday with your boring, yet handsome, father?" he teased.

"Dad, you are so lame."

"Guilty. What about Mom? You want to call her, too? She should be finishing her last class. She may not be able to meet us so don't be disappointed, okay? And sure, you can ask Sara. It's always more fun to have someone to go with."

"Okay, Daddy. What are we bringing?"

"Turkey sandwiches, apples, and brownies from yesterday's bake sale."

"Good. Don't forget. Mustard on one side, mayo on the other."

"How many turkey sandwiches have I made you? A hundred? A thousand?"

"Just making sure, Dad. I'll call Mom and Sara."

Jillian snapped, "What do you mean you're going to the park? Saturday is chore day, Chelsea. Daddy has yard work. You have to clean your room. When I finish here, I have a list of errands to run."

"But, Mom, we're only going for a little while. You can come before you go to the market." Chelsea begged, "Please, Mom. Sara is coming but Daddy will be all by himself."

"He'll live. Did you remember to write down all the things you want for this week's lunches? I'm only going once this week."

"Yes. Don't forget cookies again. I want Oreos. And get chips. I promise I won't eat too many at a time. I wrote them down but you didn't get either last week. I didn't have anything to trade."

"All right. I have to go. I have some paperwork to do before I get out of here. See you at home and I expect your room to be clean when I get there."

Blake heard Chelsea's side of the conversation. When she went into her room to get ready, Blake called Jillian. "Chelsea's growing up fast. Try not to miss it."

"Hello to you too, Blake. I'm not exactly spending the day at the spa. Somebody has to be the grown up."

"Or your definition of it." He hung up.

Frowning, Jillian supposed a short time in the park wouldn't kill her. They'd be easy to find. Blake always went to the same area, on the south side, close to the lake house and bathrooms. No surprises there.

Even if she did join them, Jillian had no desire to cut short her favorite time in the studio—when the last students had gone and she was alone in her quiet, orderly space. She brewed a cup of tea and while it cooled, she closed her eyes and took several deep breaths.

When she opened, them, a man stood in the doorway. Tall and muscular, with shaggy, light brown hair and hazel eyes, he wore an open-collared, crisp white shirt and blazer.

Disconcerted, he blushed, "My apologies for disturbing you. I'm Philip Langdon, Allegra's father."

Jillian smiled and motioned for him to sit down. "I was taking a moment to decompress," she smiled. "I'm pleased to meet you. Allegra is one of my best students."

"Ah, would she love to hear that. All she talks about is Madame Jillian this and that. She adores you." He leaned toward Jillian and whispered, "The Russian battle ax scared her."

Jillian laughed. "Sima was a bit intimidating but I don't think I've worked with anyone more caring or invested in their students."

"Maybe so, but I rather like Allegra's new enthusiasm. It's so important for our children to become proficient in an art form, is it not? Which brings me to the reason I'm here." He cleared his throat. "I have to be away for two weeks. Our symphony will be performing in LA as somewhat of an exchange program and I'm taking Allegra with me. She doesn't seem to be worried about missing school, but dance is something else entirely.

"You're a musician?" Jillian asked.

"Conductor."

Philip looked at her so intensely, she had to look away.

"Allegra must come with me. She rarely asserts herself but has absolutely refused to go. Can you imagine? You see her mother is also out of town. Like it or not, she's going. I'd like to soften what she considers an arbitrary decision with something that would thrill her. I wonder if you could spare the time to work with her privately when she returns? I'm not concerned about the cost."

Wistful, Jillian remarks, "I see so much of myself in her. From the time I was twelve, dance was everything."

"And now?"

"For years, I nurtured the illusion that I would be another Gelsey Kirkland or Darci Kistler. Now, I'm a teacher. It's gratifying to see a student with promise."

"Yes. I know. City Symphony is a far cry from my delusional dreams of conducting the New York Philharmonic, but if you demand quality and surround yourself with talent wherever you are, you can make beautiful music." Sheepish, he added, "at least that's what I tell myself." He stood. "It's been a pleasure to meet the famous Madame Jillian. Do you ever go to the symphony?"

"Occasionally," Jillian lied.

"Any time you want to go, let me know. I'll have the box office set aside tickets for you."

"That's very kind of you." Jillian smiled. "Tell Allegra we'll spend two hours together. I'll let her know when."

What a lovely man. Not bad to look at either.

Uplifted by her conversation with Philip, she poured out her tea and headed to the park.

Walking down the hill, she saw them immediately. Blake was stretched out on a blanket, leaning on one elbow; the girls were laughing, crumbs on their lips. Chelsea saw her first. "Mom!"

Blake sat up, making room for her.

"I can't stay long but I thought I'd get some sun with you."

Chelsea frowned, "Oh, no. We ate all the sandwiches. You wouldn't want a brownie, would you?" She offered her the one she was eating.

"I'm good. I had a yogurt before I came." She sat on the blanket cross-legged and leaned back. "It really is a beautiful day." Closing her eyes, she turned toward the sun.

Blake said, "We were just about to play gin rummy. Can we deal you in?"

Sara said, "Four is always better than three, Mrs. Golden."

"Wish I could, Sara, but I can't stay. Blake, guess what?"

"What?"

"The father of one of my students offered us complimentary symphony tickets. Any time we want."

"Joy. I can hardly wait."

"It won't kill you. You might even enjoy it. Chelsea, I read the flyer you brought home announcing a new middle school program for those of you that didn't begin an instrument in fourth grade. What do you think? Interested?"

Chelsea shrugged, "I still don't want to. I hate the scratchy violin and I don't think I could blow a flute. It looks hard. If I'd play anything, I'd pick drums. I have pretty good rhythm."

"Drums," Jillian repeated, flatly. "Maybe I should take you instead of your father to the symphony. When you hear the gorgeous music and the variety of instruments, you might change your mind. What about you, Sara?"

"I love being in choir and don't think I have time for both. Besides, if I did join band, my mom says I'd have to play the clarinet because she bought one for my brother and then he quit. But drums, Chelsea, that would be cool."

Heading off whatever Jillian might say, Blake said, "We have plans, Jillian. Saturday night pizza and a movie. Right now, still undecided on the movie. We've got it narrowed to *Hocus Pocus*, *Home Alone* or *Sister Act*. What's your vote?"

"Can't we do something besides pizza?" Jillian sighed.

"Movie suggestions, Jillian. The menu is set. What would you want the girls to eat? Tofu hot dogs? Veggie burgers?"

Sara piped in, "I know, Mrs. Golden. We can have carrot sticks dipped in ranch dressing."

Jillian tried not to picture the thick mayonnaise dressing masking the carrots.

"With Rocky Road ice cream for dessert," Chelsea added. "Put it on the list, Mom."

Jillian glowered at Blake. "All right then." She stood up. "Maybe you'll even get home while it's still nice and rake the leaves. Burn up some calories before tonight's feast."

He didn't tell her he'd almost finished. "The groceries can wait. Warm days like this are a gift."

She pushed up off the blanket. "There is no time during the week and I've procrastinated long enough. See you all at home."

I shouldn't have wasted my time. What's wrong with him? He'd rather watch Hocus Pocus than go to the symphony. But maybe I can get him enthused by making an evening of it. We could get dressed up. Go out for dinner.

"I'll never get out of here," Jillian muttered to herself as she pulled into the supermarket parking lot. Tense, she drove up and down the rows until she found a spot. Sprinting into the store, she calmed herself down focusing on her list.

Jillian weaved around shopping carts blocking her way and aisles narrowed with boxes piled on pallets for restocking. While waiting her turn at the deli counter, she felt a tap on her shoulder.

"Jillian," Philip smiled.

"What's a nice man like you doing in a place like this?" she flirted. Glancing into his basket, she saw organic greens and free range chicken.

"Same as you, I suspect. Trying to get in and out of this madhouse as soon as possible. I always promise myself never to come on Saturdays but you know how it is."

"Indeed. Looks like I'd rather be eating at your house tonight judging from your basket," she chuckled. "I've been informed it's pizza and movie night. I think I'll try to sneak a few veggies onto the pizza."

"Ah, there is no happy medium in our children, is there? I wish Allegra would eat some child-type food. I worry about her weight obsession. Yet, I can't get through to her."

"The grass is always greener, isn't it? I'll talk to her. A dancer needs good nutrition, not junk and fast food, but those ascetic habits we develop can have dire consequences on our metabolism." She laughed, "For a time when I was a teenager, I rationed a banana and some sunflower seeds over the course of an entire day. Bad idea." She shook her head remembering those days. "Don't worry. I'll do my best to scare her."

Philip put his hand on hers. "Thank you, Jillian. I'd appreciate that. And don't forget my offer regarding tickets. I'll be looking for a review."

"I'm sure you're fabulous," she smiled.

"I hope you're right. I'd hate to disappoint you."

She watched him walk away. The heavy curtain of annoyance disappeared as she stood waiting for her number at the deli to be called.

Lily
2003

To: asinclair@brighamandwomens.org
From: lilylerner@aol.com
Subject: I think I'm in love

You worry too much. What we do is who we are. You're in medicine, for heaven's sake. You see birth, death and all the suffering in between. Does that stop you? Of course not. It's your purpose.

And, it seems to me I haven't heard a word about James in weeks. Did you break up with him? Do you still want to talk about balance?

I'm on a mission right now. People are hardened. They see so many horrific things on the news all the time, they don't let it sink in. But if they hear it as a story with characters and a storyline that's familiar, they stop for a minute and realize that we are all the same. Mothers are mothers whether you live in South Sudan or Iowa. One mother can relate to another when she thinks about how many times she's sent her daughter to the market as this mother did, never to have her return. Or the suffering a mother must have when her child is malnourished. Not just the bare facts that yet another suicide bomb went off or there is a famine somewhere faraway. It's those connections that make a difference. Somebody will see or read a story and there will be a small change somewhere. That's what keeps me going.

That being said, I have real news for you, girlfriend. You don't have to worry anymore. I'm just a girl in love.

Hildie insisted I have drinks with her brother's friend who was in London for a lit conference. My immediate uninformed reaction was gag me. I'm doing prep for my trip to Botswana on top of my regular assignments. I don't have time to waste on some academic prig studying Shakespeare. But she's my boss, so what could I say?

I picked an iconic British pub to win Hildie points. It's always crowded and so noisy it's impossible to have a conversation. A quick drink and mission accomplished. When I got there, this guy, Stephen, managed to be deep in conversation with a short, balding guy, who it turned out was the owner of a local book-shop. When I walked toward him, he smiled and said, "Hildie described you perfectly. You walk into a room and everyone else disappears."

"Great line," I said, not letting on I felt the same way. You know how we used to laugh at those corny movies when the lovers lock eyes?

We left right away and went to a quiet wine bar. For someone who prides herself on keen observation, I couldn't tell you a thing about what was going on around us. All my preconceived prejudice fell away as soon as he began to talk about Virginia Woolf. She is undoubtedly the love of his life. He made her seem like someone even I would have loved to spend time with.

Stephen also understands the power of story. Although our work is different, we have much in common. I don't know how to explain it. Just watching his tenderness in handling the books when we went to Charring Cross Road made me fall a bit harder for him. In one shop, he held an early edition of *To the Lighthouse* like it was something holy.

And did I mention he's gorgeous? He's tall, broad, with sandy colored longish hair and has gold flecks in his coffee colored eyes. He smiles from his very core. I just wanted to melt into him. No details but now that I've been with him, I don't feel that I ever knew what it was like to have someone truly make love to me. We've spent every moment together I could steal away. I even took some vacation days.

Smug, Hildie smirked, "He must be something really special for you to give up your eighteen hour days. Good thing. You were becoming a real bore."

"What do you mean? I didn't say why I wanted the time."

"You don't even look the same, Lily. Could it be you finally let someone in?"

I didn't think I was that obvious.

You suggested I bring balance into my life. Well, it came gift wrapped in a six-foot wonder.

I don't know about sharing a life with anyone but if I could ever bring myself to do that... it would have to be with him or someone like him. All I can tell you is I felt as if we were at the beginning of something real. Odd given my two-second track record with boyfriends.

It is what it is, Amber. Chicago and London. Maybe long distance is a good solution for me. Ease into things slowly.

I feel refreshed. My time with Stephen gave me just the lift I need to work even harder.

I hope the residency isn't wearing you out and you're getting the specialized training you want in neonatal care. And don't forget, I want to know what's going on with James. You've been uncharacteristically silent.

Back to Africa next week. Call you when I get back.

Love you,

Lily

Chapter thirteen
2007

Time didn't ease the strain between them.

Willow's sadness put Denny on edge. Even when he saw small signs of the old Willow emerge—energy about her kids at school, interest in seeing friends again—she was aloof with him. Even talking to him about ordinary day-to-day things seemed forced. He knew it was only a matter of time before she would disappear on him altogether.

He put his arms around her one night and before she could pull away, blurted out "We can't go on like this. I love you too much to see you this unhappy. We'll try to have a baby."

But it only brought deeper despair. Willow suffered through one miscarriage. Then, after nearly a year of trying to get pregnant again, she lost another baby just as she got through her first trimester.

Willow asked him to come with her to her follow up appointment after her most recent D&C. Denny equivocated, "I'd rather not."

She stomped out of the room.

He followed her and spun her around. "If you really want me too, I will."

"I've never asked you before and you certainly never volunteered. If I didn't need you to go with me this time, I wouldn't have asked. This is supposedly about us. Not just me."

They sat in the cramped office waiting for the doctor for almost an hour. Denny fidgeted with the plaster model of a uterus on the desk. Willow stood by the window looking out over the parking lot to a patch of goldenrod.

The doctor opened the door, apologizing for keeping them waiting. He was a large man with a shock of white hair and deeply lined, open face. "Occupational hazard, I'm afraid," he smiled. He extended his hand to Denny. "Denny, I'm Dr. Hall. Hello, Willow. Please sit down."

They both watched him as he leafed through the pages of her thick chart. He then sat for a moment. "Four miscarriages. You've been through the ringer." He looked up at Willow, then Denny, and paused. "Let's talk about options."

"Options?" Denny repeated. "Are you kidding me? We have no options."

"Of course, you do," the doctor countered, scrutinizing Denny in a way that forced Denny to look at him. "There is medical testing that can be done. There…"

"You can't change the past. It's the damned pills I took."

Dr. Hall wrinkled his forehead. "I'm sorry. What pills?" He looked at Willow. "Refresh my memory."

Pinched, she said. "Denny believes the pills he took while he served in Iraq to counteract possible chemical attacks may be the reason for my miscarriages. He also thinks that if I would be lucky enough to hold a pregnancy, the baby would be born with Gold-enhar."

Stunned, Denny stood up. "May be the reason?"

Willow ignored him.

Dr. Hall interceded. "I remember now. Denny, Willow did share with me some of your worries. I poked around a bit. There was some speculation there might be an increase in specific types of birth defects born to soldiers who may have either been exposed to chemical weapons or to the drugs used to counteract the effects of those chemicals. But, the association is not particularly strong. In any case, that's not the problem here. Willow's difficulty is she can't stay pregnant."

Denny folded his arms across his chest. "Same thing. Damaged sperm."

Dr. Hall closed the folder. He spoke to Willow. "You've been through a lot. There are tests we can do to see if we can figure out why this is happening. But perhaps, you should give yourself a rest. Maybe even think about counseling after all you've been through. There are also support groups." He hesitated. "I sense a difference in opinion here and added stress can't be helping. And of course, you might want to consider adoption. It's a long, arduous process that you might want to get started."

Denny stood and extended his hand to the doctor and turned to Willow. "Thank you, doctor. Come on. Let's go."

She didn't move.

"Willow, we're done here. Let's go."

She glared at him. "Go ahead to the car. I'd like to speak to Dr. Hall privately."

"Suit yourself." He hobbled out.

"Let me ask you this straight out. What are my chances of ever being able to carry to term?"

"It's hard to say. You are considered high risk because of the number of losses. There is nothing in your personal history that stands out. I'm not sure about the rest. I'm not even sure the relationship between those exposures and miscarriages have even been studied. There is a colleague I can call at Walter Reed. I'll call you if I find out anything you don't already know."

Dr. Hall added, "Willow, up until now, I didn't realize the extent of the stress you are under. Suffice it to say, with your husband's attitude, it makes a difficult situation harder. I hesitate to ask you this, but does he even want a baby?"

"He's fixated on his friend's Goldenhar baby. But that doesn't mean it's going to happen to us. Having a baby is everything to me. You know that." She began to cry. "That Denny has come this far is only due to my pushing. But part of me thinks that he's grateful for each loss."

He handed her a Kleenex. Gently, Dr. Hall said, "My dear, I had no idea. You've never let on." He looked down at her sizable file. "I should have suspected. You've been through so much and this is the first time I've met him." He paused. "Willow, you are a young, capable woman. You do have options—don't think you don't. I won't presume to lay them out for you but one of them might be to take a good look at your marriage."

She stood. "Thank you, Dr. Hall. You've been most kind."

They were silent on the ride home and through dinner.

"Maybe you were right all along." she said quietly as she stood to clear the table.

Wary, he asked, "About what?"

"About having a baby, Maybe, in time, we can talk about adoption. But not now. "

"I'm sorry, Willow. But, honey, it's for the best."

His relief was palpable. She could almost touch it.

Lily
2005

To: sbrooks@chicago.edu
From: lilylerner@aol.com
Subject: sleepless and missing you

Dear Stephen,

It's the middle of the night and I can't sleep so I thought I'd just get up and talk to you.

I hated saying good-bye the other night. For a minute, I forgot the distance. I imagined we might have said let's meet at the pub on the corner. But there is an ocean between us and our phone calls and emails will have to do for now. Have I told you how happy I am you are an English professor who loves to write?

I'm heading back to Ethiopia. We want to see if conditions after the drought have improved and there is new information coming out we will try to verify. The government is supposedly moving people from their villages out to farms under false pretenses. Apparently, the real motive is to undercut the influence of rebel groups. The people have no choice. And with the customary audacity, these semi-prisoners are being showcased as examples of the government's generosity.

I also may go to Nairobi. Human Watch just issued a report estimating that over 200,000 refugees from Burundi, the Democratic Republic of Congo, Ethiopia, Rwanda, Somalia, and Sudan have fled to Kenya. They have no means of subsistence and live under continued threat of violence. I don't think it's out of the frying pan into the fire yet but there are reports of murders and kidnappings. What a world...

I'm still having that nightmare about the refugee camp. I see those dead children, flies swarming, landing on skin and bone. A ghost of a small girl rises up. She is wrapped in her mother's orange headscarf. I hear her screaming that she's hungry and wants to go home. I wake up in a sweat. It's not happening as often but I know I have to stop this. Now, I know why reporters drink. Only kidding.

I also haven't mentioned this before but since I'm in confession mode, I thought I'd tell you that sometimes, before I get on a plane, I get shortness of breath and palpitations. The first time, I thought it was a heart attack because I felt a weight on my chest. But it passed. Now, that I know it's just anxiety or a panic attack, I breathe through it and it eventually passes. It doesn't always happen and sometimes it's really out of the blue. I think I'm relaxed, well prepared, and then boom.

Maybe I just need a vacation. Let's plan a trip when the semester is over. Just name the place and time and I'll ask for the time off. Any place you want to go is fine with me. My only request is we book a hotel with a good bed and room service.

I think I'll try to sleep again now. Imagine myself wrapped in your arms with no thoughts of anything but us.

Love, Lily

Chapter fourteen
2008

"You say I never listen to you. But it's not true."

Willow and Autumn walked the path bordering Washington Park's frozen lake on a clear February morning. Autumn slowed down. "You have my full attention."

"You said I needed a diversion so I found one. I'm going to Arkansas," Willow announced.

"You're going to Arkansas," Autumn repeated, shaking her head. "For any particular reason? Want to go to a place called Hope?"

"Very funny. Actually, I'm not sure of the exact location. I've decided to try to make myself useful so I'm going to tend goats on my vacations. I just read *Heifer International* has a volunteer program. It's a really great organization."

"That's your big revelation. You're going off to tend goats." Autumn doubled over laughing. She spits out, "I bet you still have your purple bandana."

"Of course, I do. It's my lucky charm. It's in the bottom drawer of my nightstand."

"I can see it—you in braids, wearing your old threadbare bandana and faded denim overalls, feeding little goatlings," Autumn exclaimed. "I bet there are all sorts of animals you can take care of before they're shipped to Africa or wherever else they may be off to. Heifers. Llamas. Think of all the experience you have milking. But come to think of it…. you hated that job. Remember…"

Willow ignored her. "Is that what they're called?"

"What?"

"Goatlings." Willow smiled. "I like that."

"So when do you leave on this exciting new adventure?"

"Haven't gotten that far. Just thought I'd let you know I'm thinking."

Autumn nodded. "Keep thinking, okay?"

The two sisters continued to walk, both preoccupied.

A few minutes later, Willow said, "Maybe I can do some new things at school. I couldn't stand working for that battle-ax at the middle school but my new principal seems more open. I've heard he actually listens before he says no."

Autumn smiled. "You can develop something for kids who hate to read. An impossible task that's perfect for you," Autumn asserted. "More suited to you than cleaning up goat poop, I'd say."

"You think so? You haven't met any of my students. Hey. Speaking of the devil. Autumn, see that guy walking toward us with the two girls. That's him."

"Who?"

"My principal, silly."

"What? You've been holding out on me. He is good lookin'." Autumn whispered.

Blake smiled when he saw her coming toward them. His eyes lingered on Willow.

"Hi, Willow." He extended his hand to Autumn. "I'm Blake Golden. This is my daughter, Chelsea, and her friend Sara."

Willow shook the girls' hands. "I'm Mrs. D'Angelo, the new high school librarian."

"Cool." Both girls said simultaneously.

"Let's see how good I am. Eighth grade."

"Yup," Chelsea smiled.

"These are my favorites: *The Giver, Roll of Thunder.*"

Chelsea smiled, "I just finished *Little Women.*"

"A girl after my own heart. How about you, Sara?"

"Everything *Harry Potter.* They're awesome."

"Yes, they are. Readers! You just made my day. I don't know you from middle school. You must be at Hackett. I pride myself in recognizing all the students."

They both nodded.

"I'll look forward to seeing you when you get to the high school. You're almost there."

"Don't say that. Please," Blake interjected.

Chelsea rolled her eyes. "Dad, is it okay if we go straight to the lake house to get some hot chocolate before we skate? Kristina and Kerry should be there by now. You can watch us from here."

"A safe distance so I won't embarrass you?"

"We won't get abducted. I promise."

"If only you could promise such a thing," he laughed. "Go ahead. Have fun. I'll be back to get you at four."

He shook his head, amused. "To think I used to be the center of her world. Never thought I'd spend my Saturdays stalking her so she thinks she's on her own and I think she's safe. Double fantasy."

Willow chuckled. "The teen years, a petri dish for parent despair."

"Ha. Little does she know I'm honing my detective skills. Following teenagers without being seen is an art form."

Autumn said, "Forget the subterfuge and come skating with us."

"Thanks for asking but Chelsea would die of embarrassment."

Avoiding his gaze, Willow turned to go. "We should get going, then. See you Monday, Blake."

Out of earshot, Autumn said, "He couldn't take his eyes off you. Shame on you holding out on me He's got it bad for you. Woohoo."

Willow blushed. "Don't be ridiculous. In case you didn't notice the child, he's married. And so am I. You seem to forget that. You are such a jerk. Anyway, my fantasy lies in the cappuccino with fudge cake and whipped cream we'll will be having at the cafe after we skate. That, my dear sister, is the whole of my future."

"You think so?" Autumn beamed, "We'll see."

Chapter fifteen
2008

Twelve girls stood at the ballet barre. Although they all wore the same black leotard and pink tights, they were an array of body shapes and heights. As Jillian gave her last instructions, the girls tried to contain their eagerness to leave, except one. Allegra stood with rigid posture, nodding slightly as Jillian spoke. "Work on the new part of the dance we learned. You can't expect to master anything if you only work in class. Understood? The recital isn't that far off. You must become the dance. All right then. Until Saturday, girls."

"Thank you, Madame," they responded in chorus, quickly gathering their bags and hurrying out. Only Allegra hung back.

"Good effort today, Allegra. Your chassé is much better." They walked out of the studio together. "Concentrate on balance. Always pay attention to your arms as well as your feet. Practice. Practice," she encouraged. "It's what separates great dancers from the *could have beens*."

Jillian couldn't help but see herself in Allegra —the twelve-year-old who decided she was going to be a famous ballerina. Perhaps Allegra would be more successful. She was far more modest in her self-appraisal. "Why don't we wait for your father in my office? You can start your homework while I finish some paperwork."

"I'm sorry he's late again today," Allegra reddened. "He forgets everything when he's working."

"Things come up. I'm sure he never forgets you. What kind of job does your mother have that requires so much travel?"

"Is that what he told you?" Allegra made a face. "She's in Dallas. They both say it was a short-term transfer but I heard him on the phone with her." Her lip quivered. "She's never coming back. Dad just refuses to believe it. He can't face being stuck with me until I go to college."

Jillian came around her desk, sat in the chair next to her, and took her hand. "Allegra, taking care of you is probably what keeps him going."

There was a rap on the open door. "What are your two conspiring about?" Philip asked lightly.

Jillian smiled up at him. "Planning and plotting as all women do."

"About what? My darling girl isn't trying to talk you into sending her away to some awful ballet school, I hope."

Jillian blurted out, "Actually, we're going to start work on a dance next week for the recital. Do you think you're ready for a solo?"

"A solo? Really? You mean it?" She threw her arms around Jillian's neck.

"Yes. I mean it." Jillian smiled at her. "I have something in mind but let's plan on working out the choreography together."

Philip smiled, "That's marvelous. Let's go now. We've kept Madame Jillian too long already."

Allegra grabbed her dance bag and backpack.

"We're going out for dinner. Come with us?"

"No. Thank you. I've got to finish up and get home."

"Too bad. Allegra, wait for me in the car a minute?"

"Sure, Dad." She skipped out of the room.

Philip stepped forward, inches from Jillian. "You've made my girl very happy. How can I ever thank you?"

She didn't answer him but as he stepped closer, she stumbled backwards. Clearing her throat, she said, "Allegra's waiting."

Philip frowned, "I promise I won't be so late next time. Maybe then you'll join us."

Jillian frowned "Philip, I have a family waiting for me at home."

"A pity."

"Maybe so," she murmured. "Make sure Allegra eats well tonight. She worked very hard in class today."

"Thank you for taking such good care of my daughter. Good night, Jillian."

"Mom, why are you so late? I'm starving and Dad said we had to wait until you got home so we could eat together," Chelsea grumbled.

"Well, I'm here now. I hope you haven't been filling up on junk."

"Quit picking on me."

"I'm not picking on you. I can see the crumbs. How many times have I asked you not to eat or drink anything while you're lounging on the white couch?"

"I wasn't lounging. I was doing my homework."

Blake scowled at Jillian. "We had a deal. On Thursdays, you finish at six. What time is it now?"

"Sorry, Blake."

"Yes, I can see how sorry you are."

Jillian changed the subject. "The tomatoes smell great. Did you add olives to the chicken dish?"

"Nope. Change in plan. Tomatoes, yes. Chicken and olives, no. I've made an improvement on sloppy joes instead. I think we should call them cheesy delight."

"What happened to the chicken, asparagus and brown rice we're supposed to be having?"

"Couldn't stand looking at another piece of chicken."

Chelsea clucked.

"Stop that, Chelsea." She turned to Blake. "How many times do I have to ask you to cook clean? None of us need the extra calories."

"Don't start. If you aren't happy with my cooking, then maybe you should start coming home earlier and cook yourself."

Jillian seethed, "In case you've forgotten, I was at work." She shook her head. "No. Let's not do this. You go ahead. I'll fix myself a salad. It'll only take a minute," she sighed. "Did you make any vegetables?"

"Onions, peppers, and tomatoes are in the sauce."

Jillian groaned. "I'll make you a small salad along with mine, Chelsea."

"Just lettuce and carrots with bleu cheese, please. I don't like the other stuff you put in, Mom. Especially green peppers. I only like them the way Daddy cooks them in the sauce."

"It's time you learned to like them. How about a little vinaigrette instead of bleu cheese? Where did it come from anyway? I certainly didn't buy it."

Chelsea fought back tears.

Jillian fumed, roughly cutting carrots for her salad. She should have gone out to eat with Philip and Allegra after all.

Chapter sixteen
2008

Blake read the same memo three times before he realized he wasn't absorbing a word. There were a couple of contentious items on the school board meeting agenda but he couldn't concentrate. All he could think about was the way Jillian treated Chelsea. Watching his beautiful daughter suck in her stomach or slink to her room to avoid Jillian's critical eye, infuriated him. At least tonight, neither one of them had to see her — he had the meeting and Chelsea had plans with Sara.

Lately, he couldn't wait to get to work. Some of that had to do with the friction at home, but mostly, it was his interest in the new librarian, Willow. A glimpse of her working with a student buoyed his spirits. He may not have realized it but he'd been very aware of her since she first came to school, and either consciously or unconsciously looked for her in the halls, the teachers' lounge, the parking lot.

Willow stayed at school long past the time the rest of the faculty cleared out. She'd sometimes pop into his office to talk to him about a student. Blake looked forward to her visits, catching himself glancing up from whatever work was on his desk, hoping she'd come.

She'd sometimes walk in talking as if they were already in the middle of a conversation. "What can we do for Alex Wheatley? Aren't there some rules for passing a student from one grade to the next? Like knowing how to read?"

"Alex Wheatley. Doesn't ring a bell. What grade is he in?"

"Freshman. Ds in everything. His mother tracked me down. Textbooks are a nightmare for him. I'd say his comfort level is fifth grade tops."

"Care to sit down?" he smiled.

She laughed. "If you're sure. I must have interrupted you."

"A welcome interruption. Has the mother called Alex's teachers?"

"Of course not. Her son would kill her."

"But she trusted you."

"I worked with him in elementary school. Less successfully than I thought," she lamented.

He shook his head. "I hate to think about how many kids fall behind and never catch up. But by the time they get here, there isn't a whole lot we can do."

Her eyes flashed. "Identified kids are only a fraction of the need. All teachers need students who can read. It's not that hard to make change, Blake. You just have to do the work."

"Just do the work." Blake shook his head. "I think you need a slogan with more pizazz."

"How about I work on that and you make the faculty cooperate?" She grinned, "I'm officially dropping this in your lap."

He wanted to ask her if they could talk about it over dinner or if she realized how beautiful she was. Or say nothing and run his hands through her tangle of soft bronzy curls and feel the softness of her cheek. Or maybe ask her to save him as well as Alex Wheatley. It suddenly dawned on him, that he, too, needed saving. But all he could say was "So, you want to drop anchor here? I mean, not here," he blushed, looking around his office. "At the high school."

"I would. There is so much I'd like to do here. I know the deal was a temporary transfer but I want to stay if you can make it permanent." Breathless, she added, "I'm still mulling it over but when I have a plan, I'd like to bring you a list of ideas. I want to do something for the achieving kids, too. They need to be reading classics. When did it become okay to read any old garbage? Just record page numbers and number of books in a log for credit. Really! You think I can get a dozen to start? Actually, I want to run a bunch of book clubs for all levels." She sank back into her chair.

He shook his head, "You must have a serious case of insomnia." Remembering his own initial excitement when he came up with a new idea, he smiled. "One sleepless night I decided to organize a History Bowl. Teach my students that competition could be intellectual as well as athletic. Wow, did I let myself in for it."

"What happened?"

"Parents went ballistic. Didn't like the way the teams were formed. Didn't like all the extra work I required. Didn't like that their kids were in it. Didn't like that their kids weren't. You name it. They complained." He hit the side of his head. "I spent more time placating than prepping. Come to think of it, prepared me for this job."

She laughed, "I'll bet. But you were undeterred, you did it and it's still happening. Plus, the kids love it."

"Yes. All true," he admitted.

"So, I'll draft up something and then we'll take it from there." She got up to leave.

He couldn't let her go. "Listen, my board meeting isn't until six. Do you have time to get coffee or something to eat? We can start developing a plan."

He watched the rapidly changing expressions on her face as she decided. He was sure she was going to say no.

"If I can get the principal's undivided attention, I might even offer to pay."

No worries. You have my undivided attention. "How about if we just go over to the Corner Café? Do you know where it is?" Blake asked.

"Of course. Meet you there."

They had sandwiches and only talked about work. But when they both grabbed the check, their hands lingered, hers on top of his. He hoped it was more than wishful thinking that she, too, felt a spark.

Chapter seventeen
2008

They were finally going to the symphony. Jillian tore through her closet looking for something special to wear. Desperate, she went to her friend, Claire's. "I have nothing to wear."

"What did you have in mind?" Claire asked.

"A dress that's silky and sophisticated."

She pulled skirts, shawls, and dresses from her closet. "Voila!" She handed Jillian a long dress with a matching shawl.

Jillian slipped the cerulean blue and silver silk dress over her head. Looking in the full-length mirror she turned sideways, smoothing the soft material over her narrow hips.

"Made for you. You don't need to try anything else."

"Where did you get this? It's gorgeous."

"On a trip with Peter, I think. No maybe it was with Simon. Anyway, when Blake sees you in this, it might fan the embers before they grow cold."

Jillian nodded but she wasn't thinking about Blake.

Blake grumbled, "We're only going to be sitting in the dark, Jillian. Does my navy blazer, white shirt, and silver tie meet your approval?"

"Do you have to put it that way? I want to look and feel different tonight."

"I hardly feel special wearing the clothes I wear to work every day but if that's what you want, fine."

Jillian sighed.

Chelsea came into the bedroom.

"Ready to go, love?" Blake asked.

"Yup."

Jillian hugged her lightly and kissed the top of her head. "Have fun. Say hi to Sara."

Chelsea nodded.

With his back to her, he said, "Be back in a few minutes."

"Try not to dawdle. I'd like to get there early."

Jillian was admiring herself in the mirror when he came back.

Blake whistled, walking toward her. "Where did you get that dress?"

"It's Claire's. She got it on one of her trips." She held up two different earrings. "Which do you think?"

"The silver twists." He walked to the closet to get his blazer. "Boy, you've got to hand it to her. Never thought there was a butterfly in that tightly controlled chrysalis."

"Now, she's one happy woman."

He sat on the edge of the bed. "You know, I'm not the caveman you make me out to be."

"No, you're not. You couldn't be more unlike Claire's ex. He supervised every minute of her life."

He muttered, "In our house, it's the other way around."

"What, Blake?" she asked.

"Nothing."

Philip set aside excellent seats— third row center—but Blake would have preferred the aisle. There wasn't enough leg room and he couldn't get comfortable. "We've got about twenty minutes before it starts. I'm going to walk around. Do you want to come with me? Maybe get a drink?"

"No. I'm fine. I'd like to look at the program."

"Suit yourself."

From the back of the theater, Blake watched Jillian hunched over the program. He shook his head and left to find the bar.

Jillian thumbed through the pages to find the performer notes. Philip had an impressive resume, she thought. He'd studied at Juilliard, Curtis, and The New England Conservatory. Surely, if it were all true, he could have done better than this. Maybe they had more in common than she realized.

She became increasingly anxious as the time approached for the performance to begin. She imagined what Philip would look like in his tuxedo, what it might feel like for him to hold her, the strength of his muscular arms.

Blake slid back in his chair as the lights dimmed.

She tapped his arm and whispered, "They're beginning with Prokofiev's Cinderella Waltz. Does that mean anything to you?"

"Sure. It was in a showcase. You…"

"Yes," she interrupted.

Philip walked to the podium, faced the audience and bowed. He pivoted to face his musicians. Jillian closed her eyes at the first notes of Prokofiev's grand waltz. She could feel the music. Her internal metronome ticked. She saw the ballet in her mind, having watched the soloist rehearse the ball scene so often. She knew the part well, practicing it late at night alone in the empty building. Believing the role might be hers someday, she fell asleep going over the steps and rose the next morning, humming the music. Thinking and feeling the steps on her way to class, on the walk home. The choreography was imbedded in her mind, in her feet, in her arms. Everything else fell away.

She is Cinderella. The pink silkiness of the bodice is like a second skin. She performs flawlessly. Waltz in with the prince—one, two, three—turn, turn, turn. One single, one double, one rotation each step, then two. Offstage to make way for the jester. Re-enter with the prince. *Grand jeté* leaps.

Her leaps are high and fast and clean. Then at the two o'clock stage mark, *piqué arabesque* and a turning *assemblé*—feet in fifth brought together in the air, landing in fifth— and the prince catches her.

Then, a *sous-sus*, up on toe right before the prince lifts her onto his shoulder. Turn, leap sequence —*cope jeté, a sauté arabesque, glissade saut de chat, glissade saut de chat, glissade saut de chat*. Repeat two times. Then, turning leaps. *Coupe jetés* in a circle. The clock chimes. She runs off stage.

She is technically flawless but also an artist possessing the magical quality that once eluded her. On point, her arms flutter. She has met her prince. Their joy at finding one another transforms them as they dance across the stage. The frantic feeling when the clock strikes twelve hits her hard. She is shaken back to the present by the applause.

She blinked away her tears.

Blake watched her. He saw the otherworld of sheer pleasure as it washed over her. In the darkened theater, he understood what she was doing. He knew she was transformed into the radiant Jillian he remembered, her delicate face frozen into that fixed, unknowable stage smile. He felt every trace of happiness evaporate when she opened her eyes. Instinctively, he reached for her hand but she pushed it away. He heard the catch in her breath and saw the tear before she wiped it away.

She closed her eyes again and knew she had to get away. She couldn't breathe.

When the lights went up, she bolted out of her seat to escape and sat at the edge of the threadbare velvet settee in the ladies' lounge until the bell rang. She felt as raw as the day she ran away.

She said nothing to Blake as she slid back into her seat. The *Rachmaninoff Concerto* meant nothing to her. She hated its overbearing sentimentality. Her eyes never left Philip. He wore the music well. He moved with every phrase, knew when to encourage, when to quiet the orchestra, when to come full out. His arms became powerful wings as he flew with the speed of the music —all with natural grace. She couldn't help but admire him.

Maybe he would understand what no one else in her life could— not her husband, her friends, her mother. Not even Sima, who would cut her off, tell Jillian she had far too much to sink into self-pity. But it was different for Sima. She tasted it. She danced with the Kirov. At least that's what she claimed.

It may be second rate but Philip was doing it, too, she thought. Maybe that was her mistake. He might be leading the Podunk Symphony Orchestra but at least he lived with the music. What did she really have? A few good students who she actually enjoyed teaching.

Forcing herself back into the moment, she admired how the pianist threw himself into the music, wringing out every last passionate note. He held himself taut, his back curved over the keys as close as he could be, becoming part of the piano itself. He, too, probably imagined something more for himself, but he was performing.

When it was finally over, the packed house rose to their feet.

She said, "Let's just say a quick hello to Philip."

"Let's not," Blake groused.

"We should thank him."

She pulled a reluctant Blake backstage. Philip stood in the doorway of his dressing room. He had already changed from his tuxedo to a pale green shirt and jeans.

"Why Madame Jillian, you look bewitching. Perfect colors for you." He stuck out his hand to shake Blake's. "Sorry my hands are still a bit clammy. The lights are terribly hot."

Blake stood behind Jillian, lightly touching her shoulders, trying to detect what, if anything, was going on between them.

"I don't know what to say, Philip. The Cinderella brought me back to a happy time. Thank you."

"I wondered if you'd be dancing in your mind."

Jillian laughed, "How did you know? The choreography of that particular ballet is still part of me. I hadn't realized."

"Old habits die hard. I'm sure if I wasn't conducting, I'd be waving my arms around in the air and people would say, he's lost it, poor man," he snickered.

She laughed, nodding.

After an awkward pause, Blake said, "Time to go."

"It is late. I have to be on the road early tomorrow but I did promise the guest pianist, I'd take him out for a drink. Care to join us?"

Before Jillian could say anything, Blake said, "Thanks but we have plans. Let's go, Jillian. Goodnight." He walked out expecting her to follow him.

Turning to Philip, she said, "Sorry about that."

"One can see why he wants you to himself." He held her hands and kissed her on both cheeks. "Until next time."

Blake was standing in the hallway.

"That was rude."

"You think so? You don't ever see a thing as it is, do you? The world according to Jillian is a distorted place. I need some air. Let's get the hell out of here."

Lily
2006

To: sbrooks@chicago.edu
From: lilylerner@yahoo.com
Subject: How about Paris?

I have a friend with an apartment in Le Marais who'll be away this summer. He said we can stay there. Just have to give him dates soon to have first dibs. The thought of being there with you is making me—well, let me say this. I'm picturing the weekend we spent at the Georgian House and hardly left our room. That delicious splurge. Hmmm. How do I love thee? Can I begin to show you the ways?

To: lilylerner@aol.com
From: sbrooks@chicago.edu
Subject: How about Paris?

Ah, the Georgian. The best weekend of my life. Except for all the others.

I can come June 18, right after my summer session ends. I'm already counting those ways and days until I can see your beautiful naked body in the glorious Paris light. Forget what Hemingway said. You are THE moveable feast, my love. And to have you in Paris, my thoughts are now censored.

Imagine walking along the Seine in the evenings, listening to jazz on the left bank, and having an apartment there? A dream. Or we don't go anywhere. Instead, we can make love all day every day.

To: sbrooks@chicago.edu
From: lilylerner@yahoo.com
Subject: How about Paris?

Yes! Wait until you see where we're staying. It's my favorite part of Paris, with its old, winding streets barely wide enough for cars. Trés charming. It'll be great to be based there.

I hope you won't mind too much but with my job, it's never just vacation. I may have to do a few background interviews with Muslim teens while we're there. Trouble may be brewing. But I can do that while you trace your favorite ex pat writers. It shouldn't take much time.

To: lilylerner@aol.com
From: sbrooks@chicago.edu
Subject: How about Paris?

I'm sure I can amuse myself while you do those interviews. After Paris, I'll go back to London with you until the end of July. There are two colleagues I will be working with when we go home. Can I say that?

To: sbrooks@chicago.edu
From: lilylerner@yahoo.com
Subject: How about Paris?

Sounds good to me. Six weeks together. The moveable feast travels back to the next best city in the world. I'll try to take some time off. Maybe we can take some day trips. I'm sure you'd like to go to Shakespeare country.

To: lilylerner@aol.com
From: sbrooks@chicago.edu
Subject: How about Paris?

You're on!

Chapter eighteen
2008

Willow stopped at the threshold of Blake's office. It was a space with crowded bookshelves. On his desk flanked by piles of papers and files, a Mac scrolled wallpaper of student activities, light streamed in through high windows. *He is one good looking man.* She loved his dark wavy hair, his intense dark blue eyes, his easy smile. Broad shouldered and muscular without being brawny, he seemed solid in every way. She retied the satin ribbon at her waist, glad she chose her cream-colored lace dress today. He was reading a file and had his hand on the phone, when she knocked on the open door.

He looked up. "Willow. Come in." He motioned for her to sit down.

"You look busy. I'll be brief."

"That'll be the day."

"You never know. I may surprise you."

He tried to suppress a smile. "I welcome the interruption. I was about to call a parent whose son isn't going to graduate. Wouldn't mind putting that off."

She slouched in the chair and grimaced. "What's the story?"

"He's working nights to help support the family and failing every subject."

"Not Jimmy Bates."

He looked at her sideways. "How did you know that?"

She shrugged. "His father lost his job and split. He's supposedly looking for work elsewhere."

"Didn't know that. Jimmy's been sent down here countless times. Sleeping in class, multiple warnings about getting homework done, general teacher concern. He's such a good kid." He shook his head. "I tell him he's got to make school a priority. That it'll help him earn more if he graduates. He just nods and says, 'I know, Mr. Golden. I'll try to do better with my classes but I can't quit my job. We need the money.' They're in the system. Getting the social services they're entitled to. But that's never enough."

Wistful, she said, "I don't know how you do it. I'd try to take them all home with me." She added, "They love that you try so hard even if you can't fix things."

"Lot of good that does." Trying to contain a smile, he said, "So. I doubt this is a social call. Just tell me it won't cost anything."

He got out of his chair and leaned against the edge of his desk, nearer to her.

"Not a penny. I promised you that when we had dinner."

"We should do that again. It felt great to talk about the kids to someone who totally gets it."

Willow looked away. "While it was like asking them to jump off a cliff, ten teachers agreed to be in the book club. They were harder to get than the students. Too busy. No time. Not their subject area. One, who shall remain nameless but will forever be on my you know what list, said to me, 'like I don't have enough to do but what would you know, I actually teach.' But I'll stoop to any level." She giggled, "I found guilt to be most effective. The big surprise was that getting students was a breeze. I thought maybe a couple of kids would say yes but I have a dozen including your daughter, Chelsea. What a lovely girl she is."

"The light of my life."

Willow smiled. "Intelligent, helpful, generous. The whole package."

They were silent for a moment. She turned her head to avoid his steady gaze.

"Anyway, both student and teacher groups are doing the same book. We're starting with *The Kite Runner.*" She took a breath. "Then, after a few months— they don't know it yet —but I'm going to mix the groups. Teachers and students as peers."

Blake laughed, "Good luck with that."

"They'll balk at first, but once they get used to the idea, they'll be fine with it."

"In any case, count me in to help out if you need to buy more books," he offered.

"Thanks." She went on. "Next, I'm starting a group with students who are behind and need to improve their comprehension. I'll start them with Stephen King stories. They're short and the kids'll think they're cool."

He nodded.

"I'll do all of them on Thursdays so they'll make the late busses."

"You've thought of just about everything."

She looked at him quizzically. "What'd I miss?"

"The student uprising to get into the coolest club. When that happens, I'm throwing you in."

Willow threw her head back and laughed out loud. "That would be my dream. If I can do nothing else, I want them to know reading can be their passport to a different life. Or at least can take them out of their own life for a while." She looked down at her lap.

"Why don't we go over to the *Book House* to see if we can talk them into a deal. We might even get them involved."

Willow stood. "Really?"

"Why not? They've always been generous to us. We'll rope them in from the beginning. They may even want a tie in to their own book club. I'll call Jimmy's mother and then meet you."

When he got there, Blake watched Willow through the window talking to a woman behind the counter. He knew he shouldn't be doing this but he couldn't stop himself. If it were some other librarian, he would have told her to go ahead and that would be the end of it. But then, she wouldn't have been Willow. A woman who appeared airy and light, optimistic, yet tinged with melancholy. *Blake, get a grip. You don't know a thing about her.*

She'd cut a deal before he even made it through the door. "Sorry you wasted your time coming over. Deep discount for this and future selections."

"No worries. But… since we're here, how about a cup of coffee? Maybe the café next door hasn't run out of their remarkable scones."

As he held the door open for her, she asked, "On whose authority are they remarkable?"

"Mine corroborated by Chelsea. Scientifically tested in every bakery in town. Chelsea and I have been playing *Who Has the Best?*

since she was eight. It started with chocolate ice cream. She would make up all kinds of criteria and we'd record it all. Our analysis is totally objective," he beamed.

She sat down and put her shoulder bag on the back of her chair. "You're kidding." She broke into a grin. "When we were growing up, my sister and I played the same game. We called it *The Very Best.* The very best hot dog. The very best chocolate layer cake. We even did the very best brown rice and vegetables. We ate it almost every night at one of the places we lived." She smiled at the memory. "What a great thing to do with your daughter, Blake. I bet your wife is thrilled you have that kind of relationship with her."

"Perhaps, but Jillian hates this particular game. So much so, we had to complicate it by putting everything in code. I know —devious. But sometimes you need to have a little fun and bend the rules a bit. Jillian teaches ballet so her idea of food does not allow for sugar or fats, unless you're talking avocado. Come to think of it, she might play if we did the best poached fish, best sushi, best steamed broccoli."

Willow made a face.

Blake caught it and said, "I'm not crazy about poached fish either but somehow I don't think that was an I-hate-fish-look."

"Never mind. I had an unkind thought. Totally out of line. Sorry."

"Doubtful, Willow, and I'm not letting you off that easily. A cloud passed right across your face."

"I hate for you to know how judgmental I can be. The worst trait." Sheepish, she added. "Working on it."

"I doubt you have a judgmental bone in your body."

She blushed. "*Dinner at the Homesick Restaurant* has this great line that popped into my head when you said that." She looked down. "That's all."

"Out with it."

"Sorry, Blake. *"Cody cut into a huge wedge of pie and gave some thought to food--to its inexplicable, loaded meaning.... Couldn't you classify a person, he wondered, purely by examining his attitude toward food?"*"

He muttered, "There may be more truth to it than not."

"I'm sorry. It was thoughtless to intimate anything about your wife. I'm an idiot. Always watching what she eats shows tremendous discipline of which I have none," she backpedaled. "If I ever had to diet, I don't know what I'd do. What would become of me if I couldn't have ice cream every night? Or drown my sorrows in potato chips?"

"What kind? Barbeque? Ranch? Or are you a purist?"

"Sad to say, I don't care and have no brand loyalty. But I do like kettle chips if I had to pick a favorite."

Blake laughed. "I should have Chelsea talk to you. I hate the food wars in our house."

"Your wife is probably right up to a point. I never gain any weight. Lucky as my five-foot two-inch sister always reminds me. But then again, we did have different fathers."

"A child of divorce, unscarred half-sisters? That's refreshing."

"I wouldn't say unscarred and I never ever thought of Autumn as anything but my true sister. But then, I'm not a child of divorce."

"What then? If you don't mind my asking."

"My mother didn't believe in marriage. Autumn and I grew up in communes and collectives. We don't know who are fathers are and our mother was no help. "'Girls, you are creations of love,'" she imitated, spreading out her arms. "'The rest doesn't matter. All the men here are your fathers.'"

Blake laughed at the parody. "Stop. You're making this up."

"That's nothing. I'll wait until I know you better to tell you more. You have no idea."

"There's a lot to be said for *it takes a village.*"

"Like anything else, it had its good and bad points. Some of them were great, others were nasty, dangerous places we were happy to leave. I never attended a real school until high school. When I finally got there, I fell in love and decided I was going to spend my life in one. Books were always a safe haven for me and I've always wanted to give that same gift to my students. Oh, listen to me. Going on like this." Her eyes misted.

"What is it, Willow?" He placed his hand on her arm. "What's wrong?"

"I'm fine. It's just… Well, it just hit me that I don't have much fun anymore. Just laughing with you now…" She shook it off.

"You're not alone there," he murmured. "So, back to the matter at hand. We haven't chosen our dessert."

"You lured me here on false pretenses, Mr. Golden."

He blushed, "What do you mean?"

"Here I thought you were all about business but you just wanted me to be your excuse for deliciousness. I'll be your willing partner in crime. Carrot cake if there aren't any of the remarkable scones left."

He stood, "Coming right up. Anything else?"

"Coffee. Wait a sec." She took her wallet out of her pocketbook.

"Don't be silly. How about next time, it's your treat? I mean…" Flustered, Blake raked his fingers through his hair, never taking his eyes off her. How lovely she looked, he thought. He knew that beneath the façade, this woman in lace, dressed as if she were going to a garden party, was a complicated woman who he wanted to know, layer by layer, perhaps, more than he was willing to acknowledge.

She looked at him squarely. "Next time. Chocolate layer cake at Java's."

Chapter nineteen
2008

Willow opened the front door, flipped the lamp on the cherry console table in the foyer, and bent down to pick up the mail that had fallen through the delivery slot. She leaned her purse and canvas book bag against the table leg and looked through the mail. "Telephone bill, credit card offer, Macy's sale ..." she murmured to herself as she shuffled through the envelopes. A postcard fell out of the pile onto the floor. She stooped to pick it up and smiled when she saw the picture of three little girls wearing gauzy white dresses, standing in a golden, hazy field. The girl standing in the center wore a daisy wreath in her hair. It was a book cover. *Growing up Hippie: From Drop City to The Farm and Beyond* by Laurel Somers.

Willow smiled. "Denny, I'm home."

"I'm right here. You don't have to shout." He was at the kitchen sink getting a glass of water. "You have the mail? I'm expecting two checks."

"Didn't come." She handed him the stack of envelopes.

He rifled through them. "Been waiting a week. That on top of delay on the maple I ordered and get this, Bob Whitman called to tell me they want me to change the finish on the cradle."

"They'll pay for it, won't they?"

"Not the point. They want it painted friggin' white. I bought that beautiful piece of cherry. I could've used pine."

"They probably bought a white nursery."

He shook his head. "You don't understand."

"Enlighten me. Shouldn't the customer get what he wants?"

"Never mind."

"No tell me," she insisted.

"Nothing to tell. Painting that gorgeous wood is a sacrilege."

Willow gauged the extent of his bad mood. "What else? What did you work on today?"

"Stuff."

"Stuff," she repeated. "Okay, then. Moving right along. How was your day, Willow?"

"And how was your day, Willow?" he mimicked.

She frowned. "It appears consistent with the way my evening is going to go. I worked with a boy whose mood was just about the same as yours. Brewing tantrum. Thanks for asking." Her shoulders tensed. "You've been irritable for weeks."

"No I haven't." He threw the mail on the table.

"We did get something interesting today." She held up the postcard she'd slipped into her pocket.

Barely looking at it, he asked, "Where's the hippie mother now? Wish we could get around like she does."

"Sure, you would. You don't even want to go to the park."

"Don't start."

"Just once I'd like to come home to ...well never mind." Willow sat down at the table and flipped over the post card. "It isn't from my mother. It's from Laurel."

"Who's that?"

"What do you mean who's that? We spent a week at her lake house."

"Oh yeah. I remember now. She had that douche bag boyfriend."

She handed him the postcard. "Look at it, Denny. Anyone look familiar?"

He squinted and shook his head.

"There's Autumn wearing the dress she loved until it fell apart. And that's me." Willow pointed to the little girl on the right.

He looked at it more closely. "How old are you in this?"

"It looks like it was taken when we lived on the farming collective so I must have been seven. I'm so proud of Laurel. She hasn't had it easy."

Denny flipped the card over. "Book signing here next month. Autumn will want to go with you."

Willow snatched the card from him. "We're all going and then we're taking her out to dinner. Oh, wait a minute. Here is a note in her famously terrible handwriting. She wants to stay with us."

"Great." He made a face.

"She's the only friend Autumn and I have kept in touch with. You'd love her if you gave her a chance. You have other plans?"

"Guess not," he grumbled. "Call me when dinner's ready." He walked into the living room and turned up the TV volume.

Willow, Denny, Autumn, and Laurel sat in a booth at a quiet restaurant. Willow squeezed Laurel's hand. "Your reading was stupendous."

"Thanks to you two for packing the house. I can't tell you how many duds I've been to. Two or three people browsing come over to chat because they feel sorry for me sitting alone behind a mountain of books."

"That's the publicist's fault, not yours," Autumn said.

"Maybe so but it's still demoralizing. But for the most part it's been pretty good. I've met some very interesting people."

Autumn turned to Denny. "Aren't you glad you decided to come? Wasn't Laurel great?"

"Yes. Great."

She suggested they order. "Everybody know what they want? I know I'd love a glass of wine. Beef stroganoff is their specialty if anyone's in the mood."

Focused on the menu, he said, "Yeah. I'm ready."

Autumn motioned to the waitress and they ordered their food and drinks.

Willow said, "Okay, so now tell me your best book signing story."

Autumn and Laurel burst out laughing.

"What's so funny?" Denny asked.

Laurel giggled, "Willow was always asking everybody to tell her the best story they knew. She'd follow them around until they'd relent. Finally, someone figured out they should teach her to read to get her off their backs."

Willow protested. "Totally untrue. I was reading by the time I was four, in case you've forgotten. I just liked to hear stories when we were doing our chores. It made them fun. Remember Cynthia? She'd spin tales around whatever we were doing —cooking or planting or sitting around during those never ending rainy days."

"I learned a lot from her about how to tell a story," Laurel mused.

Autumn said, "I remember her as always patient and serene. Now, I'd love to know where that peacefulness came from."

Denny fidgeted, his mouth was firmly set in a frown.

Laurel turned to him. "Denny, do you have a favorite childhood memory? Ours must be boring you to death."

He clenched his jaw. "Not really. Listen, I'm going over to the bar to see the scores."

Willow glared at him.

Laurel nodded. "Sure. We'll call you when the food comes."

"Why did you drag him here, Willow?" Autumn asked.

"He spends too much time alone. I think he's losing his people skills."

Autumn muttered, "You can't lose what you never had."

Willow ignored her. "I'd hoped he'd snap out of the funk he's been in." She shook her head. "Never mind about him. Best book tour story."

Laurel said, "In a minute. Who's that guy Blake you introduced me to? He couldn't take his eyes off you. Remember Javier who was so crazy in love with your mother. He'd look at her as if she was the only woman in the world? Blake looks at you just like that."

Willow flushed. "Don't be ridiculous. He's my boss. He was probably trying to figure out if it was me in that chapter you read."

Autumn rolled her eyes. "Sure, honey. That must be it." She turned to Laurel. "I met him eons ago and it was obvious then that he was smitten with our Willow."

"Dark curly hair and what would you say, Autumn? Sapphire, navy, or just plain glistening ocean on a sunny day blue eyes?" Laurel chuckled.

"Cut it out, you two. He's married and so am I. A story now, Laurel."

"Okay. We'll drop it for now." Her eyes lit up. "This one really is the best. I was in Seattle at an indie bookstore, one that was struggling beneath the shadow of a *Barnes & Noble*. It was gorgeous with its high ceilings, exposed beams, and brick walls. The café had every literary journal you've ever heard of and served me the perfect latte.

"What a contrast to some of my other signings. You could just feel how the booksellers love writers and are proud of their store. They promoted the signing. Even got somebody from the local paper do a phone interview."

Laurel drank some wine. "But just my luck, there were torrential rains that evening. I didn't think anybody would show but I was mistaken. At least twenty people came. Raincoats were saturated, umbrellas dripped puddles all over the floor. But the fact that they got there despite the storm made them a bit giddy.

"There was a man who sat right in front of me. Talk about someone who couldn't take his eyes off a woman. He made me very uncomfortable. A big guy in a long, black coat. I whispered to one of the booksellers that I was nervous about him. She said not to worry. He was a regular and never caused a problem.

"I did my usual shtick, read a chapter, and then opened it to questions. He was the only one to raise his hand. I was uneasy about what he might say but what could I do? 'Miss Somers,' he asked, 'was there a man at that ranch who taught you how to groom and feed the horses, exercise them? Was there a particular horse named Skylark, that you absolutely fell in love with and considered him yours even though the ranch philosophy was that nobody should own anything?'"

Laurel smiled joyfully. "My heart sped up as I realized who he was. He continued with his questions. 'Did you once get stung on your butt by a bee and scream holy hell for an hour?'"

Willow and Autumn cried out together, "Jordy! Jordy was there!"

Laurel laughed. "I practically jumped over the table to hug him. I couldn't believe I didn't recognize him. He still has that tic in his right eye. His hair is graying now but still in a neat ponytail. He came up to the table and sat with me. People were really interested in what the life was like. Many of them thought of communes as filled with filthy hippies who did nothing but do drugs and have sex. There was that, of course, I told them. But not all of them were like that.

"Did you tell them our runaway story?" Autumn asked. "That's the most dramatic, I think."

"Yup. I told them how we left in a hurry because some nut job, flying high, thought it would be fun to give us kids Kool-Aid laced with LSD. But we also talked about the ranch and the farm. The good parts of that life."

"Jordy," Willow smiled. "He used to hoist me up to kiss the horses."

Autumn asked, "What's he doing now?"

"He married the woman who called herself Hyacinth. I think I remember her. They lived in Oregon for a while and then moved to Seattle to care for her mother. They have a small horse farm."

Autumn asked, "Since the book came out, have you heard from anyone else?"

"Some emails either saying they loved it or I was a liar. But the general feedback has been good. Nobody but Jordy ever showed up."

The waitress came with the food. Willow asked her to bring Denny's plate to the bar. Autumn and Laurel looked at each other.

Laurel said, "Willow, you're breaking my heart. You have to do something."

"Amen," Autumn chimed in.

Willow's mouth was set. "It's complicated."

"When school's out this summer, I want you to come stay with me at the lake indefinitely. Figure things out."

Sour, Willow snapped, "What's to figure out? Things are what they are. Period."

"No." Laurel reminded her. "You're suffocating and sad. You don't even look like my Willow."

"Some quiet time at the lake is just the thing. I'll make sure she gets there," Autumn said.

"Hello, you two. I can hear you, you know." Willow said, "Nobody knows what goes on in a marriage."

"That's true," Laurel admitted. "But a little space, some time for reflection, never hurts. I can't say much about Denny since he won't talk or look at me but he is bitter. Anyone can see that. And you know how insidious that can be. It spreads and infects everything around it. And no one is immune to it. Not even you, Willow."

Autumn added, "Laurel doesn't know half of the story and she zoned right in. Why can't you see something so obvious?"

"I'm not as naïve as I look. Let's just drop it, okay? I want to enjoy the evening and catch up with Laurel's life."

"Fair enough. Hey," Autumn wondered, "Laurel, what happened to Seth? I thought you were pretty serious."

"I thought he'd be the one to stick. But when it came right down to it, he was all about his work, traveled a lot, and it didn't leave a lot of time for us. Gradually, we just drifted apart. I will say that when it was working, it was the best relationship I've ever had, but I'm not sorry it's over. I'm enjoying my life now, meeting people all over the country. Not bad for someone who was once so shy, she thought her heart would leap out of her chest if someone asked her a question."

Autumn said, "Too bad Grace isn't here. She'd be swooning with pride."

Laurel lifted her glass. "To Grace, mother to all, wife to none!"

"Well put," Autumn snickered. "In a way, I think she always felt men were disposable though I know she loved hard."

"Disposable?" Willow repeated, incredulous. "That's how little you two know about her or about me for that matter. That couldn't be farther from the truth."

Denny downed his second beer before the food came. When the waitress set his plate before him, he looked over and caught Willow's eye. If a look could wound, hers would be lethal.

A guy two stools over said to him, "Those girls sure know how to have a good time. And good lookin'. You know 'em?"

Denny grunted, "Yeah. I'm married to one of them."

"Then what are you doing over here? Were you sent away for bad behavior?" he guffawed. "Ya know, I wouldn't be opposed to an introduction. You're not married to the small, perky blonde one, are you? She's hot."

"Her? Hell, no. She's my sister-in-law, a real ball buster. Consider yourself lucky you don't know her." Denny felt a fist in his gut tightening. He tried to shake it off, ignore it, ignore them. Goddamn hippies. He hated the way Willow was with Autumn. And now, there was Laurel, an even bigger asshole. Maybe he'd sleep at Joe's.

"So why are you here and not out there with them?"

"It's none of your business. Can't a guy have a beer and a meal in peace?"

"Sorry, pal. You don't have to get your back up. I'm just saying there are some of us who would love to be married to one of them instead of sitting here drinking alone." He slurped down his beer and wobbled off his stool.

Denny watched him stumble out and then turned to watch Willow. There would have been a time when she would have been miserable if things were wrong between them. Look at her now. She could care less.

Lily
2007

To: asinclair@brighamandwomens.org
From: lilylerner@aol.com
Subject: Paris

Dear Amber:

As promised, my update from Paris.

We've been here a week. The apartment is trés Parisian but lacks my one criteria. There is NO BED. Albert must have lots of guests. He's furnished the living room with three couches that open. Not the same but what can you do?

Other than that, the apartment is amazing. There are six floor to ceiling windows with a view of the complicated, angled rooftops we both love. The bathroom is marble with the best bathtub. A large table set by the windows is perfect for working side by side and eating our delicious in-home meals— baguettes, pain au chocolat, fruit and cheese. What could be better?

Being together after the long separation has been very natural.

Stephen brought a map of literary cafes with all known history (roll eyes). I think we've been to every cafe on the left bank. We also trekked over to Shakespeare and Company, the English bookshop near the Sorbonne. He's decided to work there one day in exchange for a night's lodging. It's been the custom for decades— probably since the first store opened in the 1920s. There are beds tucked in among the books for those who have nowhere to sleep.

"Lily," Stephen says, "It's a dream. I scouted out the beds but I can't decide whether or not I want to risk sleeping under the precariously leaning, overstuffed poetry bookcases or stay upstairs in classics. I keep thinking it's more than possible I'd be buried alive under a poetry avalanche. If only this were the original site, then, perhaps, Sylvia Beach, Joyce, or Hemingway would stop by. At the very least, I'll have a great anecdote for my students." That's my Stephen. Everything's a story.

While he's lolling in literary history and good books, bad news calls me. I don't know if you heard there was a bombing here. I doubt it got much international press. There were a couple of injuries but no deaths, thankfully. A Muslim group took responsibility. I was supposed to interview some Muslim teens anyway for background on a bigger story we've been working on but now with this, it changes the questions. Maurice, my very cool looking, Moroccan colleague will accompany me as trans-lator. Hopefully, if they don't want to talk to me, they'll connect with him.

Don't say it. I'll do the work and then enjoy my time with my terrific guy.

Love, Lily

To: lilylerner@aol.com
From: asinclair@brighamandwomens.org
Subject: what?

Have Maurice do the story. He's fully capable.

Try something new. Stay in the present. Don't fast forward to what you are going to ask some bad boys. Plumbing the depths even when you are on your first real vacation in two years is a terrible idea. You are separated from Stephen for months and in Paris you do this??

MEN LIKE STEPHEN COME ALONG ONCE IN A LIFETIME. He's so right for you.

Listen to me, Lily. I am a doctor. This is my prescription.

Eat.

Drink.

Tour the city of love.
Walk in the rain.
Go to jazz clubs.
Make love.
Live a little.

To: asinclair@brighamandwomens.org
From: lilylerner@aol.com
Subject: what?

I can do both, Amber. This is how I enjoy myself.

April 15, 2007
Blog Post: *As I See It*
Lily Lerner, WNN.com

Trouble Brewing in the City of Lights

Last year, a series of riots broke out in the Paris suburbs. A group of teens scattered in order to avoid questioning. Two boys hid in a power station and were electrocuted; a third suffered serious burns. The incident inflamed a clash fueled by youth unemployment and police harassment in poor neighborhoods. The riots resulted in the deaths of three bystanders. There were police injuries and 3000 arrests. A state of emergency lasted three months and the government cracked down on immigration and fraudulent marriages.

The two incidents— the riots and bombing— appear to have different causes. One is the usual story of the disenfranchised and the other is increasing radicalism.

To give the situation context, the BBC reported that French society's negative perception of Islam and the social discrimination of immigrants has alienated some French Muslims and may have been a factor in the cause of the riots: "Islam is seen as the biggest challenge to the country's secular model in the past 100 years." France has never been hospitable to immigrants and the Muslims flooding in from North Africa are no exception. The fact they are brown further exacerbates the animosity.

The boys I will be talking to tomorrow are similar to the gangs of black youth in our cities. They are angry. They have energy to harness. Their discontent is fed by alienation. The unemployment rate is high. I don't think these boys really understand the concept of jihad but the idea of being a hero, having purpose, hurting those who have hurt them is appealing.

I'm trying to formulate the right questions. Maurice Lahsini, from WNN North Africa, will accompany me as translator. Hopefully, if they don't want to talk to me, they'll connect with him.

So… here we are again. The haves and have-nots. I am grateful to be in the plus column. While I gorge on croissants and breathe in the magic of the city of lights, dark undercurrents don't seem to affect us whiteys. At least, not yet.

Chapter twenty
2008

It was Blake and Jillian's wedding anniversary. Blake was able to leave school earlier than he'd planned and decided to surprise Jillian at her ballet school. She had redecorated the waiting area and he thought this would be a good time to see it. It had been awhile since he'd been there but he remembers how old world it seemed to him with Sima's furnishings. This was no longer the case. Jillian had been very excited about the architect she hired who enlarged the space by taking out a wall and modernizing the look. Gone were the old movie posters. In their place were modern, brightly colored paintings of young dancers. The furniture was now modular and could accommodate more students and waiting parents.

Hearing a man's voice in her office, he stopped in the waiting area to listen.

"Jillian, what you've done for Allegra is nothing short of a miracle. She's eating better. She's the happiest she's been since her mother left. She actually twirls around the house."

Blake edged forward. Philip's back was to the door. He saw how close together they were standing, how Philip held her hands, the way Jillian gazed at him.

Jillian jerked her hands away the moment she saw Blake. "Blake! I thought we were meeting at the house." She backed away from Philip. "You remember Philip? From the symphony?"

Blake glared at her.

"We were discussing his daughter's progress."

"Discussing his daughter's progress," Blake repeated.

Philip reached out to shake his hand but Blake ignored the gesture. "Your wife has done a great deal for my daughter, for which I am extremely grateful."

"How nice. But then, she cares about all her students. Isn't that true, Jillian?" He looked over at her, then back at Philip. "If there isn't anything else you need to discuss, we should get going. It's our anniversary and we have plans."

"Of course. I'm sorry. I didn't mean to delay you." Philip's nervous smile quickly disappeared.

Blake asked, "Where is your daughter, anyway? Odd she's not here."

"Jillian was kind enough to let her practice in one of the studios after class because I was a bit late."

"Probably the reason she's been coming home late so many evenings. You should get your daughter and tell her it's time to go."

"Yes. Indeed. We'll be out of here straightaway. Enjoy your anniversary celebration."

They could both hear Allegra in the hall. "What's the hurry, Dad? Ow. You're pulling my arm."

The door slammed behind them.

"Did you have to be so rude?"

Blake hissed, "I was rude? He's lucky I didn't punch him. Holding your hands? Didn't he ever hear of personal space? Did you see the way he looked at you? Or the way…"

She interrupted, "Don't be ridiculous. So, what's our plan?"

He glared at her.

"Blake?"

"I thought we'd go to La Serre," he muttered.

"Look at me. I'm not dressed. I planned on going home to change."

"You look fine. Let's go."

She hurried to catch up to him and linked her arm through his. "I guess I have no choice. You seem like a man in a hurry."

He didn't answer.

Speed walking to keep up with him, she said, "I love La Serre. It always makes me think we're someplace else. Like in a Paris bistro or a brasserie in New York."

"You'd like to be anyplace else, wouldn't you?"

She pulled away. "I didn't mean anything. I was just saying…"

Jillian took two steps to each of his strides. When they reached the restaurant, he opened the door and looked at her. "What was it you were saying, Jillian?"

There was a small table open in the window. Jillian sat down. "I was saying it was a good choice."

A waiter came for their order. "What can I get for you?"

"Are you hungry or do you just want a drink?" Blake asked.

"Why don't we get a drink and an appetizer? Remember the clams casino we ate at the Plaza in New York?" She looked up at the waiter. "Do you have them?"

"Of course."

"How is the stuffing made? Prepared with chunks of clams, light on breadcrumbs?" Jillian asked.

"I'm sure you'll like them very much, Madame."

"Blake?"

"Scotch on the rocks."

"A glass of wine for me. Pinot Noir."

"Very good."

The waiter brought them their drinks. "Let's have a toast," Jillian suggested.

"Knock yourself out."

"Come on Blake. We're supposed to be celebrating."

"Just like that."

"I know it hasn't been a great year for us but can't we just start fresh? Get back our magic?"

"That would be quite the trick—a stunning illusion— wouldn't it? Maybe we could just make Philip disappear while we're at it. I know this is beyond your scope but just because he's a conductor doesn't say anything about him."

"Stop. Nothing is going on. Just drop it."

"I'm putting you on notice, Madame Jillian. Do I have your attention yet? The poison you're nursing is destroying our lives and I've had it. If you don't open your eyes and see how good your life is, it's going to vanish just like your ballet career. Although maybe you wouldn't care as much."

Jillian's eyes filled. "Is that a threat?"

"It's a fact. You don't seem to care about Chelsea or me. If only you cared about Chelsea the way you do that Philip's daughter. The way you talk to Chelsea is borderline abusive. There is no reason for you to be so hard on her." Blake slugged down his drink and ordered another.

"Like you're Mr. Perfect."

"I'm not talking about perfection. You never seem to notice us except when we're disappointing you."

She looked at him, miserable. "You just don't get it." She slowly shook her head.

"I'm sick of living with your ballerina dream. Time to have another dream."

She traced the condensation on her water glass.

"You're right, Blake. Of course, you're right. But there is so much you don't understand."

"Enlighten me."

"You don't know what it's like to live for something and have it blow up so there is nothing to do but turn your back on it. I've…"

"Wait. Stop right at the blow-up part. I'm living with the wreckage of a crash and, even now, you don't have the decency to tell me what caused it." He frowned. "One minute, you're on your way to becoming a professional dancer. With my blessing and sacrifice, by the way. And then in a flash, boom, you're home. No explanation. I give you the space I think you need, but you never recover. As far as I'm concerned, that gig is up. The least you can do is tell me what happened. You owe me at least that much."

Jillian looked down at her glass of wine.

"I'm waiting, Jillian."

She looked directly at him. "You don't even sound like yourself."

"Don't shift this. And no hedging. Just spit it out." He slammed his glass on the table.

"I don't know if I can. It may be history to you but not to me."

"We're not leaving here until I get the truth."

She faltered, "I hope what I'm going to tell you won't make you think less of me."

"For God's sake, Jillian. If you think that, you don't even know me."

Jillian took a sip of wine. "First, I'll tell you exactly why I came home. Then, I'll try to tell you what it's done to me since."

"Fine."

"You remember, I was auditioning for a featured role for the student showcase. It's an important event. The ballet community comes to the performance and careers have been launched from it. I worked as hard as I could. Lived the part day and night."

"Tell me something I don't know," he interrupted.

"Let me tell this my way, Blake." She took a deep breath. "I was sure I had it. Especially... when after auditions...the ballet mistress asked me to come to her office." She stopped. Her throat was dry.

"Go on," he urged. "Take a drink."

She swallowed hard, and in a voice barely above a whisper, she told Blake word for word what happened from the moment she stepped into the office until she called him. As Jillian recalled the day, every smell, sight, and touch was as vivid as if it just happened— Olga's stale breath, the way her own feet barely touched the stairs as she fled the building, the pungency of chestnuts roasting in push- carts as she ran home, the sourness of the hall outside her apartment. Olga's face was clear, unlike the contorted face in her dreams. Her face, pulled tight by her bun, the red lipstick smudged around her top lip, set in firm disapproval of everything Jillian was. The years hadn't dulled any of it. Neither did speaking it aloud— which she had never done.

Lost in the layers of the memory, she jumped when she heard Blake say, "So one lousy opinion and you gave up?"

She shuddered, trying to recover from the power the memory still had over her. "Don't think I haven't gone over this a million times in my head." She was quiet for a few minutes while Blake finished another drink.

"I went home and got in bed. I still remember how safe I felt wrapped up in the dark. I thought about my choices. Endless days of hard work with no chance at the good parts, starting over in a new school, or coming home to you. In those hours, the white picket fence seemed very inviting."

She motioned to the waiter for another glass of wine. "So, in- stead of taking my time to digest what happened, I was home with you and pregnant before I figured anything out." Wistful, she said, "You were incredibly loving and supportive. Even making me a studio." She thought about her first uncertain steps into the room. "But rather than shrinking, the loss seems bigger as the years go by."

They were both silent.

"I'm sorry, Blake."

"For what? For not telling me what happened or treating me like a bad second choice."

"Is that how you feel?"

He scowled at her.

Lightheaded, she reached for him but he pulled away.

He held her eyes with his. "You think I didn't know?"

"What? What do you mean you knew? What did you know? I never told anyone," she insisted.

"I didn't need you to tell me. I know you. I may not have known the exact words she used but I knew what she must have said to have you react like that."

"You knew and yet, over all the years you never stopped asking me to tell you what hurt me more than…"

"I thought you finally saying it might help you put it where it belongs but I was wrong about that and just about everything else. You're beyond hope." He stood up. "Listen, if you can't see what you have, what's the point? You have much more than you've lost. Me. Chelsea. Do you know what it would mean to women who actually want a child and can't have one to have a Chelsea? And you own a ballet school to fuel your ego. But you don't see any of it. Grow up. Make our life a dream worth having."

Jillian looked down at the table. Quietly, she said, "You don't understand because you never wanted anything enough to make sacrifices for it or feel like something vital to you is missing."

"Do you even know what you just said?" Defeated, his shoulders slumped. "You are dead wrong, lady. I'm tired, Jillian. That you don't know what and how much I want is astounding. You just don't care enough to see what that might be. It's always been about you. And… I don't know what's going on with that prissy conductor but it better stop." He stood. "I'm out of here."

She held up her glass of wine. "I'm not finished."

He threw some cash on the table and left.

She stood up intending to go after him but sat back down, too tired to move. Jillian stared out the window, feeling as lonely and deserted as the street. She didn't know how long she sat there when she saw two men walking toward the restaurant. She panicked thinking one might be Philip. It was dusk. The window was somewhat masked making it hard to see. But he was the same height and body type, wore a sport jacket with jeans as Philip often did and his head was tilted toward the man he was walking with, something she always noticed about him. She turned away from the window hoping they would just walk by.

Jillian absently tucked the hair that had fallen from her bun and dabbed her eyes. She couldn't let him see her like this.

The door opened. It wasn't him.

Did Blake see the chemistry between them? Is that what set him off? No, she thought. Everything he said tonight was true. And in all their years together, she had never heard that kind of anger in his voice.

She slugged the last of her wine mortified to realize how well Blake knew her.

Lily
2008

To: lilylerner@aol.com
From: sbrooks@chicago.edu
Subject: wanting to be with you

Sometimes our distance really gets to me. I come home at night and wish we could share our day over a bottle of wine. I could spend my days thinking about what it will be like to make love each night. I wish I could be there to comfort you when you're having that horrid nightmare but... that's not our life right now. I don't really know what to say about all those dreadful things you encounter in your work. Coping with it is a tall order. We really are little more than the sum our experiences, aren't we? That's what makes you my incredible Lily but sadly, I don't really know what it's like except through you and my tried and true way— research. I'll try to find some memoirs by journalists to get some insight on coping. Otherwise, I have nothing to say that you haven't told yourself. We just have to figure out how to stop the nightmares. But I am worried. It's beginning to sound to me a little like PTSD.

To: sbrooks@chicago.edu
From: lilylerner@yahoo.com
Subject: wanting to be with you

PTSD? That's crazy. I just have some bad dreams. I love my work and wouldn't trade what I see and do for anything in the world.

Don't worry. You're beginning to sound like Amber. Have you two been talking?

    To: lilylerner@aol.com
    From: sbrooks@chicago.edu
    Subject: wanting to be with you

No. But if we're both saying the same thing maybe you should consider it. I can see the face you're making so I'll change the subject.

On my work front, good news. The paper I coauthored with Andrew was accepted in the Journal of Modern Literature. I'm thrilled. It will certainly help keep me on tenure track although I may not want to stay here. I don't like the direction the department is taking. We'll talk.

Love, Stephen

Chapter twenty-one
2008

The dread of monotonous evenings and sleepless nights kept Willow at school late and took her on errands she didn't need to run—a browse in a bookstore, a drink with Autumn, a walk around the mall. Sometimes she'd go to Tess's to play with Jason.

Blake would occasionally stop in at the library after dismissal. "You're still here? Did you know the custodian thinks you work late because you have a crush on him?"

Willow smiled, "Who else knows?"

He laughed. "Seriously, you keep longer hours than I do. You haven't become homeless, have you?"

She straightened a pile of books on her desk. Faking exasperation, she exclaimed, "Stop coming in to check up on me, Blake. I'll be going home soon. Just like to miss the traffic."

She wants to miss the traffic when school gets out at three? Stop thinking about why, Blake berated himself.

Denny said nothing about how late she was coming home. Sometimes when he worked, he'd lose track of time until her car turned into the driveway. But often, an alarm precise as the dismissal bell would go off in his head, and he'd count the hours before she finally arrived.

Willow never shared where she'd been. When she finally had no more energy to wander, she'd pick up dinner. The Willow who loved to cook was also gone.

"Denny, I'm home," she called out. "Picked up Chinese."

Always hopeful she'd morph back into the real Willow instead of this vague, distant woman, he tried to be enthusiastic. "Terrific," he said. "What did you get?"

"The usual. Moo Shu pork, Mongolian beef, and cashew chicken."

They sat opposite one another. Denny looked at the white cartons covering the table. "That's a lot of food considering how little you eat."

"Oh, I thought we could have it tomorrow, too, or you could have it for lunch."

Denny opened the cartons and filled their plates. He didn't look up at her. "Where do you go? After school, I mean. You can't be working this late every day."

"I'm either at school late or running errands. Nothing earth shattering. I just don't feel like cooking anymore."

"I can. Why don't I plan on making dinner for a while? You used to love my chili. And my stew."

"Sure. That would be nice."

"Or we could go out tonight. Get something we never eat? I heard there is a new Ethiopian restaurant that just opened. Can't say I've ever had that," he rambled. "We could put this food away and have it tomorrow. Or maybe we could see a movie."

"No, not tonight. I'm too tired." She looked at the plate Denny fixed her and stood knowing she couldn't swallow a bite. "In fact, I think I'll go to bed now."

He should bring up adopting a baby. That would make things better. But he couldn't seem to push out the words.

Willow undressed and got under the covers. She fought the tears that inevitably came each night. She didn't know how long she would mourn her unborn babies and she didn't know what, if anything, she felt for Denny any more. She only knew her chest hurt and a wall of tears, always there, lay close to the surface, threatening to flow without provocation. The only time her spirit lifted was when she was at work and with Blake. Maybe she was just lonely for conversation. Maybe that was all it was.

She rolled over and fell into fitful sleep populated with people she didn't know, in places she'd never been.

Lily
2008

To: sbrooks@chicago.edu
From: lilylerner@aol.com
Subject: Happiness

You've managed the impossible—a sabbatical year in London—and made me unbelievably happy.

We've often talked about how hard this long distance can be. Now, we'll be like normal couples who take all the time they have together for granted.

It's spectacular on all fronts. Professionally, it will be a great addition to your already impressive resume and personally, well... I see it all now. Long, lazy Sundays, walks in the park, going to sleep and waking up together. I'm in heaven. My travel is still pretty heavy but coming home to you will be a dream.

I'm emptying out drawers for you right now.

Hurry up and come.

Love and more love,

Lily

Chapter twenty-two
2009

The diner was filling up and Jillian snagged the last booth. She smiled when she saw Georgia come through the door and waved her over.

"Georgia, thanks for meeting me. I know Mondays are busy days for you," Jillian said.

"No problem but I have to get back for a two o'clock meeting. What's up?" Georgia put her napkin on her lap. "How was the anniversary dinner?"

"A total disaster. We didn't even get to dinner. Blake left me in the bar. Can you believe it? He actually threw money on the table and left," Jillian said.

Skeptical, Georgia said, "What? That's hard to believe."

"Whose side are you on, anyway?"

"Come on, Jillian. Something must have happened to make him that angry. He has a very long fuse."

"I think he suspects I'm having an affair with Philip."

"The conductor you've been talking about?" Georgia raised her eyebrows. "Why would he think that?"

Jillian didn't answer.

"Are you?"

"Of course not. What he saw was innocent but I think he misconstrued it. Besides, he's been weird for weeks. I thought going out for our anniversary would help diffuse how irritated he's been with me."

"What did he see?"

"Nothing."

"Jillian?"

"Blake surprised me at the studio just when Philip took my hands. Don't look at me like that. It was innocent, Georgia. I swear. He was just thanking me for taking care of his daughter and moved in too close. Blake's been pissed off at me because I've been coming home late. I think he jumped to conclusions."

Georgia looked hard at her. "You haven't answered me. Why have you been late? Is there anything going on?"

"It's only a flirtation."

"How serious?"

"It's nothing but Blake was ticked anyway. From the second we got to La Serre, he picked on me and then goaded me into telling him the real reason I left New York. He demanded it in a different way than he had before. So, I sucked it up and told him the mortifying truth. Then, you know what he said?" she gasped. "He's known all along." Jillian's face reddened. "Can you believe he did that? He knew all these years and let me swing in the wind, always pressing me to tell him. Then he accused me of being a bad wife and mother."

"What did he actually say, Jilly?"

Jillian looked down at the table. "I don't think he likes anything about me. He criticizes the way I am with him, with Chelsea, that I'm never home and that when I am…"

Georgia scrutinized her. "When we get together with Claire, your one-note song is a complaint. Everything about them lets you down. They must both know they can never live up to your expectations. Don't get mad at me, but lately nobody gets anything right in Jillian's world."

"That's not fair," Jillian objected.

"I've known you better and longer than anyone. You think you should have married someone like that conductor. Maybe you should have. But you didn't. Things are never as they seem so you'd better be careful. You could lose everything if you play with fire like that."

"You think I don't know that? But I look at a man like Philip and wonder what my life would be like with someone like him. I can't help it."

The waitress came over. They quickly looked at the menu and ordered.

Georgia shook her head. "I worked with a man a couple of years ago who was a real flirt and, whew, movie star good looking. Complimentary but never over the top. Just enough to make me feel great about myself." She sighed, "I can't believe I'm telling you this. It's both embarrassing and adolescent."

"You've never told me anything about him."

"I'm only telling you now to make a point. I felt beautiful around him. I could feel electricity surge through me any time he was close. He had no concept of personal space. I'd think to myself, would it hurt to have a fling? Jerry probably wouldn't even notice.

"After months of serious infidelity in my head, which by the way cost me hundreds in new clothes and trips to the beauty salon for blonde highlights, I walked past my co-worker Sherry's cubicle and there he was, bending over her, charming her in exactly the same way. I felt like a total idiot. Thank God I didn't do anything I'd regret."

"What's your point?"

"My point? I could have jeopardized everything for a professional flirt I knew nothing about. Ditto about Philip. You don't even know the story behind his phantom wife. You better think hard before you do something reckless, Jilly."

The waitress delivered their food and Georgia lifted her fork. "Remember Mr. Bartlett who lived down the street when we were kids?"

"Of course. We all thought he was the dreamiest man alive." Jillian laughed. "He used to wear those well-tailored suits with flashy ties, making our fathers look pathetic. I even used to fantasize about dancing for him and he'd fall in love with me. Whatever made you think of him?"

"His son, Eddie, is a client. He's trying to shore up the family business his father ran into the ground. Seems old Mr. Dreamboat was both a gambler and a drunk."

"What does that have to do with anything?"

"Any jackass can buy a good suit and sweet talk little girls. Or big girls, as the case may be."

"Blake doesn't look at me the way he used to."

"And you need to be adored. That's been your problem since we've been kids, Jilly. You've always needed an audience of admirers.

I'm afraid for you. You're on a runaway train. For your sake, I hope you figure out how to get off before it crashes."

"Blake," Jillian said after they got up from the dinner table, "Can we talk? I'll do the dishes later."

"About what?"

"Us." She set down two glasses on the coffee table. They sat down on either end of the couch facing one another.

"Red wine near your white couch? That's a first. This must be serious. What's up?"

"I want to diffuse the tension in the house. I thought maybe the three of us could go away next weekend. We could rent a cabin at Schroon Lake. Bring board games, our bikes, watch movies."

Blake sighed. "You're a couple of years too late. Chelsea would have loved that then but she's a teenager now, in case you haven't noticed. Listen, I have an early meeting tomorrow. I'm going to look over my notes and turn in."

Deflated, Jillian nodded, "Okay. Goodnight, Blake."

She drank her wine and then his. *It isn't too late. I'll show them. I'll deposit my unreasonable expectations in the recycling bin. Chelsea and I will do mother-daughter things together like lunch and shopping, maybe a trip to New York. Blake doesn't think I can do it but I'll prove him wrong. If I win her, I'll win him back, too.*

Jillian poured herself another glass of wine and surveyed the living room. When they first bought the house, she imagined they'd decorate it together, carefully choosing each piece of furniture and artwork.

"Blake," she said during the walk-through before they signed the papers, "I don't want this to be an ordinary house. Wouldn't a stylish leather couch along this long wall look divine?"

Blake balked. "We have furniture that's functional and for the time being will have to do. After closing costs, we're tapped out."

"Of course. But in time, the furniture we have now is either going down to the family room in the basement or out the door."

"No, Jillian. Leather. I don't think so."

When she was in ballet school, she visited relatives who lived in an apartment building opposite Gramercy Park. Her cousin greeted her wearing black leather pants and an expensive looking taupe silk blouse; her husband wore a turtleneck shirt and a gray cashmere sweater. Their apartment had beautiful artwork and unusual furniture. It screamed taste and sophistication to Jillian. She was a teenager then, easily impressed. But she always held fast to the wow she felt when she walked in their door. That's exactly the kind of home she wanted for herself and was determined to have.

She looked around the living room as it was now. As with most things, if she insisted, she eventually got her way. When she was out shopping one day, she passed an upscale furniture store. There it was. The couch she had to have. Sleek with a graceful curve to the back and arms and what's more, it was white leather. She cajoled Blake into getting it. "Just this one piece for now, Blake. It's spectacular."

"Who buys a white couch when they have a family? Besides leather is cold in the winter and you stick to it in the summer. If you want something new, let's be more practical. What about microfiber like Claire's? It's nice looking and good with kids. Even if you pick a light pastel."

"Just this one piece, Blake. Then we'll wait to get anything else."

He grumbled, "I don't see what's wrong with what we have."

It was on the tip of her tongue to say she didn't want to live in a house that looked like his parents', complete with a recliner and tacky knick-knacks. He'd been right about the leather. And, as she looked around the room at the chair she chose, she knew it should have had an ottoman, and the glass coffee table wasn't a good choice for Chelsea and her friends. But she still admired the overall appearance every time she walked in.

"Okay. If you want the kind of living room you just look at, I'm furnishing the family room in the basement my way." He remodeled the space so Chelsea could have a playroom that would grow into a teenage hangout. And for the family room, he used their old furniture, adding a lounge chair, a big TV, and a music system.

She suddenly realized they had separate, perhaps, unequal living spaces. What must people think when they come here?

Jillian finished the entire bottle of wine. Blake was sleeping deeply when she went into the bedroom. She sighed. He was still so good looking.

Jillian applied herself to her marriage in the same way she did everything else. She made lists in her head. What would make Blake happy? Be home on time for weeknight dinners. Do not complain about whatever he may have cooked. Invite his parents over. Offer to go with him to school events. Compliment him: *The bushes look terrific. Great chili. Good speech at school the other night.*

Same with Chelsea. *You got a 98 on your math test. Well done! I saw this bracelet when I was out today. I hope you like it. Sure I'll drive you and your friends to the mall right after my Saturday morning class. My pleasure.*

But her effort went unnoticed.

Blake and Chelsea had their own rhythm. Chelsea was in the school play and had rehearsals almost every night. They came home together, ate quickly, and then Chelsea disappeared into her room to do homework and chat with her friends. Jillian often stood outside her door listening to Chelsea's laughter. Her daughter had a teenage life that she couldn't relate to. Ballet consumed her at that age. Georgia was her only friend. The others were only girls she danced with.

Blake was unimpressed with her effort. "Do you want a medal for finally noticing your daughter? Too bad you waited so long."

It can't be too late. I'm trying. Why can't they?

Chapter twenty-three
2009

The bell rang, a stampede of students piled onto the late buses, and suddenly the school was eerily quiet. This was Willow's least favorite time of day. It was the mornings she loved most. Standing just outside the library door to greet the students as they trudged in, she'd notice who was sleepwalking, who was bursting with gossip, and kept her eye out for those she knew came in hungry. As they passed her, she'd slip them breakfast bars, fruit, or trail mix from a stash she kept in her storage room.

What would the day bring for them and for her, she wondered? Something better than the night before, she thought, never allowing herself to fully acknowledge how miserable she'd become.

Scanning her now silent library, her mind wandered as she pulled books off the shelves for her Black History Month display.

When she was twelve, they moved to a community on an apple orchard. A man named Alfred Eton inherited it from his father. He believed in the benefits of communal living and the need for self-sufficiency and organized a thriving community. Everyone shared in the responsibility of caring for and planting new trees, picking apples, maintaining vegetable and flower gardens —essentially working together to make the lifestyle work. In this case, it also meant running a shop around autumn harvest time, making cider, doughnuts, pies and crafts.

The communes they lived in before were rarely considered part of the larger community but it was different there. Town residents and tourists came for the melt-in-your-mouth cider donuts, organic vegetables, and handmade quilts rather than to gawk at them as if they were a sideshow.

It was in this collective that the girls were the happiest. But Grace wasn't satisfied with the education her girls were getting there. In the past, if anything didn't meet her standards, they left. But this time, rather than leaving, she was willing to deviate from the communal philosophy of one for all and took over her daughters' education. This was pure bliss for Willow and Autumn. Grace quietly found reasons to pull them out of the cider mill classroom run by a teacher who smoked too much weed.

They studied the geology of the area, how things grew, read books with regional settings. They spent time with the man they called Apple Alfred, who gave them their own ledger books and tasks. This was the last and best of all their educational experiences in the life.

"Willow," Autumn said years later, as they were driving to Laurel's. "I just realized something."

"What?"

She sputtered, laughing hard. "You know how Grace wrangled Alfred into her plan to educate us? We thought we were so special not having to listen to that idiot Lydia drone on and give us stupid homework."

"Apple Alfred? I loved hanging out with him. He even gave us our own trees to name. Said not to tell anyone there was a Willow and Autumn Orchard that grew the best apples. What were they again? Galas for me and Empires for you. What made you think about that?"

"Alfred was banging Grace. They were as close to a couple as you could be in the land of free love. You know all that time they said not to bother them because they were making up our lesson plans out in the fields somewhere." She giggled, "That's why Mean Lydia was so pissed. She didn't care about us. It was Grace and Alfred. All the women wanted him. Ha! It just came to me as a lightning bolt."

Willow sniffed, "No way. For god's sake, Autumn. What a way to talk about our mother."

"Never mind, little sister. I'll ask Laurel what she remembers. I know you don't like to think about that side of things. For you, it's all pure and happy memories. And of course, Grace loved every man she ever slept with." Autumn turned up the radio.

Willow smiled, thinking perhaps Autumn was right. *I wish I could still be that naïve girl or be more like my mother. She wouldn't stand my life for a second. Her whole way of living was taking what she needed, and then if it didn't seem right anymore, moving on.*

Sorting through the poetry books on her desk, she thought of Theo from the orchard days. He was a big smiler, with a mouth full of teeth lining up every which way. He memorized a new poem to recite every week. His adolescent voice creaked but Willow always heard the rich voice that she knew would come later. That first fall, after the crush of the apple harvest, he was obsessed with Claude McKay. *There is joy in the woods just now/The leaves are whispers of song.*

While the rest of the kids would be dreaming of becoming rock stars, wanting to join the *Stones* or the *Sex Pistols*, Theo would chant poetry in his distinctive creaky-voice, adjusting his work cadence to the rhythm of his poet of the week. The other kids teased her. Willow's got a crush on Croaky, they would taunt. But she knew Theo would become a man with a big heart. He trusted her with his own poems. They were soulful. He understood the contradictions of love even at that age.

She lost track of him. It was the nature of that life. But she would really love to know what happened to Theo.

She smiled to herself. Come to think of it, Blake reminded her of Theo in that way. Genuine. Robust, with a soft underside. Wonder if he had a croak as an adolescent. She'd have to ask him sometime.

Blake waited for everyone to clear out before walking to the library. He stood outside the door watching her. Today he replayed the conversation they had when she told him how she wanted to acquire more contemporary books for the library. If that meant taking on the small group of parents who monitored what their children should or shouldn't read, she was ready.

"I've learned not to invite their interference. Instead, why don't you put together a flyer about Black History month and the books we'll be featuring. Chances are they never heard of most of them. They aren't the usual lightning rod books. Are you still going to try to do a poetry slam?"

Placated, she said, "I'm not sure if I want to publicize it. Maybe we'll just call it poetry café night."

"Good idea."

"I've got four language arts teachers on board. It's a start."

His eyes sparkled. "I like it. You're going to make me look really good."

Now, he watched her arrange the stack of books she insisted upon —*Go Tell It on the Mountain, The Ways of White Folks, Their Eyes Were Watching God, Life is Short but Wide, The Piano Lesson,* an anthology of Harlem Renaissance writers.

Oblivious to him standing there, she read the notes on a Nikki Giovanni CD and flipped through a book of Nujorcan poetry slam winners.

Blake cleared his throat. "Willow, when you can pull yourself away, come down to my office. I want to show you something."

She raised her eyebrows. "Give me a hint."

"You'll have to come and see for yourself."

"I'm intrigued. Be down in a bit."

Willow rearranged her display until she was satisfied. She was shelving books left on tables, when the custodian came to clean up the library.

"Hi, Leonard."

"Why you still here when everybody's gone? It's near four thirty. Go home. Put your feet up."

"I'm going. I'm going," she smiled, grabbing her bag. "Have a good night, Leonard."

He waved her off. "You, too."

With her coat over her arm, she strolled to Blake's office.

"Let's see." She looked at his desk piled high with files, his crowded credenza, the conference table. "Hmm...wait a minute. Is that what I think it is?"

He closed the door behind her.

"Tired of the mud we've been drinking at the end of the day so I bought one of those one-cuppers. Fresh cup every time and voila! To go with it, I bought scones from *Bountiful*."

He made room on one side of his desk, put down a cloth napkin, and set the scones down.

"I love surprises I can eat or drink. This is perfect." She clasped her hands together. "You are a thoughtful man."

He set a mug down before her. "Don't let me fool you. This is more for me than for you. You have no idea."

"Aren't you afraid of gossip? People misunderstanding?" she grimaced. "This," she swept her hand over his desk, "could become a problem for you."

There was an excited rapping on the door before it flung open. "Dad, I just had to tell you." Then, she saw Willow. "Mrs. D'Angelo. Hi! I'm sorry to interrupt your meeting but I have great news! Daddy, I passed. I have my driver's license!"

Willow stood. "Congratulations, that's wonderful. You passed your first time? I failed twice before I finally got mine."

Chelsea blushed. "Thank you. Well, I'll be going now. Sorry to interrupt your meeting."

"Hey, just wait a minute. Where do you think you're going without a hug from your father and some stern words of advice?"

Chelsea looked at Willow and rolled her eyes. She turned to her father. "I promise to look in my mirrors, drive the speed limit, keep the music down, drive only one friend at a time. Did I forget anything?"

He smiled. "Seatbelt."

"Dad," Chelsea groaned, "It's automatic. I've never been unstrapped in a car my entire life. Whoa. What do I see here?" She grabbed one of the scones and took a bite. "These are *Bountiful's*, aren't they? The best! Nice of you to get my favorite scones in celebration of my liberation." She turned to Willow. "It really isn't fair. Mom puts us on carrot stick diets and Dad cheats with scones and chocolate cake. Hey, wait a minute! Now, I can, too. I have wheels!"

"Come here, you." He hugged her, brushing her dark hair off her forehead. "Just stay safe."

"I will, Dad," she pulled away. "See you later. Bye Mrs. D'Angelo and by the way, thank you for the help on my story. It's going to be in *The Clarion's* next issue. I was going to tell you tomorrow."

"It's a wonderful story. Congratulations on all counts, Chelsea. And listen to your father. Be careful."

"Thank you. Bye, guys!" She went to the door but then turned to her father. "Don't worry, Dad. I'll keep your secret."

Flushed, he looked at her.

"The scones, Dad."

"Whew. Thank you. Maybe we'll even sneak out for a sundae to celebrate."

"You're on. Bye, guys."

Willow sighed, "She's a lovely girl, Blake. You're very lucky."

"I am, indeed. But damn, now you're going to have to share." He took a bite out of her scone.

"Have it all. I've got to protect my girlish figure."

"Right," he said, breaking the scone in half and giving her the larger piece. "So, where were we?" he asked, lightly stroking her hand.

"Savoring the last moments of the school day."

Neither of them said any more than that but they both knew every time they crossed a threshold together, they were inching toward something they might not be able to stop.

Lily
2009

To: asinclair@brighamandwomens.org
From: lilylerner@aol.com
Subject: mental case

I just left Stephen at Heathrow. I should be in pieces but I'm not. Why am I not bereft as I walk through my flat's empty rooms? Maybe Mom's rules for her men have made more of an impression than I realized. She never let them stay. I think I overheard her once saying to your mom that she was never going to put herself in a position of getting used to something that would inevitably go away.

I know I'm going to miss him. I was happy when he was here. Coming home to him after assignments away was glorious. One homecoming was better than the last. He is the best friend and lover anyone could ever want. He's smart, loving, great to talk to, understands me in a way I sometimes don't understand myself. I was good with the whole thing while he was here. I dreaded his leaving.

It was all on my terms. I didn't have to change a thing.

So why am I not heartbroken or thinking about a way to be together? Why didn't our year together move me toward wanting permanence?

Stephen is no wuss. He says some things are worth compromising for. I know he likes the freedom of our relationship, too. It's just that he sees our future. Why can't I?

And yet, I never want to be without him.

WHAT'S WRONG WITH ME?

Love, Lily

To: llerner@aol.com
From: asinclair@brighamandwomens.org
Subject: I've got nothing for you

I don't know what you want me to say. Maybe it hasn't sunk in that he's really gone and you won't see him again for months. You've always said you don't want to have your mother's alone life. But that's where you're headed. Can't you see that?

Nobody can help you with this, Lily. But in fairness, if this is how you feel, it's time to cut Stephen loose. He's making all the effort in good faith.

I know you're on your way back to Africa. See how you feel when you come back to a dark flat without Stephen there to welcome you.

Love, Amber

Chapter twenty-four
2009

Jillian set down her green smoothie and poured Cheerios into a bowl. She called out, "Chelsea, if you don't hurry, you'll miss the bus. Breakfast is on the table."

"I'm looking for my math homework."

"I think I saw it on the coffee table. Why does every morning have to be like this? How many times do I have to tell you to pack your backpack before you go to bed?"

"I needed some help from Dad on the last problem."

"Always a reason," she sighed. "Here's your cereal."

"No time. I'll just take a banana and a bar with me."

"Lunch money?"

"Dad packed our lunches."

"Good." Surprising herself, Jillian said, "You know, it's been a long time since the two of us had a day together. Do you have plans for Saturday afternoon? After I teach, we could have lunch and go shopping."

"Really?" Chelsea stuffed the homework into her backpack. "I was going to the mall with Sara, Jen, and Stacey."

"Okay. We'll do it some other time," Jillian said, pouring the cereal back into the box.

"Is something up? I can go with them any old time."

"Nothing's up. Just wanted to spend time with my daughter. Is that, okay?"

"Sure. I guess so," she said, running out of the house just as the bus pulled up.

Jillian and Chelsea slid into a booth at *The Standard*, a new restaurant at the mall.

"This place is gorgeous. Look at the old movie posters. I love those big round lamp shades." Chelsea's head was on a swivel. "Sure beats the food court."

Jillian laughed. "You certainly have your father's joie de vivre."

"I hope so. He's usually in a good mood but lately, he seems even happier. When he walks the halls at school, he's nothing like the monitors who live to catch you doing something wrong. He's like a Wal-Mart greeter. The school is huge but he remembers stuff about everybody. Kids get that he cares."

"As he always says, it's the little things," she prickled. Looking around, she said, "The decor is from the time when Frank Sinatra was popular. Have you ever heard of him?"

"That's probably why it's called *The Standard*, Mom. The American songbook? Of course, I know who he is. See that poster over there? It's the Rat Pack. Sinatra was a good actor too. Dad and I watched *From Here to Eternity* one night. Wow."

"You did? Where was I?"

Chelsea hesitated. "Please don't get mad but if I get my homework done early enough on Thursdays, we watch a movie when you're out on with Georgia and Claire. He finds them at the library. Rule is it has to be a classic since it's a school night," she snorted.

"What else have you seen? Now that I know you do that, you'll have to give me a review on Fridays."

Chelsea looked away. "Really? I thought you'd blow."

Jillian shuddered. "No, Chelsea. I'm not going to blow. I wish you didn't think you have to walk on eggshells around me."

Chelsea was tickled. "That's a funny expression," she said, laughing. "You could probably walk on your toes and not crack a single egg."

Jillian smiled. "You have to wonder where some of the old sayings come from." She looked at the menu "What do you think you'd like?" Jillian asked.

"Uh, I don't know."

"That's not like you. You always know exactly what you want to eat."

"Um. Which one of the salads are you having, Mom?"

"I feel like splurging today. I think I'll have a cheeseburger." She looked at her daughter and smiled. "I hear they're very good here."

"What?" Chelsea's mouth hung open. "I don't have to get salad?"

"No salad today. For me or you."

"Mom. You're acting weird. Something's wrong."

"Everything is fine. Why would you think that?"

"Well... you never have time to do anything fun on Saturdays. Chore day. Right? Then, you didn't yell about the movie. And then," Chelsea opened her eyes wide, "you're going to order something you'd never ever eat. Something you don't want anyone else to ever eat either. What's going on? You're gonna tell me something awful. I know it." Her eyes filled up. "Are you and Daddy getting a divorce?"

"No, Chelsea." Jillian took a sip of her water. "I have no dire announcements to make. Your father and I have our differences but we aren't getting divorced over them."

"That's what you guys always say. You have differences but you don't seem to have any samenesses. You're always so mad at him." Chelsea's heart raced, frightened she'd cause her mother to blow up.

Jillian sighed, "I'm trying to do better, aren't I?" She looked back down at the menu. "What do you say we get two cheeseburgers and split an order of fries. This isn't exactly on my diet plan so I better be careful."

"Of what?"

"Did I ever tell you what I did when I decided to leave ballet school in New York?" Jillian asked.

"No. You never talk about it at all. I bet you have all kinds of cool stories. I was thinking I might want to go to college there."

"Really? I always pictured you on a big campus with rolling hills and a famous football team."

"Why would you think that? I hate football. It's a stupid game with guys who think they're something special just because they huddle and fall all over each other on the field."

"No crushes on the high school quarterback, then?" Jillian smiled.

"No, Mom. Ew. New York has everything. Theater and art, music and all kinds of exotic food and people and parks. Well, you know that. You lived it. Tell me that story about when you were there."

"The eating regimen was very strict. I basically subsisted on salad, poached fish and other lean, tasteless protein."

"Yuk."

"In many ways, it was. I rarely left school. I wasn't able to take advantage of so much that was around me. The environment was very competitive and I had to be in top form. On Saturdays, I allowed myself a treat —an ice from the Italian truck across from school. I always chose lemon. With his heavy accent, the vendor would say, 'today try my raspberry. Always lemon, no good. Dulce sometimes better.' But I couldn't be convinced—lemon once a week."

"You still only eat lemon," Chelsea remarked.

"True! Still my favorite. Anyway, after I decided to quit, I thought if I could have anything to eat, anything at all, what would it be? First I thought, hot dog. Nathan's with spicy mustard on a good roll, not a doughy white bread roll but one with texture and flavor. Then, I thought no. When was the last time I had pizza? New York pizza is famous. And I could have anything on it. Pepperoni, sausage, oily, salty anchovies. But then," Jillian smiled, "then I smelled French fries. Yes, that's it, I thought cheeseburger and fries."

Chelsea laughed, "I can't believe you never got to eat anything good. I agree with Grandma Irene. She says that good food is one of life's pleasures."

"Grandma Ruth thinks the same thing. Before she finishes one meal, she's planning the next." Jillian arched her eyebrows. "The big question is what constitutes good food? We all think about food differently, Chelsea. Some people think if it's greasy, it's good. Others think that only macaroni and cheese will comfort them when they're sad or depressed. And then there are people who depend on their bodies to perform and need to eat a certain kind of food for high energy and performance, like dancers and athletes."

Chelsea groaned, "I know, Mom."

"Right. Sorry. Back to my story. I decided I'm free and can eat whatever I want. I chose a cheeseburger on a big fat grilled bun and fries, ate half of it, and then had to run to a trash can to throw it up."

Incredulous, Chelsea exclaims, "You threw up right on the street? So embarrassing."

"I wasn't embarrassed though it was a long time before I realized how smart my body was for rejecting it."

"I'm confused. Are we getting cheeseburgers or not?"

"Yes. We're getting cheeseburgers. All I meant was then, my body couldn't take it because it wasn't used to such heavy food."

"Like the time you smoke your first cigarette, you cough your brains out?"

"Wait. How do you know that? You're not smoking, are you?"

"No, Mom. But I do have eyes and ears."

"Course you do. Great comparison," Jillian backpedaled. "The thing is… there is a whole lot of food out there that is better tasting and more nutritious than any cheeseburger," Jillian instructed. "I just want you to be more open to better food. As you're becoming a woman, the last thing you want is to stay chunky." Jillian gasped as soon as it was out of her mouth. "I didn't mean that Chelsea. You're perfect. You're beautiful."

It was too late. Chelsea was in tears. "Yes, you did. I'm sorry you hate me and I'm not one of your precious, skin and bones ballet students." She stood up. "This was a big mistake."

"No. Please forgive me. You are beautiful. It's just that my standards for ballet are always creeping in. I don't mean for them to…"

"Yeah, Mom. I know," Chelsea cried. "But I'm not a ballerina. I hate everything about ballet. It's stupid and boring. All the dancers are anorexic with deformed feet who have no life. I know nothing else matters to you but I'm in the school's Acting Troupe. You have to audition for that, Mom. I'm in the literary society. I'm on the honor roll. I eat what normal kids eat. I have friends. I don't want to be anything like you."

Jillian pleaded, "Chelsea. Wait. I'm sorry. You're right. I know how accomplished you are and …"

Chelsea couldn't get away from her mother fast enough and bumped into a waiter as she bolted.

She ran after her, but Chelsea was gone. Jillian sat on a bench near the food court hoping to see her daughter walking arm in arm with her friends, laughing, recovered from her big mouth. She tried not to think about all the hurtful things she had said to Chelsea over the years.

She waited and waited but with no Chelsea in sight, she got in her car, slumped in her seat, and called her mother.

"Jillian. What's wrong?"

"Something doesn't have to be wrong for me to call you. How's Daddy?"

"He's doing better. I think the new medication is helping."

"That's good. And you, Mom?"

"I'm fine. So now that we have that over with, what happened?"

Jillian swallowed hard. "I'm a terrible mother. Even when I try to do the right thing, I make everything worse."

"Dear me, Jillian. What now?"

"Things just come out of my mouth that are, well, devastating. It's bad enough Chelsea's a teenager with all those moods and insecurities and everything. I couldn't even take her out for lunch without creating a catastrophe," she whimpered.

"Jillian, you have to love Chelsea as she is. That's all Chelsea needs from you."

"Of course, I love her," Jillian barked, "That's not the problem."

"Then, what is?"

"I seem to have Tourette's around her. I can't help myself. I know what I should and shouldn't say. And then the worst things come out."

"Honestly, Jillian. You don't have Tourette's and you can help it. Just see her for the wonderful kid she is for a change, not who you were for god's sake or worse yet who you want her to be."

"Great. Even my mother is against me."

"Don't be petulant. There are many things in this world to value, Jillian. Dance is hardly the only prize. You're not the ballerina spinning in the jewelry box anymore. You have Blake and Chelsea. They need you and they deserve better. Instead, of having your nose pressed to the window of your own home, it's time to open the door and walk in."

"That's it, Mom? Open the door and walk in," she repeated.

"Yes. Stop living in the past or that's all you'll ever have. I begged you to face whatever happened and you refused so now all these years later, you're still stuck. Don't make your ballet school the sole replacement for what you think you've lost. Look at what you have, not at what you don't. You could have a full, well rounded life if you let yourself."

"Look around me? Open the door? These are your pearls of wisdom. Not helpful, Mom."

It was quiet on her mother's end but Jillian knew more was coming and braced herself.

"I have more and I'm sorry if it's hurtful but here it is. You were a self-centered, demanding child and you've grown into that kind of woman. Things can't always be on your terms. That's why you could never keep friends when you were growing up except for Georgia, who never let you get away with anything. Your father says I spoiled you for life. Do me a favor. Prove him wrong."

Barely audible, Jillian said, "That's so cruel, Mom."

"I'm sorry. You know I only want the best for you but things cannot go on as they are, Jillian. I don't know what happened today but you better go home and fix it."

She sat in the car too tired to drive. When she finally got home, Blake asked, "Where's Chelsea?"

"She'll be home later. I think I'm going to lie down for a while."

Blake watched her practically crawl down the hall. Where was the woman he married? He hardly recognized this pinched stranger who casts a pall over them. He couldn't allow Jillian to harm Chelsea any longer. He didn't know what to do, but something was going to have to change.

Chapter twenty-five
2010

Sunlight streamed through the kitchen window and Willow, standing at the sink, felt its warmth on her face. Holding her coffee mug in both hands, she watched the activity at the bird feeder. A tufted titmouse turned away from a strutting male cardinal. Baby black-capped chickadees squeaked their song, sparrows flew back and forth. Birds spit sprays of discarded husks to the ground.

Denny sat at the table, flipping through the newspaper. "What do you say? How about a date tonight?"

Standing with her back to him, she shrugged. "If you want."

"You used to love going to the movies. We could go to the *Fountain* for pizza afterwards like we used to."

"Okay."

"That's it. Okay? Your enthusiasm is underwhelming."

She turned around and leaned against the sink, looking past him.

He slid the newspaper across the table toward her. "I don't know what to say or do anymore," he said, defeated. "Let me know if there's anything you want to see."

"Okay."

He scraped his chair against the floor almost flipping it when he stood up. "Do you have anything more to say than okay?"

Willow sighed. "Having lunch with Tess."

"Hope seeing her improves your mood."

"Doubtful," she murmured.

"What?" he asked. "I didn't hear you."

"Nothing, Denny." She turned her back to him to look out the window.

"You know it would help if you tried a little harder. I'm not the enemy, you know."

He slammed the back door.

"Maybe you are. Maybe we are at war. That might be something you understand." She gathered all the words of war she knew in her mouth and spit them out one by one: attack, skirmish, battle, encounter, conflict. None of the words she needed to draw upon for peace — negotiation, détente, engagement, truce—seemed possible anymore.

Just being around him made her angry. Clueless, egotistical, self -centered Denny. Why hadn't she put her finger on his basic character flaw before? Everything that was wrong happened because he did whatever the hell he wanted. Now that work was coming in regularly and the baby matter was settled, he thought they could la-di-da back to the way things were a hundred years ago when she was a girl in love and didn't know any better.

Denny spent days and some evenings in his garage workshop. Furniture from the house was finding its way out there. She knew he was giving her space and she should stop him. But the less she saw of him the better.

Anger had been a stranger to Willow. She never understood raging drivers yelling obscenities out the window or the wrath that came with an argument that left people sputtering with fury. Now, it filled her. She didn't know what to do with it except to avoid its source as much as possible.

Willow washed and dried the breakfast dishes and crumpled the newspaper into a ball without looking at the movie schedule. She was too irritated to stay in the house.

As soon as she felt the light breeze on her face, she began to relax. Willow went for a long walk in the neighborhood, chatting with neighbors along the way who were taking advantage of the sunny day. When she got home, she showered, dressed, threw some books in a bag. The new café Tess wanted to try was on a block with a bookstore, a pharmacy, and a thrift shop. Perfect entertainment until she arrived.

The puffy white clouds drifted aimlessly across a Crayola sky blue. She put on her sunglasses, rolled down all the car windows and sang to Paul Simon's, *50 Ways to Leave Your Lover*.

She felt better immediately.

Willow parked in front of the café and chose a table in the sun. She willed herself to stay present, as her mother would have advised. This is the kind of morning when you can smell the earth waking up and feel the strong sun melting winter away. Bushy planters of yellow flowers —daisies and spider mums, pansies, and primrose—bordered tables decorated with multi-colored pots of blue cornflowers. But as soon as she sat down, whatever energy she had on the ride over evaporated. The ever-widening pinhole sapping her stamina won out.

"What can I get you?"

"I'm meeting someone for lunch later but I'll have a cappuccino now."

"Sure. No problem." The young waitress sported a high blonde ponytail and wore heavy black eye makeup. "It's about time we had a good weather day like this." She glanced at the book Willow had with her. "You're reading *Broken for You.* One of my faves."

"An homage to all that is broken. Exceptional characters. I don't know who I love more— Wanda or Margaret. But I'm not finished yet so don't tell me anything," Willow warned.

"Would never. That's like telling somebody the end of a movie. My mom would kill me. Books were like her religion. Got me a library card as soon as I could read. Every Tuesday night all through school we had a standing date. We'd go to the Pine Hills library and then talk about the book I just read over pizza at the *Fountain.*"

"You're kidding? My favorite place. You must have an exceptional mother."

"Yeah. I thought she was dorky and embarrassing most of the time. But now, I'd give anything to have our Tuesdays back." She paused, "Anyway…"

Willow said, "Come sit with me when you're on break. I love book talk. By the way, I'm Willow."

"Zoe." She turned from Willow and wiped down the table next to her.

Blake was leaving the drugstore across the street when he saw Willow chatting with the waitress. The sunlight gave her long wavy hair a golden cast. *Sitting among all the flowers in a yellow and green sundress and matching green sweater, book in hand, she would have been a perfect subject for an Impressionist painter.* Without hesitating, he strode across the street.

He beamed. "It doesn't look like you're going to get much reading done with all these interruptions."

She looked up and smiled. "Looks like this is my lucky day. First I meet a young book lover and now, here you are."

"May I sit down for a minute?"

She moved her bag off the other chair. "Sure. I'm meeting a friend for lunch but I'm very early. What are you up to?"

"The usual Saturday stuff. Paperwork at school, errands. Otherwise unplanned. I say that with some trepidation," he scoffed. "Jillian would be horrified to hear that anyone would just want to enjoy a sunny Saturday. I'll probably find a rather extensive to-do list when I get home. And then again, I may ignore it and rake out the gardens."

"That's what I should be doing. I love doing the spring cleanup imagining all the new varieties I'm going to try. Every year, I decide I'm going to do a yellow garden or a pink one. I love the look of a solid mass of color but then once I go to the nursery, I can't do it. There are too many colors beckoning."

"What a dilemma," he teased. "You do it all? The heavy work, too?"

"Yup. It's totally my domain. All those years working on farms and orchards made me a pro." She blotted the foam from her mouth. "You should have one of these. It's absolutely delicious."

"Never had one. No idea how a latte is different from a cappuccino. And Starbucks is a foreign language."

"Come to think of it, I'm not really sure either. But here, have a taste. Cappuccino."

Willow pushed the cup toward him and he took a sip.

Instinctively, she took her napkin and wiped the foam from his mouth. Willow blushed, "Sorry, Blake. Reflex."

"Thanks. I'm glad not to be sitting here like a commercial for *Got Milk?*"

They were both quiet.

Zoe came out. "Can I get you something, sir?"

He turned to the waitress. "I'll have one of those." He pointed to Willow's cup. "And a toasted bagel with cream cheese."

"Sure thing."

They sat for a moment.

Willow broke the silence. "People will get the wrong idea if they see us together like this. I'd hate to have a starring role in the school gossip mill. And it could start trouble for you with the school board."

They both looked down the street. Several downtown blocks had been renovated to reflect its historic character. Cobblestone was added to the intersections, black light poles resembling the old gas-lights lined the street. New awnings dressed up the tattoo parlor, the used furniture shop, the liquor store.

Two young girls in black with Goth make up, a slender boy with shorts falling to his knees, an old woman stooped over her shopping cart, shuffled past.

"Which of our esteemed colleagues do you think we might run into down here?" Blake asked. "Maybe Watson, the music teacher, in search of old jazz records at the *Blue Note*, or maybe Holly Jarvis, who might be scavenging the used bookstore on Dove Street. But I wouldn't worry about either one of them."

"How about Howard?" she suggested. "A tattoo might help him finally get the lunch lady he's been after."

Blake laughed, "How do you know these things?"

"People talk to me. They always have."

"I'm not surprised. You're so easy to talk to. And wise." He paused. "Jillian's ballet studio is about six blocks down the street but she never ventures into the neighborhood. She's become strictly suburban."

"What would you say to her if she walked past?"

"Same thing I'd tell anyone else. Two colleagues running into one another having a cup of coffee is not a big deal."

She smiled. "So if we see anybody from school looking at us oddly, we'll ask them to join us."

"More likely we'd see some kids and I doubt they'd even notice us."

"You're right about that. A very self-absorbed age."

"Understatement. Speaking of which I promised Chelsea she could have a sleepover tonight. That means pizza, a lot of giggling, and losing the big screen TV because they want to see Channing Tatum up close and personal."

"Who?"

"That's what I said. I'm glad her friends always want to come to our house, despite my job."

"I envy you," Willow said, suddenly feeling weary again.

"You have a crush on him, too?" he teased. "I hear he's got a six-pack and the movie they want to see is about male strippers."

"Forget about him. There must be nothing better than a house full of teenage girls. Sorry, Blake." Her lip quivered. "I'm a bit off today."

"Talk to me, Willow."

She brushed away the tears. "I'm sorry."

Without thinking, he gently tucked her hair behind her ear.

"I listen to mothers at school complaining about their kids and want to scream at them, 'Don't you know how lucky you are?' I'd give anything to be a mother to one of them." She shuddered. "Four miscarriages and a husband who was relieved each time."

She looked down. "Denny came home from the Persian Gulf War with health problems. My friend, Tess, who I'm meeting for lunch, is the wife of one of his marine buddies. They have a son with a birth defect which totally turned him off to the idea of having kids. Needless to say, we have different reactions to all the loss."

Blake's eyes softened. "I'm so sorry. I..." he stopped himself.

"Right. There's nothing to say. I've heard enough platitudes to last a lifetime."

The waitress came back. "Here you are, sir. Let me know if you need anything else."

"It's your turn. I told you something personal and painful. Revealing really. You have to do the same."

He sighed. "I'm a pretty boring guy."

"Untrue."

"Ask my wife. I'm not sophisticated or cultured enough."

"Enough for what? What does that even mean?" she asked.

"It means that she'd really rather be married to a violinist or a choreographer, maybe even a conductor."

Willow furrowed her brow, "If that's true, she's a foolish woman."

"What's worse is she doesn't share your view of motherhood. The way she treats our daughter is hard to figure."

"Ah, isn't that always the way? We always want what we don't have."

"You can say that again! Let's just leave it at that. Enough for one morning."

"You are so easy to talk to. Too easy." She paused and tapped the book. "This book is about transforming broken things. Taking those things that have made you unhappy, smashing them, and re-forming them into something else. It's something to think about on a spring morning when everything is coming alive again, don't you think?"

"Yup. You know the Greek restaurant on Maiden Lane? The owner gives people plates to smash. We should go there and ask if we can be the smashers one day."

She chuckled, "Now that would be fun."

Tess walked to the table. "Hi, Willow. I'm actually here a bit early. Didn't realize you double-booked today." She winked at Blake.

"Hi, Tess. This is Blake Golden. Tess Hennessy."

"Glad to meet you, Tess." Blake stood and shook her hand. He popped the remaining bagel in his mouth. "I'll see if I can set up a time to smash plates." He put some money on the table.

Willow picked up the money and while giving it back to him, let her hand stay in his an extra moment to draw in its warmth. "I've got it, Blake. Really."

"Okay. But next one's mine."

"Pleasure meeting you," Tess said.

"Likewise. See you Monday, Willow."

They both watched him cross the street and get into his car. Tess admitted, "Confession. I got here early and lurked. I haven't seen you that engaged in months. No let's make that years."

"We've become friends."

"That's not the principal you've been having coffee with?"

Willow nodded.

"Here I was imagining someone close to retirement with thinning hair and a potbelly. You shouldn't leave out such interesting details."

"Didn't think it was relevant," she smiled. "He is great looking, isn't he?"

Tess nodded. "Absolutely. So where are you two smashing plates?"

"At some Greek restaurant."

Tess smiled, "Very cathartic. Can I join you?"

"Why do you need to break plates?" she asked.

"Joe wants to come back. He says he's miserable without me but I'm still not getting any signs that tells me he's made any real progress about Jason."

Willow grimaced.

"I still miss Joe in ways I never thought possible. Part of me really wants him back. But he really hasn't changed. On a brighter note, Jason's amazingly resilient and is healing well from the last surgery. I think my little man is stronger than the big one."

"Ha! What did they do exactly?"

"The speech therapist felt he had too much nasal tone making it harder to understand him. She explained that this happens when the muscles at the back of the throat and the soft palate let air leak into the nose. So, we took him to a surgeon."

"We?" Willow asked.

"Yes. Joe's been better about that."

Willow nodded. "Glad to hear it."

"In any case, the surgeon felt Jason would do well to have pharyngeal flap surgery. The recuperation wasn't too bad but the doctors warned us of two things. First, that it may take a few months for the nasal tone to even out and that children can snore for up to a year after surgery. If I thought Joe was bad, Jason is rattling the house."

Willow laughed. "Guess he takes after the old man after all. Jason has so much to say even if we can't understand him now. I'm sure he'll be an interesting conversationalist one day."

Tess shrugged. "At least, he'll whistle less when he makes certain sounds. The taunts from other kids I imagine in my sleep are starting to fade a bit."

"Oh, Tess."

"Look, it's a beautiful day. I want to just enjoy it. Leave my worries behind, so to speak. Let's order."

Willow motioned for Zoe to come over and she gave them menus.

Tess tilted her face up toward the sun and smiled. "It's obvious you and Blake are intensely connected."

"Silly. We were just talking, passing the time."

"Sure you were. I'm not pro or con. Just saying."

Willow said quietly, "I probably like talking to him more than I should. And now that you mention it, I look forward to that. But that's all."

"Just know that whatever you decide to do, I'm with you all the way." Tess studied the menu. "What's up with Denny?"

"In what way?"

"Any way you want to talk about."

"The truth? I can't stand being around him. Everything he does annoys me. He acts perplexed. What's to be angry about? Is he dumb or just unable to take any responsibility for all the ways he's sabotaged me? Us?"

"Wow. Sabotage. That's a strong word. Have you thought about seeing a therapist? It might help to talk things out."

"I have thought about it," Willow mused. "But for right now, I just want space. Not a separation but I just don't care to be around him. He actually wants to go on a date tonight for movies and pizza." She snarled, "Like that's going to fix anything."

Tess started to say something but then thought better of it.

"It's okay. What were you going to say?"

"Well, it sounds like he's trying and even that makes you angry. Think about that."

Chapter twenty-six
2010

Jillian apologized to Chelsea over and over for what she said when they were at The Standard. She understood how devastating her words were to a teenage girl who had grown up with her caustic criticism. Although Chelsea told her to forget what happened, it was clear she hadn't and avoided her mother as much as possible. To make amends, Jillian went overboard on a campaign to bolster Chelsea's confidence.

"Let it go, Jillian. She won't tell me what happened but whatever it was can't be fixed with your phony cheerleading."

Jillian was diligent about coming home on time. She let many of her expectations around the house go, and tried to be upbeat and supportive. But it seemed all the concessions were hers. Coming in at the end of a long day to see the house in disarray, books and papers everywhere, dishes in the sink, infuriated her.

What began as conciliation began its turn.

She tried to squelch her rising anger but couldn't seem to contain her shrill disappointment. Chelsea was Blake's child in every way. If she didn't know Chelsea came from her own body, she would think she was someone else's child. As much as she would lecture herself on the drive home to exorcize her bad mother thoughts, as soon as she entered the house, her resolve disintegrated. She'd walk in on the two of them, so comfortable with one another, united against her, and begin her sniping.

Jillian was furious one Sunday when Blake was sprawled on the couch watching football when he was supposed to be fixing the drip in the kitchen sink. She didn't want to start another argument. At least, not while Chelsea's friend was there.

She stormed out of the house. Trying to calm herself down, she found herself wandering the aisles at Target to blow off steam when a solution presented itself in the form of a dry erase board. Ah ha! Pay dirt. *The perfect solution. I'll never have to talk to them about chores and errands again. I'll write down the week's list and what they haven't done will just stare back at them. I won't have to say a word.*

When she got home, the game was over. The Giants won and Blake was in a great mood. He had gone to the hardware store to get the part he needed and was fixing the sink. But she couldn't let go of her find and hung it on the kitchen wall.

Her old habits gradually crept back. Jillian threw herself into work with focused intensity. She hired another part time teacher who had been a professional dancer to enhance the prospects for her school and had her eye on a building next door that had come up for sale.

After meeting Blake, Philip had become better about picking up Allegra on time but didn't sustain it. If it had been anyone else, Jillian wouldn't have allowed it but she adored her. Serious, introspective Allegra reminded her of herself at that age. How old were you when you went to ballet camp? Was it hard to take so many classes in a day? Were the girls nice or were they mean and competitive? The questions would come one a day, as if Allegra had to choose them carefully and store the answers one at a time. All the patience she could never access for Chelsea was given to Allegra.

And if she were honest, she looked forward to even a moment alone with Phillip.

"Madame Jillian, I'll be going home with Michelle this afternoon."

"I'm glad," she smiled. "It's good for ballerinas to hang out together. Is Dad out of town?"

"No. He thinks I should make some friends, too."

Jillian was disappointed. While she spent only a few sexually charged minutes with Philip several days a week, they were becoming big moments to her. Her fastidiously imagined fantasies changed. The imaginary Lance became the real Philip. She would take a magic carpet ride to a place where Philip and Allegra were her family. He was a conductor, an artist, a sensitive man. Allegra was a child with Jillian's sensibilities and nature. They had money and lived in a contemporary townhouse downtown.

In her mind, Jillian furnished every room with modern, up-scale furniture and vibrant abstract art. The kitchen gleamed with stainless steel appliances and copper bottom pots hung from a rack over a granite island. There was a music room with a grand piano and a ballet studio. Their friends were artists and successful businessmen who were eager to come to their fabulous dinner parties. In her alternate reality, she didn't mind not dancing as she did in her real life. It didn't hurt as much because she had all the rest.

She was putting the day's attendance sheets away when she heard the door open. She thought she had locked the front door but perhaps she'd forgotten and an intruder had come in—they were downtown after all. She reached for the phone but as they came closer, she recognized the footsteps.

"Philip, what are you doing here? Allegra left with…"

"I had to see you alone."

He closed the door behind him, walked over to her and pulled her close to him. He held her face in his hands and began to kiss her— tender, soft kisses at first— quickly turning deep and hungry.

She hadn't known until then how much she wanted the real man, not just the fantasy. His kisses felt so right. She was a woman living the wrong life. Wasn't she? Could Philip fix that? If this man could do that for her, she would not deny herself.

"Lovely Jillian," he crooned, "I haven't been able to think of anything but you. I study a new score, the notes blur and your face emerges. I often see you dance across the page." He pulled her close. "We should be together."

Jillian separated herself from him. She knew she could not speak while he touched her. Short of breath, she said, "I would be lying if I told you I hadn't thought about the possibility of us. But…"

His eyes sparkled, "Come out for a drink with me. We can plan our future."

"Our future?" Jillian laughed. "My future tonight is having dinner with my husband and daughter."

"Tomorrow night, then? I know an out of the way bar where we'll never be discovered. A place we can get to know each other better."

Offhandedly, she mentioned to Blake after dinner that she'd be home a bit late the next night. She was going to have a drink with a prospective teacher.

"Good. Maybe she'll be able to take some of your late classes. We'd love to see more of you. Wouldn't we, Chels?"

Chelsea looked up from the book in her lap. "Sure, Dad."

"Yes," Jillian said. "It would be nice to get some relief."

The deception began with stolen hours at an out of the way wine bar in Schenectady's Stockade area. It had a shabby chic elegance she thought suited them — dark paneling, low lights, cozy red cushioned booths, jazz standards playing in the background. There were a few regulars at the highly-polished bar but it was otherwise a quiet, safe place for them to meet.

Much to her surprise, he always arrived first. He sat at the same table waiting, never failing to break out into a broad smile when she arrived. She looked forward to seeing him. It was so easy. He talked. She listened. She never thought she'd meet a storyteller as gifted as Blake.

"Have I told you about the European tour when I was at Curtis?"

She laughed. "Yes, Philip. At least once."

He cringed, "I'm sorry. I must be boring you with my chatter. For some reason, I feel I have to impress you. You're a bit intimidating, Jillian. I'm afraid it makes me ramble."

"I love hearing them. It's obvious how thoroughly you enjoy yourself. You've had some marvelous experiences."

"It's just a cover. I'm talking so I won't rip off your clothes."

"Well then, when will you?"

"When will I do what?"

"Not here," she teased. "I think that might shock the old geezer at the bar into a heart attack. But yes. It's time for us."

Without hesitation, he said. "I know just the place."

"I'll bet you do," she flushed.

His smile faded. "I don't do this, Jillian. I've never done this before. Never. I've just been hoping that you might…"

"You're kidding? I thought you'd have a woman on each trip," she baited.

"I'm not that kind of man. I'm sorry you think that."

"Just trying to figure you out. I'm not exactly adept at this kind of thing. What to think? What to say? Is it worth the consequences?"

He sipped his martini. "If you're sure, the place I'm thinking of is out of the way so we won't be seen and it's charming."

And how often have you been there? "Sounds perfect."

The next Thursday, on a night she would have been out with Georgia and Claire anyway, she hired a substitute teacher to cover her day classes. With hours stretching out before them, they traveled to an inn in the Berkshires. On the drive, they spoke little. She was nervous. As the landscape changed from city to country, she began to relax but just as she did, the first CD he put on was the wretched ballet that ruined her life.

"Please, Philip. Play something else," she insisted.

Surprised, he said, "I could imagine you dancing it."

Sharply, she repeated. "Please, Philip. Turn it off. Now."

"Of course."

"Thank you, Philip." She closed her eyes. "Coppélia and I have a history I'd prefer not to be reminded of."

Philip laughed, "Only my charming Jillian would have a personal relationship with a musical score. We are meant for each other."

But he didn't ask her why. In fact, he didn't try very hard to get to know her at all. She couldn't help but compare him to Blake who would want to know why she didn't want to listen to a certain piece of music. The details in our personal narratives, he often said, are as important to who we are as our cells. At least the old Blake said that. *Go away, Blake,* she thought, trying to push him out of her thoughts.

To fill the silence, Jillian initiated small talk. Had he spent any time in this town before? She'd heard they have a good theater there. How was Allegra? Was she making friends?

The interminable ride was over and there they were, in a fussy dining room crowded with blue-haired ladies having lunch. The décor supported the clientele. Heavy, velvet flocked wallpaper, chairs upholstered in chintz, thick white table clothes set with Blue Willow china and Waterford crystal.

Jillian felt out of place and conspicuous but soon could have cared less. As soon as they ordered, Philip jolted her. Always reticent, he now had one hand under her dress, pushing her panties aside, fingers inside her. He smiled, encouraged at how wet she was. She felt hot. Ready. She closed her eyes, threw back her head, gulped a glass of champagne.

They didn't wait for lunch.

He pulled at her as they walked down the hall to their room. Once he unlocked the door, Philip pushed her down on the bed, hiked up her dress, tore open the front buttons and pulled her breasts out of her bra.

She slid out from under him. "Philip, I need to go into the bathroom. Slow down. We aren't renting the room by the hour, are we?" she joked, sliding out from underneath him. Once in the bathroom, she splashed cold water on her face and looked at herself hard in the mirror. What was he thinking? This was nothing like the romantic encounter she imagined. *Jillian, cut it out. You're just nervous. Go out there and live in the real world for a change.*

She left her clothes in the bathroom and walked toward him. He had taken his clothes off and lay on the bed. His pasty, loose paunch was hidden well under his well-cut clothes, she thought. The shine in his eyes scared her.

Jillian suddenly wished it was dark.

She lay down next to him and he rolled over on top of her. It was over before she knew it. She was stunned. No foreplay. Not even a kiss. The risk she had taken. Not only was he uninitiated in the art of real conversation, he was a terrible lover. Inconsiderate. Selfish. Uninspired. Lacking in every way. She never expected that. She expected his music to inhabit him. Something enchanted to be worth the jeopardy.

He didn't seem to notice that he treated her like a receptacle. *Worse than a teenage boy in heat*, she thought. *Where was his self-control? What about her?* Jillian only had Blake to compare him to. Blake knew how to make love to a woman because that was the kind of man he was— generous and sweet, tender. This was the first time she'd been with a man who didn't love her.

Jillian grabbed the sheet and ran into the bathroom. She was a fool. Wrapped in shame, she sat on the toilet and cried. When there were no more tears, she got into the shower, adjusting the steaming water as hot as she could stand it, hoping it was not too late to purify the poison within her. She dressed and woke up a snoring Philip, who was deep into a dream with a smile on his face.

She shook him roughly. "I want to go home."

Lily
2010

To: asinclair@womanandbrighams.org
From: lilylerner@aol.com
Subject: what have I become?

Delete this email after you've read it.

What I've done isn't the same but...remember when you were feeling suffocated by James. You had been dating for two years when you had the obsessive lusting for the intern you were working with? You knew what it was but you did it anyway?

Okay. I can hear your irritated sigh... you know what's coming. My confession couched in rationalization.

Given what goes on when nomadic journalists live together like college frat boys, my self-control has been amazing. (I warned you I was going to rationalize my behavior, didn't I?) Wild flirting when I'm drunk is as far as it's gone. Well, maybe sometimes a little more. But I really crossed the line this time.

I was on assignment when this insanely good looking French photographer set his sights on me. I knew what he was— a womanizer with enough charisma and arrogance to think he could woo Mother Theresa. But, there was something irresistible about him. It was just raw sex. His wild experience took me places I never imagined. And murmuring about my beauty in his French accent didn't hurt. I pushed Stephen out of my mind and enjoyed every minute of it. Sex for its own sake —hot, reckless sex—in this sad place seemed to me to be part of whatever experience I was after. Though not an excuse, falling into bed with him was a welcome relief from all the awful parts of this African trip. Sick irony. I don't even want to tell you what is happening to the village girls in this remote part of the country. It is probably the most horrifying I've ever seen.

It was only when it was over and he moved on to the next girl, did I begin to panic. I'd never want to hurt Stephen in any way and this was such extreme betrayal. Now that I'm back home, I've been waking up sweating, petrified he'll find out.

My mother has said in no less than three letters that I have to face facts. It would be one thing if there was a time limit on our separation but there isn't. According to my free-spirited Mom, she isn't advocating for something traditional with Stephen, but wants me to know it's time for me to decide something before it gets decided for me. I wonder if she had ESP about a conversation he and I had after he left London.

"Lily, we're going to have to find a way to live together. Didn't our year together show you what our life could be like? I don't know about you but the longer we go on like this, the harder it is to let go when we see each other. Simply said, I need and want more."

"Me too, Stephen. Sometimes I miss you so much, I just want to jump on a plane and go to you. But for right now, I can't give this up."

"Or me?" he added quietly. "We have to start talking about our future. I don't know what that looks like, but it has to be more than it is now. You've got clout now. It's time to think out of the box. Do you hear me, Lily?"

And then I go and do this?

I'm scared. I love him. He is the light in the dark world I've chosen to live in. I can't lose him yet I don't know how to change my life. I think my reaction when he left London was just that—me being scared. What am I doing, Amber? You've always known me better than I know myself.

Love, Lily

To: llerner@aol.com
From: asinclair@womenandbrigham.org
Subject: sigh

Lily, I'm not your conscience.

News bulletin: Successful journalists do get married. I read somewhere that even your idol, Christiane Amanpour, has a husband and child. And I think they all live together in the same country. What's more, there are pretty good jobs for journalists in the good old USA.

I'm with your mom. Make the choice yours. But I will say this: Guys like Stephen are rare and even though you may not realize it, you depend on him for all the intangibles. If that were gone, it would devastate you and would be mighty hard to replace.

Love, Amber

P.S. I may have deleted your last email but I have the ones you sent when Stephen was in London. Even though you are too thickheaded to realize it, you've never sounded happier.

Chapter twenty-seven
2010

Denny was desperate to win Willow back. To please her, he pursued alternate ways to control Demon. He had acupuncture twice a month not wanting to disappoint either Willow or the petite Chinese acupuncturist determined to heal him—biting her lower lip, referring to her hefty books of meridians and pathways, quietly talking to herself. But when he lay on the table feeling like a patchwork quilt, he'd look up at the paper crane origami mobile over his head and wonder how he could stop these futile treatments.

His Chinese herbalist did much more to help him manage his allergy attacks, and he finally found a migraine medication that didn't reduce the frequency of headaches but shortened them. There was nothing much to be done about his leg. The pain was synchronized to the barometric pressure and change of season. For that, he loaded up on Advil, which often was all he needed.

He'd come so far from those debilitating years but the recurrent nightmares never faded.

Just thinking about going to the beach conjured a return to an empty vista of sand, whipping every part of his body, stinging his eyes, burning his throat, sleeping in what seemed to him like a shallow grave.

In summer, the buzz of flies brought back the very real feeling of their assault. They were in his mouth when he was eating, up his nose, in his ears. He'd sometimes wake up in a sweat feeling tiny insects crawling on him, so many of them, they appeared as a black mass.

A neighbor's bonfire would bring him back to fiery skies, searing his skin, or to the burning oil wells blackening everything —soot on his food and body, oily water when showering.

Before her sympathy for him petered out, Willow tried to calm him. "Just think of the sound of the waves and the feeling of sand between your toes. The sun warming your bones. Think of that."

He didn't have the heart to tell her those thoughts were the problem. Or that extreme heat and cold also would set him off. The hot, scorching desert in daytime followed by night patrols in frigid cold. It was a part of him and he didn't want it to be a part of her.

Jason's lopsided face and deformed ear also found its way into his nightmares. Willow, his mother, his uncle, Joe all had his deformed face. In his dream, he would turn away from Willow, not wanting her to see his revulsion. He'd wake up quickly and ashamed, relieved it was a dream.

His suffering now was compounded by Willow's recent apathy. She never rebounded after losing the babies and blamed him. It lay between them cold and unrelenting. The reminders were constant—aside from his issues, he'd go with her to a school program only to have the lesion reopen. That her students would attach themselves to her maternal magnetic field emphasized her losses.

It all made him work hard to feel worthy of taking up space on the planet.

He turned to work. When Denny felt his business was secure, he took out a loan to buy all the high-end equipment he needed and to fully winterize the garage. He told her repeatedly there also was money to update the house, but she was uninterested.

After Willow left for school in the morning, he would start his day as well, taking a second cup of coffee out to his workshop. He'd remind himself he was no longer a disabled man who stayed home all day. Demon made fewer visits. He was a sought-after carpenter, successful and skilled enough to pad time estimates for lost days and not have to account to anyone for them anymore.

Denny knew he'd have to do the one thing he didn't want to if he was ever going to get Willow back. He sucked in a deep breath and called the Vet Center to find a therapist, hoping there'd be a huge backlog like every other military benefit he tried to get. He broke into a sweat when a Dr. Kogan called him back later that afternoon telling him he had a cancellation the next day. But what could he do? He tried to answer the therapist's basic questions as best he could and agreed to come.

He fidgeted in the spare, wood paneled waiting room. A couple of Audubon prints in cheap frames hung on the walls. Outdated news magazines were stacked on a scratched-up table flanked by plastic chairs.

He was staring at the door to the therapist's office when it opened and a weathered man with military bearing, nodded at Denny and left. A few minutes later, a slight man with thinning, longish, white hair came out. "Denny, I'm Dr. Kogan. Come right in."

The office had two armchairs and a couch across from a small desk. Dr. Kogan sat in one of the chairs. Denny looked at the couch and made a face. He sat in the other worn chair. "Today, I'd like you to tell me about your military experience and more about the difficulties you're having. Then, we'll talk about the kind of therapy we do here."

"Let's do that first." Denny folded his arms across his chest. "The kind of therapy thing."

"Of course," he nodded. "Basically, if someone has suffered trauma, it is not unusual to stay stuck in it. It's hard to get past it when you're constantly reliving something painful, when you never know when and how it's going to pop up. It's too much to be expected to come back home and slide back into your life as if you'd never left."

"Tell me about it," Denny agreed.

"Cognitive therapy helps you get a handle on your distressing thoughts or recurring dreams. Its purpose is to give you the skills you need to help you deal with flashbacks and other reminders. It's not complicated and we'll go through it together. So, Denny, let's start with some basics."

"Let me ask you some questions first, Doc."

"Of course."

"Have you ever served?"

"I don't see how that's relevant. But no, I did not."

Denny's heart pounded. "How the fuck can you help me if you've been sitting in this office your whole life?"

Dr. Kogan leaned back in his chair. "Let me see if I understand this. Your assessment is since I haven't had your experiences, I can't help you."

"Yeah. That's right. How could you? Sitting here safe all these years."

He looked directly at Denny, not responding right away.

The silence unnerved Denny but he didn't look away.

Finally, Dr. Kogan said, "Therapy only works if you want it to, Denny, and trust the process. I don't have to justify my practice to you. Nor tell you about all the clients I've successfully treated."

Denny sat ramrod straight, his face blank.

"Let me offer you this. Cognitive therapy works in group settings as well. I didn't propose that at first because from our phone conversation you struck me as reluctant and private. But maybe you'd like to consider it.

"The Vet Center holds group meetings run by a psychiatrist. Everyone in the group has served in a war zone. You share the experiences that haunt you. That is essential. You are part of a whole. Just as you each had your own job within your unit, you are a cog in the wheel there, too, so to speak. You write, you share, you talk, and by talking it through repeatedly with your group, you gain the tools to manage the symptoms."

Dr. Kogan walked to his desk and grabbed a business card from the middle drawer. "The thing is, Denny, you have to make a commitment. That means you have to agree to attend a set number of sessions in fairness to the group. But it's worth the time and effort. Here is the information."

He shook Denny's hand. "Think about it and feel free to come back here if you're ever ready to work with me."

Denny nodded. He knew he should give this guy a chance. But he couldn't. He just couldn't. His mouth was so dry, he could barely swallow.

He folded the paper in his pocket and left without saying a word. His only thought was what am I going to tell Willow?

Chapter twenty-eight
2010

Barcelona's was filling up. When Jillian got there, Georgia and Claire were already seated at their regular table. Georgia was irritated. "What happened to you last Thursday? You didn't even call to say you weren't coming. And we didn't hear a word all week."

Jillian sat down next to Claire across from Georgia. "Okay. I'm sorry. I couldn't come. I was… and then I needed time to figure out …" Jillian gulped the wine Georgia poured for her.

Georgia glowered. "No. Don't tell me."

She blurted, "You were right, Georgia. I shouldn't have. It was a disaster."

"I don't know why I even bother talking to you."

"Okay. I should have listened. It was a huge mistake. All of it. Turns out, I've been fantasizing about a guy who's a big zero."

"No surprises there," Georgia mumbled.

Claire prodded, "It's okay, love. Start from the beginning."

"You know we've been flirting, circling each other for ages. The sexual tension was intense. When Philip finally suggested it was time, I didn't hesitate. We'd been meeting for weeks at a wine bar."

Georgia scowled. "You've been meeting him for weeks? Couldn't have been feeling too good about it if you didn't even tell us?"

"Never mind. If that's how you're going to be, I'm leaving." She stood up.

Claire shot Georgia a look. "Stop, you two. Sit down, Jillian. Come on, Georgia. Enough now."

Jillian sat down. "Please. Let me just get this out. It's hard enough without your commentary."

"Okay. Sorry. I'll shut up." Georgia patted her hand.

"What can I say? For the first time in years, I felt beautiful and desirable and sophisticated. That should count for something, shouldn't it? Especially since Blake is hostile and angry at me all the time now. Things at home are worse than ever despite all my good intentions."

She shook her head. "I don't know. Maybe I just wanted to do something rash. I fantasize about things and never do them. Isn't that what you always say, Georgia?" Jillian cringed remembering the daydreams she had about Philip, finished her drink and reached across the table for the bottle. "What can I tell you? I did it and now I feel disgusting."

"Slow down. Getting drunk isn't going to help," Georgia said, taking the glass out of her hand.

Jillian pulled the glass from Georgia's grip, spilling some on the table, and took another drink. "Philip and I drove to the Berkshires. We went to an inn there I'd never heard of. At lunch, I was so turned on I could barely get to the room." She shook her head horrified all over again at their tawdry behavior in the restaurant. "As soon as we got to our room, it all fizzled. He took off his clothes and started tearing at mine, worse than a teenage boy. No kissing, no foreplay, Jack rabbit over. Rolls over and falls fast asleep. Snoring sleep. I expected a hot, electrifying sex lead up and what do I get? A quick minute thank you ma'am."

She looked past her friends into the noisy space around her. She took a tissue from her purse to blow her nose. "There I was, in a strange room with all its heavy furnishings—the chintz and draperies and too many pillows and old building mustiness—and I couldn't breathe. I was wide awake in the middle of a bad dream."

She looked at Georgia, then Claire. "I showered, practically scalding myself clean, and when I woke Philip up to leave, he had this big smile on his face like something wonderful happened. No wonder his wife left him and he doesn't know why." She shuddered. "The silence on the way home was excruciating. He kept looking at me sideways but never asked a damn thing."

Claire leaned in. "Do you want to say anything else?"

"What else is there to say?" Jillian shrugged. "And quit shaking your head, Georgia. I'm sorry enough about taking the risk for nothing."

This time it was Claire who spoke up. "If that's all you got out of this fiasco, I'm going to say something harsh, Jillian. But it needs to be said." Claire took a very deep breath. "What happened with Philip is a look in the mirror. He's a male Jillian."

Jillian blazed, "What? That's mean, Claire. You with your flavor of the week."

"Don't be nasty, Jillian," Claire went on, unflustered. "We've been friends for too long to be dishonest. Being with Philip gave you a peek into what it's like to be with you."

"What? How can you say that to me after what I just told you?" Jillian sucked in a breath. "I expected some sympathy and what do I get? The two of you just sitting there judging me. You're not even listening. Let alone trying to understand what just happened to me."

Claire softened her voice. "Not true, Jil. We always listen and this is the thing. It's always about you and never about what Blake or Chelsea want or need. And now, you've come up against it in Philip who doesn't even know that anything is amiss because his needs were met."

Jillian began to cry.

Georgia said, "Make it count for something, Jilly. Look what judging someone by his resume got you. You float around in dreamland thinking he's your possible out. You'll be with him and have a life that isn't as good as being a ballerina but is better than life with Blake." Georgia rested her hand lightly on Jillian's arm. "You either have to say, yes, I still love Blake and want to work things out, or no, it's time to get out. Your constant dissatisfaction is exhausting everyone. And pushing you to make bad decisions."

Jillian grabbed her coat. "I can't listen to this. You may think you're helping but you're not. Not one goddamned bit. Some friends." She ran to the car, rested her head on the steering wheel, and burst into tears.

Blake was dozing on the couch when she got home. She nudged him awake and sat down next to him. Her face was puffy and streaked with dried tears. Subdued, she said, "Blake, we can't go on like this. We have to do better. What would you say if I went away for a week? To think? Try to sort things out?"

He said, "Good. Do it."

She was stung. There was neither gentleness nor compassion in his voice. The tender way he used to look at her was also gone. She tried not to panic. What if she'd come home and told him she wanted to leave him? Would he say the same thing? Good. Do it.

At three-thirty, Blake woke up. Jillian hadn't yet come to bed. Thirsty, he headed for the kitchen. Music drifted from her closed studio door. He assumed that if he opened the door, he'd see Jillian dancing, elegant as ever. It was the only place he thought she showed any grace at all anymore. But over the music, he could hear her racking sobs. He had his hand on the knob but stopped himself. There was nothing to say.

Chapter twenty-nine
2011

Smiling with anticipation, Willow sat at the kitchen table jotting down questions for her faculty/student book discussion on *The Elegance of the Hedgehog*. There was a cool breeze blowing through the gauzy café curtains. A patch of sunlight arced across the table but Willow didn't notice. Nor did she notice Denny come into the kitchen to pour a cup of coffee. He stood watching her, willing her to look up, but saw that wasn't going to happen.

"Willow," he sputtered, "can we talk?"

"I'm in the middle of something. Can't it wait?" She looked up. When she saw the insistent look on his face, Willow put her pen down. "What's wrong?" she sighed.

"Everything." He sat down across from her. "We have to do something. You're disappearing. Even when you're here, you're not here."

Willow refused to look at him.

"This is what I want to say to you." There was a bead of sweat on his forehead. He faltered, "I'd give anything to be able to undo everything I did and… said." He reached across the table to grab her hand but she jerked it back. His voice cracked. "Once you loved me enough to accept what I'd done and move on from there. Can you do it again? I miss us. I want to get us back."

Willow's eyes flashed. "Which *us* do you mean, Denny? The *us* in which I contort into a pretzel, shape myself to fit around your needs and wants? Or the *us* when I say, okay, Denny, anything you want is fine, screw what I want? Or how about the *us* when I say Sure Denny, be anti-social or rude to my friends, my sister, it's okay.

You aren't feeling friendly. Sure. Be a shit. Which *us* exactly are you talking about?"

He flinched.

"What do you expect from me?" she seethed. "I'm open to suggestion. Our life hasn't been anything near happy for years, in case you haven't noticed."

Denny knew he had to do something, say something, but it had to be the right something. Fear crept in as he really looked at her. What he saw startled him. He'd been telling himself she was distracted, sad, maybe even a little angry but that wasn't it at all. He hadn't let himself see what had been staring him right in the face. The truth was she no longer loved him.

Desperate, he babbled, "Let's get out and do something fun. We could drive to New York to see a show. It's still early enough. Or how about going to Stockbridge to the Rockwell museum? We could eat at the Red Lion Inn after. We could plan a trip to see Grace."

"Denny, stop."

"I can change. I can. We were so good once. We can get it back." Desperate, he jabbered on, "Call Laurel. Maybe we can spend some time with her at her lake house?"

Willow couldn't look at him. Staring at the light shifting on the table, she said, "Denny, I don't need or want an away. I need simple things right here. When I come home at night, I'm sick of not knowing what the temperature will be like in the house. Hmmm. Let's see. What kind of day did Denny have? Will he be sullen or animated? Grouchy or happy? Conversational or brooding? Will the lights be on or off?"

"Come on, it's not as bad as that anymore? We could try to slough off the past and start over. Remember how much fun we used to have just being together. We could…"

"Slough off the past? You've got to be kidding." She closed her notebook. "Think, Denny. How long has it been since we've been good together? All your backpedaling makes things worse. You behave badly, realize it and say sorry, sorry, sorry, Willow. I'll do better. But you don't. Nothing ever changes."

"Please. Give me another chance."

Willow looked at him, speechless, Finally, she said, "Denny, for your own good you should go to therapy. I don't know whether or not it will help, but you should try to figure yourself out. Not understanding anything about why you do what you do is…"

Denny forced a smile, interrupting, relieved he hadn't told her things didn't work with that Dr. Kogan. "Yes. Ma'am. I'll get on that. I promise, But what about tonight? Are you free? I know it's short notice but there is an award-winning French film at the Spectrum. And to get in the mood we can go to L'Auberge. Get us a French dinner. What do you say? How about I pick you up at six?"

She sighed, "No. I don't want to do that. How about just giving me a hand in the garden later. I have to get out of the house. I need air."

Denny stood. "Love to. Let me know when you're ready." Relieved, he sprinted out of the kitchen before she could change her mind.

Willow stared out the window. She pictured herself pulling out rotted roots, cutting away old branches, pinching off the dead blossoms and imagined planting a row of sunflowers somewhere else. Far from here.

Lily

Dear Mom,

I HAVE BIG NEWS. I've landed my dream job. The network is piloting a thirty-minute program to show what's happening in a location after a big story is no longer newsworthy. Each show will be devoted to a single story giving time to do in-depth reporting. They've asked me to anchor. My big break, Mom!

Okay. Now to what you really want me to talk about. I'm not ignoring your last letters.

I understand what you're telling me. You want me to make my choices in life based on something real, not some illusions I may have about independence or even codependence. I'm no dummy. I know men like Stephen come around once in a lifetime (if you're lucky). I also know part of him likes the long distance, too. Otherwise, he wouldn't have gone along with it for so long.

But, you're right. He's ready for a change. He didn't take the news about the new job well at all and has been disturbingly silent since I told him. I really blew it when I accepted before discussing it with him first. I didn't stop to think about how he'd feel about that. I was just flying from the offer.

I'm giving him time to cool off. I'm self-absorbed enough to think he won't issue any kind of ultimatum when I've finally reached the next rung on the ladder.

Maybe this isn't what I'm going to want forever but I want it now. And I want it badly. I've worked hard to get where I am. What am I supposed to do? Go home and get married? Find a job at a local TV station covering car accidents? Not Possible.

I have a few more things to accomplish first.

I'm sorry you decided to end things with Michael. I was hoping he might finally be the one. I understand what you said about being on your own so long, it gets harder to let someone in. I just wasn't sure who it was you were talking to.

I'm out on assignment next week. I'll call you when I get back.

Love, Lily

Lily

To: lilylerner@aol.com
From: sbrooks@albany.edu
Subject: You're right. I'm very angry

When you told me what you'd done, I was so angry I couldn't speak. I wanted to wait until I calmed down but I haven't and don't know if I ever will. Signing a new three-year contract that puts you on a different trajectory without even talking to me was audacious. I imagine a conversation would only have been a courtesy but I reeled from your blatant disregard anyway.

You have no idea what it means to be in a relationship.

It's easy to say you love someone. I know in your Lily way you do love me. The question to consider is what does loving someone mean to a singularly ambitious woman who only thinks about herself?

For me, being separated is getting harder. Being together during my sabbatical year was a blessing and a curse. The contrast of our life together (even with your long assignments away) and apart is painful, but I wonder if that's true for you, too. I've been a fool not to understand that you will always make decisions with only you in mind.

It's unacceptable Lily. Will you ever be ready for a real partnership? What do I mean to you in the scheme of your life? I'm not talking about you giving up your career any more than I would give up mine. You know as well as I do that people do manage both.

I started seeing someone. A faculty member in the history department. We started as friends and then it became more. It lasted three months. I had to end it. She's a great woman and is probably better suited to me than you are but I had to break it off precisely because she is not you. And I don't feel as if I need to ask for forgiveness.

You are brilliant and resourceful. Time's up, Lily. You're either all in... or not.

S.

Chapter thirty
2011

The fragrant lilacs in full bloom buoyed Willow's spirits. It was a bright May morning and Willow kneeled in her garden deciding how she would plant flats of purple pansies and marigolds. *What would I do without my flowers?* she murmured, after she laid them all out on the grass. *Pansies with a marigold border. Definitely.* She looked at them. *Perky pansies. Maybe I'll catch their mood.* Reaching for the trowel, she heard the phone ring.

Dashing to the kitchen, she picked up. "Hello."

"Hi, Willow. It's me."

"Blake?"

"I hope it's okay I called. You sound out of breath."

"I was in the garden planning how to plant the flats of flowers I bought yesterday."

He laughed, "Major decision. How many times have you re-arranged them?"

"Too many. It's an important decision, don't you think?" She lowered her voice. "Glad to hear you laugh after the hellish week at school."

"I know. I can't help but think I could have done more. The boy driving the car was troubled. Did you know him?"

"Only by sight. I know there were problems with drugs and alcohol. But I also know that the school psychologist, social worker, and some teachers, worked with him. We can't save every kid," she said gently.

"So now we have one lost life and another is destroyed. It's a nightmare for both families."

Willow sighed, "Yes."

"I'm going to go over to see the Bentons in a little while."

"I don't know how you live after you lose a child like that."

"You never recover."

"Blake?"

After a prolonged pause, he said, "Can't tell you how many times I've hugged Chelsea since it happened. Now, she's had it. 'I know you love me, Dad. But it's enough.' Then, she'll look and me and relent. 'Okay, if it'll take that traumatized look off your face, but that's it. One more hug.' I tell you the world would be a much dimmer place without her. And I'm sure that's just what the Bentons are thinking. Ricky was a great kid."

Willow poured a half-cup of coffee and sat down. "Has the boy been charged yet?"

"His brother found him in the garage with the car engine running after he was released from police custody. Got to him just in time."

She gasped. "I had no idea."

"Yes. It's heartbreaking. But that isn't why I called. I phoned the Greek restaurant and they said we could throw plates at lunch time today. If ever there was a plate-smashing day, this is it. Can you get away?"

"Yes. The perfect thing after you visit the family. We'll break plates and have lunch." She was thoughtful. "Sometimes just being alive hurts," she exhaled.

"Meet me at the Acropolis at at one?"

Quietly, she asked, "Are you sure about this?"

"Yes. Absolutely."

She nodded and gently hung up the phone.

The storefront restaurant was on a short, cobblestoned street near the Corning Preserve. It was on a block with a couple of other restaurants, an antique dealer, and dress boutique. Lamb roasted on a spit in the window.

The owner stood just inside the door, holding a stack of white plates.

Blake said, "I called yesterday about breaking plates."

"Yes. I'm Theo. Happy you come."

"I'm Willow." She shook his hand firmly.

"I give you ten plates. You see people walk down street, you smash, but be careful. Want only good publicity." He smiled broadly. "How you know custom?"

Willow said, "When my sister was at the Sorbonne, she saw it for the first time. She said it was great fun and she had lamb sliced from a spit just like the one here." Willow pointed to the window. "She claims she's never tasted anything as delicious since then. Wait until I tell her."

Theo clapped his hands. "Wonderful. I don't know why custom but I'm gonna tell people each plate they break, bad memory goes away. Maybe true. Maybe not," he said, pleased with himself. "Sound good?"

"Just right," said Blake.

Theo gave them each ten dishes. "Kyra," he called out. "Get samples for crowd."

"Vai, Papa."

"You first," Blake said.

"Okay." She took the first plate, tossed it low, and watched it shatter. *For Denny joining the Marines.*

Blake's first plate seemed to bounce before it broke into pieces. *For Jillian's sins of omission.*

Willow. *For choosing the wrong man to love.*

Blake. *Jillian's narcissism. That night at the symphony. The way she talks to me.*

Willow. *Denny never wanting children.*

Blake. *For hurting Chelsea.*

Willow. *For the lost babies.*

And on it went until the end of their stack. Intent, they didn't notice the crowd they drew. Theo was thrilled. "Come in, come in, you two. I make you nice tasting plate. But first, I better sweep for next show."

Blake said to Willow, "After you, Madame."

The restaurant was narrow and deep. Great care had been taken to recreate a slice of Greece. A mural of the Parthenon filled one wall. The other walls were painted bright Greek blue. They sat in a high-backed booth in a corner surrounded by paintings of the Aegean Sea, Mykonos, a cityscape of Athens. Willow's eyes sparkled, her face flushed. "That was fun, wasn't it?"

Blake threw his head back, laughing. "If I knew heaving a dish would be this satisfying, I'd have done it years ago."

"Especially when you don't have to clean up the mess."

Theo came to the table with two shots of ouzo.

"Oh, I don't know," Willow hesitated.

"It's good," assured Theo. "You will enjoy. You nice couple."

He left them and Blake lifted his glass. "What shall we drink to?"

"To better days and Theo's success!"

"Yes. Opa!"

They clinked glasses and drank.

"Whoa." Willow's eyes teared. "I never thought I'd be breaking dishes and drinking ouzo when I woke up this morning."

"I'm glad you said yes."

"Blake, what are we doing?"

"What we should have done a long time ago." He took her hand. "It's come to me very slowly but I realize how I've shortchanged myself. The truth is marrying Jillian was a mistake from the beginning. Except, of course, for Chelsea."

Blake confessed, "It never occurred to me to leave her. It was what it was… until the day you first walked into my office and I started to come back to life." He looked at Willow. "I was a kid myself when I rushed Jillian into marriage, making all kinds of concessions to make her say yes. Only five years older than Chelsea is now. It seems crazy when I think about that. I was reeling from a family tragedy. In some ways, she was my life boat."

She furrowed her brow. "I'm so sorry. What happened?"

"Let me just finish this first before I lose my nerve… I didn't realize what pushed me toward her then, but I've had plenty of time to consider and understand that. Thing is I can't blame her. When we first met, it was all on her terms and that hasn't changed. Fast forward twenty years. To you."

Willow whispered, "I know."

"I want to erase your sadness."

"That would be a job for a superhero, Blake," she chuckled. "Besides, that's up to me. The idea of rescue is for romance novels." She closed her eyes for a minute and nodded. "It's time for us to tell our stories, isn't it? We both have so much in our past that has brought us here."

"Start anywhere, anytime," he coaxed. "It doesn't matter."

"It's tough to know how or where to begin. There is so much to say and at the same time, peeling back the layers of what went wrong won't really describe what actually happened to us." She paused. "I thought I had such simple ambition for my life. I was young and in love and thought that would carry us. I didn't look closely at the man I thought I loved. I didn't see who he really was even when he waved big red flags in my face."

She was still flushed from the ouzo. She lay her head against the banquette and recounted everything—how they met, the disappointments, the regrets, the lost babies. It all came pouring out, each part of the story leading to the next.

"He's in better shape now. But when I look at him, I see everything he did or didn't do, want or didn't want. I realized..." Willow smiled at Blake. "Not too long ago, Denny was trying to placate me as usual. At that moment, I realized that all the love I once had for him now belongs to you."

His eyes sparkled. "And you didn't think you should share that with me?"

She laughed. "Never occurred to me."

Blake hesitated, "I didn't know Denny growing up. You know how it is. I was a few years older and that makes a difference when you're a kid. But I'd see him hanging around with his uncle."

"Yes, Uncle Terry. He's the one who taught him carpentry."

"And about fast cars."

She raised her eyebrows.

Sheepish, he said, "I asked my mother what she remembered about him when he was in her class."

"This is new to me. What did she say?"

"The uncle filled in for Denny's father after he took off. He didn't have a family of his own. Aside from carpentry, the uncle rebuilt and raced cars. When Denny was a sophomore, he was drag racing with the uncle and got stopped by the police. The cops gave

Denny a warning and let it go but his mother forbade him to go near one of Uncle Terry's cars ever again. About a year after that, the uncle was speeding across an icy Dunn Bridge and died."

"What? He never mentioned a word of this."

"From what my mother remembered, Denny was at loose ends, edgy, cutting class. His mother was worried and badgered him to try to get involved in school. Since he was always athletic, she asked the football coach to encourage him to try out. Evidently, he became a football star who got the most beautiful girl at school." Blake stroked her cheek.

"I knew he didn't have a great childhood. I should have understood that his father taking off was important. But growing up the way I did and having no clue who my own father was, I never connected the dots. Dummy that I am. It never occurred to me that it could be the main reason he didn't want to become a father. Not the other excuses." She looked out into the restaurant. "He never told me anything about the cars but it makes sense."

Cynical, she said, "I guess I always knew he didn't join the Marines out of patriotic duty. It must have been wrapped up somehow with all that." She played with her spoon. "I think he wanted to be the man I was in love with but wanting doesn't make it so."

Kyra came to the table with a platter of stuffed grape leaves and squares of moussaka, mini gyros and souvlaki, eggplant salad, and olives. She also brought a small plate with lamb slices.

In unison, they said "Wow."

Kyra smiled, "Kali orexi! Bon appetit!"

"Saved by the food," Willow said.

At first, they picked at the food but with each bite, they put the past behind them, enjoying the new flavors, sharing a bite of this in exchange for that.

Over tea, Willow said, "What if I told you the great romantic is now skeptical about love? What if we're wrong about what this is?"

"We'll just have to spend more time together and find out. And I don't mean a few minutes together at the end of the school day." Blake kissed her hand. "Do you want to go down to the river? There's a jazz band playing on the Landing."

"No, Blake. Someone might see us."

"I don't care." Blake said.

"Yes, you do. I have a better idea."

"Sure. I'm game. Do you want to leave one of the cars here or drive separately?"

"No sense coming back downtown. Follow me."

He smiled as he pulled behind what the students called her propaganda car. The otherwise unremarkable blue sedan was covered with bumper stickers about the joy of reading.

Twenty minutes later, they pulled into a park. She grabbed his hand and pulled him toward such a perfect scene, it seemed surreal. A narrow waterfall, framed by thick pines, dropped into a sparkling pool. She backed up to him and he wrapped his arms around her. They listened to the rushing water. Willow broke the silence. "I stand here sometimes thinking about everything disturbing and after a time, it just falls away."

He pulled her closer to him. The fresh smell of her hair mixed with the piney scent of the trees, the moving water, the cloudless sky, overwhelmed him. Blake turned her to face him and they kissed. They both pulled away at the same time to look at one another.

"Mmmm," Willow said. "More."

Breathless, she pulled away and grabbed his hand. "Come, Blake. There is something I want to show you but first you have to promise me you won't tell another soul."

He kissed the top of her head and then followed her on a narrow trail. At a curve, Willow said, "Here's the turn."

"Off the trail?"

"Just a bit. Come see."

They ducked under some low branches and walked through moss into an opening. "Ta da." She spun around, arms out. "Isn't this absolutely amazing?"

A circular stand of white pines shaded a grassy area at the edge of a pond. A small clearing was dotted with patches of wildflowers—clover, violets, lily of the valley and a field of Queen Anne's lace. A slice of pond reflected the afternoon sunlight.

"How did you happen upon this?"

"On one of the unhappiest days of my life, I was walking on the trail. I thought I saw a patch of light and decided to investigate. At first, I thought it was a mirage. Then, the unexpected beauty seemed cruel."

They sat down near the pond, absorbing the sun's warmth.

"In what way?"

"Well, growing up in communes like I did you learn things…"

Blake laughed. "I'll bet."

"Not talkin' about that," she smiled. "The only thing normal about our education was gathering with other kids every day. Sometimes we went to a makeshift classroom, but often it was a porch, a field, a kitchen. We learned the usual stuff but much more about other things.

"See the field of Queen Anne's lace over there? I spotted it on that day. It's not just an innocuous flower— it's so invasive it chokes out the roots of anything growing near it. One of the guys who tended the fields told us the history and lore of different plants and how they could be used for food or medicine. I remembered his story about this flower because I thought it had magical powers. It was used as a diuretic to prevent and eliminate kidney stones, settle GI problems, and even cure hangovers.

"What stuck with me, though, was that the seeds were used for centuries as contraceptives and even as a morning after pill. I overheard one of the women telling my mother she ate a teaspoon full of seeds a few days before, during ovulation, and for a week after. She told Mama that she didn't know if it was preventing or aborting but it was working. So, when I came here bereft from another lost baby, I thought it was some kind of uncanny coincidence that these were the flowers that sought me out."

Blake shook his head. "For argument's sake, let's say that you were just brought here for their beauty."

"Yes, let's concentrate on their beauty."

"An interesting way to grow up."

"My mother, Grace, is an absolute original. She walks the walk, as they say. We moved around a lot. Autumn and I didn't attend a traditional school until we reached high school. And that was only because of my unrelenting begging."

"I won't ask when she was born, or was it conceived?" he teased.

"Very funny. At least, she got a season. Mama loves the sweeping grace of willows. Says it every time she sees one. I thought it might be too much information to ask her if I was conceived under one," she chuckled.

Blake grinned, "Where is your mother now?"

"California. She had breast cancer several years ago and was helped by the weed she smoked while getting chemo. Ever since, she's been on a campaign to make sure everybody has access. 'Whatever helps shouldn't be denied' is her slogan."

"She sounds wonderful," he nodded. "Guess the apple doesn't fall far from the tree."

Willow punched him lightly. "Yes. I'll tell you about life on an apple orchard sometime." She took his arm. "Enough about me. Your turn."

"This is hard. I never talk about this."

"If you can't…"

He revealed, "My only sister, Emma, died of leukemia when she was a teenager."

"Oh, Blake." She leaned into him. "Going to the Bentons' home this morning must have been hard."

He nodded. "After all the years, it took me right back. I could see myself in the face of that kid —the younger brother." He looked through the trees and composed himself. "After Emma died, I floundered. For two years, everything was about the next best treatment to cure her. She died the summer after I graduated. I went to college with not much more than a big hole and guilt for being alive and leaving my parents, too." He was thoughtful. "I met Jillian a month after I got there. I never knew anyone like her. She was delicate yet strong, dedicated, disciplined, wanting something so badly she worked tirelessly to get it. Me. I never had burning ambition to be the best at anything. I wanted to be a teacher like my parents. Supporting her dream, maybe even thinking I was a part of it, was enough for me. Maybe even a reason to be. Maybe I even thought Jillian's zeal would rub off on me. Faulty reasoning. And as we both know too well… life takes surprising turns."

"What do you mean?"

He shook his head. "When her personal dream fell apart, all she had left was mediocre me." He hesitated, "and a child I'm not sure she ever wanted." Blake swallowed hard, "I think it's fair to say, neither of us gave her what she needed."

"What was her dream?"

"She expected to become a soloist for a major ballet company. It was a young girl's dream she carried into adulthood and when she failed, it soured everything around her."

"Doesn't she own a ballet school?"

Blake laughed. "Apparently, she still subscribes to the view that those who can't do, teach. Another one of my failings. Needless to say, we don't have a happy house." He looked at her directly. "I want you, Willow. You're the woman I should always have been with. Every minute we spend together makes me sure of that."

Willow looked away

Blake said softly, "Without knowing it, I've been waiting for you."

"You and I have something in common. We were never right for our partners."

"Their loss. But then again. They were never right for us either."

She grinned, "You're right. Can I tell you how naïve and absurd I was? I was the little girl who drew the house with the neat shutters and tulip garden. When I attached myself to Denny, I thought I was going to live in that house. Can you believe it?"

Blake held her. "I'd be happy to live in that house. Some dreams shouldn't be given up."

"And how do we make this happen?" she cried.

"We'll start making plans. We'll begin to put us first."

"You make it sound like we can."

"Yes."

"A principal and school librarian. Great example."

"No. It won't be like that. As soon as you're ready, we're doing this right." He slid closer and brushed the hair from her face. "Now, let's change the memory of Queen Anne's lace forever."

They laid on the carpet of grass, the sun low in the sky, and made slow love, taking their time to learn one another's bodies, savoring each touch and kiss. The field of Queen Anne's lace seemed to watch over them, their gentle puffs blowing in the soft wind.

Chapter thirty-one
2011

At breakfast, Denny said, "I'm meeting a new client tonight. Do you want to meet me when I'm done? Get something to eat?"

Willow opened the refrigerator to put the juice away. "Not tonight. I have something," she said, vague.

To Denny, Willow was as lovely as ever. Time hadn't diminished her graceful curves from her long, slim neck to her tapered thighs. To him, she was still the beauty she'd always been despite the frequent frown that had replaced her quick smile. He was still aware of her every move though he doubted she noticed him at all. She reacted to his touch more like an unpleasant electric shock than the entrée to tender love making that used to be their life. Now, she couldn't wait to get away from him.

She pecked him lightly on his cheek, grabbed her lunch, and headed out the door.

Denny looked forward to meeting this new client. She was rich, one of those entrepreneurs with a successful dot-com business, whatever that was. He hoped she'd recommend him to other high-end clients.

Tonight was their first face-to-face meeting. The doorman buzzed him up, and with his carefully prepared renderings rolled up under his arm, he knocked on her door.

She answered in a sports bra and running shorts.

"Nicole? Am I early? I thought you said seven." His cheeks burned.

"You're right on time, Denny. Sorry for the way I look and probably smell. I was held up in a meeting and needed to squeeze in a run before you came."

She was damp with perspiration. He tried to avert his eyes but it was impossible. He had expected a computer nerd, not a Barbie doll. She had a lean, muscular body with a tiny waist and disproportionately large breasts. They were so oversized on her small frame, he wondered for a moment if they were real.

He cleared his throat. "No, you're fine. I brought three designs for you to look at."

"Great. Would you like a drink?"

"No, thanks." Denny's hands were too sweaty to unroll and separate the pages. The papers fell between them. Off balance, he kneeled to retrieved them and laid them on the coffee table.

She put up her hand and smiled, "I get it. This is a work meeting. Let me rinse off. Be back in a flash."

While she showered, Denny moved the designs to the large dining room table, spreading them out and securing them with hefty martini glasses from a tray on the table. He stood looking out the window at the city skyline at dusk and beyond that to the river.

Nicole walked to the window as she toweled her long blonde hair dry.

He moved away from her. Clearing his throat, he said, "Here are my three designs."

Nicole bent over the dining room table. She was so close he could smell vanilla on her skin. She took her time studying each one, moving slowly from one to the other but kept returning to the one in the middle. Pointing to it, she said, "This one."

"Good choice," Denny agreed. "It has great lines and maximum function. I'll build in a drawer for your jewelry in the center. Line it a fabric you choose. I have some wood and stain samples to show you."

"Not necessary. I want you to paint it with a high gloss red lacquer."

"Red lacquer?" Denny swallowed. "You sure about that?"

"Yes. When you've finished, I'm going to hire an artist to paint black poppies. I want a reverse motif."

He forced a smile. "As I always say, the client is always right. It wasn't what I had in mind but... I suppose that could make it an interesting piece."

"And maybe the first of many." She picked up the estimate from the table. "I still want the good wood you've factored in but choose one with the least grain. How much do you need to start?"

"Fifty-percent."

"No problem. I'm assuming you want a check. You don't seem like an online banking kind of guy."

"Right." Denny began rolling up his plans.

"Come with me. I want to show you where I plan to put it." She took his hand and pulled him into the bedroom. The beginning of her Japanese motif was evident. His eyes rested on a shoji rice paper screen.

She watched him. "You have good taste, Denny. Isn't the screen a beauty?

"I haven't seen anything like it since I was in Japan."

"Yes. It's the real deal. I wouldn't settle for anything less and I'm building the room around it. See the red in the pattern. That's the color I want." She locked eyes with his.

Denny looked down. "I won't be able to start right away."

"It's okay. I'm sure it will be worth the wait." She took his arm to walk him to the door. "Call me for a consult whenever. Or just drop by." She toyed with his collar.

"Sure." He opened the door to leave but then remembered his drawings. Walking to the table, he grabbed them.

She laughed, "And don't forget this." She waved the check.

He grabbed it, hurried to the elevator, and kept his finger on the down button.

He was stunned by the encounter. Rock hard, he imagined burying his head between her breasts, sliding his tongue across the firm mounds. He tried to think about Willow, imagine her body, how responsive she used to be. But that was becoming a distant memory. He didn't even feel like much of a man around her anymore. She had trouble looking at him and flinched at his touch. But this Nicole? She didn't seem to care that he was a lame, middle aged guy. Maybe she even thought he was attractive. Secure in the way she looked, how she had the world knocked, maybe she could infuse him with pure sexual energy, make him feel like a man. Or maybe he could take charge. Bang the certainty right out of Nicole, leave her spent, and walk away. What if she was half his age and a player? Maybe she could give him back something that got lost along the way.

Lily
2011

To: sbrooks@ualbany.edu; lstern@wow.org
From: lilylerner@aol.com
Subject: a poetry story

I wanted to send you both this blog.

Stephen: Poetry in action. Like you always say: poetry is where the truth lies.

Mom: The strength of women helping women. Your life's work.

Love you both. I'm due some time off and I need to see you both. I'll give you some dates next week.

The serendipity of you both living near each other is not lost on me. And now, with the news from Amber that she is joining a practice in Albany, everyone I love will be in one place.

Yours for always,

Lily

December 30, 2011
Blog Post: *As I See It*
Lily Lerner, WNN News

The Real Cover Up: Beneath the Burqa, Poetry Thrives

We write haikus in elementary school—three lines, seventeen syllables. 5-7-5. For many of us, they are the only poems we ever write.

I'd never heard of a landay. It's also a structured poem. With its twenty-two syllables, it is part of an oral tradition that's been around for generations. They are recited by mostly illiterate people, including Pashtun women living in Afghanistan and Pakistan. Traditionally, they are sung to a drumbeat.

Although the Taliban banned them, landays don't belong to anyone. Women have found laughter and power by creating them. This is evident in these three poems:

You sold me to an old man, father/May God destroy your home, I was your daughter.

For God's sake, I'll give you a kiss. /Stop shaking my pitcher and wetting my dress.

I call. You're stone. /One day you'll look and find I'm gone.

Out of necessity, women find surreptitious ways to cross the gap between who they pretend to be for survival and who they are. Forbidden to work, they go underground to find ways to create income. Forbidden to sing, dance, speak out, they find ways around this as well.

Quite surprising (but maybe not so much), there is a women's literary group in Kabul with a call-in radio show. They have set up a hot line for girls in the rural provinces to call in their poems. Imagine, living in isolation and having a place to be heard.

I don't know about you, but I found this to be an amazing story given the restrictions of Shariah law in Afghanistan. It is a call to all who feel voiceless. Share your words whenever and however you can.

An old adage is true. Nothing can keep a girl down.

Chapter thirty-two
2011

Denny wouldn't let Nicole embarrass him this time. He'd deliver the bureau, get his money, and leave. He wouldn't jeopardize the lucrative referrals she gave him. He wouldn't offend her. All he had to do was remember to keep whatever dignity he had left and resist her.

He'd never known anyone like her. She'd call to ask detailed questions about the bureau and then morph into raunchy phone sex. He imagined her standing naked in front of the big window, hoping someone would see her touching herself as she talked. He was aroused. Of course, he was. He wasn't dead yet. But he wouldn't play her game. There would only be one winner and it wouldn't be him.

Relax, Denny, he reproached himself. He wouldn't let the spoiled brat get what she wanted. He didn't like her and he didn't like himself when he was with her. Who did she think he was? Some pathetic loser? No, he still had some self-respect. Maybe he had a few moves of his own and could shift the odds to his side. Let her think she had him and then walk out.

In spite of himself, he showered and shaved, dabbed on some aftershave, and wore a new shirt.

She stood at the door waiting for him.

"Hi, Nicole." Denny tried not to look at her in her clingy, white silk kimono.

She flashed her perfectly whitened smile. "I'll call down to have someone help you bring it up."

"Not necessary. I got it. I just wanted to make sure you were home." Denny's armpits were already damp. *Jeez, what the hell?* He tried not to think about what her body looked like under that robe.

"I've chilled champagne to celebrate the first of many pieces I hope you'll make for me."

"Champagne? You really shouldn't have, Nicole. Can't stay."

"We'll see," she smiled.

He took his time walking to the truck, even sat in to compose himself before he maneuvered the chest onto the dolly. *Get in and out fast. No drinks. Maybe pick up some Rocky Road for Willow at Ben and Jerry's on the way home.*

The elevator door opened. He wheeled the gleaming red bureau into the bedroom, set it in place and unwrapped it.

"Denny, it's positively gorgeous!" She jumped up and threw her arms around him. "It's a masterpiece." She held him close and began to kiss him.

He tried pulling away but gave in to her deep kisses, in spite of himself. "Nicole," he murmured, pulling away, "What are you doing?"

"Seducing you, obviously. It's what I've wanted to do since I first laid eyes on you." She untied her robe and dropped it to the floor. "What's the matter?" she crooned. "I'm not turning you on. Let's see what I can do about that."

She leaned into him and tugged at his belt. He backed away from her flawless, airbrushed Victoria Secret body.

He hated the way she looked at him—a dare— as she put his hands on her breasts. He pulled away as if they were blazing.

Undeterred, she moved closer, put her hand on his crotch. "Oh, that's better, my wounded carpenter. I've been fantasizing about you, Denny, and I always get what I want. I want to screw you here on the couch, on the terrace, on the kitchen floor. You'll be a good boy. Let me trace all those ghastly scars you must have on that lame leg of yours. You will do everything I ask and I will keep telling all my rich friends to call you. And when you make them beautiful furniture, I will imagine us on it." She whispered, "My old, wounded carpenter, I'll spoil you. You'll never get me out of your head."

Her words cut him, thundered in his ears. Fuck the new clients she might get him. He stepped away from her. His breath ragged, he said. "No, Nicole. Get away from me. I don't want you. I'm not some pitiful toy you play with and then tell your friends."

She ignored him. "Just think all I can teach you to spice up your tired, old marriage." She began to touch herself. With her free hand, she pulled him to her.

Denny pushed her roughly. "I don't do this, Lady. Tough as it may be for you to get, I'm just not into you." The last thing he saw was shock on her face.

Afraid she would chase him out of the apartment naked or open her foul mouth, he tore down the stairs. He got in his truck and gripped the wheel to calm his shaking hands. His leg was on fire. *I'm a fucking freak show with a sign on my forehead flashing Loser. Willow doesn't see me anymore and this fucking nut job thinks I'm a pathetic experience. I wish I never survived my crash.*

He sped out of the parking garage on two wheels.

Lily
2011

When we talked, I said it. But let me say it again: Having hurt you breaks my heart. I don't blame you one bit for what happened with that other woman. I deserve it. I'm holding on to the fact that you said you broke up with her because she wasn't me. Don't give up on me yet, Stephen. Please.

I promise you I will never make another decision without consulting you. It was a terrible mistake. I am scared. I can't lose you. Please forgive me.

The program is tanking. Viewership is too low for the cost. At another time, I would've been devastated but now, I think I'd be relieved if it's cancelled. Maybe we should talk about my putting in for a stateside transfer. Would you still want that?

I have one more follow up story in Ethiopia and that's all that's solid for now. My producer suggested that I do some work here in London next. She wants me to explore the impact of the "troubles" between Ireland and Brits all these years later. It may be the last program and will mean I've come full circle.

I feel unmoored and lonely. And I miss everything about you.

Love, Lily

To: lilylerner@yahoo.com
From: sbrooks@albany.edu
Subject: We have a lot to talk about

Lily,

I'll call you Saturday at four my time. We have a lot to talk through. It's not a matter of forgiveness. It's about figuring out where we are headed. Together or apart.
    S

Chapter thirty-three
2012

Jillian pushed through the crowds at Penn Station. She stopped under the arrivals and departures board to get her bearings and noticed a young couple. A lanky boy, held on to his petite Asian girlfriend, clearly not wanting to let her go but her eyes were fixed on the board. She pulled away from him and kissed him lightly. He watched her walk away but she never turned around. They reminded Jillian of the many protracted goodbyes with Blake. He, holding her tight; she eager to get back. Perhaps, this boy was like Blake, clinging, but never saying don't go.

Rolling her suitcase behind her, she rushed past the competing smells of *Rosa's Pizza and Pasta*, *Zaro's Bakery*, and *Penn Sushi*, onto Eighth Avenue. Once outside, she began to feel more comfortable and slow her pace. The cold air was refreshing.

Georgia's sister, Heather, was out of town. 'It's yours for the week,' she said. 'Relax and enjoy it.' Jillian couldn't imagine being more unrelaxed. Her mission was daunting. She had to understand and accept what she'd avoided for twenty years if she was ever going to find any peace.

If fear was a motivator, it was working. When not irritated with her, Blake was completely disengaged. To make matters worse, she overheard him making plans with Chelsea for their own getaway while she was gone. He got tickets for *Les Miserables* and made appointments to visit several colleges in Boston. They never even told her.

Heather, lived in one of New York's most famous art deco apartment buildings, London Terrace, in Chelsea. Jillian would have to remember to tell her daughter she stayed in a neighborhood that shared her name. She'd think that was very cool.

It was once the largest apartment building in the world, occupying an entire square block. Now a centerpiece in Chelsea's gentrification, few of the long-standing rent stabilized apartments remained. The original mastermind of this magnificent building plunged to his death during the Depression before his vision was completed. Was that an omen? Jillian banished that thought.

Before going up to the apartment, she stopped at Joe's Café on the ground floor. She stood in line behind a woman and her thick set, teenage daughter.

"Just order something, Mom. People are waiting. I'll taste whatever you get."

"What if I don't want to share?" the mother teased, looking at Jillian. "The muffins here are to die for."

Familiar territory reversed. She'd never encourage Chelsea to have a treat. Note taken.

The mother turned to Jillian. "Look at you. You're probably getting black coffee."

Why do people think New Yorkers are unfriendly?

"Mom," her daughter reddened. "You're so embarrassing."

"It's our job. My daughter feels the same way. Ordinarily, I'm a coffee only girl but today feels like an everything bagel day." Jillian felt her chest open.

"Which is why you're a size two," the woman lamented.

"I have to watch what I eat. I teach ballet."

"It must be fascinating to go to a performance with you."

Flashing back to their night at the symphony, she grimaced. "I don't think my husband would agree."

"At least, he goes."

Jillian joked. "He does but he'd rather go to the dentist."

"You ladies want to order something or what?" the counter man growled.

The woman ordered and left with a large bag, her daughter dragging behind her.

Jillian finished her coffee, left most of the bagel, and stopped next door for a bottle of wine.

The doorman buzzed her in to an amber colored marble lobby. Jillian's jaw dropped when she unlocked the door to Heather's apartment, remembering what it once looked like. Georgia and Heather's aunt lived there for forty years but wouldn't recognize her apartment in its gutted, updated form. The brightly colored fabrics covering mission style furniture and lemony walls, took her breath away. A king-sized bed, covered with a downy comforter and soft pillows, was tucked into an alcove. She felt right at home.

Suddenly exhausted, Jillian dropped into Heather's inviting bed and fell into a deep sleep. She dreamt she was in dress rehearsal. She knew the steps to every note but her feet were crazy-glued to the floor. The music stopped. Everyone laughed at her. The other dancers' faces were contorted right out of Munch's painting, *The Scream*. Ugly open mouths shouted she should get out. The ballet master and musicians just watched. Their silence, a tacit agreement she didn't belong there. Somehow she leapt out of her shoes, leaving them stuck to the floor and ran out of the building. The cold sharp air left her panting. She woke up gasping and ran into the bathroom to splash cold water on her face.

Welcome back to New York, Jillian.

After a long soak in Heather's deep tub, she felt better and went for a long walk. Aimless at first, she walked to Lincoln Center. What a fool she'd been to think she'd ever dance there. How many girls had that same dream? About a million.

She sat on the edge of the fountain people-watching until the well-dressed crowd disappeared into the theaters. Walking a few blocks further, she stood in front of her school. It was an unremarkable stone building but it still contained Jillian's damaged spirit. She wondered if she'd muster the courage to go back inside.

Then, it occurred to her what she would do. She'd buy a notebook and write through each part of her life that led her to now. Simple spiral notebooks to keep her words honest.

She bought one at a Duane Reade and then stopped at a bodega for yogurt, fruit, and a pound of coffee. Jillian wanted to tell Blake her plan but he told her not to call him. Perhaps that was for the best. Nothing would be said to deflate her resolve, confuse her, color her intention.

Jillian woke early the next morning, brewed a pot of strong coffee, and sat at the table overlooking the courtyard. Staring at a blank page for what felt like hours, she began:

My heart pounded when Mom and Daddy brought me to school. This wasn't ballet camp. This was the real do or die. I told myself that if I weren't the best, I'd work double time to get there. I was scared walking into my first class. My legs were shaking but at the barre I went into my happy place. The repetitious familiarity was a salve. I was home.

It poured out—the sureness of the dream, the need to be the best and then the difficulty relating to the other girls (except for Jessica who tried to be her friend), the punishing schedule, her rise from the nervous little girl, to the hopeful one, to the expectant one, to the failure.

She wrote through the morning, into the afternoon, crying as she relived the conversation she let define her. She carried a big dream in her young body, worked tirelessly to achieve it, and then just walked away. Why didn't she fight to stay? Was Blake part of it or her excuse?

When she couldn't face any more, Jillian walked again until she was too weary to take another step. Back at home, she took her notebook and melted into the concave nest of Heather's multi-colored Papasan chair. With a glass of wine in hand, she opened the notebook and read. When she came to the end, there was only one thing to do. She ripped out the pages she'd written, set them in a pan in the sink, and lit a match to them. She watched the flame blacken and eat up all the words, curling in on themselves. When only ash was left, she doused it and threw it in the trash.

Jillian felt parole was in sight from her twenty-year sentence of regret and self-doubt. She couldn't change what had happened but she could be on her way to letting it go.

The next day was devoted to Chelsea. *I cheated her from the beginning. I never felt that overwhelming I'd-throw-myself-in-front-of-a-bus-to-protect-my-child. What kind of mother did that make me? Some women shouldn't have children. Was I one of them?*

A thought suddenly gripped her. *I was indifferent to her from the beginning.* She reeled from a pain that left her breathless. How could she not have seen this before? And then…she did to Chelsea exactly what was done to her. Judgment. Criticism. Her watchful eye that made Chelsea wary. Always telling her what she couldn't do, shouldn't do, painting her into a box that was the wrong size and shape.

As she wrote on, she exalted Chelsea's exuberance, her friendships, her delight in small things. Everything Jillian never experienced. As she thought about their relationship and her behavior, she felt herself shrinking. Shredding the pages as she wrote them, she sobbed, "I'm just like my friggin' father. The world according to me." *Chelsea blossomed only because of Blake… if left to me…Can I ever make things up to her? Of course, not. But maybe we can start from a new place.*

Although nausea overwhelmed her whenever she thought about Philip, he was part of how confused she was. *I knew from that first encounter, I would do something unforgivable.*

With each sentence, she tried to expel more of him, still horrified she'd slept with him. She filled pages feeling sick with shame because it was never just about him. It was Allegra, too. All of it circled back to how she cheated Chelsea and Blake.

After writing, she'd leave the apartment, wander through galleries, boutiques in Soho, touch silky fabrics, admire well cut trousers. She was determined to buy Chelsea just the right gift. Something Chelsea would choose for herself, not something Jillian would want her to wear. At last, she found exactly what she was looking for. A pair of boot cut jeans made of the softest fabric she'd ever felt. Distressed denim, just the right color, faded, yet not stonewashed. She found an oversized sweater in the sea green Chelsea loved, soft as cashmere without the itch. Finally, she felt she got something right.

She avoided writing about Blake until she could no longer put it off. As painful as it was, she thought, wasn't figuring out her marriage the main purpose of the trip?

Memories of Blake took her on a rollercoaster of happiness, regret, tenderness and anger. She relived how he stalked her at college before he had the nerve to approach her and how touched she was by that. His shyness mixed with resolve was irresistible.

After scratching out pages in which she continued to lie to herself, she made herself face facts. There it was right in front of her. The unflinching truth plunged her into an ice water bath. All the bitching and moaning about Blake and Chelsea's failings only masked her own. In her warped mind, she blamed him for her decision to walk away from dancing. The ifs drove her crazy....and ugly. If he hadn't been there to run to, would she have stayed? Found another company? Adjusted her dream? Was she so full of herself, so unyielding, that a life in the corps would not have been better than what she'd done? It was all so unfair. Blake was an innocent bystander to wreckage, a witness, a comfort who was then blamed for it. He never deserved the way she demeaned him in that self-righteous way of hers. A good man she cheated in every sense.

They'd never had a real partnership. She always wore him down. Always got her way. She couldn't even give him credit for what a good father he was and worse, ignored all the cues he gave her to do better with Chelsea herself. He more than pulled his weight in the important things and yet, she always found him wanting.

During a disagreement years earlier, her mother asked her if she was capable of loving anyone other than herself. She'd have to say now that while the first was in question she didn't love herself either. Not one bit.

The thought of living without Blake was crushing. Was that love? She didn't know. But she was going to believe that it was and that she could find a way to make him love her again. That is if she could she leave that young, spoiled girl now woman in New York.

Time was running out. She had to go to the school and confront Madame Olga. She phoned to make an appointment but hung up before anyone could answer.

After a brutal morning tossed about in the undertow of her emotional life, she decided to go to a ballet matinee. That morning, she thought about her own ballet students. In writing about Allegra, she tried to focus on the girl rather than the girl and her father—who never came into the studio again, never asked her what happened.

There were few students in her school like Allegra. It occurred to her as she wrote her litany of complaints about the others, she might be able to teach them what she thought most important regardless of what they did with it. If nothing else, they would learn good posture, grace, attention to detail, the value of discipline. Maybe she could inspire them to always love ballet. Perhaps bring them to see ballet at its best. This was an entry she would keep in her desk to read before the noisy, influx of students arrived each day.

Walking through the lobby at Lincoln Center, she was drawn to a tall wood block sculpture decorated with text. It reminded her of how much Blake and Chelsea enjoyed playing *Jenga*. They'd laugh hysterically when the tower fell. She never joined in and then resented them for it. Now, one block stopped her: love and kisses/nothing lasts forever.

She instructed herself to just sit back and enjoy the dances. She'd seen them before—George Balanchine's classics. He was known to have said, "One is born to be a great dancer." *How did she think she could bend that truth to her will?*

When the curtain finally fell, she realized it was possible for her to admire a dancer's fluidity and ethereal athleticism without comparisons.

Walking out of the theater, she felt ready to face the dragon and hurried to school before she lost her nerve. Despite butterflies and lightheadedness, she took the stairs two at a time. It was much smaller than the cavern of her memory. She sat down on the bench near the office to slow her heartbeat.

A gray-haired woman walked toward her. "May I help you?"

"Perhaps. I was a student here. May I look around and perhaps, speak to Madame Olga?"

The woman shook her head. "I'm sorry to tell you this, my dear, but she is no longer with us."

Jillian faltered. "Not here? Where did she go?"

"You misunderstand me." She sat down next to Jillian. "She had a stroke. Died right in her office."

Jillian's eyes burned.

"Most of the girls thought she'd give them a stroke. And she didn't improve with age," the woman smiled. "When were you here?"

"About twenty years ago."

She peered into Jillian's face, "After all these years…"

"She may not have remembered me at all."

"I doubt that. Have a look around. I doubt anything has changed since you were here. Maybe that will help you."

She stood up. "We keep clippings of our students' successes in the office. Feel free to look through them. I have a class now. Should you decide to take a look, the scrapbooks are on the shelf behind the receptionist's desk organized by decade."

"Thank you. You've been very kind."

The woman lamented, "There are more disappointments contained in these walls than triumphs, I'm afraid." She stood. "I hope you find what you came for."

Jillian walked down the hall and peered into the studios. Empty, they were all the same. Barres. Mirrors. Floors. It was up to the dancers to bring them to life. Jillian took off her shoes and walked into the room she practiced in for that elusive part. She didn't feel a thing. It was a studio like any other.

She knew she couldn't leave without knowing who made it. Opening the scrapbook, her trembling fingers could barely separate the pages. There were five articles from around the time she was there. They were all about a Jamaican dancer she didn't recognize who ultimately joined the Dance Theater of Harlem. The one girl she tried unsuccessfully to emulate evidently didn't make it either.

Walking back to the apartment, she decided she to call her old roommate. *I was awful to her. No amends could make that right but maybe I can apologize and see how she is.* Heather had a phone book and she found a Jessica Jarreau listed in Brooklyn.

"Jessica, this is Jillian Golden, used to be Kent. Did you study ballet at…?"

"Holy cow, Jillian!" Jessica exclaimed.

Jillian smiled. "I'm here visiting."

"What happened? You were my roommate and best friend one minute and the next, you vanished."

"It's a long story."

"I've got all the time in the world. I've been waiting years for this mystery to be solved."

"I just got homesick."

"Bull-ony. You wanted it worse than any of us."

"So, what are you doing now? Married? Kids?"

Jessica ignored her. "'We thought you had a nervous breakdown. Ogre was a monster. Remember Mary Moran? She disappeared on us, too, and we heard she killed herself. She always seemed too fragile for life in general, let alone the kind of stress Ogre put on us."

"That's awful," Jillian swallowed.

"Well, no getting out of it. I've waited a long time. What happened? Nobody would tell us a thing. For all we knew you could have been kidnapped. You didn't even take all your stuff with you. I wouldn't have known you were okay if your husband hadn't called. He badgered me wanting to know what happened. And when I called you, you wouldn't even talk to me. I don't mind telling you how hurt I was."

"I'm sorry, Jess. I really am. I was all messed up back then. It wasn't all that dramatic and none of it matters now. How long did you study there?"

"Two years after you left. Foot injuries. Three surgeries. After a while, my need to walk superseded my desire to dance."

Jillian laughed, "Good decision."

"Yeah. Plus, I met a great guy. Now, I'm a realtor with three kids."

"And happy?" Jillian asked.

"Hell, yes. What about you?"

"We have a daughter and I own a ballet school."

"That's awesome. Gives you the best of both worlds, doesn't it?"

Jillian hesitated for a moment. "Did you know that Olga died?"

"It's too bad the witch didn't die before she ruined even more lives. God, I hated her."

"You did? I just thought she just pushed us to be the best."

"You're kidding, right? She wanted me to dance with three broken bones in my foot. Called me names when I wouldn't. She was a sadist. Her only joy was causing misery."

Barely audible, Jillian asked. "Is that what everyone thought?"

"Oh, honey. She was one sick ticket. The only thing she lived for was to break the most vulnerable girls. I always hoped she didn't scar you for life."

Jillian didn't answer.

"Well, I'm sure you're the kind of teacher little girls need."

"I try to be."

"Great to hear from you. Glad everything turned out well."

"Take care, Jessica."

Numb, she sat in the chair as the day faded.

On the train ride home, Jillian braced herself. It was now clear to her that she never valued what was staring her right in the face. She understood repairing her damaged marriage would be an uphill battle but she could do it. She would do it. They loved each other once. She would make him remember the girl he once loved and he would once again become the wavy-haired boy who took her breath away.

But as the train sped toward home, she had to push away the sinking thought that sometimes injuries can be so damaging, there can be no recovery.

Chapter thirty-four
2012

To get into group therapy at the Vet Center, Denny had to sign an agreement that he'd attend all sessions. *What are they going to do? Sue me if I drop out?*

When he got there, a couple of guys were milling around in front of a closed door. Denny nodded to them, thinking they looked as unenthusiastic as he was. When the door finally opened, a tall, balding man, with wide set brown eyes and acne scarred face came out. Denny stared at him, willing himself not to run.

"Follow me," he said, showing them into a windowless room with blank walls. There were metal chairs around a long table and a cart with a coffee pot reeking of burnt coffee and Styrofoam cups. He gestured to them to sit.

"I'm Ed Turner, psychotherapist. From the looks on your faces, it's apparent none of you want to be here. It's okay," he joked. "I'm not sensitive."

No one reacted.

"Okay, then. Here's my speech. The concept behind cognitive processing therapy has been explained to you. The work we do here is hard, but it works. Before we get down to business, I'm going to answer your unasked questions. I've been doing this work a long time and have seen the most hesitant of you helped. Those of you who think it's bullshit need to lose it if you're tired of living in your own versions of hell."

Dr. Turner looked around at the impassive faces. "Next. I'm not military. I haven't gone through basic or any of the deployments that have brought you here. That being said, I've been serving longer than anyone here. For twenty-five years, I've been doing the work Department of Defense should be doing but doesn't. Until they step up, I'm all you've got."

A few of the men nodded. Denny tapped his foot.

"Just because you're not living under a bridge doesn't mean you aren't suffering. Recurring nightmares, sleeplessness, sweats, headaches, flashbacks, periodic confusion. Any of that sound familiar to you? I'll bet it does. I've sat in rooms just like this collecting and managing all the terrors and guilt that have brought hundreds of soldiers to me. And I've helped.

"But it only works if you're honest and, believe me, I've been doing this long enough to know when I'm being jerked around. These are the ground rules. We're a unit. You follow orders as you did before, only they come as assignments. You agree now or you leave. The work we do is hard but worth it." He looked at all of them one by one. "Okay. I'll give you five minutes to decide."

Denny stared at the door. If he left, what then? He'd be back home with his sorry self and a disappointed Willow. What the fuck? He'd give it a try. He nodded to Dr. Turner, grabbed some coffee and sat down. A round faced guy with a potbelly and a couple days' growth on his face, sat next to him.

"I'd rather have a beer," he mumbled to Denny. "I'm Hal."

"Denny."

One guy left, three others who looked like they were thinking about it eventually sat down.

Dr. Turner took a seat. "Okay. Let's get started."

Denny pulled up to the dark house. He went through each room flicking on lights, as if to say to the absent Willow, I'm trying. He didn't remember where she said she'd be. She probably didn't.

He took a beer out of the refrigerator and slapped down the yellow tablet and pen the shrink gave him. He stared at the empty page through his first beer. By the time he was halfway through the second, he was ready.

The dream: We landed on a makeshift runway in Eastern Saudi Arabia and were transferred to a busy base called Scud Bowl. I felt safe there but that was short lived. A dozen of us were sent north to...

Lily
2012

"Stephen, I know it's late but I had to hear your voice," she quavered.

"Lily? What's wrong? What's happened?"

Lily sobbed.

"Babe, what is it?"

She didn't answer.

Alarmed, he asked, "Lily? Are you still there? Are you hurt? Where are you? Are you on assignment?"

"Give me a minute." She blew her nose and then walked around the living room. A moving light outside caught her attention. It was only a car. She sucked in a breath. "There was a bombing…"

"Are you hurt? What happened? Tell me."

"I'm fine. It's just. Well. I freaked out. I couldn't do what I had to do. Couldn't do what I always did. I just…"

"Slow down, okay? Take some breaths and start from the beginning."

Lily sat down on the couch. Then, she stood and moved to a chair by the window. "A bomb tore through a restaurant here in London. I got there with all the responders. The usual chaos was all around me but it's mostly fuzzy." She stood up, closed the curtains, and moved away from the window.

"It's okay. Just tell me what you remember."

"A woman lying in the street. Her leg was blown open. I was confused, seeing things. Flashbacks, I guess." She hiccupped. "I think I knew I was in London but —I saw a row of African girls covered in their mothers' headscarves. They were wavy at first. Then clear. I wanted to go to them but before I could, they disappeared. I had to stay with the screaming mother. The noise was deafening but all I could hear was her pleading to find Ella. I think that was her daughter's name. No, maybe it was Joanna. I don't remember. I don't know if she found her. I have to find out… I can't even remember how I got home. I have a pounding headache. Have had one since…"

"Do you want me to come?"

"I don't know. I'm so tired, Stephen."

"I know you are. You need a break."

She said flatly, "That's what my boss said."

"She's probably right. I'm sure it's not the first time she's seen someone…"

"She said she could transfer me stateside for a couple of months, if I wanted. I could have a *less stressful assignment* until I was ready to come back full throttle. But first, I had to take time off and talk to someone." She whispered, "I don't think I can."

"You need to talk to someone, sweetheart. This has been building."

"No, not that. The work," she shuddered. "I can't do it anymore."

"Talk to me."

"I just want to come home to you."

He didn't answer her.

"Stephen, are you still there? You don't want me to come? After all…" her voice trailed off. "Please. I'm so sorry I was stupid and selfish. Will you ever forgive me?"

"This has nothing to do with that. Listen to me. You're going through something really big. I was afraid of this. I'm sorry this happened, babe, very sorry. But in some way, it's a good thing." He paused, "You've been headed here. Now, you are forced to stop. Consider alternatives. We'll figure this out together but coming back like this is a no-go. You have to come to me to go forward. Not to say yes to something you couldn't agree to until now."

Her voice dropped. "I thought you'd be ecstatic."

"How could I be when you're this low? You have a world of options. There are many paths for you to consider if you need a break from reporting. But first, you have to talk to someone who has experience with this kind of trauma."

"If I'm not a reporter, what am I?"

"Quit the drama, Lily."

She laughed in spite of herself. "No reporting? No drama? Will you recognize me?"

He laughed, too.

"I'm serious. Isn't what I do part of what you love?"

"Of course. But it's not who I love." He soothed, "See someone who counsels reporters. Take your time. We'll talk it all through. Every day. We've waited a long time to get this right. And, Lils... know that I'll be on the next plane if you need me now."

Chapter thirty-five
2012

After the ruckus of changing classes, Willow stopped Blake in the empty hall. "You remember Laurel, my friend from…"

"Of course, I met her at the book signing."

She smiled. "Of course, you did. She called last night sounding urgent about needing help at her lake house. She insisted you come with me. Now that I tell it, she was pretty vague. But she never asks anything of me so I'd like to go. What do you think? Take a couple of days at the end of next week? Maybe extend it into the weekend? It would be glorious."

"Couldn't agree with you more." He sighed, "I hate to lie but there is a conference in Boston I could conceivably attend. This duplicity is no good. It's time, Willow."

"I know."

"Tell her yes."

She beamed. "I already did. And Lucy Randall, who just retired from the middle school, said she'd cover for me."

His eyes twinkled. "That sure of me?"

"Absolutely."

"Denny, I'm going to the state library association meeting next week. It's from Wednesday to Sunday."

He lowered the volume on the remote. "Great! It'll do you some good to hang out with other librarians and I'll be fine." He paused. "By the way, I went to the Vet Center last night. Met some good guys."

"I hope you aren't doing it for me."

He curled his lip. "Yeah. Well, whatever."

She turned away. She hated her lies but had no idea how to tell him the truth.

It was an hour drive. "There's a great oldies station I think we can get." She fiddled with the radio and found it. She started singing along with Mama Cass. He laughed, joining in. One song led to another and they sang off-key all the way.

She pointed to the sign coming up. "We're here already." Willow directed them off the main road and through the village center. "Turn here," she pointed. A narrow gravel road took them to the lake.

"Can see why they call it Glimmerglass."

"It's actually Otsego Lake but when James Fennimore Cooper called it Glimmerglass in his *Leatherstocking Tales*, it stuck."

Blake smiled at her. "Always the librarian."

Laurel's house was a chocolate brown clapboard A-frame on the lake. Dressed in flowing palazzo pants and matching tunic, she waved from the front porch. As soon as they turned into her driveway, Laurel ran to the car, pulled Willow out and wrapped her in a tight hug.

Blake gave the women a minute.

Laurel came around the car to hug Blake. "Welcome to mi casa."

"What a spot!"

"Sure is," she agreed. "Hungry?" she asked. "I thought we'd have breakfast together before I leave."

Willow exclaimed, "Leave? Where are you going? I thought you needed…"

"I'm going to New York. I lined up a bunch of meetings and interviews to keep me away."

"Hey, did you cook this up with Autumn?"

Mischievous, she grinned, "No. I do need you. If you're here, I don't have to worry about the place. Now get your stuff. I'm making my famous pancakes with lemon blueberry butter."

"I'll get our bags, Willow. You go in with Laurel."

They walked into the house with their arms around each other's waists.

"I knew I had to 'need' you to come. That Willow hasn't changed. Maybe while you're here you'll think about what you need for a change. I'm hoping that if you spend uninterrupted days with Blake here, you'll stop wasting time."

After Laurel left, they took her boat out. There wasn't another soul around on this unseasonably warm spring day. Blake rowed with ease. Willow brought her small pocket book of Persian poets. "Listen to this, Blake." She softly recited a Hafiz poem that always made her feel grateful but never more so than at that very moment.

He reached across and pulled her close to him. "Read me another. Surely you have some Rumi in there as well."

"How do you know that wasn't Rumi?"

"You forget. I'm an educated man. There is Hafiz and then there's Rumi, Hallmark's new discovery," he teased. "Personally, I'm all about Ganjavi. *He who searches for his beloved is not afraid of the world.*

"You are always surprising." Unable to resist for another moment, she pulled off her dress, straddled him and they made love. Afterwards, the sun warmed them as they lay on the floor of the flat-bottomed boat and floated on the glassy lake. Willow closed her eyes, listening to the lapping water beneath her, the birds whoosh through the air, the ripples of the pooling water made by the schools of fish just beneath the surface. "I don't think I've ever been this happy. It scares me."

"Don't let it." He pulled her closer. "We've waited too long to do anything but savor and appreciate this. You're a miracle."

"If you want miracle, wait until you see the sunset. The lake reflecting the sun takes on the appearance of striated color on mirrored glass."

"While that sounds incredible, all the beauty I need, well, I'm looking at her."

Laurel anticipated all their needs. There was a freezer full of meat and fish. She bought fruit, vegetables, eggs, artisan cheeses, fresh pasta, and pie. Several bottles of white wine were in the refrigerator and there was a case of red. Two fishing poles and a tackle box were in the mudroom. She left a note on the nightstand.

Dearest Willow and Blake,

We never know what can befall us between the breaths we take. The great lesson of our communal childhood was to become masters of our lives. There is no reason to squander any more time. Whatever debt you both feel you owe your partners has been fully paid. Be happy together.

With love and hope,
Laurel

Blake took the note from Willow. "She's right, you know."

The loft bedroom had a wall of windows facing the lake yet they were high enough to feel private. They made slow, lazy love because for once, they had time.

While Blake still slept, Willow slid out from under him and took a bubble bath. Then, she went to the kitchen, poured herself a glass of the cabernet. She hummed as she cut vegetables for the pasta they would have tonight. The simmering sauce brought Blake downstairs. "Something smells awfully good."

"It's just about ready. Foolproof deliciousness."

"Is that a word?" he asked, as he always did, and poured himself a glass of wine.

"Here," she dipped a wooden spoon into the pot. She blew on it. "Taste."

"You're right. There's is no other way to describe this other than definite deliciousness. I'll set the table. Want me to make the salad?"

"Sure."

They each set about their tasks, working around one another, as if they'd done this all their lives.

As they got ready for bed, Willow asked, "What do you want to do tomorrow?"

"That's an easy one. I want today to be our Groundhog Day for the rest of our lives."

Willow and Blake were swaddled in their own world. They finally had a solid mass of time just to be. To wake up together, prepare a meal, read to one another, take a walk. They tasted life together and understood there could be no going back.

Blake talked about Chelsea. "It will throw her even though she's asked me countless times why we stay together. No kid wants divorced parents. But she'll adjust if we do it right. And it won't be long before she's in college falling in love herself. Besides," he smiled, "we may not be young but we're not too old to give Chelsea that sister she's always wanted."

"I wouldn't count on that."

"I wasn't counting on you showing up in my life either. And yet, here we are."

They made their plan. Willow, still uneasy about telling Denny, knew she'd have to find the words. Blake was gone in his own mind even before Jillian left for New York. He finally felt the cloud eclipsing the sun roll from view.

They would waste no more time. As soon as they returned, they would tell Jillian and Denny they were leaving them. Then, they would meet at a downtown inn and begin their life together.

Part Three

Aftermath
2012

Forgiveness does not change the past
but it does enlarge the future.

– Paul Boese

"It's never too late to be
what you might have been."

– George Eliot

Chapter one

There is little sleep for anyone that night except for the still unconscious Willow. Denny circles, paces, and sits in the waiting room and in the ICU, terrified. At daybreak, he goes home to shower, hoping to wash away his dread.

Under the streaming water, he screams *no* over and over. He doesn't care what the doctor said about her luck and strength. They're all liars anyway and can't hide the truth from him. She's a pincushion with drips and machines buzzing, beeping, breathing for her. Even if she does pull through, he knows better than anyone what happens when pain, like his Demon, becomes your life. Hell, if those miscarriages rocked her, what would this do?

He blew yesterday morning. If only he had a clue about what would happen later that day. They hardly spoke. This parallel living had become their new normal. She'd been distracted that morning as she had been for months. Why didn't he say Willow, where are you? Talk to me. He's a coward, that's why, afraid to hear what she might say. If he hadn't been his tortoise self, pulling his head back into his shell, maybe she wouldn't be unconscious and broken. Maybe, if he finally woke her up, she wouldn't have been preoccupied and gotten into an accident.

He blubbers, "What did I think? If I made dinner. Or more money or pretended to want what she wanted, she'd love me again?"

Out of the shower, he curls into a ball on the bed, sobbing.

Spent, he reaches for his migraine pills. The intense throbbing has blurred his vision but he realizes he can't take them. It might knock him out. He almost welcomes the burning inside his skull. *Come on, Demon. I deserve every last needle stick of pain. Bring it on.*

Disjointed sleep comes but it's filled with elongated shadows, crushed cars on slick roads, police sirens, Willow gone.

When he wakes up, the headache still throbs but he'll have to manage. He gets out of bed, makes it and straightens up the room. Willow always nagged, 'last out of bed should make it.' But he rarely did. It annoyed her, yet he refused. *Why couldn't I do something as simple as make the bed if it was important to her? Stubborn asshole.*

Life without her is unthinkable but the doctor said she'd be all right, that he fixed her injuries. Maybe, at last, a doctor is right. He has to be.

Chapter two

The thought of seeing Willow lifeless in the ICU makes Denny want to punch walls. He walks slowly down the eerily lit hallway, past a nursing station with blinking computer monitors, to her cubicle.

"Mercy, I want to know everything," Autumn insists. "What do all these machines do? What can she feel? What exactly is an induced coma?" she gulps.

"Whoa, honey. One thing at a time. Let's start with…" Denny walks in. "Come in. I'm Mercedes Bianco. But everyone calls me Mercy. I'll be taking care of your wife today. I assume you are Mr. D'Angelo. No party crashers allowed here. Immediate family only."

"Denny," he nods, finding a sliver of wall to lean on.

"Where was I? Dr. Sheldon is her intensivist."

Autumn frowns. "Intensivist?"

"Critical care specialists do one-week rotations here. Dr. Sheldon's also a pulmonologist. Good for Willow since her lungs are an issue. We're big here on continuity of care and every patient has a team. I'm her day nurse and I have only one other patient. Her night nurse will be Jack Morris. The nurse practitioner, Kerry Lockhart, works directly with Dr. Sheldon and will check her throughout the day. Specialists will come in —her trauma surgeon, a neurologist, a GI doc. A therapist who…"

"Therapist?" Denny interrupts. "She's unconscious, for Christ's sake."

Amused, Mercy laughs, "Not that kind. Respiratory."

Autumn ignores Denny. "Tell me everything."

"Okay. Stop me if I'm giving you too much. Let's start with her lungs. She has a tube to help her breathe. As the amount of fluid in the chest tube decreases, we'll get a chest x-ray to see if the lung is inflating properly. We'll do breathing trials by pulling back on the induction medication. As things progress the way we hope they will, we'll wake her up slowly. We may have to keep her on the ventilator a bit longer because of her rib fractures. They'll make taking deep breaths painful.

Autumn grimaces.

"A chest x-ray, oxygen levels in her blood, and breathing strength will tell us when she's ready to breathe on her own. When the tube does come out, she'll be hoarse. The tube irritates the throat, but within a couple of hours she should be able to speak."

Autumn points to all the apparatus. "Tell me what all this does."

"We need to keep track of blood pressure, pulse, oxygen level, temperature, heart rhythm. The ventilator will set off an alarm if any parameters are off. The bags give her fluids, antibiotics, and other meds."

"What about her brain?" Autumn's voice shakes. "The surgeon said she hit her head. How do we know if it's a coma you're controlling or a real one?"

"Don't worry about that now. She probably banged her head hard given the deep laceration but that's all we know. Even though she's still unconscious, they can do a basic neurological assessment. They may do a head CT scan to check for bleeding or other things, but let's not go there yet. And while Dr. Horan isn't a plastic surgeon, he's meticulous. I doubt she'll be left with much of a scar."

"He didn't mention any of that to us," Autumn sighs.

Mercy smiles, "No surprise there. He's a trauma surgeon. He was probably focused on all the possible problems he may have headed off, no pun intended."

Looking at their somber faces, she continues, "Try not to let your minds wander to what could happen." Mercy squeezes Autumn's hand. "She's conserving energy to allow her body to begin healing. We'll check her often to make sure the surgery site isn't red or swollen, that the sutures aren't infected. But for now, all is good. Concentrate on that. Questions, Denny?"

"No," he mumbles.

Autumn asks, "Can she hear us?"

"She's out but I wouldn't say anything you wouldn't want her to hear. Hearing is the last sense to go and family drama can cause problems."

"What do you mean?"

"Once I was taking care of a patient and her sons began arguing. One actually punched the other. The mother must have heard it all and her blood pressure skyrocketed. She was clearly in trouble. We call it 'bucking the vent' when a patient fights the ventilator and can go into respiratory distress."

Mercy shakes her head. "I've heard and seen it all. Here's a classic. Two daughters hold vigil at their mother's bed. Lord, those two were something else. Every time I came in, I interrupted their infernal bragging about who was the favorite and conjecture about the will. First thing the mother said when she came to was, "'Don't you wretches have anything better to talk about while I'm lying here?'" I tried to contain myself. Either, she wasn't in as deep as we thought or maybe she just knew her girls," Mercy laughs.

Autumn smiles, "We all want to be best loved, don't we?"

"Sure do. Do you still have your mother?"

"Yes. She's on her way from California. Mama's always been convinced she's a healer. Let it be true."

"Grace is coming?" Denny scowls. "Just what we need."

Mercy ignores him. "Any more questions?"

Denny shakes his head.

"Okay then. Stay positive. All things considered, she's doing pretty well."

Autumn clutches that last bit of optimism and holds it tight.

"Kerry will be here soon to check the incision."

"Thanks so much for explaining everything so clearly, Mercy."

Mercy nods and looks from Autumn to Denny. "You know, maybe this would be the time to mend fences. This space is too small to hold baggage and it's not good for Willow."

Autumn balks. "That fence is way beyond repair, all the boards are thoroughly rotted."

"That's your business. But if your conversation isn't cordial, take it outside. Willow's needs are front and center. As hard as it is to get in the ICU, it's that easy to get thrown out," she cautions.

Autumn sits close to her sister with her back to Denny. He hovers for a while and then positions his chair so he can focus on her pale, still face, looking for traces of his once vibrant Willow.

Chapter three

Willow and Autumn are children planting seeds in the big garden at the commune in the Finger Lakes. The field is vast. Jesse, a tall, tanned man with round wire-rimmed glasses is an experienced farmer. This is a vegetarian community and they have a short growing season. Everyone is required to pitch in, even the children.

It's Willow and Autumn's turn this morning. They love to work with Jesse and run to the fields holding hands. They know their jobs. He has a tool to dig holes in long straight lines. Willow drops the seeds. Autumn covers them.

Jesse's a gentle man who makes up stories and silly rhymes for the children. Willow and Autumn giggle so hard, they double over in laughter. The morning flies by. Jesse says, "We're finished, girls. Count how many rows you've planted. You'll see it's more than you think." Willow starts at one end, Autumn at the other. Counting, they skip toward each other.

Willow loves the sound of Jesse's gentle voice. She squints, trying to pull his face into focus and sees it's not Jesse at all. It's Blake.

The planting finished, it's time for them to go in for lunch. Blake takes her hand. She looks at Autumn who nods for her to go with him. Autumn smiles at Blake. She trusts him and Autumn doesn't trust easily. Willow knows he must be good. He wraps his warm hand around hers. She looks up at him and seeing his smile, grasps it even tighter.

Chapter four

All night long, Blake wanders from one part of the hospital to the other. Now, he sits in the large lobby that doubles as a surgical waiting room. People sit in clusters, ready for their long wait— knitting, doing crossword puzzles, staring at the TV blaring CNN.

He watches a petite, white-haired woman's lips move, rosary beads in hand. A couple sit gripping each other's hands, worry etched in their young faces, a threadbare bunny propped up on the woman's lap. A drooling, golden retriever therapy dog, bounds through the room allowing the worriers to pet him before turning back to their distractions.

Blake can't sit in this room overflowing with anxiety when his own is cresting. He walks outside to the courtyard. A fountain with a marble statue of St. Bernadette is in the center, forcing him to walk in circles. *How can he get in to see her? He has to see her.*

He replays the newscast in his head. Shaking his head vigorously to obliterate the ghastly picture of Willow's crushed car, he realizes he should call school. He is stricken all over again when he sees all the calls he made to Willow before he knew.

"Nora," he cleared his throat. "It's Blake."

"Thank heavens. How is she?"

"You know? Of course. The news."

"Tell me."

He knew so little. "She came through the surgery and is in ICU now."

"I see." She let a moment pass. When he didn't say anything more, she said, "Well, don't worry about anything here. I've cleared the week's meetings."

"How did you...?" he sputters.

"Don't give it a thought, Blake. Stay where you need to be." She breathes hard. "Listen to me. She's going to be fine. She's strong willed and has a lot to live for. We're all pulling for her. And you."

"She has to..." His voice breaks.

"Please keep us up to speed and if you need anything at all, consider it done."

"Just look out for Chelsea, okay? I don't know what she knows. She'll be devastated about the accident." He hesitates, "And what must she be hearing?"

"Is there anything you want me to tell her?"

"Just that I'm at the hospital and I'll text her when I have news. I'll see her as soon as I can."

"Of course. Blake, for what it's worth, I've been a school secretary for thirty years. Schools can be a breeding ground for malcontents, but the gossip mill is heavily in your favor. Even though she annoyed the hell out of some of the teachers with all she demanded of them, they admire her. I'll keep my eye on Chelsea. Don't you worry."

"Thanks, Nora. I appreciate that. I'll call you later." He clicks off and goes back into the hospital.

Not knowing what to do next, he passes the chapel and reluctantly goes in. He's alone. Early morning sunlight illuminates the stained-glass windows, warming him. He lights a candle and sits in the front pew.

The last time he had been in a church was for Chelsea's baptism. Blake quipped that if Jillian had any religion at all, it was dance. When Chelsea was born, having her christened didn't cross their minds, but Blake's mother insisted. It was surprising. She never interfered and stopped going to church when Emma died. "A christening is a milestone for the family as well as the baby. Even if you don't believe in original sin, it's a celebration of a new life. Nothing will happen to her but if it does..." She never finished the thought.

It was a small thing to do for his mother but Jillian didn't see it that way. "If you give in to this, what's next? Never pegged you as a mama's boy."

That stung. Although he let it pass, he knew then she didn't fight fair.

As it turned out, his mother was right. It was a wonderful day for them all and Blake was glad she insisted. He suddenly realized something that never occurred to him before. Jillian felt there had been sides to choose and he chose his mother's. Maybe this was the reason she was always cold to her mother-in-law. He shook his head to push out the past. None of that matters anymore.

He tries to pray but can't. After his sister died, he didn't have much use for God. He didn't know if he could bring himself to bargain or plead again. If there were a truly merciful God with any interest in the people Blake loved, He or She would not have let this happen to Emma or Willow.

Lighting a candle is all he can muster.

Blake feels too far away from Willow in this silence. He heads to the cafeteria. Maybe the surgeon will be there. He buys a cup of coffee, scans the room, and sees Autumn sitting at a nearby table. Her blonde bobbed hair is tangled, standing on end; her face is blotchy and her blue eyes are rimmed red. She clutches an untouched cup of coffee and idly crumbles a blueberry muffin.

Blake takes his coffee over to her table. "Autumn?"

She looks up at him and motions him to sit.

"I waited and waited for her, panicking, thinking Denny threw a fit. I never imagined it could be something like this."

She smacks her head. "I should have realized. She must have been trying to figure out what to tell Denny. Why else would she have gotten into a senseless accident? It's always him. God, I hate him."

Blake said, "Never mind that now. Tell me everything."

Autumn mangles her muffin with a plastic knife. Looking down at the crumbled mess, she tells him all she knows and starts to cry.

Blake, willing his own tears away, holds her as she cries into his shoulder. When she's able to stop, she sits up straight in her chair, blows her nose, and breathes deeply.

"Denny went home for a few hours so I had some peace with her. When he came back, I had to leave. I can't stand being in such a confined space with him."

He shakes his head. "Our plan was no good."

Autumn clenches her teeth. "She should have sent him a tele-gram. Or better yet, a text message."

"She's Willow. She wanted to tell him in the least damaging way. It was the wrong way to go about it. We should have known that."

"No, don't go there. We just have to take care of her from here." She stirs her coffee round and round. "I'm going to believe the worst is over and her recovery has begun. We're going to get her though this. We'll just have to tell Denny ourselves it's time to get the hell out of her life since she didn't have the opportunity to tell him herself."

Blake smiles. "Willow didn't do you justice. She described you as a force of nature but I didn't have quite the right picture."

"You think I am? Wait until you meet our mother, Grace. She'll be here in a few hours. Sisters are close for a lot of reasons but for us, it's symbiotic. We always depended on each other. The only time that got screwed up was when Willow was hell bent on staying with that loser, no matter what he did."

"I'm happy you're on my side."

"Don't take it personally. To be honest, my eye was totally on the prize—get her away from Denny. The truth of the matter is, I wanted her to leave Denny and come live with me. Give herself time to sort things out. But, no. Willow was in love. She didn't want another second away from you." Autumn sighs, "You better be who she thinks you are."

She concentrates on her destroyed muffin. "We need a strategy. She will need you to draw her out. She has to hear your voice. What to do? What to do?" She mashes the blueberries. "They're so strict up there. You practically need proof of citizenship to get into ICU. Wait a minute. I know. Blake." She looks at him squarely. "I've al-ways wanted a brother."

"Your mother will go along?"

"Grace believes family has little to do with legal details, or blood for that matter, so in her mind if Willow needs and loves you, that's it. The way she thinks, you'd be the real husband, anyway. That's our Mama."

"I can't wait to meet her." He stands. "Let's go up."

"Can't. Denny's with her now. Hang on. I'll get you in.

Chapter five

Denny stares at her. Willow's skin has a bluish tint. The breathing machine, drainage tubes, IV drips, and filling urine bag, make her look more dead than alive.

"Willow, you've got to get through this," Denny whimpers. "I can't lose you. I know things are strained between us, you angry at me about the babies and all. But you still love me. I know you do."

He closes his eyes and squeezes out the tears blurring her face. His breath is ragged. "We'll get past all the old stuff. I was always screwed up, you know. Uncle Terry stepped in to straighten me out. He taught me how to make stuff so I wouldn't be at loose ends. He thought he was helping me get shit out of my system by racing but he was dead wrong on that. Putting me behind the wheel of a fast car was like giving a junkie smack.

"I never told you about any of that. I was afraid to. I know I should have talked to you before I joined up, too. I was young and stupid, but mostly, I couldn't take the chance you'd talk me out of it. You could've, you know. You had that kind of power over me. I guess I'm glad you made me go to that shrink. I'm learning a lot about myself."

He looks away from her and then rests his hand on the sheet.

"But that look in your eyes—that stunned look when I told you about the Marines— I still see it, you know. I'll be trying to fall asleep or working on something and there it is."

Denny walks to the door and back, shaking out the stiffness in his leg. He sits down again, leans in close to her.

Autumn comes back. When she sees Denny bent over Willow, she stands in the doorway, listening.

"The thing about you, Willow, is that you never see anything the way it is. The whole family thing wasn't right for us. I couldn't pull off pretending to want what I didn't want. But you, with that crazy childhood of yours and your whacked-out mother telling you if you want something badly enough you can make it happen. All that bullshit talk about destiny and karma and chakras. It's so fucked up.

"I know you blamed me for the miscarriages. I can hear you and Autumn now. You saying, it's bad karma, the babies knew what they'd be born into. And your bitch sister telling you to lose me and start over." Silent for a moment, he sniffles, "And then I found out you were gonna leave me over it."

Autumn is about to step forward but stops.

"I saw the adoption application papers and that you checked the divorced box. I couldn't believe you'd pick raising somebody else's kid over me. I wasn't going to let that happen so I told you I was ready to adopt. I didn't want you to know I snooped so I convinced you I really changed my mind." Wistful, he sighs, "But you didn't go ahead with it because you knew we were what always mattered most."

Tears roll down his face. He smooths the wrinkled covers and gently rests his hand on hers. Backhanding his tears away, he exhales deeply. "Anyway, it's all history. I forgive you for all the things you did behind my back. And finally, you'll just have to forgive me. Life's going to be hard for you now. It's good you don't have children depending on you. I don't know much but I know pain, and it's nothing compared to what you're facing. But I'll take good care of you. I promise."

Autumn feels herself growing taller, ready to pounce. She can no longer contain herself.

"You forgive her? You would do her a big favor by letting her adopt a baby? You know all about pain?" she seethes. "Well, so did Willow long before last night."

Denny jumps, startled.

Autumn can't stop. "Forgive her, you selfish bastard? You think she needs to hear about all the pain she'll be facing? Stupid moron. Get out."

Denny's voice trembles. "You have no right. What I say is between my wife and me." He stammers, "I, I... have every right to be with her. You can't bully me."

"Yes, Denny." Her voice freezes, sharp as icicles. "You have a legal right to be here. But this is what's happening. We're making a schedule so I don't have to see your pathetic self. I'm picking Grace up at the airport in an hour. We'll rotate. I'll be back at two. You'd better not be here," she orders.

Hang-dogged, he agrees. "I'm only saying yes because the feeling's mutual."

"Good. And another thing, Denny. Didn't you hear what Mercy said? Willow might be able to hear everything we say. Try not to make your conversations about poor Denny. It may make her not want to wake up."

Before he can answer, she's gone.

Chapter six

Jillian roams after leaving Blake at Dunkin' Donuts. She tries not to think of him rushing to that woman's bedside. She drives through town finding herself at family landmarks— Washington Park, Chelsea's schools, their favorite diner, *The Gateway*, because Chelsea thought they made the best, gooiest, grilled cheese. She realizes she winced every time Chelsea said it, hoping now it went unnoticed.

She then stops in front of La Serre, thinking back to the awful night Blake caught her flirting with Philip and then exploded; the night he revealed her corrosive secret had never been a secret after all. She felt sick all over again remembering his disgust.

She parks in front of her ballet school. It was there that she knew how to be a good wife. Her devotion, pride, love, attention— qualities all wrapped up in those walls.

What now?

She rolls past her in-laws' house. They were disappointed their son chose her but they were always thoughtful. Her mother-in-law baked her an angel food birthday cake each year, respectful of Jillian's disdain of sweets. In return, Jillian oblivious to the gesture, would murmur a thank you and barely eat a forkful. Yet, despite Jillian's rudeness, they sent flowers when she opened the studio and at recital time, appreciated whatever she'd contribute to holiday meals. But they couldn't love her. She wouldn't let them.

She heads home. The dark houses on her quiet street frighten her. Rolling slowly toward her own house, she realizes she never really looked at them, never saw their distinctiveness. She hadn't made friends with any of the neighbors beyond a nod or forced smile. The only names she knew were the ones that Blake and Chelsea spoke about and the parents of Chelsea's friends.

If I disappeared, no one would notice. She imagines a reporter or the police going house to house as they did when a crime was committed. The neighbors would say we really didn't know her very well. She seemed pleasant enough. Maybe a little snooty. But she did buy my daughter's Girl Scout cookies and my son's Pop Warner candy bars. That was nice. Now, her husband and daughter. Well, that's another story.

Exhausted, Jillian goes home. Georgia's asleep on the couch; Chelsea's curled on her side, a bunch of crumpled, wet tissues have fallen out of her hand. Jillian sits on the edge of her bed watching her sleep. *I have to step up in a way I never have. Am I capable?* She smooths Chelsea's quilt, collects the tissues, and goes to her room to lie down.

Jillian hears Chelsea and Georgia in the kitchen but can't get up. She may have slept but doesn't feel the least bit rested. Her limbs feel like lead and her head hurts. She wants to cry but an icy numbness creeps in.

"Honey, here's some lunch money. I have to go in to work but call me if you need anything."

"Dad will be at school, won't he? C'mon, Georgia, there's something else. Tell me. I can handle it."

"I don't know much of anything. If, and I only mean if, he isn't there and you want to come home, I'll get you. Now, go so you don't miss the bus." Georgia gathers her up in her arms. "Don't worry, sweetheart. It's a rough patch. But everyone will get through it."

"A rough patch? Mom's a basket case and Dad's gone." Chelsea wails, "And when I get to school, it's all going to be about Mrs. D'Angelo."

"On second thought, I'll drive you."

Chelsea hiccups, "Do you think she'll die?"

Georgia dabs her face with a tissue. "Let's be positive. She's under good care. Primo trauma center in the northeast."

When Jillian hears the car start, she sits up and puts her feet on the floor. One foot after another. That's how you dance. That must be how you continue to live.

Chapter seven

Sitting at the kitchen table, Lily works on her laptop and Stephen is reading the newspaper.

"Done. Just sent Rich today's blog."

Stephen looks up.

"When I first started writing a blog, WNN was trying to pad their website and thought it was a good intern job. I've written through everything I covered, even some things I didn't if the subject interested me and it was newsworthy— I didn't realize it would become one of my favorite things. And this morning, I can see us writing books here right at this table."

His eyes gleamed. "You can, can you? What kind of books would you like to write?"

"Oh, I don't know. Investigative Reports. The story behind the headline. The history of something. I'm babbling." She closes her laptop. "Anyway, back to the blog. Of course, I volunteered. I volunteered for everything wanting to become indispensable and visible."

He smiles, "No surprises there. It was a great idea. It foreshadowed the way we get our news now."

"What do you mean?"

"The lines between news and opinion is blurred. Opinion, reflection, and analysis all interpret the facts."

"I suppose. Even bozo Rich said yes to a regular post and I didn't know he knew how to say yes."

Stephen frowns. "He's not the only one."

"I think I'll ignore that crack for the moment. Stephen, what if…" she stops herself.

"What if what?"

"Oh nothing." She checks her phone. "Rich should be calling any minute. You watch. He's going to come up with a lame assignment today as payback for last night. And I have to get back to the hospital."

He shakes his head. "Lily, no. You have to back off. The family needs privacy."

She glares at him.

"Think about it. What if it were you? Would you want your anguish observed?" He crinkled his forehead. "Why do you want to go anyway? Hanging out at hospitals has never been your thing."

She pours herself a second cup of coffee. "I can't tell you why. In my gut, I know this accident shouldn't have happened."

"That's what makes it an accident, Lils. Be honest. Is your interest news or curiosity? Or just plain resentment that Rich won't let you do whatever you want."

"Harsh, Stephen." She darkens. "I don't know what's driving me. The only news left in the story is whether or not she'll recover. The human-interest part of it is the why. Doubtful there was something wrong with the car. It's the triangle that makes it compelling. Maybe I got all embroiled in this because of well, you know, even while following a car accident I come across it again."

Stephen finishes his coffee. "Come across what?"

"Love blazing into destruction."

"Lily, you don't know anything at all about whatever is going on. And... they're not us."

"Maybe not now."

He grins. "How can you possibly resist us after last night? It was pretty spectacular and here we are sitting in the morning sunshine. Love is hard to knock. That's why we all chase it so hard." He sings, "*All you need is love.*"

She laughs.

"This is all I've got to say. Follow your gut right back home to me tonight."

She kisses him. "I've got the bread crumbs all laid out. This is an awfully nice way to start the day."

"Keep that thought. Gotta run. I have to meet with a student before class."

After Stephen leaves, Lily looks through the newspaper. The council meeting is on page one, not the local section. *What a lousy paper.* She looks for the item on the accident. It's buried and taken from the police log. *Name, accident location, hospital. Pathetic.*

Procrastinating a bit longer, Lily calls her mother, Lisa. "Morning, Mom. Got a sec?"

"Morning, sweets."

"I have a question."

"Shoot."

"Are you sorry you never got married?"

"Lily, for heaven's sake, I haven't even had a cup of coffee yet."

"Pour yourself some and then answer me."

Lisa sighs, "I don't know what more to say. We've talked this to death."

"It seems everywhere I turn, I get signs that scare me."

"What kind of signs?"

"I covered an accident last night."

Lisa was silent for a moment, pushing aside her memory of another car accident. One that changed the course of her own life. Finally, she said, quietly, "I know. I saw your report. Poor woman."

"I spent most of the night in the hospital."

Lisa didn't answer.

'Mom, are you still there?"

Lisa shook it off. "Why would you do that?"

"Her husband is a beat-up mess. He can barely walk and has this haunted look in his eyes. And he was alone."

"Haunted how?"

"It's hard to describe. He just seems off. Anyway, he was alone, so I stayed with him. Then after a couple of hours, his wife's sister arrives. They obviously hate each other. Around the time the woman gets out of surgery, Blake Golden shows up."

"My neighbor Blake?"

"None other. There's no question he's in love with the accident victim. Ha. How many times have we said he and Jillian look like they have it all? So much for appearances. Then, there is the accident itself. I don't think it was an accident. How could it have been? She was stopped at a red light and then just sped through it. So…"

"Stop right there. It could very well have been an accident. Maybe her brakes weren't working right or something unusual happened. Your imagination is working overtime, my dear. Although I do think the politics of love can get pretty interesting," she snickers. "So, what's this all about? You think you're involved in this mess for a higher purpose?"

"Don't mock me, Mom. It's a sign and it's smacking me right in the head. I'm sure of it. Why after all my months of losing my reporter self, did I come back to life to follow this particular story? First time since ... since London."

"You sound like your great grandma. She saw signs everywhere it was convenient. Her imagination was a runaway train," Lisa laughs at the memory. "But let's not get off the subject. The real story is not the one you're obsessing about. My darling, the only thing you need to decide is whether or not you love Stephen enough to take a leap with him. That doesn't have anything to do with anybody else." She paused. "What happened to those people is their story, not yours."

"I'm scared, Mom. If I try to put him off, it's the end this time."

"Progress. You finally understand that. I know you're under a lot of pressure. You have big decisions to make on all fronts."

"Are you sorry you never married?"

"Back to that again," she sighs. "What can I tell you? The answer is yes and no. It would have been nice to have the right someone to share my life with. I wanted more at one time. But once I had you, it didn't seem as important. I had the Women's Center. Maybe I never got over my losses. Who knows?"

"What about Daddy? Aren't you sorry about that?"

"It just didn't work out for us. But Stephen is nothing like your father. Listen. You were a journalist when he met you. That's who he fell in love with. Think about what life would be without him and I think you'll find your answer. Who did you call when you fell apart? And what did he say? Come home, get married, and have babies. No. He said, come home and we'll figure out your next move together."

"How do you know this? I never said."

Gleeful, Lisa said, "I have powers."

"Very funny."

"This is what I wonder."

"What do you wonder, Mom?"

"What's so hard? Think of your life apart and together. And I mean really without him in it at all. If you're honest with yourself, you'll realize just how much space he's always taken up. He's been your lover and confidant for years. Don't kid yourself." Lisa sighs deeply. "You know hours after you were born, I knew Daddy wasn't going to come through for us. I realized right off I was going to have to be strong for the two of us and thought naming you Lilith would give you an edge. My thinking then was that by naming you Lilith for the first woman, the one born as her own person, not the one from Adam's rib, I was giving you something important. You chose not to use it, opting for Lily, but in some ways, I think it binds you. You don't lose your strength or independence when you share a life —if it's the right life."

"I don't want to repeat Daddy's mistakes. He's always loved you and I know he's sorry he blew it."

"Probably. But bad judgment isn't necessarily hereditary. Gee. That's a good one. Sometimes I even surprise myself with my wisdom."

Lily laughs. "What if my next move was a new job in a different city. A more commutable one."

"You got a job offer?"

"It's just a hypothetical," Lily hedges.

"This is all I have left to say. You have many options. You live in a time where you can work from anywhere and with your experience, you can do many interesting things. But that being said, if you want to do what you've always done and fly solo, then get on with it. End of story. Some people can't manage a personal and professional life. I don't happen to think you're one of them. But, what do I know?"

"Any other momilies this morning?" Lily smiles into the phone. "You seem to be on a roll."

"One more. Every decision has risks. There are many meandering trails in our lives. If you make a wrong turn, it might be bad for a bit, but then something else opens up. Say you're right about what's going on at the hospital. Maybe they were planning a second chance at love."

"Ew, Mom. Corny."

"Maybe. Listen, I've got to get going. If you have time for lunch tomorrow, call me."

"I will. Thanks, Mom. Call you tomorrow."

No sooner had she hung up, the phone rings.

"I have an assignment for you."

"Well, hello to you too, Rich. Did you get my blog? Good. All right. Where am I going and what am I doing?"

She takes down the details. The middle school's trying out some new, healthy menu items. Soda machines were pulled yesterday. See how everybody feels about it. *Big whoop. Maybe I can swing past the hospital on the way back to the station.*

Lily decides she's still hungry. She grabs a bagel from the bag on the table and smiles. Stephen is going the distance to make her feel at home. Even down to making sure she has sesame bagels and veggie cream cheese.

Preoccupied, she holds the bagel in her hand to cut it in half when the knife slips and gashes her thumb. "Damn," she cries out. She holds her hand under cold water and presses a paper towel to absorb the blood. One sheet after another turns red. The bleeding doesn't stop. The slice is deep and hurts.

Lily wraps her hand in a dish towel. "This was not how I planned to go to the hospital," she cries.

May 9, 2012
Blog Post: *As I See It*
Lily Lerner, WNYS News

By the Grace of God: Local School Librarian Injured in Car Crash

This is the headline. A beloved high school librarian was seriously injured on her way home from school last night. She was in surgery for several hours and now faces an uphill battle back to herself.

Let's be honest. When we hear about or see an accident like this we think *that poor woman*. Her family. How life can change in a second. It could happen to anyone. It could happen to us. But by the grace of God.

We think about the "if onlys." If only she had taken a different route home. If only she had been a minute later. If only she was driving a newer car with side airbags, or a heavier car that might not have crumbled, or one higher off the ground. If only the florist had one less delivery that day.

You get my drift.

This particular accident is hard to explain away. And we always need to hear there are reasons for an accident to make us feel safer. Her car was stopped at a red light and inexplicably flew through the intersection.

What happened?? Understanding why and how this accident occurred seems important to us for our own sense of safety. Perhaps one day, she'll be able to tell us.

But what about this thought? A quote attributed to Napoleon: There is no such thing as an accident, it is fate misnamed.

Do you think there is any truth to that?

Fate. That's unsettling. It takes control out of our hands altogether and casts it to the wind.

And then there is outcome. If she survives, what will her life look like? Will it be the life any one of us would want to live? Or,

350

perhaps, there will be a miracle. She will have crossed the line we all fear and returned to her life. A relief.

None of us are really untouched when we hear a news report like this. The precarious nature of our lives is something we try not to think about. From one breath to another, whether we are breathing deeply or holding it, everything we take for granted can dissipate as easily as a child's bubble floating through the air one minute, disappearing the next.

Think about that and make today your best yet.

Chapter eight

Grace grips Autumn's hand as they're buzzed into the ICU. "Prepare yourself, Mama."

Willow's mother stands at the foot of the bed, motionless. She backs away and runs to the bathroom down the hall.

Autumn stands outside to give her mother privacy. Retching over the toilet, Grace empties herself. When her sobs peter out, Autumn goes in to make sure she's all right. Grace turns on the cold water full force to wash her face and then takes the pin out of the long gray-streaked blonde hair piled on her head and reworks it into a knot at the nape of her neck.

"I'm ready now. We have to let Willow know she has no choice but to get well."

"That's right, Mama."

Grace smiles. "You haven't called me that since you were a young girl. It feels right today." They hold hands as they walk back to Willow's room.

Mercy is resetting one of the machines.

"Mercy, this is our mother, Grace."

"Hello, Grace. Autumn, you must be happy to have your mother here."

"I sure am. Are there any changes?"

"No. The surgical resident, Dr. Whiteman, just left. Nothing unexpected has come up. Dr. Horan will be in later. Why don't we give your mother a few moments with Willow?"

Trying to squelch her panic, she walk-runs to match Mercy's long strides. They stop in front of the nurse's station. "What's wrong? Is there something you didn't want to say in front of Grace?"

"Sometimes I may soften up the truth but I never hide anything. Not for me to decide such things." She peers over her half glasses.

"This unit is for family only. It's important to minimize disruption. There is a man who has been in the waiting room all morning. He stops every staff member leaving the unit and pleads with them to tell him what they know about her."

"Blake."

"Lordy, he's a mess of a man if I've ever seen one."

Autumn was silent a minute. "He's our brother."

Mercy snorts. "Your brother. Odd he didn't mention it." She shakes her head. "Autumn, understand this. There is no room for drama here. Willow is my only concern. Anybody and I mean anybody who causes her distress gets the boot."

"Willow needs Blake. It's Denny you should keep out."

"Nice to see such close siblings."

"We're taking shifts to stay out of each other's way. As family, Blake will be with us. Can you bend the rules to allow the three of us? Please, Mercy."

"You see all kinds of comings and goings here. Too many labels —husband, wife, mother, sister— that don't mean a damn thing. But the hospital has rules and I have to follow them. Hear me, Autumn, if I see or hear anything, and I mean anything, that's not good for my patient, all bets are off."

"Thank you. Willow will also thank you when she wakes up."

Blake is still sitting in the waiting room, attuned to every footstep in the hall. When he sees Autumn, he jumps to his feet. "Any change?"

"The surgical resident says the incision looks good. Listen, Mercy didn't believe me but she'll accept you as our brother. We're splitting shifts with Denny and we have to make sure there's no overlap."

"Let's go." He sprints to the door and rings the buzzer.

Autumn can't suppress her smile.

Blake is startled when Grace turns around. Like Autumn, she is petite but her face is the image of Willow's. Though her eyes are puffy, the shape and blue are the same. Her complexion is toughened by too many years in the sun but she has the identical splash of freckles across her nose and cheeks, the same texture hair, and the same open face.

"Blake," she whispers. "We'll help make her well, won't we?"

His eyes shine. "We will."

"Stand back and let me look at you. Yes. You're just as she described." She points to the chair. "Sit and talk to her while Autumn and I grill the staff. I'd like to do Reiki, if they'll allow it."

He nods and stands where Grace had been, willing himself not to cry. "Willow, when you wake up, we'll all be here. You'll get well and then…"

Blake takes everything in at once —the rhythm of the machines, the blinking monitors, her stillness. He closes his eyes for a moment to block it all out and then makes it all fall away. It is only the two of them. He then looks into her face, strokes her arm avoiding the tubes, and kisses her palm. It is when he covers her hand with his that he feels hers move.

Chapter nine

If a painter stopped here, he'd spend his life capturing its exceptional beauty. Against the backdrop of sky blue, a parade of floating cotton balls wander the sky as we drift in a rowboat on the sparkling lake. It feels as close to a perfect moment in all the clichéd ways. It must be what heaven is like. I am so light; the air is moving through me.

It feels somewhat familiar but there is a surreal quality to it. I feel like I have been lifted out of my colorless, familiar life and placed in one deep with color— but vast and unformed.

Whoever is rowing has his back to me. His aura is calm and steady. I know it can't be Denny. He is never calm.

I am in the boat and yet I'm watching. I should be afraid but I'm not.

I want to keep going. Drift across the lake, late into the day when the sky turns pink and coral and violet and gold. Farther and farther away from what I've always known.

The rower will always hold my hand firmly so we don't lose one another. I will squeeze it to make sure he knows not to leave me. Map, destination, time are irrelevant. If I'm with him, wherever we go is where I should be.

Chapter ten

Grace and Autumn come back with Dr. Horan. He glances at Blake. "Would you all step out for a few moments?"

The three of them huddle. Blake remarks, "The family resemblance is unmistakable. If the two of you had your backs to me, I wouldn't be able to tell you apart."

"I got the body and height or I should say lack thereof. Willow got the face. We never knew our fathers, but there was no mistaking our mother."

"I know you might think it's wishful thinking, but she squeezed my hand. I'm sure of it."

"I don't doubt it for an instant. You should leave before Denny gets back." Grace instructed, "Bring back some of her favorite books? You can't really know her and not know what they are."

"True enough. I'll bring Neruda and Dorianne Laux, oh, and Mark Doty — one of her new favorites. And let's read her the *Secret Life of Bees*. She's doing it in book club this…" He chokes, catching himself. "It's her book this month. Maybe it will make her remember she has someplace to be."

"Perfect." Autumn says. "I'll get her music. Grace, you stay here with Denny. I walked in on him saying awful things to her. About how she was going to have a lifetime of pain…" Autumn whimpers.

"Denny didn't mean harm. What he says doesn't come out quite the way he means them. I'll talk to him about staying positive."

Autumn grimaces. "Oh, no. Here he comes."

Denny limps toward them, his leg wooden. "Grace."

She embraces him.

Awkward, he pulls away and glowers at Blake. "Who are you? Young for Grace, aren't you?" he snipes.

Blake doesn't answer him.

"Wait a minute. I recognize you now. The school principal. What are you doing here? Family only. Can't you read?" He points to the sign.

Blake's tone is even. "I came to see Willow."

Denny is about to say something but his vision blurs. He leans against the wall to steady himself.

Blake ignores him. "I'll get those things you asked for, Grace."

"Remember, Denny," Autumn glares. "Two hours and then it's our turn."

"I don't want you here. Don't come back," he says to Blake's back.

"What you want doesn't matter," Autumn retorts. "Grace, I'll be back as soon as I get Willow's CDs. We'll catch something to eat before Denny leaves. And Denny, remember, conversation that will make her want to wake up." She runs to catch up with Blake.

"Well, Denny, my boy. It's just you and me." She takes his arm to steady him and they walk back in. "I have a salve that will help your knee."

Denny mops the sweat off his forehead with his sleeve and looks down at her. "You never change."

"Ah, yet I do. Life is change."

Grace motions for Denny to sit. She takes a tube out of a large macramé bag.

"No, Grace. Don't need it."

"I can see you do. Come now. It will ease the burn." She kneels and rolls up his pant leg. "I made the paste myself." She rubs the salve on and around his knee and down his shin. "There. You should feel relief as it penetrates. How about if I put some on your temples? I saw you were dizzy before."

Gruff, he snaps, "I'm fine. Sit down."

"I prefer to stand. Especially when I tell you something you won't want to hear."

"There's enough going on without listening to your crap. Let's just sit without talking."

She ignores him. "Willow's accident has shadows around it. Something happened to her in the car before the crash. I can intuit her state of mind. If she wasn't bracing herself for something difficult, she wouldn't be lying in that bed, broken."

"For God's sake, Grace."

"If you allow yourself to think about it, you'll know why. It's time for you to face your life as it is."

He squirms. "Cut it out. I'm in no mood for your mumbo jumbo."

"All right. Never mind that now. Just talk to her. Let her know you're here. I'm going to get some tea so you can spend some time alone with her."

With Grace gone, Denny's nervous. Seeing Blake spooked him. *What the hell was he doing here? The three of them looked pretty tight. Face your life, Grace says. Next, she'll be pulling out her tarot cards. No wonder Willow can be birdbrained.* He shook his head.

He moves the chair and bends low to talk to her. "I'm back. I don't like being home without you. Even though you didn't talk much lately, you were always moving, spinning around the house. It's too quiet without you."

"I was thinking." He takes in a deep breath. "As soon as you get out of the hospital and rehab, we'll go somewhere new. I could use the change in scene, too. I've been dizzy and lightheaded. You being sick is already taking its toll. If you were awake you'd be saying, I know you have a headache, take a pill, make Demon go away. But I can't. I can't risk missing you wake up."

What can I say to make her want to wake up? Got to keep talking. Happy times. "Remember the *Seeing into Our Life Game* we played. I'd describe a place—somewhere in the Adirondacks, or a dune cottage on Cape Cod, or the French Quarter in New Orleans— and you'd fill in all the details. But..." he croaks, stopping before he can go on. "But in the end, you'd always say, anywhere I'm with you, Denny, is the best place to be. When did you stop thinking that?"

He stops rambling and stares at her. Scared, he goes on. "But it was the name game you liked best. We'd play it when we went to the overlook at Thatcher Park. Remember? We'd stand looking across the escarpment with the long view of the valley. You'd rest your head against me and you'd say, 'Denny, I want four or five kids. We'll give them meaningful names, real names, not like Autumn and me. Joshua. It means leader. Andrea or Andrew means strong. Matthew is a gift from god. But most of all, I love the name Blake. *I am in you and you in me/ mutual in divine love.* It will be a gift to our son to name him after the poet.'"

"'Really? I'd ask?' And you'd say. 'Absolutely. That line is one of my favorites. It's us.'"

Denny cringes. He hadn't thought of those conversations in years. Why did he even bring it up? And he hadn't remembered she liked the damn name Blake, either. Shit. No, he wouldn't think about that.

She was always clear about what she wanted. He made it all impossible, destroying that love. Through all the years, he never cried. Now, it was all he could do. The years of holding back coursed through him as a ceaseless river. He's drowning.

Grace comes back and gently strokes his back. "Denny," she croons in his ear. Placing her hands on his shoulders, hands practiced in soothing colicky babies, angry teenagers, the heartbroken, the bereft, Grace says, "You can pretend and avoid, but in the end, truth grounds us. You know she's already left you. You may not believe it now but people adapt to things they don't think they'll survive. And so will you."

Just as she thinks she feels his shoulders relax, he jerks away. "Shut up, Grace."

Chapter eleven

Jillian is standing at the counter waiting for the coffee to brew when Georgia gets back. "You look like hell. Where'd you go last night?"

She shrugs. "Everywhere and nowhere." Jillian takes two mugs from the cabinet. "I have to ask you something." Fearful, she gulps, "Georgia, have I been a good friend? Have I been capable of at least that?"

"For about thirty years. Otherwise, why would I hang around?"

Jillian's eyes well up. "I don't know what I'd do without you."

Georgia smiles, "In case you haven't noticed, I'm here to stay."

"How upset is Chelsea? Did she talk to you on the way to school?"

"I won't lie. She's had her life turned upside down. And then there's the accident. She's never had anyone close to her die or be seriously hurt. But she'll be okay. Kids are resilient."

"She has to be."

"Jilly, you'll be fine with her. Don't worry."

"Don't worry? I've never done a thing right with her." She shudders and pours the coffee with a trembling hand. "Can I ask you a favor? Call Madeline and tell her to cancel classes for the next two weeks? I know she'll want to know why and I just can't talk to anybody right now."

"You sure? You need your routines. Otherwise, what…"

"I can't."

"Sitting here with nothing to occupy you?" She pauses, looking at a shrunken, tentative Jillian she's never seen before. "Never mind. Maybe it is a good idea." Georgia takes cream out of the refrigerator and fixes her coffee. "So where did you go last night?"

"Here and there."

Georgia arches her eyebrows. "Where?"

"I drove to all the old familiar places. That was a song, wasn't it?"

"What places?"

"The diner, the pizzeria, the park, the high school, the bar where I should have noticed my marriage was over, the hospital."

"What? No."

"Don't worry. I didn't go in and make a scene." She exhales deeply. "Before I got to the hospital, I realized something awful. I've been sleepwalking through my life. I've spent every minute of every day calculating what's next. The memories I should have been fondly turning over in my mind or the ones that should have been ripping me up just weren't there. I wasn't thinking about this good time or that, or even for a way to become a family again. I felt like a visitor in my own life. Pathetic."

Georgia opens her mouth to interrupt but thinks better of it.

"I don't know what I thought I'd do when I got to the hospital." Tears trickle down her face. "Fine time for me to be spontaneous." She tries to smile. "Even in the state I was in, I knew it was wrong to go in. But I wasn't ready to come home so I went over to the Dunkin' Donuts across the street from the hospital and who's sitting in the window? Blake."

Georgia arched her eyebrows.

"Yup. You could see the pain he was in and it sure wasn't about leaving me," Jillian sputters.

She sniffles, "I was desperate to turn things around when I came home from New York. Even before. Maybe I knew it was too late but couldn't face it. I don't even know what pushed things over the edge. Was it me or her?"

"What exactly did Blake say to you?"

"Very little. He was consumed with worry. You could even see fear in his eyes." Jillian dabs her face with a crumpled tissue. "He didn't have a thought in his head about what he left behind. Even if she dies, he won't come back. He loves her. Of all the terrible things I realized tonight, you know what was the hardest?"

"What, honey?"

"He once loved me like that," she laments. "What I saw in his face tonight is that I'm erased. Disappeared."

"Oh, Jilly."

Jillian feels like she can't get a full breath.

Georgia interjects, "May I remind you how unhappy and dissatisfied you've been. Think about why Philip happened. You're scared. You feel rejected. But in the end, Blake just isn't the guy for you. Never was."

"Just keep reminding me. I'm terrified."

"I know you are. The circumstances are awful but it may be the best thing for you. I'll call you when I'm about to leave work. See if you want me to come back. A night alone with Chelsea might be best. Claire wants to stop by but I told her to call first. Another friend, by the way, who loves you." She kisses her cheek. "Get some sleep now."

Jillian drags her comforter to the living room couch. "I can't bear sleeping in our bed. I'm going to try not to think about anything except what to say to Chelsea." She lies down and covers her eyes with an arm. "Thank you for everything, Georgia."

Chapter twelve

Lily calls Amber while she waits for a doctor to stitch her gash. "I'm in the ER. I sliced my thumb open cutting a bagel."

"I'll pop down as soon as I can."

Just as the doctor finished stitching her up, Amber whisks in. "You okay?"

"Weak-kneed but otherwise fine. Boy, did that hurt."

"Those cuts are real bleeders." Amber yawns. "Sorry. Long night. My patient delivered two six-pound twins this morning. She was positively heroic."

"Wow. Amazing." Guarded, she asks, "Do you know anything about the woman in the accident?"

"Let it alone, Lily."

"I just want to know if she's going to be okay."

"That will never be enough for you and you know it."

"I don't know why, but I can't let it go," Lily concedes.

"I'll tell you why. In your warped mind, you want this to be about a love story gone south. But I've got a news bulletin for you. Love getting off track isn't news. And an accident is sometimes just an accident."

"I suppose. But I want to know the full story."

"Out of the question. It's none of your business. I'll check on her condition only if you promise me you'll leave the hospital right now." Amber gets in Lily's face. "I want you to listen to me. You have a new assignment. Says me. Find a new job. Not the same old, like that ridiculous radio cop-out you told me about. Something that uses your experience and talent in a different way. Be creative. Follow some subject that interests you. If you decide your next move is to write a romance novel, go for it. But focus on your own life, Lily. Now, I'll call and you're leaving."

"Okay," Lily grumbles.

"This is all you're getting. She's on track. No complications yet. Still under. Now, go."

"Thanks, Amber." Holding her arm up in the air, she gives her a hug. "I heard you and I'll try."

Amber pulls away. "I expect results."

Lily nods. "Yes, ma'am."

Chapter thirteen

Blake takes a taxi to the inn to get his car and drives to school. He parks in the back lot and ducks into his office. Nora comes out from behind her desk, "Blake!"

"I'm just here for a few minutes. Two things, if you don't mind. Will you get Chelsea and also go to the library for these books? They may even be on her desk." He hands her a list.

She looks at it and smiles. "*Secret Life of Bees*. Willow loves this. She was, I mean is, especially fond of the idea of the Wailing Wall. She was using it for both the adult and student groups. You know she asked me, the school secretary, to join? She's one of a kind." Nora tears up. "Any news?"

"The line is she's doing as well as can be expected." Barely audible, he adds, "But Nora... you should see her..."

"We'll take the good news and hang on to it." She nods and looks down at the list. "Okay. I'm on my way."

He closes his door and puts on the fresh shirt he keeps for evening meetings.

Chelsea opens the door and runs to him. "Dad, what's going on? Where were you all night? Kids are talking. They say Mrs. D'Angelo's going to die."

Holding her tight, he strokes her long hair and kisses the top of her head.

She pulls away and wipes away her tears. "Dad, you better tell me what's going on. Sara overheard two teachers talking. They said you're having an affair with Mrs. D'Angelo. It's true, isn't it? Everybody's looking at me weird."

"Let's sit." He moves her to his conference table. Blake's eyes fill with tears. "Honey, I'm so sorry about everything." He reaches for her hand.

Chelsea jerks away from him. "Just when were you going to get around to telling me? I have to hear you're having an affair from my best friend? It affects me, too, you know, and you don't even bother to give me any warning. You're not just leaving Mom, you know," she blubbers. "You could have trusted me."

Blake measures his words. "You know things have not been good with your mother for a long time. It's true. I should have trusted you. I should have talked to you but I thought there would be plenty of time for that."

"Is that why Mom went to New York and was so sweet when she got back? Did she know?"

"I can't answer for her. You'll have to ask her. But in any case, I wouldn't call my relationship with Willow an affair. Our friendship developed over many years. It…"

"It is what it is, Dad," she lashes out. "No matter how you say it."

"Chels, come here." He holds her, lets her cry. When the tears seem to be stopping, he releases her.

"Now that Mrs. D'Angelo, I mean Willow, is hurt OR DEAD, will you come back home?"

"No. Our marriage has been troubled for a long time." Softly, he adds, "I think you know that."

"You're getting a divorce no matter what?"

"Yes."

"I'm such a dummy. Remember when I barged in on the two of you when I got my license? You know what I thought? I wished you could look that happy and relaxed with Mom. I mean, I didn't think anything of it. I should have. I'm an idiot."

"No, you're not. We'll talk about all of it later. Right now, I'm getting Willow's favorite books and music to help bring her back. She's in a drug-induced coma to help her get stronger after her surgery."

"You're going to read to her? That'll be good. She'll like that." Chelsea's anger slips away. "You're really good at doing voices and stuff."

"It'll be hard but put all this adult stuff out of your head. School is what's important."

"Oh, sure, Dad. My life is a garbage dump and I'm supposed to just forget about it. I'll go home after school and Mom will be a basket case and Georgia will be giving orders."

Blake smiles. "It's good she's there. She'll keep you both moving. She loves you, you know."

"She's a pain but what would Mom do without her," Chelsea admits. "Is there a Mr. D'Angelo?"

"Yes."

Chelsea asks, "Doesn't he mind you being there?"

"Right now, everybody just wants her to get through these next critical days. The rest can wait."

"This sounds like a sad movie I'd never go see."

"I know."

"What should I tell everybody? All the kids will be asking me stuff."

"Just tell them that Mrs. D'Angelo was hurt very badly and everybody needs to pull together to send her positive thoughts. Nothing matters but her recovery."

"And the rest?"

"Tell them it's none of their business."

Chelsea stands. "You know, Dad, I always thought Mom might leave us. I never imagined you'd be the one."

"Chels, you are my heart. I may not live in the house anymore but I'll never leave you in the way that matters."

She teared up.

"I'm sorry but I really have to get back to the hospital."

"Okay. Text me. I want to know what's going on. Even if you have nothing new I want to hear from you. Promise me."

"I will, sweetheart. I'm so sorry for the way this happened. I really screwed up."

"It's okay, Daddy. I'm not a little kid anymore."

"You'll always be my little girl. I hate that you're caught in the middle of all this. Try to remember this mess is for Mom and me to figure out. You and me, the two of us, we're forever." He hugs her and when she turns to leave he frowns, noticing her sagging shoulders.

Why didn't I think to tell her first? This was no way for her to find out.

Chapter fourteen

Mercy buzzes Blake into the unit. "If you don't mind my saying so, you look awful and your nice pressed white shirt makes you look even worse. Go home and get some sleep. You shouldn't be here now, anyway. It's not your shift."

"Can't. She needs to know I'm here."

"If my experience holds true, we won't be cutting back on the anesthesia for hours. Maybe even another day. Exhausting yourself isn't going to help her. Besides, Denny's with her now." She stands in front of him, blocking his path.

"How long has he been here?"

"I'm not sure. But Autumn just got back, so I imagine he'll be out soon. Go. I don't want both of you here at the same time."

She walks down the hall to check on her other patient just as Denny appears. He flares, "Why are you still here?"

Blake doesn't answer.

"Family only and you're not, so get the hell out. Leave us all alone," he roars.

Blake's fatigue settles deep into his bones. Quietly, he says, "I'm not going anywhere, Denny."

Denny lunges at him, poking his collarbone hard with two fingers. Caught off guard and off balance, Blake falls back several steps. Dropping the books in his hand, he catches himself, and finds his footing.

Mercy rushes toward them. "Stop it right now," she orders.

Denny's eyes bulge. "Great …you ran your errand… now leave. You're worse than that reporter girl last night, hanging around, thinking if she brings me sandwiches, it gives her rights. You're all revolting."

Mercy wedges her ample body between them. "Get out now. Both of you."

Blake walks straight to the waiting room. He crumples into a chair, exhausted from worry, lack of sleep, an upset Chelsea.

Menacing, Denny follows and looms over him. Blake wills himself to contain his rage, to stand and face him while keeping his own clenched fists at his side.

Inches apart, he peers into Denny's dull eyes. "Denny, consider this a warning. Don't ever touch me again. Like it or not, I'm here to stay. Even now, you can't think of anybody but yourself. No wonder Willow collapsed under the strain of life with you." He catches his breath. "I'm not leaving. In fact, I'm never leaving."

Grace saunters in. "What's going on in here?"

Denny snarls at her. "This your idea, Grace? Bringing him here, thinking we all can have world peace? Since, you brought him here, you can get him the fuck out."

"Game's over, Denny. If you weren't such a weak, selfish bastard, Willow wouldn't be fighting for her life." Blake strides past Grace and walks out.

Denny punches the wall. Shaking, he grabs the arm of a chair and sits down. Grace sits next to him and reaches for his swelling hand.

He flinches. "Don't touch me or say a word. I don't want to hear anything out of your big mouth. Not one goddamn word."

Grace also leaves the waiting room. Denny sits as he did during all the hours of Willow's surgery, hunched over, staring at the floor, hoping the footsteps in the hall pass by, dreading news he can't live with. He puts his throbbing head in his hands and begins to rock.

Autumn is trying to adjust the sound on the DVD player so Willow can hear it over the drone of the machines. "Kreisler's, *Liebeslied*, is one of her favorites. She used to drive me crazy, playing it over and over. I would tell her to stop. It was making me suicidal. She would patronize me. 'Autumn, it may sound breathtakingly sad but its beauty is so intense, it fills you with a kind of happiness. Just listen and feel it,'" she imitated. "I didn't have a clue what she was talking about. I was the black and white sister. To me something is good or bad, tragic or happy, nonsensical or meaningful. She could always meld opposites. I think it explains Denny in a way."

Blake says, "He just tried to throw me out."

"Oh, great. Grace with him?"

"I think so." He looks at Willow, lying so still. "I think I'd like to read her a poem."

They change places. He opens to Dorianne Laux's *For the Sake of Strangers.*

Willow listens to a man's voice at the end of a long tunnel. He's faraway but his words are traveling toward her. She wants to tell him she knows what he'll say next… we rise and gather momentum… but that's all she remembers. Oh no. He's disappearing. The words are growing faint. Steady whooshes and beeping and violins overpower the man's deep voice. She hopes he comes back later. She likes the sound of his voice. She thinks she'd like to wrap its richness around her.

There's a woman with him, but she's talking over waves, muffled, under a flutter of notes.

Chapter fifteen

Mercy comes in with Dr. Sheldon, a rotund man with a shiny bald pate. His tortoise shell horn-rimmed glasses slip down his nose. "Anesthesia disrupts normal breathing so we use a ventilator to help keep breathing steady during and after surgery. Soon, we'll begin pulling back a bit on these meds, wake her up just enough for her to move, react to stimuli. We'll decrease how much the ventilator is doing, in order to get Willow breathing on her own."

He pushes his glasses up on his nose. "Getting her off it is a process. You should try to keep your expectations real. Sometimes initial movement is involuntary—the eyelid moving, a hand squeezing, wiggling a toe. It might be the beginning of the awakening, but it doesn't happen like in the movies. The body takes its time."

"How much time?" Blake asks.

"No way to predict. Also, we have the bowel issue. When there are tears, we worry about sepsis." He points to the drip bags. "She's getting antibiotics through one of the IV lines to avoid that."

The nurse practitioner, Kerry, joins them, adding, "We can tell a lot through physical exam and so far, so good."

Dr. Sheldon continues, "If the blood levels stay stable, we're less worried about internal bleeding. So far, everything looks good. Later today, neurology will evaluate her. There are things they can do while she's still asleep. I know the waiting's hard but just hang in. All things considered, she's doing well." He nods to Mercy and leaves with Kerry.

Blake, Grace, and Autumn stand at the foot of the bed watching her, trying to find comfort in the steady lines on the monitors and rhythmic beeping of the machines.

Chapter sixteen

Chelsea bangs the front door shut and shouts, "Mom, I'm home."

Jillian, lying on the living room couch with an ice pack across her forehead, waves her arm in the air. "Right here, Chelsea."

"Oops. Sorry."

"It's okay. I'm in and out of sleep. I don't know what's worse. My distorted dreams or what's really happening. If school's already out, I must have slept longer than I thought." She sits up. "I think I'll have a cup of tea. Do you want a snack?"

"I'll have tea with you."

A rumpled, uncombed Jillian, still wearing yesterday's clothes, fills the kettle, and takes out two mugs. She looks at them, puts them back and takes out two others." She turns to Chelsea, holding up a purple glazed mug. "This one, okay?"

"Sure, Mom. Fine." Chelsea frowns, watching her mother open and close cabinets.

Jillian flips open a tea box. "Chamomile okay or would you rather have something else? Let's see what's here. There is peppermint and peach…"

Chelsea interrupts, "Mom, it's just tea. I don't care."

"What do you want with it?" She takes out Oreos and vanilla wafers and hesitates trying to pick out a plate. Finally, she chooses one and arranges the cookies in a circle, then fans them out.

"Mom, sit down." Chelsea makes the tea, puts the cookies away and toasts wheat bread, careful to spread a very thin layer of butter and honey so her mother will eat it.

"Thanks, Chelsea. Toast is the perfect thing. Here, have some."

"No. You eat it, Mom. I bet you haven't eaten a thing today." Chelsea sits down and blows on her tea. "I saw Dad."

"He was at school? I thought he'd be at the hospital hovering over her. But then again, her husband probably booted him out." Jillian gasps, realizing what she's said. "I'm sorry. I don't know what I'm saying."

"It's okay. I know."

Jillian narrows her eyes. "How long have you known?"

"Today."

They both stared at their tea. Finally, Jillian broke the silence, "You'll probably want to live with him rather than me."

"Mommmmm, why would you think that? Don't you want me?"

"Of course, I want you but I was thinking about how you might feel. I was thinking maybe he should stay here and I could live at the studio, at least temporarily. I'm guessing that if she lives, she'll be in the hospital for a long time and he'll need and want to be with you."

"Why would you think you should leave? Geez, you're really thinking crazy." Chelsea's lip quivers. "Or don't you want to be stuck with me?" She gets up. "I'm going to my room." The hot tea splashes her hand and the floor. She leaves it and slams her door closed.

Jillian waits a few minutes. She brings the mugs to Chelsea's room and puts them down on her nightstand. She's lying on her bed with a pillow clutched to her stomach, staring at the ceiling. Her face is tear stained but she isn't crying. Jillian sits on the edge of the bed. "You know, one of the reasons I went to New York was to face myself and figure out how I could get things back on track with you and me, as well as with Dad. I did really hokey things, trying to figure out how to make things better."

Chelsea sits up, still hugging her pillow tight. "Like what?"

"You know how I always make fun of touchy feely, new age stuff?"

"Always."

"Well, I sat in that apartment kind of looking at all the different parts of my life trying to figure out why I did some things and didn't do others. I wrote everything down and then burned it in the sink. Bonfire New York City style."

"No way."

"Yes way. I also went back to the places where things had happened that I never dealt with. You know. Returning to the scene of the crime, hoping to finally figure it all out. Just like those detectives on all the *Law and Orders* you watch."

Chelsea shivers, "Did you figure out what you were going to do with a daughter like me?"

"No. It wasn't that way at all. Just the opposite." Her voice breaks. "Ours is a story about the daughter who did everything right and the mother who got it all wrong." Jillian tries to compose herself. "I know there's no way I can make things up to you. What I did is the worst thing a mother can do. I transferred disappointment in myself to you and never realized it. I don't know if you'll ever be able to forgive me or if I can ever manage to be a good mother to you, but I want to try. I felt like this before last night. The big if for me was not knowing whether or not it was too late for us or… Dad and me." She sighs. "Apparently, it was for him."

Jillian takes a damp tissue from her pocket and wipes her face. "This is what I think. It's been a god-awful night and day. Let's not try to figure anything out. Let's just hang out together tonight."

"And do what?"

Jillian's slow to answer, trying not to take in all the question implied. "This is pathetic. Mothers and daughters have places, a sweet spot, that's theirs alone— a favorite restaurant, a place to shop, movies to watch for the hundredth time. I can think of a million things you and Dad could pick." Stricken, she realizes, "We don't have one special place, do we? Not a single, solitary place that is just ours."

"That's just occurred to you? Every time we went someplace, it was a disaster." Her face clouds. "You know something? You're right Mom. We are pathetic."

They look at each other and burst out laughing.

"Good thing this isn't a deathbed conversation," Jillian exclaims.

"Yeah. Or our talk when you drop me at college."

"College? Don't remind me. It doesn't seem far enough away."

"So what are we going to do? We don't want to go anywhere. You don't like cards or board games."

"But I could…"

"No, if you're not honest, it won't work."

"You're right." Jillian stretches out next to Chelsea, grabbing the other pillow.

"How about just veg'ing out in front of the TV or watching a movie?" Chelsea suggests.

"That's a Dad and you thing."

"Doesn't have to be. We'll watch something he'd never want to see. Something girlie. We'll have a chick flick night."

"Okay. Do you want to order pizza or should we make grilled cheese?"

"No. Let's have broiled fish and salad!"

Jillian opens her mouth.

"Only kidding, Mom. Gotcha!"

Jillian throws a pillow at her.

Chapter seventeen

From the waiting room, Denny sees Grace, Autumn, and Blake walk down the hall. He shoves an article from the newspaper into his pocket and races back to the ICU, bumping into the surgeon.

"Dr. Horan? Denny D'Angelo. You operated on my wife last night?"

Looking down at his phone, he says, "Yes. Heard she tried opening her eyes and squeezed your hand. All good. But don't expect too much too soon."

"Hard not to."

He puts his hand on Denny's shoulder. "All in good time. She's been through a lot and keep in mind, we still don't know if she sustained any head trauma."

"Trying not to get ahead of myself."

The doctor's already down the hall.

Who told him Willow squeezed my hand? Doctors. He's probably got her confused with somebody else. Impatient, Denny rings five times before a nurse buzzes him in. She scowls at him. "Calm down. We've got patients to care for, you know."

"Sorry." He dashes into Willow's cubicle. "Willow, the doctor says you're doing great. You won't believe what I just read. Smack in the middle of the waiting room, there's a newspaper open to this." He pulls the torn page out of his pocket. *"Brain Scans Find Abnormalities in Gulf War Veterans.* After all this time, they're owning up to what we've known all along. It's not psychosomatic or nonspecific or whatever the hell they said to give us the brush off. You'd say, Denny, it's a sign. Who knows what that will mean for us? Maybe now, they'll fix me and pay us disability or something."

He touches her hand, careful of the tubes. "This could be a new start for us. You'll get better. I'll get better."

Grace and Autumn trudge back in. Blake stands in the doorway.
"Has there been any change, Denny?" Grace asks.

"No." He doesn't turn around, keeping his eyes fixed on Willow.

"I called Tess and Joe. They'll be here soon."

"No, Autumn. You have no right," he flares. "How many times
do I have to tell you to stay the fuck out of my business?"

*The voices are coming closer. I can hear them but I'm still foggy.
Something heavy is pressing on my chest. I'm thirsty, too, but my throat
hurts. My eyes are taped shut but I want to see who's here.*

Willow's eyes flutter several times before they open. She blinks
to clear them. She sees Denny. He's wavy at first but then clears. Her
eyes linger on him for a moment before they travel to Grace and
Autumn. It isn't until Autumn moves toward her that she sees Blake
standing in the doorway. Then, she closes them again.

Mercy pushes her way into the room and sees Grace smiling.
"What's up?"

Grace whispers, "She opened her eyes and looked at us all. It's
sleep now, isn't it? Ordinary sleep?"

"You know the drill. Let us do our thing. Vitals, fluids, blood
work. Denny, let me in there. I'll let you know as soon as I'm done
here and gotten a doctor to take a look."

Willow feels the room empty. She thinks she hears their steps grow
faint. When she opens her eyes again, the room feels alive with beeping
and hissing, monitors lit with lines and dips and peaks. What is she
doing in this strange room with weird light and humming machines and
antiseptic smells? Bags are inflating, deflating, dripping. There's something heavy on one leg and pressure, coming and going, on the other.
Her throat has something in it. She wonders why it's so hard to stay
awake. Maybe she can sleep a little longer and still be on time for school.

Willow wakes up again several hours later. There is a woman in
the room with her who seems very busy. She is heavyset but agile and
is wearing a blue and purple flowered jacket with white pants and
the comfortable shoes with squishy soles Willow wishes she could
wear to school. Gray hair threaded through chocolate dreadlocks
frames her mocha skin.

Sensing Willow watching her, she sits down. "Willow, my
name is Mercy Bianco and I'm a nurse at Lourdes Hospital. Don't

try to talk yet. We'll get that tube out of your throat soon. You'll be very hoarse at first and it will be hard to make understandable sounds, but that will work itself out."

Willow stares at her, blinking.

"I know you must have a lot of questions but we'll go slow. You were in a car accident. You have some serious recovering to do but you should be okay. Now, close your eyes and rest while I get a doctor to take a look at you. Your family is here but I'm going to keep them out until we get you squared away and comfortable."

Willow raises her eyebrows.

"Ah. You want me to tell you who's here. You saw them all but were groggy. Your mother flew in from California. Your sister, Autumn. Your husband, Denny."

Willow stares at her, struggling to talk.

Mercy sighs, "Yes, love. Blake's been here from the start."

When the group trudges back to the waiting room, Tess and Joe are there.

Tess runs to Grace. "Willow won't let this second chance slip out of her grasp."

Joe pulls Denny into a bear hug. "Hey, man. How you holding up?"

"She's starting to come out of it. But Joe, you should see her," he squeezes his eyes shut. "Pale and bruised and bandaged, hooked up to all kinds of machines and tubes. White as the sheet on her bed."

With Denny's back to her, Tess then approaches Blake. "I didn't think you'd be here."

"Where else would I be?"

She frowns at him. "What about Denny?"

"He thinks Willow's going to jump out of bed and life will go on as always."

"Good lord, Blake."

"The important thing is they've pulled back on the anesthesia and she's coming to. She just opened her eyes, looked at all of us and then closed them. That's the best it's been."

Lily walks in.

Denny grows feral and gets in her face. "What the hell are you doing here? Get out, you goddamn ghoul."

"I didn't mean to upset you, Mr. D'Angelo. I won't stay. I just stopped by to see how she's doing. That's all."

"You people are vultures, picking our bones clean."

Lily feels everyone's eyes boring into her. "I was here for another reason and just hoped to hear some good news. I'm so sorry to have intruded." She held up her bandaged hand.

Head bowed, she runs out. Tess follows her. "I'm sorry. He doesn't know where to direct his anger."

Lily holds back tears. "I used to be a pro. Never let anything I covered get to me. At least that's what I thought until a few months ago. But this? The strange accident, the complicated love story, the sadness of it all," Lily rambles. "It has some kind of crazy hold on me. Like I need to be paying attention."

Tess nods.

"Blake Golden is my mother's neighbor. He and his wife seemed to have it all." She sighs. "Nothing is ever as it seems, is it?"

"I don't know what to tell you." Tess shrugs, "Life just has a way of happening to us."

"I'd like to meet her sometime."

"I hope you will. I'm sorry about Denny's rudeness." She turns to go and stops. "Willow would tell you underneath it all, she's an optimist. She would just warn you of the dangers of magical thinking."

Lily watches Tess go back into the waiting room, puzzling over what the woman might have meant.

Chapter eighteen

Shaken, Lily decides to stop at Starbucks before heading to the middle school. Since she won't get there in time for lunch, she'll have to get footage of the new vending machines in an empty cafeteria and talk to students later. Oh, well.

She has to get a grip. Maybe a latte and some quiet time forcing her to think about what Amber said will center her and get her mind off her aching hand—and the mess she's making everywhere she turns.

She spies an open table in the corner. Somebody left a newspaper. An article about Persian Gulf War veterans catches her eye. Skimming it at first, her interest is peaked. She goes back to reread it carefully —vets with chronic illness, experimental drugs, possible chemical exposure, government denial. Surfing the web, she begins taking notes. One article leads to another. Searching Amazon, she orders books: *Against All Enemies: Gulf War Syndrome, The War Between America's Ailing Veterans and Their Government. Gulf War Syndrome: Legacy of a Perfect War. Gassed in the Gulf: The Inside Story of the Pentagon-CIA Cover-Up of Gulf War Syndrome.*

Immersed, she jumps when her cell phone rings. Her stomach clutches when she sees the time and Rich's name on caller ID.

"Lily. I've been wanting to say this since I made the mistake of hiring you. You're fired."

Chapter nineteen

Mercy pops into the waiting room. "Awake and asleep. That's how it will be. Slow but she's coming out of it. The tube is out but she really won't be able to talk for a while."

They all rush toward the door. "No. Two at a time. Mother and husband, first. And remember, leave all your baggage at the door. Any trouble and you're out."

Joe snickers, "Reminds me of our sergeant."

"Sure does. Nothing gets by her."

Grace says, "Come, Denny."

When they're out of earshot, Mercy taps Blake's shoulder. "I'm not a hundred percent but I'd swear on something sweet that when I was taking her vitals, she croaked something sounding like, 'Blake late.'"

Relief smooths the lines in his face. "Are you sure?"

"I wasn't at first but when she tried lifting her head and again said something, it sure sounded like Blake."

Denny holds her hand carefully. Grace looks through the stack of books on the nightstand. "What would you like to hear first? I'd bet on Neruda."

Leafing through the book, she looks for one of Willow's favorites. "Here's one. *Ode to a Tomato*. Oh, does this book bring back memories. It reminds me of our time in California—fields of tomatoes, peppers, zucchini. The scent of citrus blowing through our windows at night. And the avocados. You ate enough of them to turn you green. You were some little girl. Not all children could adapt the way you did. You thought of life as an adventure. 'What's next, Mama? I don't like it here anymore. Let's move on. I want to go to a place that doesn't look anything like here, Mama. Let's go!'"

Grace sighs, "It was only when you became a teenager that you lost faith. You didn't have a father, or a house— or any semblance of a teenager's life. I struggled. I didn't know whether to keep you in the life or take you into what you called the real world. Whatever that was. Seems to me from the first day in that 'regular' high school in real world, you entered into a pact you never understood. Thanks to me, you were unprepared for it and have suffered greatly." Grace's voice cracks.

"Stop, Grace. You're dead wrong. As usual."

"I know my daughter, Denny. She's been bound, cut off from who she is, and she's been doing it for so long, you don't even see what it's done to her. She was trying to get back to herself." Grace shudders, "And this happened."

"Your life is all messed up. Our life—Willow's and mine—is what's true."

"Denny, you are galling." She looks at her daughter's peaceful face. "Willow, we'll start with *Ode to a Tomato.*"

Yes, Mama. Neruda's tomatoes. Star of earth, recurrent and fertile.

Chapter twenty

Grace sits on the floor meditating. Joe and Denny are staring out the window at the parking lot. Tess chats with the parents of a woman who had a brain tumor removed.

"It was nice talking with you, Tess. We're going for a bite to eat now while our son-in-law is with her."

The couple leave and Tess joins Autumn. "When I worked in intensive care, I learned more about families than I ever wanted to know. Some can't rise above their pettiness no matter what's going on. And then, there are others who are so loving, your heart breaks for them. Like that family."

Autumn wonders, "In your professional opinion, how would you rank our motley group?"

Tess laughs, "A disaster waiting to happen. I never expected to see Blake here. How is Denny taking it?"

"Mostly passive, then overtly aggressive. He knows Blake is trouble for him but can't seem to figure out why. Aside from ordering him to get out a couple of times and punching him once, it's been okay."

"What? If I were Willow's nurse, I'd never allow Blake to stay. What's the deal? She gives off that folksy manner but I've worked with women like her and they're tough as nails. All about the patient and not giving a hoot about the family."

"You've nailed her. Technically, she's in the clear. We told her he's our brother. She knew we were lying but sized Blake up right away and figured out the situation. It's a gamble. But Mercy is clear. She's warned us repeatedly that if there's any trouble, she'll throw us all out."

Denny leaves Joe standing at the window and sits down. The claustrophobia of Willow's cubicle is bad enough but now the waiting room is worse. Too many people. He pulls at his shirt collar.

"No, Tess. Don't sit there. I need space."

She looks at Joe but he just shrugs.

Sitting down anyway, she says gently, "Denny, look at me."

"Didn't I just tell you not to sit there? Leave me alone."

"I stopped by the house to get your pills. I thought the stress might bring on a headache or your neuralgia. And I can see that it has."

She signals to Joe who takes a bottle of water out of the fridge.

Tess peels back the tab from the pill card and hands it to him but Denny won't take it. "It's only going to get worse."

"No. They knock me out."

"Hold on to it just in case."

He slips it into his shirt pocket.

Tess knows she has to say something before he recoils into his own world. She can barely recognize the man he's become. The Denny she first knew was sociable, spurred on by Willow's enthusiasm. Tess remembers the first time he and Willow came to their house. Denny was lively, energetic and he doted on her. She thought, lucky Willow. She certainly got that wrong.

"Denny, remember what you said when Joe left Jason and me. Our break up was hard to take but you understood why he had to leave."

"Yeah. So what?"

"Because Joe couldn't cope, he felt he had no choice? Willow has to do the same thing."

"No. Your talking out your ass."

"Things don't always work out the way we want them to. We are Jason's parents but could never be Tess and Joe happily ever after."

Joe interrupts, "What are you talking about Tess? They aren't us. Nothing happened to them."

"You two are some pair," Tess laments. "You change the road map when things get rough and then go to pieces when we don't fall in behind you."

"Shut up, Tess," Denny snarls. His head hurts. He can't listen. *Why is everybody on my case? Know it alls when they don't know dick about me and Willow.*

Defeated, Tess sighs. "Think about what Willow…"

"Why the fuck does everybody keep saying that? She's all I've ever thought about. Get the fuck out of here. I hate you all." He ambles across the room to get away from Tess.

Shaking her head, Tess makes a cup of coffee.

Autumn and Blake stand by the window talking. Denny glares at them. He can't figure it out. *Maybe Autumn met Willow's boss and they're a couple now. Yes. He's here for Autumn.* Demon is getting the best of him. His head is getting worse. He starts the deep breathing Willow always encouraged him to do. Repeat anything, she'd say. Pick your mantra and say it over and over to get you into the zone. Willow. Wake up. Willow. Wake up, he pleads silently.

He watches Grace close her eyes and breathe long deep breaths. Then, right in the middle of the waiting room, she moves into a yoga flow. *Am I in hell? Why can't all these ridiculous people just go away? It was that damn reporter insisting on calling Autumn. If she hadn't been here making me crazy, nobody would be here. Fuck.*

Conversation around him is hushed but he thinks he hears someone say Blake and Willow. Their names linked. Hearing that, he's overcome with fury— at Willow's accident, his illnesses, Autumn who wants him gone, his so-called friends whom he now realizes he despises. And that cocksucker standing there like he belongs. All his anger and fear and resentment rolls into a fireball.

Grace finishes her practice and walks toward him, determined.

He grits his teeth. "Go away, Grace. I mean it. I don't want to hear any of your bullshit."

Oblivious to his crazed look, she says, "Denny, you've made it clear what you think of me. Now I'm going to tell you what I think of you. You abused Willow's love for you. You made her an unequal partner by making unilateral decisions. Despite that, she nurtured you, tried to heal you, tried to make the best of the empty cage you locked her in. Well, my boy, you've taken enough from her. No more. Do you understand me?"

"And you think she wants HIM? He'd be better for her than me?" he growls, his eyes widening. In a single movement, quick as a cat, he lunges across the room, spins Blake around, slugs him in the jaw, and punches him in the gut.

In a quick move, Blake flips him around into a strangle hold.

With Blake's hands at his throat, Denny spits, "I've had it with you hanging around. Get out of here or else."

Trying to catch his breath, Blake pants, "Or else what, Denny? What are you going to do? You think Willow's accident is going to give you another chance? She would have been long gone if you weren't such a weak…"

Denny breaks Blake's hold and pummels his back. Joe is on him in an instant, pulling him off Blake and steers him by the shoulders across the room. "Pull yourself together, man. Willow would hate this."

He slumps in the chair. The spinning room turns dark. The throbbing inside his skull immobilizes him. His face is hot with tears.

Everyone does their best to avert their eyes.

Denny dries his face on his sleeve and stumbles over to Blake. "She's hardly been home. I should have known something was up but I never thought she'd cheat on me."

"Interesting choice of words since you cheated her out of everything she ever wanted and needed," Blake seethes. "Did you ever ask her where she was? If you had, she'd have been honest. She was on her way home yesterday to tell you she was finally leaving. Yet, she still worried about you like you were a helpless puppy. She was probably so absorbed in figuring out what to say, she crashed into the…"

Denny backs away from him and bolts out of the room. Autumn has been standing near the door and sees Denny buzz himself back into the ICU.

The room is silent.

Grace touches Blake's face. "Autumn, see if you can get some ice packs."

Joe and Tess sit together. Grace makes tea for Blake, resumes her lotus pose. Autumn returns with ice packs. Blake holds one to his jaw, puts the other at the base of his spine, leans against the back of the chair, and closes his eyes.

Standing by Willow's bed, a numbing shame creeps into every pore. Just last week, she came home exuberant after a student book club. "Everyone in the group was animated, warring over the characters they loved and hated. It was sublime, Denny. Absolutely sublime."

Out of the blue, she was the old Willow, animated, excited, actually talking to him like she used to. But did he ask her anything? What book was it? Who was in the group? No, dumb shit. He only said, that's good. Glad. He wanted her to keep talking, fill the house again with her chatter but he didn't encourage her. He'd forgotten how. It should have occurred to him that she'd found someone else to talk to. Willow needed to share things to thrive the way plants need water.

When Denny can bear to look at her, he sees she's staring at him.

"Willow." He wipes his face with the back of his hand. "Hi, babe."

She looks up at the fluorescent lights, down at the tubes in her arm, up at the bags of fluid.

"Everything's going to be okay."

She croaks something he can't understand.

"Don't worry. It's all okay. I'm going to get your nurse."

Chapter twenty-one

Denny and Grace watch Mercy adjust the clips on the tubes. "The neurologist, Dr. Beesley was just here. Willow has a concussion but for now, he isn't worried about neurological complications beyond that. He'll be back tomorrow to check on her again."

"Head hurts. Don't remember anything." Willow strains.

"That's a blessing, honey. No need. It's not surprising your head hurts after all the anesthesia and trauma, too. We're still going to keep you as pain-free as possible so you'll stay foggy."

She rasps, "Tell me."

"It can wait."

"Now."

"Broken ribs, broken left leg, bruising, contusions. A splenectomy—took out your spleen— but that shouldn't cause any problems. Tears in your intestines that've been repaired. Your left lung collapsed but it's already inflated again. The tube that hurt your throat is out. You're remarkable and have quite the fan club. Now, rest a bit."

Willow whispers, "Mama stay. Denny, go home. Headache."

"You can barely keep your eyes open. How do you know if I have a headache? Maybe I look happy. Handsome even." Denny tries to smile.

"Headache. Go."

"If that's what you want, I'll go home for a while. But I'll be back."

She watches him leave.

"Mercy."

"Yes, hon."

"Can I still have babies?"

"Don't worry yourself about that now."

"Tell me." Willow stares Mercy down.

"Told you all that I know. Nobody's said anything more. That's something you best talk to a doctor about later. You have some healing to do first." She covers Willow with another blanket. "Warm enough?"

Willow nodded.

"Good. There's someone else waiting to see you. Let's give Denny time to leave. Then, I'll get him."

"Blake?"

He bends toward her. "Yes, love."

"Plan no good," she squawks.

"You think?" he laughs. "Well, this is the new plan. You're going to get better and then our life together begins just where we left off. But this time we go to the Inn together."

She tries to clear her throat. "You and Denny. Here. Together. Awful." She struggles. "What happened... to... your...face?"

"Punched me once. No, make that twice. Good thing I was on the wrestling team. The Kardashians have nothing on us. Seriously."

Grimacing, she moans, "Worse than TV reality show. It's real."

"Except for us the fighting's over. No new season."

"Mama. You'll look after Denny while you're here?"

"No, Willow. No more. Denny has to figure himself out."

She struggles to keep her eyes open.

"Sleep now. I'll be here when you wake up."

"Love you."

"Then, I'm a happy man."

Autumn strokes Willow's hand. "She doesn't seem as far away. Is it my imagination or does it seem like less scary sleep?"

Blake agrees. "It's probably us though. We aren't as afraid."

"Why don't you go home for a while?"

"I told her I'd be here when she wakes up. Besides, I don't really have one."

Grace interjects, "What were your plans? Knowing you for five minutes, Blake, I know you had one."

"We were going to spend a couple of nights at the Beverwyck Inn. Then, we found a small house on Thompson's Lake to rent for a month to get our bearings and decide where to go long term."

Autumn muses, "She should have had that."

"She still will. I'm going to call the owner and tell him what happened and try to push it back a few months."

"And in the meantime?" Grace asks.

"I'm not sure. Maybe I'll go to one of those rent-by-the-week motels. All I need is a bed and shower."

"Think about staying at my house." Autumn pulls out her keys. "At least, go there now. Shower. Take a nap."

"That's generous of you, Autumn. But you and Grace should have the time together. I'll stay one more night at the Beverwyck and then tomorrow find the best of the fleabags…"

"Invitation stays open."

"I appreciate it. Maybe I will leave and freshen up. Want to look my best when Willow wakes up."

"As if she would care," Autumn laughs.

Denny is waiting in the hall outside the ICU.

"No more scenes, Denny."

Denny inches closer to him and blocks him.

"Move out of my way."

Denny warns, "Don't come back. Whatever happened between you and Willow is over. She's my wife."

"You should have thought about Willow when you were breaking her heart. You're done. She's going to get better and I'm going to give her the life she deserves; the life she should have had all these years. Now, get out of my way."

Denny doesn't move. Blake pushes him aside and he loses his balance, nearly falling. He catches himself and follows Blake.

Blake turns, startling Denny. "Listen to me. If Willow needs anything from you it's to man up."

He notes Blake's long strides, his straight back, his confident walk as he disappears down the hallway. Denny feels himself shrinking.

Joe watches from a distance. When Blake is safely out of sight, he puts his arm around Denny and says, "Let's go, buddy. Tess will call us if there is any news."

Denny staggers backward, staring down the empty hallway.

Chapter twenty-two

months later

"Knock-knock." Georgia raps on the open door to Jillian's office.

Jillian waves her in as she hangs up the phone. "Lovely surprise. What are you doing downtown?"

"I had a meeting on Lancaster. Lucky for me the client had a lunch date. She is the absolute queen of digression. I thought she'd never stop talking. I'm predicting she'll have a very successful political career. On the upside, she did like the mock up I did for her ad campaign. Probably worth all my nodding, pretending she's a genius." Georgia stretches out on the chair facing Jillian. She picks up a brochure on the desk. "What's this?"

"With no husband and a daughter with one foot out the door, I'm thinking of doing something new."

"Really?" Georgia sits straighter in her chair. "You've got my attention. RAD?" she reads. "What's that? Radiology? Ha! Can't picture it."

Jillian laughs. "Hmmm. Now, that would be quite the makeover. A white uniform and thick soled shoes? Can you picture it?"

Amused at the image, Georgia's asks, "So really? What is it?"

"Royal Academy of Dance." Jillian is thoughtful. "For years, I found reasons to stay at the studio later than I needed just to avoid going home. Now, my time is practically all my own and I don't know how to fill it. The irony is not lost on me," she sighs.

"I'm listening."

"At first, I planned to convert the top floor to an apartment but decided that wasn't the best idea I ever had. Never having to leave the building seemed like I was giving up."

"Good thinking."

"Instead, going to add two studios up there for other types of dance. Sima's advice has been haunting me. She chided me for years that if I couldn't be open minded, I should at least be business minded. There is also the building next door. It's been on the market a long time so maybe I could get it for a good price. I called that terrific architect I worked with once before, David Lerner, to do a preliminary assessment. Perhaps, if I could swing it, one building could be ballet and the other an array of other dance classes. Join the buildings somehow."

"And the RAD thing? How does that fit it?

"I want to bring my ballet school to the next level. The Royal Academy of Dance is a worldwide dance education and training program. They have member studios in nearly a hundred countries. I want their certification. It'll give me a goal and who knows what could happen from there?"

Georgia laughs.

"What? You think it's crazy?"

"Crazy? What was crazy was my worrying that you'd never get up off the couch. But here we are, a few months later and you're planning a future. It's just the thing. Tell me everything. What does it entail?"

Jillian grins. "It's a big commitment— a two-year program with both distance learning and onsite classes. After that, there are annual seminars. I just got off the phone with a woman who runs a RAD certified ballet school in Florida. I'm going down at the end of the month to take a look at her school, observe some classes, and pick her brain. She says it's made all the difference for her personally and for the reputation of the school. It's also helped her keep her best students. You have to be taught by a RAD certified teacher in order to qualify for their exams. That's critical for students who hope to dance professionally."

"You could become an examiner and travel the world meeting all kinds of interesting people. Or at least the country. Scout out the next soloist for the New York City Ballet."

Jillian laughs. "None of that anymore. The focus is on my school. That's it."

"On the practical side can you afford it? The renovation, the training, the travel?"

"It won't be easy but it's doable. I got a whopping surprise from my mother. When Blake left, she called to tell me she's been saving money for me as a *just in case* fund. I think she was surprised my marriage lasted as long as it did."

"How did she ever get away with hiding money from your cheapskate Dad?"

"She didn't. As it turns out, my mother is both resourceful and talented. She's also done a bang-up job investing her money. When I prodded her about the real source of the money—first for the school and now this— she told me she launched a knitting business while I was still in high school. She said the reason it was so easy to cart me all over creation for lessons was the knitting. She was doing something for herself as well as me. First, she sold them on consignment. Now, she sells high end, one of a kind designs to boutiques and online. I knew she was good but when I looked at her website, yes, website, I was amazed. Her work is original and sophisticated. You wouldn't believe how much she gets for a sweater. I can't believe she never told me."

"If you just listened to me ..."

"But that's just it. I couldn't listen to anyone. Since I came back from New York, I keep replaying the conversation I had with my old friend from dance school. You know, the one I called after I found out the ballet mistress was dead."

"Of course."

"That one conversation made me realize how I sabotaged myself. Why did I listen to a woman I knew was cruel? Why did I have so little confidence? Then, I hid under Blake's cover and then blamed him for it. Even worse was I never saw myself in the life I had with him and blamed him for that, too."

"Don't go there, Jilly. Today is a going forward day, not back."

"Right. I also see no reason to keep the house unless selling it breaks Chelsea's heart. At worst, I can keep the home fires burning for her and sell it say, when she graduates college. I only need an apartment. Or, maybe a condo. I know Blake will be amenable to whatever Chelsea needs. There might be money there, too."

"This is cause for celebration. Come on. I know you don't have a class today until four. Let's go to that new French bistro. My treat."

"Georgia, I don't know how I would have survived these past few months without you." Jillian comes around the desk and hugs her. "As long as I keep moving I'm okay. It's when I'm not busy that I get scared and insecure about everything."

"Of course, you do. You've taken a big hit." Georgia breaks away from Jillian and pirouettes around the office. "Do you think I'm teachable?"

Jillian laughs and puts both hands on Georgia's waist to steady her. "With a little work, the most unexpected things are possible."

Chapter twenty-three

Willow closes her eyes and tilts her face to feel the sun through the garden window.

Grace smiles. "I bet your sister had you in mind when she first saw this sunroom."

"Maybe so but I'm sure she never imagined the three of us together here."

"You can be sure of that. So, my love, how are you today?"

"No inventories this morning. It's too daunting. Let's just say I'm a bit better than I was." She stretched her neck. "Let's focus on that."

Her mother sits down on the love seat and silently assesses her daughter. The bruises on her face have faded. The stitches are out and the scars have faded. Her broken and cracked ribs have healed although she has residual pain. She's on her second cast and needs crutches to walk. Getting in and out of a chair is still difficult. Her cough lingers after fighting a lung infection, pneumonia, and stubborn bronchitis. Her abdominal stitches have dissolved but her skin is still raw from a severe allergic reaction to the hospital adhesive tape. She has headaches and some dizziness but they are less severe and less frequent. "Then, tell me what's good today."

"I'm celebrating a fairly good night's sleep in a bed, which, of course, is top of the line because it's Autumn's. I woke up to the aroma of my mother's coffee, and I know if I ask, she'll make me her famously delectable blueberry scones. Most of all, I'm looking forward to Chelsea's visit."

"It could be stressful," Grace cautions. "And anticipating the predictable eye rolls that you and your sister have perfected, I want to remind you that Thich Nhat Hahn says, 'In order to heal others, we first must heal ourselves.'"

"It's far too early in the morning for him. He should heed his own advice and meditate silently."

Grace chuckles. "I suppose you're right. But you have the physical therapist coming later. That always takes so much out of you."

"Regardless of Chelsea's visit. Wait until you meet her. She's a wonderful girl. And she said she has news. I want to know what that is. No offense but it would be nice to have a fresh voice in here. Aren't ours becoming monotonous?"

"Can't argue with that. Do you want anything now?"

She taps the books piled on the table. "All set but if you bring me a cup of coffee, that would be lovely."

"I'll make another pot. Maybe Chelsea would like some as well."

Willow nods and when her mother leaves the room, she rereads the card Chelsea sent her.

Dear Willow,

I hope it's okay if I call you that. We all miss you. It's hard to pass the library in the morning and not see you standing there. You should know that someone found several cases of granola bars in your storage room and passes them out in the mornings the way you used to. Bet you can guess who it might be!

Although we all razzed you about your car, it's sad not to see it with all the dorky reading bumper stickers in the school parking lot. We want you to come back soon driving an equally librarian-like car. With airbags, this time.

Dad fills me in on how you're doing and I'm really happy you're getting a bit better every day. Would it be all right for me to visit you when you feel up to it?

I have some news.

Let me know when might be a good time.

Chelsea

Willow smiles and folds the card. She hears a car door slam. "Mom, I think Chelsea's here."

Grace gathers her long hair into a ribbon as she walks to the door.

"I'm Chelsea Golden." She holds a plate of cookies in one hand and extends the other to shake Grace's hand.

"I'm Willow's mother, Grace. Look at those beautiful cookies." Grace takes them from her. "She's really looking forward to seeing you but she tires easily."

"Don't worry. I won't stay long."

Listening, Willow frowns.

"She's in there," Grace says, pointing to the sunroom. "I'm making coffee or would you prefer tea?"

"Coffee is fine. Thank you."

When Willow sees her, she grins. "Chelsea, you've become a woman since I last saw you."

"You think so? If only it were true. I look so much younger than my friends," Chelsea laments.

"That will make you happy someday. Come sit here with me. There's plenty of room." Willow slides her legs to the side of the ottoman.

"How do you feel?"

"Well, most days I still feel like every inch of me has been assaulted in some way. But sometimes, there are moments during the day now when I actually forget I hurt. That's something miraculous, all things considered."

"You must have been really scared."

"That's for sure. Enough about me. I can't stand the suspense. Your news. Dad won't tell me a thing."

"He's good at keeping secrets." Chelsea reddens. "Oh, I'm sorry. I didn't mean that. What I meant is he'd never tell one of mine," she stammers.

"It's fine, sweetie. I know what you mean."

Relieved, she says, "You know those essays you helped me with. The ones you said would help me get accepted wherever I wanted to go?"

"Of course, I remember them. You were able to turn the typical essay about building self-esteem in a very unique way."

"Well, maybe with your suggestions."

"A little tweaking. I get no credit."

Chelsea's face lights up. "As you suggested, I submitted one of them to a national high school essay contest and won a prize. Five hundred dollars!"

"Bravo. That's fantastic. Wonderful news!"

"Well, I wanted to thank you. If you didn't help me then…"

Willow interrupts. "It's all you, Chelsea. Don't think otherwise."

Grace comes in and puts down the tray, heavy with a coffee pot, mugs, and Chelsea's cookies. "There is excitement in the room. Do tell."

Willow nods to her.

Chelsea grins and repeats her news.

"Congratulations, Chelsea. That's marvelous. Your parents must be so proud."

Grace pours the coffee.

"You two have a lot to talk about so I'll leave you." She turns to Willow, "You sure you're all right?"

"Yes, Mama."

She rolls her eyes and Chelsea and Grace both laugh. "Sorry, love. Can't seem to help myself. Let me know if you need anything. I'll be in the kitchen."

"So… what are the top two?"

"Boston University and Penn State."

"Urban versus big campus. But both are very good schools."

"I know. I'm going to visit them once more before I decide."

"That's good. Dad didn't mention it."

"Um. He's not going. We planned to go together before well, you know. Not that it would have happened, anyway. But now, there's no way. Dad and I already checked out B.U. Mom and I did something we'd never done before, after he… We went on a road trip to see my top choices. It was…" She stops. "I don't think I should talk about her."

"Fair enough."

Chelsea is quiet. "I guess I want to say this." She takes in a deep breath. "I'm sad. Who doesn't want their mother and father to stay together? But when I think about everything, I wouldn't want a marriage like theirs." She chokes up. "It's easier on Dad because he has you but I think in the end it'll be better for Mom, too."

Willow nods.

"If Dad had to be with someone else, I'm glad it's you. It's just…"

"We'll figure this out. Your coming here this morning is big. And I appreciate it more than you can imagine. It's more than enough."

Relief spreads across Chelsea's face. "I have a surprise." She pulls an envelope from her bag and hands it to Willow.

Willow reads the card and looks at Chelsea. "The book club is coming here?"

"When you're up to it, we'll come after school. We picked a book we think you'll like."

Willow can barely contain herself. "Tell me. What is it?"

She hands her a copy of *The Book Thief.* "We all signed it."

"This is the best gift I've ever gotten. It will give me something special to look forward to. Thank you so much, Chelsea." Tears spring to Willow's eyes. "I'm so touched."

Chelsea hands her a cookie.

Willow bites into the soft sweetness. "Heavenly."

"I added Reese's to the batter."

"Pure deliciousness. Boy, do I love a good cookie. I'm surprised I didn't gain weight from all the cookies and brownies people sent over when I first came home." She laughs, "I guess it's no secret I'm a sweet-o-holic."

"And skinny. No fair."

"You're a beauty, Chelsea. Not everyone was meant to be a string bean. I would have killed for your body. The skinny ones want curves and visa versa. Same thing with curly hair and straight." She makes a face, twirling one of her thin curls.

Chelsea laughs. "You're so right on that one." She picks up her bag. "I have to get going."

"Thanks for coming by. Let me know what you decide, okay?"

"Sure." She hesitates.

Willow takes her hand and squeezes it. "This is new for me, too. We have all the time in the world to get this right, Chelsea."

"We do, don't we?" She bends down and kisses Willow's cheek.

Chapter twenty-four

The smell and touch of wood calms Denny's nerves. At his workbench, there's no room for self-recrimination nor space to wallow. It's the only place he feels in control.

Not that he's accomplishing anything much. Every day he wakes up intending to begin the jobs he got through the Vet Center. The wood sits in a neat pile but he never seems to get to them. He keeps working on old projects started before…his demarcation line. Before the accident. Before Willow left him. Before the world went quiet.

When he's in his *how could she have done this* phase, he rages. That morphs quickly into his mea culpa in which he obsesses about all the things he did or didn't do that led him to where he is now. Without her.

Joe lives with him. Denny asks him to leave every day and every day Joe's answer is the same. "No way, man. I'm not going anywhere until I see some change. You want to get rid of me? Show me something new. I want to see you as sick and tired of your sorry-assed self as I am."

Denny can't agree with him more. He looks for something to work on that doesn't remind him of her. Maybe he just doesn't want to finish anything for the simple reason she won't be there to tell him how beautiful it is. Even when he could tell she didn't care anymore, she went through the motions to the very end.

He's shaken out of his self-pity when he hears a car pull into the driveway. Who the fuck, he wonders, hoping for a split second it's Willow. But when he looks out the window, he doesn't recognize the car. Jackass, he mutters. As if she could—or would— drive over. She still refuses to see him. Whatever he has learned about her recovery has come from Joe through Tess.

"I don't think he's going to like us showing up like this," Lily says, getting out of the car.

"We'll keep it short. If he's working, he'll be in the garage."

Stephen knocks and opens the door. "Hi, Denny. Remember me? Stephen Brooks from the Vet Center?"

Lily walks in behind him.

"You. I hoped I'd never see you again."

"And I wasn't sure you'd remember me," she teases.

"How could I forget? You were an annoying bee who wouldn't stop buzzing me on the worst day of my life."

Lily smiles. "Stephen, I told you. I have an unforgettable effect on men."

Denny leans against his bench. "What do you want?"

Stephen walks toward the bookcase Denny has partially stained. "This is beautiful. I love the detail on the molding. Very different."

Denny nods.

"We were wondering about the desk."

Denny tightens his ponytail. "Haven't started it." Under his breath, he mutters, *if I knew it was for her, I wouldn't have taken it on.*

"I heard that but it's okay. I wouldn't like me either if I were you."

"Maybe you should get somebody else to do it. When do you need it?"

Stephen laughs. "As far as I'm concerned, yesterday. But I'm sure she doesn't care. Now that she's working from home, I think the desk might help contain her, though I'm not sure. Right now, there are books and notes and paper in every room."

Lily punches his arm. "It's not that bad. Don't exaggerate."

Stephen shakes his head, smiling. "We do need the desk but we have another reason for coming over."

"What?"

Lily takes a step closer to Denny. "I want to apologize. I was going through something around the time of Willow's accident that I didn't really understand then. I know it doesn't help much but looking back, I'm mortified at the way I behaved and I'm sorry for that. You'll be happy to hear I got fired."

"Good. You were way out of line."

Lily laughs. "I thought you'd be glad to hear that. So now, I'm freelancing and just got the green light to go ahead on an in-depth story about Persian Gulf War veterans."

Denny crosses his arms. "No."

"It'll give you the platform to tell your story. All of it. Finally."

"I said no," he thundered.

"No? How can you just flat out refuse? It's time the story came out. You've been suffering all these years and…"

Stephen shoots her a look.

"At least think about it. It won't just be about you. When I spoke to Joe down at the Vet Center, he said he's in. So is Tess. And there are others. Hal, a friend of yours, agreed to an interview. I'm talking to a bunch of men and women who have been in and out of VA hospitals, and I have a contact at a national birth defect registry."

"I'll bet Joe thinks this is a great idea. One more attempt to get me out of my own way." Denny turns away from her and sits down at his bench to rearrange his tools. "Forget it. I'll start on the desk next week."

"Don't you want to even think about it before you say no?"

"No."

"I don't get it."

He spins to face her. "I'm tired, lady. All the hoops I went through to get a diagnosis wore me out. Now, the VA and Defense Department are starting to own up to what happened there? I'd say twenty years too late."

"It's never too late, Denny," Lily sighs.

"Find somebody else." Denny turns to Stephen. "Once I get started, the job should go pretty quickly."

"Not a problem. C'mon Lily, time to go."

She frowns at Stephen and mouths *not yet*.

Denny goes to his bench and hands her a drawing from a pile of paper. "This is the design. If you want to make any changes, now is the time."

She takes the design, sits on the couch, and studies it. "I want file drawers on both sides. And as much surface as possible even if it overhangs the desk Also, I'd like you to polyurethane the top or at least protect it as much as you can against my coffee rings. Other than that, it'll be a beauty. Love it."

He scribbles a few notes on the paper. "Okay. Don't call me. I'll let you know as soon as it's done."

Lily follows Stephen to the door but stops. "I just have to say this. This is what I see. Everybody puts up with your *why don't I just lay down and die shtick*. What more do you have to have happen to you? It's time for you to stand up and start fighting back."

His back is to her but she knows he heard. She flinches as soon as it's out of her mouth. Even Lily knows she's said too much.

Chapter twenty-five

Chelsea knocks on the door to Blake's motel room. She carries a carton and a shopping bag from *Forever 21*.

"Hi, babe. What's all this?" He looks at the bag. "You either don't like my wardrobe or you're moving in?" he jokes.

"Not on a bet. Only good thing about this dump is it's across from the mall." She hands him the box. "Don't say a word. I know you keep saying it's temporary but it's been months. Time to bring some things over to make it seem like you actually live here." She shakes her head. "This place is gross with its dirty, lumpy furniture and ridiculous excuse for a kitchen. Excuse me. Kitchenette. Which is what? French for tiny and unusable?" She looks at it and makes a face. "So, I brought a few things."

Blake sets the box on the coffee table. "What have we got here?" He takes out his favorite lopsided blue coffee mug that Chelsea made when she took a pottery class.

"I can't believe you even use this but since you do, it's in case you have company or need something to remember me by." She then pulls out the green swirled mug they bought at a craft show. "You've used this one every day since we bought it. At the very least I know you are making coffee here, so that one was a must. I also brought Aunt Emma's snow globe. You've never been without it. And here are some dvds and your favorite books."

"This box is bottomless. What other treasures do we have here?" He unrolls two prints he had of *The Grateful Dead* and the *Rolling Stones* that hung near his recliner in the downstairs family room. His eyes lit up. "Chelsea, you've hit all the important memorabilia."

"At least, if you went to a *real hotel*, they hang stuff up on the walls. This place is the pits. They don't even try to cover up the stains.

Here's my Indian print tapestry." She unfolded it and covered the couch. "I don't know how long you're going to be here but you have to have something of yours here. It doesn't seem fair that we are in the house and you're here. Are we broke or something?"

Blake puts a bag of popcorn in the microwave. "I'm hardly here. It's just for a while and I couldn't see wasting money on anything more than this. The bed isn't half bad. That's the important thing."

"No bed bugs or other creepy crawlers?" she shuddered.

"Haven't seen anything crawling? Have you?"

"What about drug dealers or pimps?"

"Haven't seen them either. I hear they're only around past my bedtime."

"Dad!" Chelsea cried.

"Only kidding. It's fine, honey. Don't worry. I'm perfectly safe."

The time in between pops decreases and Blake pulls the bag out of the microwave before the popcorn burns. He opens the fridge and takes out two bottles of iced tea, lemon for him and raspberry for her. "Come. Let's have some popcorn. Maybe we can watch one of the movies you brought but first show me what you have in the bag. Did you go shopping?"

Chelsea sat down and took a drink. "No shopping." She took out some folders, a catalogue, and application packages.

"What's this?"

"I've been thinking. With everything that's going on, I think it would be a good idea for me to go to the University here. If I hurry, I can get all the paperwork in on time."

"No. There is no reason to change your plans. You never wanted to go there."

"But, I looked into it. There is a lot for me besides being here for you and Mom. And it would cost so much less money. They have a great creative writing program, the New York State Writers Institute, a strong theater arts program and if I decide that isn't what I want, the overall liberal arts program is very good."

"While that's all true, there is no reason to do this. This is your time, Chels. You wanted a brand-new experience. Did something happen to change your mind when you went back to visit Penn and BU with Mom? Did she say something? I thought you were still excited about both. What happened?"

Chelsea sighed, "Nothing happened. Just like you, she wants what I want. It's just. Well, I've been thinking it's just not the right time to go away. And besides, it's too expensive."

"Ah, my sweet girl. It's exactly the right time. We've all been planning for this since you were born —Mom, me, all your grandparents. Plus, you've gotten some scholarship money. Nothing's changed."

"What? Everything's changed. Mom is just putting up a front that everything is good with all the new things she's planning. You say you're fine but you insist on living in this you- know-what hole and I went to see Willow. She's far from fine."

"Important thing is we're all getting there. This is a time of new starts for all of us, including you, kiddo. These new beginnings are not for the weak of heart. But that's okay because we're all pretty strong. You are going to your first-choice college and we grownups will try to follow suit and do the best we can to find our way in our new lives. So…" he pops a kernel in his mouth. "Which is it? The big city or the beautiful campus?"

"If you're absolutely sure," she breaks out in her wide, Chelsea grin. "Boston, here I come!"

He wraps her in a bear hug. "It will never be the same."

Chapter twenty-six

Grace calls out, "I'm going now. I'll be back in an hour."

"We're fine, Mama. Don't worry."

It's taken Willow months to agree to see Denny. She needed time and had no desire to talk to him or see him. When he called repeatedly, all Grace would say is that Willow wasn't ready.

Willow had persistent early morning dreams about him that were brief but disturbing. In these nightmarish episodes, he tied her to a chair to keep her from leaving and nailed boards on the windows of their house so she couldn't look out. The dreams were jumbled, unreal, a carnival-like fun house of distortion.

One dream drifted into another but one night, months after the accident, she dreamt with total clarity. They sat on top of a hill, overlooking a broad valley. Both she and Denny were lame. His leg was in a cast broken from one of his joy rides; hers was broken when she ran from him.

He said, "I knew all along you weren't enough for me. I thought maybe it would be okay when I got stuff out of my system but the thing is first, I lied to both of us and then just to you. I needed you but I craved something you couldn't give me. You didn't know it but you pushed me to find it and then I was punished for it. You got your way. That stupid house you had to have became my prison. You won, Willow. Now, you won't leave me alone in it. I forbid it."

Willow's anger rose in her so fast and hard she thought it would blast off the top of her head. Then, it was gone. She woke up at peace. She was free. She sat up in bed, her face wet but she felt lighter. In that truth about him, she understood he was never enough for her either.

Now, she could see him.

"Mama, just go. Denny is here and I can actually get from one room to the other with my crutches." Willow laughs. "Enjoy yourself."

"Really, Grace. It will be fine. No scenes. I promise."

She looks back at Willow and then gently closes the door behind her.

Nervous, Denny asks, "Can I make you some eggs? French toast? How about an omelet?"

"No. I'm good."

"You look better than I expected."

"Getting there. Working hard at it. I hate how slow the healing is. The blessing in all of this is the three of us living together. I never thought that would happen again." She notices how drawn he looks. "Tess tells me Joe is still with you. He's a good friend."

"He thinks he's on suicide watch. I have to get to where he thinks I'm okay alone. He's got some kind of idea I'm going to change. Only you know what I'm really like. Can't change an old dog."

"It's time for you to do the work, Denny."

"Yeah, right. Has that news woman, Lily, been to see you?"

"Just once. I like her enthusiasm."

"Is that what you call it? She's writing a magazine article about PGW vets. Wants to interview me. Was really ballsy about asking. She's a total nightmare. You were out of it, but she was in everybody's face at the hospital."

"Don't be so hard on her. She's idealistic enough to think she can make a difference. You're going to do the interview, right?"

"No way."

"After what we went through? It's time for the entire story to be told."

Denny doesn't answer.

Willow tries to conceal her agitation. "Whatever. Whether or not you do it is your business."

"You're pissed."

"What I am doesn't matter anymore."

Denny moves toward her. "Please, Willow. I don't know how to live without your expectations. I let you down a lot but I at least knew what I was supposed to do. What can I do to make you come back? I'll try to be everything you want. I'm still going to the therapy group."

"And I hope you'll continue to go but no, Denny. I'm not coming back. I think you know that." Willow reaches for her crutches. "I think you should go now. And think about this. If everyone is telling you the same thing, maybe you should consider what they're saying. Or figure out what you want and then just do it."

"Sure. I'll do just that."

"Cut the sarcasm. It's old and tiresome." She walks toward the door. "By the way, Lily asked me, too, and I said yes. Why? Because I don't want any other couples suffering the way we did. I'm not thrilled about rehashing all that anymore. But I will. And my final gift to myself is forgiving both of us for not understanding what made each other tick. All of it. The truth is we never really saw each other for who we were. Now, it's time to do that. A part of me will always love you Denny. But it's time to put the past where it belongs."

Chapter twenty-seven

Every evening when Autumn comes home from work, the three women have happy hour—wine for Grace and Autumn and tonic and lime for Willow until she is totally weaned from her medications. As always, there is a glass waiting for Blake who might be late, but always comes.

There is an easiness among all of them. Slowly, they are telling each other the stories that create family. Sometimes Willow tunes out the sound and watches them talking together. She sometimes feels underwater as she did after the accident but finds a peacefulness sitting in a room with people she loves.

When Blake comes early enough, they take a short walk and then sit on the front porch and begin making simple plans around her recovery, which the doctors project to be complete.

Tonight, Willow is feeling particularly peaceful. Sitting by the window, she watches Blake walk up the path to Autumn's house with a package under his arm. It is wrapped in swaths of color. This is exactly what their life will be like. Together, they will unwrap this bright package slowly, turning it in all directions, examining it closely to truly see what they are looking at from all sides. They will savor the depth of each layer, wanting to explore and understand exactly what is in front of them.

Headline: Parasailing Blog Revisited

Looking back at a blog I wrote comparing marriage to parasailing, I cringe at my cynicism. Just to set the record straight— in focusing on the very few reported accidents, I falsely painted a pretty dark picture. Admittedly, the National Safety Transportation Board doesn't have good user statistics but they estimate that of the three to five million people who have parasailed since 2009, there have been eight deaths reported. Pretty good odds for a good time if that's your thing.

At the time, I was trying to make a point. I wrote that blog when I was running for and from my life. I was skeptical about the whole idea of a happily ever after for me or anyone else. In the interest of true disclosure, I was covering stories in the saddest places on the planet, on my way to emotional and physical exhaustion.

On a leave of absence back in the city I grew up in, sleep-walking through a stint at a local TV station, I was shaken out of my malaise by the jolting sound of a car crash. While my supposed journalist instincts to get the story kicked in, everything I did thereafter was a jumble. Whatever I saw, or thought I saw, or heard awakened me. Not in service to the story but to my existential personal crisis. The closed part of my mind refusing to consider a broader, more compassionate view of the world was forced open.

My gratitude for that can't be overstated.

In some warped part of my mind, I thought the capacity for what you could love was either limited or one dimensional. In my case, I didn't think there would be room for anything in my life except my job. I had a long-distance relationship with a man I knew

I loved deeply but I was afraid a commitment to him would jeopardize the other. In my inertia, I came close to losing both.

Back to that wakeup call in the form of a car crash—

When I should have been covering the facts of that story, I was instead getting big time life lessons. I learned first-hand that I didn't need to go to Africa to learn about the effect of our own personal conflicts and the impact of foreign wars right here at home.

I was aware enough to see a group of people—like me— who clutched an idea of love that shortchanged them. The accident was precipitated by two marriages dissolving. Now, a woman who lived on a diet of regret and resentment, is free to transform her disappointments into something that may not be the big dream she once had, but may satisfy her. A woman who never thought she would have a family may get her wish. Her new husband, a man shaped by a family death, finally married a woman with the same idea of what constitutes a good life. Sadly, the man who suffered health effects from a war he never meant to fight is still stuck. But with help from friends and the Vet Center, maybe he'll give himself a push.

As for me, I'm no big expert on love or how to get what you want out of life but in all my travels around the world, I've learned that people really are who they seem to be. What we love is a pretty good indication of what and who we are and what we want. Interior change comes slowly and it can't be forced by someone else.

In total reversal to my previous blog, I'll say "Go Parasailing!" Take a look down at the world from a new vantage point. Believe that the wind helping you glide through the air will push you in any direction you wish to go.

-THE END-

About the Author

Jan Marin Tramontano is a novelist and poet. Her books include a novel, *Standing on the Corner of Lost and Found*, three poetry chapbooks, *Floating Islands, A Woman Sitting in a Café and Other Poems of Paris* and *Paternal Nocturne*, and her father's memoir, *I am a Fortunate Man*. Her poems also appear in her poetry collective's anthologies, *Java Wednesdays.* and *Peer Glass Review.*

Her short stories, poetry and novel excerpts have been published in numerous literary journals, magazines, and newspapers such as *Adelaide Literary Magazine, AOIS 21, Up the River, Poets Canvas, Chronogram, Women's Synergy, Knock, The DuPage Valley Review, Moms Literary Review, New Verse News* and *Byline.* Her work also appears in *Ophelia's Mom* and *Surviving Ophelia.* In addition, her poems have won several poetry contests including *Poets & Writers.*

She has participated in writing workshops throughout the country including the New York State Writers Institute, Florida Gulf Coast University's Renaissance Academy's Writers Collaborative, the Iowa Summer Writers Festival, a summer writing workshop at Mabel Dodge Luhan House in Taos, New Mexico, and the International Women's Writing Guild.

After a long career in public health, Ms. Tramontano turned to her first love and worked as an independent writing consultant offering research, writing, and editing services to a wide array of clients.

Tramontano belongs to the Marco Island Writers Association and served on the board and as program chair of the Hudson Valley Writers Guild. She now lives with her husband in Naples, Florida.

Acknowledgements

Writing a novel is a very solitary endeavor, however, if you are very lucky, you find the right people to help you shape the story along the way. My particular village is extraordinary. Many people have their handprint on this book.

My thank you list is very long.

First, I'd like to thank everyone associated with Adelaide Books, particularly Stevan V. Nikolic, Editor and Publisher.

I have many readers to thank. My devoted early readers were steadfast in helping me to shape the story after initial drafts. They are: Amy Berkowitz, Marilyn Day, Christine Tramontano Faga, Jodi Ackerman Frank, Cecele Kraus, and Muriel Wilson. Their careful reading, conversation, and encouragement throughout this very long process were way beyond expectation.

Thank you to Joan Tramontano, Kathe Kokolias, and Janay Cosner for adding to the layers of excellent feedback as the book progressed.

A boundless thank you to the members of the Renaissance Academy's Writers' Collaborative under the guidance of the brilliant, insightful Jim Robison. Special thanks to Karla Araujo, Cece Harway, Tina McNiece, and Jory Westbury, for their on-going, thoughtful critique. Also, a thank you to the Naples Fiction Group.

Thank you to Stacey Marin Goldaris for her research assistance in both dance and medicine. She brought to life Jillian's dream dance sequence, step by step. Stacey also gave me terrific insight from a student perspective. Her interviews with emergency room doctor, Steven Mednick and nurse Laura Tramona got me started on the medical thread. Along the way, nurse Amy Berkowitz was extremely helpful in giving me color to add to the storyline.

A special thank you to Kerry Lockhart who walked me through the medical details and helped me figure out what Willow would go through and how she would recover. She is amazing. Generous. Funny. Just the person you would want to take care of you in any situation —medical or otherwise.

I can't say enough about Crate Voerg who served in the Persian Gulf War. While I want to emphasize he is not in any way Denny, he gave me incredible insight and context. I am grateful for the time he spent with me and how he grounded me with enough fact to proceed in developing the character. Also, to Ryan Smithson, who joined the Marines in response to 911 and served in Iraq.

Thank you to Sybil Burt, director of Etudes de Ballet in Naples, Florida, who had aspirations to be a performer and then ran a very successful ballet school. She introduced me to the Royal Academy of Dance accreditation program. Also, to Gail Tasserotti, owner of Albany Dance and Fitness Studio. As a young girl, she too took the train to New York City to study and then became a beloved teacher. She is perpetually expanding the classes she offers so that all of us can, at least for the time spent with her, feel like dancers.

I learned so much from Barbara Borst, a former international journalist and current professor at the Arthur Carter Journalism Institute at NYU. She spent many years in Africa covering stories in Nairobi, Ethiopia, Burundi, Sudan and others. She also covered Paris and London. It was Barbara who first made me aware of the unrest among immigrants from North Africa in Paris in the 1990s and told me about her experience at a 2007 London bombing. Thank you, Barbara.

I read many books and articles to enrich my understanding of the subject matter. Here are a few that were most helpful as background.

- *Gassed in the Gulf: The Inside Story of the Pentagon-CIA Cover-up of Gulf War Syndrome* - Patrick G. Eddington (former CIA analyst)
- *Against All Enemies: Gulf War Syndrome: The War Between America's Ailing Veterans and Their Government* - Seymour M. Hersh

- *Thank You For Your Service* - David Finkel
- *Gulf War Syndrome: Legacy of a Perfect War* - Alison Johnson
- *Voices in War Time Anthology:* A Collection of Narratives and Poems edited by Andrew Himes
- *Ghosts of War* - Ryan Smithson
- *It's What I Do: A Photographer's Life of Love and War* - Lynsley Addario
- *Ballanchine's Complete Stories of the Great Ballets* - George Balanchine and Frances Mason
- *Off Balance* - Terez Mertes Rose
- *Girl Through Glass* - Sari Wilson
- *Drop City* - T.C. Boyle

Thank you to Preston Browning of Wellspring House Foundation of the Arts for providing such good space in which to think and write. And also, to fellow writers from the Hudson Valley Writers Guild, Albany Poets, and the Marco Island Writers Association who are my partners in crime. A special thank you to Mary McCarthy and Joanne Tailele.

I am very proud of my large and loving blended family whose encouragement is always there when I need it. I want to name them all—Allison and Ryan, Amelia and Brian, Christine and Angelo, and Marisa and Dave. I love you all very much. And to my mother who made sure I always had books to read and notebooks to write in. While her memory may now be fading, she kept her own version of an archive which helps me remember this is always what I've wanted to be doing. Only my mother would keep the novella I wrote when I was ten to help me remember how long I've been at this!

And to my husband, Ron, who has been with me every step of the way. His critique is invaluable. His belief in me is what keeps me going. He has been the love of my life from the moment I first met him. How lucky am I.

Credits

THE MOON GARDEN, Adelaide Literary Magazine, Number 8, July 2017

THE VISIT, AOIS21 ANNUAL 2016

Book Discussion Guide

In Lily's opening blog, she suggests a romantic ideal for marriage:

*We want to be held but we want the hold to be loose. We want our
partner to admire our speed and grace in flight but not to tug on the
towline. We need to make sure the line doesn't tangle or knot. We try to
balance who gets the flying time and when.*

Mostly we want our partners to understand what we want and need,
admire it good and worthy, and help us to fulfill it. If that is the
underlying principle of a successful marriage then our couples were
doomed from the very start. How could these characters have been
so wrong?

Willow wanted quiet and stability after a life on the go, a man she
could dote on, children, and a stable job. The man she chose had
some loose wires. He knew Willow would be good for him but
wanting isn't the same as being.

Blake fell for Jillian's single-minded ambition. Did he think that
would translate to a life that would be good for him or did he just
not think beyond the now? Jillian couldn't believe anyone could
take her and ballet on as an equal partner. If Blake could do that,
could she overlook whatever other shortcomings he might have?

Regardless of Stephen's dissatisfaction over time, Lily couldn't see
anything but a long-distance arrangement. She just didn't have the
imagination or trust for compromise. So where did that leave them?

1. Willow and Denny were at odds from the beginning. Willow was very clear about the life she expected to have with him. When Denny joined the Marines, he was sending a clear signal to her. Why do you think she stayed and waited for him?

2. Do you think that love or what they thought was love obscured the truth of troubles ahead to either Willow, Denny, or both of them?

    Could Denny possibly have believed he could be what Willow wanted? More importantly, why would he even have wanted that if it was so far from who he was?

    And Willow? She was an 18-year-old girl with her whole life ahead of her? Why did she pin everything on a boy who was obviously not ready for the responsibility she demanded?

3. Willow wanted a baby more than anything in the world. Do you think it was wrong to deceive Denny and try to get pregnant without him knowing or could it be justified?

4. Denny and his friend, Joe, shared similar experiences as Marines. Yet, they had very different personalities. Do you think Joe's inability to accept his son's birth defect and the trouble in his marriage strongly influenced Denny or did it not make any real difference?

5. Jillian never wanted anything more than to be a ballet soloist. What was it that initially attracted her to Blake? Why do you think she married him before her career got started?

    Blake knew that ballet came first in life when he decided to marry her. Was it an unrealistic romantic idea he had of her or something else?

6. Jillian worked tirelessly from the time she was a child toward one goal. What do you think allowed her to be so easily cowed by Madame Olga and give up all she ever wanted?

7. Blake knew firsthand how strong her Jillian's need was to be a dancer. Yet, he hardly questioned her decision to give it up. Why? What stopped him?

Why did they get pregnant right away? Jillian experienced post-partum depression that was never addressed. What were the repercussions of that throughout their marriage?

8. Lily convinced herself that she couldn't have the career she wanted and a relationship. Do you think it's true that in some careers a choice has to be made?

9. Why did Lily push herself so hard? Were there similarities between her and Jillian? Do you think the pressure they both put themselves under contributed to making bad decisions?

10. Through all the years of their marriage, Blake and Jillian have different sensibilities and values from the big things to the daily tasks. Blake tries hard to make up for what Jillian can't or won't give Chelsea but Jillian also tries, in her own way. What do you think either one of them could have done differently to make for a better home life?

11. Why did Jillian have such a hard time with Chelsea? Did her fascination with Philip and his daughter, Allegra, exacerbate the problems, or did it make no real difference at all?

12. Blake and Willow's relationship develops slowly. Neither of them are intentionally looking yet what they need is right in front of them. How did you feel about that? Did you feel it was wrong from the start or did you want them to fall in love?

13. Does the information Blake discovers about Denny and shares with Willow help create empathy for his actions or inactions? Does it create better understanding for Denny's motivations and inability to give Willow what she wants? Do you think there is anything Willow might have done to help Denny or help her get what she wanted from him?

14. Lily doesn't see the impact her job is having on her. We don't have to be witnessing world crises to be traumatized and not realize it. Can you think of other examples within the novel of extreme stress that is not acknowledged or simply avoided?

15. Friendship between women is key in this story. Willow and her sister, Autumn. Jillian and Georgia. Lily and Amber. What role did these relationships play in the trajectory of their growth and change?

16. How do you think the three women—Willow, Jillian, Lily— are similar? How do they differ? Do you think the ending was right for them? Did it get them closer to what they wanted all along?

17. What about the men? Where do you see Denny, Blake, and Stephen in ten years?